FAREWELL DINNER FOR A SPY

ALSO BY EDWARD WILSON

THE CATESBY SERIES

The Envoy
The Darkling Spy
The Whitehall Mandarin
The Midnight Swimmer
A Very British Ending
South Atlantic Requiem
Portrait of the Spy as a Young Man

A River in May

EDWARD WILSON is a native of Baltimore. He studied International Relations on a US Army scholarship and later served as a Special Forces officer in Vietnam. He received the Army Commendation Medal with 'V' for his part in rescuing wounded Vietnamese soldiers from a minefield. His other decorations include the Bronze Star and the Combat Infantryman's Badge. After leaving the Army, Wilson became an expatriate and gave up US nationality to become a British citizen. He has also lived and worked in Germany and France, and was a postgraduate student at Edinburgh University. He now lives in Suffolk where he taught English and Modern Languages for thirty years.

FAREWELL DINNER FOR A SPY

Edward Wilson

First published in Great Britain in 2024 by

Arcadia Books
An imprint of Quercus Editions Limited
Carmelite House
50 Victoria Embankment
London EC4Y ODZ

An Hachette UK company

A CIP catalogue record for this book is available from the British Library.

ISBN (Hardback) 978 1 52942 907 7
ISBN (Ebook) 978 1 52942 909 1

1 3 5 7 9 10 8 6 4 2

Typeset in Minion by MacGuru Ltd
Printed and bound in Great Britain by Clays Ltd, Elcograf S.p.A.

Papers used by Quercus Books are from well-managed forests and other responsible sources.

To our grandson, Ollie Gore-Manton

"Man is the only animal that can remain on friendly terms with the victims he intends to eat until he eats them."

Samuel Butler

Julot's Restaurant, Marseille: October 1950

They all loved the American – and even those who didn't love him were told to love him. The boss wanted to show that his personal gratitude was shared by every section of the Marseille underworld. It was going to be the grandest of farewell banquets and no expense would be spared – which was why the gang members were expected to pitch in, and generously, too.

Julot's restaurant was packed with more than a hundred guests. They spilled out onto a candlelit terrace, where the lesser mobsters were seated. The meal kicked off with the traditional Marseille *amuse-bouche*, a tapenade of marinated olives served on tiny rounds of toast. The simplest of nibbles, intended to stimulate the appetite for the more complex creations that were to follow. The *amuse-bouche* plates had just been cleared away when the unfortunate news began to percolate. The guest of honour wasn't going to be there. Everyone wanted to know what had happened. The rumours filtered out from those seated nearest the boss. Lester, the much-loved American, had suddenly been summoned back to Washington as a matter of extreme urgency. This confirmed the impression that Lester, despite his easy-going ways and love of partying, was indeed a *très, très important Américain*. One strand of conjecture was that it had something to do with events in Korea: the president was planning a move and needed Lester's advice. 'He is, as we know,' whispered another gangster, 'Washington's number one man on Asia.' 'Which is,' laughed another *voyou*, 'why he was so useful to us in *Indochine*.' Another put his hand up, 'Shhh!'

The boss stood up and motioned for silence. 'I have just received a message from Lester.' He smiled. 'I will not try to imitate his inimitable accent, but, oddly, his written French is better than his spoken.'

He smiled again, put on his reading glasses, and began. "'To my dear friends. The pilot has assured me that the control tower will copy this message and deliver it to a waiting car. The driver, who once won the Tour de Corse, should arrive at Julot's well before the *bouillabaisse*. Your wonderful sea, by the way, is beautiful from up here. The sky is a perfect cloudless blue and the air hostess has just brought me another glass of champagne which I now raise in a toast to all of you.'" The boss gestured and everyone stood up. He then continued reading. "'To all my friends in Marseille, the best friends in the world!'" Everyone raised their glasses and drank. The boss put down his champagne flute and folded his reading glasses into a case. There was concern on his face.

It was now time for the *bouillabaisse,* a speciality of the house. Julot's recipe was so highly esteemed that a world-renowned film director and author sometimes came to partake. Julot claimed that his restaurant and *bouillabaisse* had inspired one of the man's films – a claim that, however merited, was never verified. As the legendary fish soup made its entrée, borne in a huge steaming tub by two brawny waiters, a few of the guests called out, *bullabessa*, the name of the dish in Provençal Occitan. A true *bullabessa* contained at least five different types of fish and shellfish. The most essential ingredients were *rascasse* – a lethal red fish with poisonous spines – olive oil and the best saffron you could find. If available, monk-fish, conger eel or even an octopus could be added. But shellfish were more important for the flavour. Sea urchins, small spiny creatures that cling to rocks or wrecks, were abundant in the seas around Marseille and easy to gather. Spider crabs were a delicious luxury that everyone hoped to find in their portion of *bouillabaisse*, but you savoured the broth and *rouille* first before tucking into the crab meat and fish. The waiters had already finished laying soup plates and other waiters were now ladling the soup from steaming metal bowls and placing out smaller bowls containing the *rouille,* a sauce concocted of olive oil, egg yolks, saffron and garlic. You consumed the soup with pieces of grilled bread on which you spread your *rouille.*

William Catesby and Kit Fournier were the only guests who didn't come from Marseille, Corsica or Italy. Fournier was on the opposite side of the table from Catesby, but not directly. The guest facing Catesby was a Corsican with a scarred face and one and a half fingers missing from his right hand. They had chatted briefly about wine – the Corsican had already instructed the wine waiter to find a couple of bottles of white wine from a small Cassis château for their table. 'It is,' he said, 'an Ugni blanc, one of the few wines that pair well with *bouillabaisse*. Let me know what you think.'

'Thank you,' said Catesby, but he was hardly going to disagree with a gangster who knew the turf. Catesby spread a dab of *rouille* on a round of toast and inhaled the wonderfully fragrant broth. He fully appreciated that it had been cooked with infinite care. He sipped a spoonful. It was delicious beyond measure – a world away from austerity Britain, where some foods were still rationed. Catesby popped the toast into his mouth and washed it down with a gulp of Cassis Ugni blanc. He smiled at the Corsican. 'You chose well, monsieur, it is perfect. Full bodied with a herbal aroma.'

Catesby looked over to Kit Fournier who was wolfing down the soup. 'Take your time, Kit, there's a lot more to come.'

'I'm looking forward to the crabs. I grew up with them.'

Catesby decided not to make a lame joke.

'We used to catch Chesapeake blue crabs in the river and when we had a dozen or so my mother would steam them with Old Bay seasoning. They made a helluva racket in the big pot trying to escape.'

Catesby nodded. The gangsters of Marseille were capable of great cruelty, but their cooks didn't boil their crabs and lobsters alive. But how, thought Catesby, do they kill them? The techniques necessary were not taught on the Secret Intelligence Service's induction course. The best kills, of course, were those that could pass as death by suicide or natural causes – but who was going to get a crab drunk and push him over the railing of a tenth-floor balcony? Drugs, thought Catesby. Drugs were ugly, but quiet and effective. The Russians loved them, but the toffs running the British Secret Intelligence Service were squeamish about poison.

The waiters were now passing around trays of crusty bread to soak up the *bouillabaisse*. The staff were all men in smart serving gear. There was not a woman to be seen among either the guests or the servers. As far as the mafia were concerned, women were stay-at-home wives, child bearers or prostitutes. The older ones, however, could be elevated to the status of background advisers.

'I love crab too,' said Catesby looking at Kit, 'but I'm also looking forward to a big slice or two of monkfish – and maybe some conger eel. I remember one *bouillabaisse* that contained the head of a conger – an enormous beast.'

Julot was now standing centre stage like a magician behind the huge steaming tub of *bouillabaisse*. The treasures of the depths were about to appear. The first morsels to emerge steaming and dripping from his tongs were whole *rascasse* and spider crabs; the next were chunky fillets of monkfish that were still whole after the long cook. Julot smiled as he piled high the serving tray. He dipped his exploratory tongs deep into the tub – and then started probing. A look of consternation crossed his face. He looked at the diners and laughed. 'I don't know what my sous chefs have been up to.' He turned towards the kitchen and shouted, 'Hey, Fabio, what have you put in the *bouillabaisse*? A shark's head?'

A voice replied, 'Only the usual, Julot.'

'I don't think so, Fabio. Come and help me lift this monster out.'

Fabio came out of the kitchen in a chef's toque and neckerchief. He wiped his hands on a napkin and stared at the tub of bouillabaisse. Julot handed him a pair of tongs. The chef prodded into the steaming cauldron.

'It's pretty solid,' said Julot. 'Try to find a hole to get a grip.'

A human head slowly arose out of the *bouillabaisse*. The victim's hair was stained orange from the *bouillabaisse* broth and his mouth was hanging open, more in surprise than agony.

Meanwhile, Kit Fournier had begun to retch. Catesby passed over his napkin and said, 'Let me help you.'

'No,' said Kit, 'I'm okay.' He stifled another vomit and headed towards the lavatories.

As Catesby watched Fournier disappear, he thought: *CIA agents should be made of sterner stuff.* He shrugged and mechanically poured himself another glass of Ugni blanc. Kit's vomiting had made him want to wash away the taste of the *bouillabaisse.* Catesby was a little ashamed that, rather than feeling shock and repugnance, he had already begun to analyse the situation. He was cold-blooded and would have made a good cop. And his first question would have been: *Whose head is it?* The second: *Who killed him?* And one more: *Why?* He then strained to hear a whispered conversation between the Corsican mobster sitting opposite him and another who had joined him. They were speaking *Corsu*, a language that Catesby struggled to comprehend. The only words he picked up were: *Hè Roberto, un venditore di Napuli* – which he construed as 'It was Roberto, a dealer from Naples'. The other Corsican shook his head rapidly and said, *Innò, nò, nò. Roberto hè sempre vivu è vàcù u capu* – which led Catesby to assume that Roberto was still alive and on fine terms with the *capu*, the boss. The rest of the conversation was incomprehensible to Catesby. There was a lot of shouting in the restaurant and the tub of *bouillabaisse* had been removed with some haste. A waiter had joined the two Corsicans and as he shepherded them out of the restaurant, he said something that made them laugh. The waiter then looked at Catesby and addressed him in standard French, 'No problem, *monsieur,* the head belongs to a drowned sailor. Another restaurant owner put it there because he wants to destroy Julot's reputation as serving the best *bouillabaisse* in Marseille.'

'Whoever put that head in the cooking pot certainly ruined a marvellous *bouillabaisse,*' said Catesby in amical agreement.

The waiter bowed as he backed away. 'I am sorry, *monsieur,* if this unfortunate event has ruined your evening.'

The drowned sailor tale, thought Catesby, was exactly the sort of explanation that the local police would accept with gratitude. Case solved. The alternative, investigating the mafia, was both difficult and dangerous. Marseille was a town where the parade of killers, victims and motives was long and complicated. If Catesby was a local cop, the

5

first person he would call in for questioning would be Lester Roach. He reckoned there were two likely reasons why Lester hadn't turned up for his farewell dinner. One, he was the killer. Two, he knew there was at least one person at the dinner who was aiming to kill him.

Kit Fournier had reappeared from the lavs. He had scrubbed away every trace of *bouillabaisse* from his lips, but his face still looked stunned. Catesby took the American firmly by the elbow. 'We've got to get out of here.'

'Good, I need some fresh air.'

They began walking in the direction of Le Vieux Port. There were a lot of questions that Catesby wanted to ask Kit Fournier – not as a cop, but as a member of Her Majesty's Secret Intelligence Service. London needed to know the latest.

Dunwich, Suffolk: February 2018

It was only very late in life that Catesby began to tell the whole story, not just the highly classified intrigues of the secret state – but secrets of the inner mind. Members of the Secret Intelligence Service were not just spies, they were also human beings – although some of them didn't realise it. Maybe it was because they had never found someone they could talk to; someone who really wanted to listen and understand. Catesby was lucky. He had Leanna, his granddaughter. Part of the reason that Catesby had taken early retirement was to help look after Leanna after her mother had died in mysterious circumstances in Africa. As a teenager, she had found her grandfather non-judgemental and totally impossible to shock – and even a little outrageous in his own right. Consequently, she told him everything, no matter how shameful. Later, Leanna became a professor of modern history at a London university. Now, it was Catesby's turn to tell her everything, no matter how shameful.

It was a clear cold winter's day, and they were sitting on a bench overlooking the sea at Dunwich. Catesby had made a flask of hot rum toddy and passed a tumbler to Leanna.

'This is delicious, Granddad – and a perfect treat for a day like today.'

'I got the idea from Henry Bone, but I'm sure it doesn't follow his recipe entirely. Henry put a lot more rum in his, and the wine was a good-quality Burgundy.'

'I bet you were sitting on a bench in Green Park passing on information that was too sensitive to be discussed in the office.'

'No, we were sitting on a bench in Dorotheenstadt Cemetery in East Berlin, next to the grave of a resistance fighter executed by the Nazis. We were waiting for a contact who never turned up, so we finished the rum toddy – which we needed because it was a very cold day.'

Leanna stared hard at the winter sea. 'Did ideology ever get in your way, Granddad?'

'It did, but I hope I never let it blind me – as it did some others.'

'You knew them all, didn't you?'

Catesby laughed. 'Who do you mean by "all"?'

'Let's start with Philby, Maclean and Burgess.'

'Yes, I knew them, but not terribly well – but then again who did? In fact, at first, I thought that Philby and Burgess were Tory right-wingers who had signed up for America's anti-communist witch hunt. Your grandmother, who had just started working at Five, had a much better idea of who they really were.'

'Granny says that Philby and Burgess were the reason you ended up in Marseille.'

'Part of the reason. I'm sure there were other factors. Maybe they chose me because I was a young and junior officer who was expendable – a cheap pawn sacrifice to buy off the Americans.'

'Could your fluent French have been a reason?'

'If language skills were a factor, they should have sent someone who spoke Corsican, Italian and the local patois as well. No, Leanna, I was a useful stooge, someone easily manipulated to do the bidding of my betters.'

'I think, Granddad, you are too harsh on yourself.'

'Hmm, how kind of you to say so. Well, to be less harsh on myself, I joined the Secret Intelligence Service because I needed a job. I had just married your grandmother and acquired two stepchildren who were toddlers. I was also flattered that someone like me, a rough kid from the Lowestoft docks, had been invited to join an elite secret club. But the Marseille business cleared away any illusions I had of ever becoming one of them. Sure, I got pretty good at affecting their voices and manners.' Catesby smiled. 'We ought to send spies to drama school. Even Michael Caine learned how to play a credible toff. Marseille taught me that the intelligence service regarded me as a disposable tool for doing their dirty work.'

'But you eventually rose to a very high post.'

Catesby shrugged. 'Low cunning – and I learned to play their game.'

'What are the rules of their game?'

'There are no rules – that is the very essence of the game. The most important thing about the Marseille op, and many others, was deniability – not the faintest fingerprint leading back to Her Majesty's Secret Intelligence Service.'

'And you still haven't said how you, then a German desk specialist, ended up in Marseille.'

'I still don't know.'

'Granny says that you were falsely framed as a Soviet double agent by actual doubles who were trying to save their own skins.'

'An interesting theory.'

Berlin: August 1949

When you fish a body out of a canal the presence of Jesus should be welcomed with solemn piety. But not when it's James Jesus Angleton, a rising CIA star making a name for himself in Europe. Angleton's devout Catholic Mexican mother had insisted upon his middle name – and, like his holy namesake, Angleton seemed to turn up everywhere.

The divided city was a playground for spies, but a dangerous playground where kids shove other kids off climbing frames and hide sharp spikes at the bottom of a fast slide. And don't trust the kind-looking old granny who offers to push your swing. She keeps a stiletto and poisoned sweets in her handbag.

Catesby was first assigned to the city at the beginning of the Berlin Blockade, when the Soviet Union cut off all land access to the city and tried to starve the allies out of West Berlin. The only option was a massive airlift of 2,000 tons of supplies per day to sustain the allied troops and the two million civilians in the western sectors. There were casualties. On one occasion, Catesby had to make a risky trip into the Soviet sector to collect the bodies of a British aircrew after their Vickers Viking collided with the Soviet fighter that had been buzzing it. Collecting the body parts was gruesome – and the stern faces of the heavily armed Soviet soldiers watching Catesby and his team didn't make it any easier. Being marched off into internment for crossing into East Germany was a real possibility. But it didn't happen, and Catesby began to develop a reputation as someone who could do the dirty work.

Even when the blockade ended in June 1949, Berlin remained a city under siege. It was, more than ever, an espionage swamp full of double-dipper spivs wanting to make a fast buck. Double dippers were greedy agents who sold intelligence to both sides. It was a dangerous occupation – as one of Catesby's double dippers found out.

The branch of the Landwehr Canal where the corpse had been found was firmly in the British sector – and had been cordoned off by Royal Military Police. The dead man's face was glistening in the summer sunshine as Catesby leaned over to confirm his identity.

'Dieter was one of yours,' said Angleton. He sounded sober but his voice was raspy.

'Yes, he was.'

'He was one of ours too.'

'We'll have to arrange a post-mortem,' said Catesby.

'And where will this autopsy take place?'

'I assume at the BMH.'

'The British Military Hospital?'

Catesby nodded.

'We'll send observers and one of our own pathologists.'

'And flowers too, if you like.' Catesby looked at Angleton and was pleased to see that he was getting on his nerves. Meanwhile, two RAMC corpsmen were making their way up the canal path carrying a stretcher. 'I think,' said Catesby glancing at the body, 'it's time to say goodbye.'

The post-mortem ended up being quite a big deal. London sent over a leading forensic pathologist and the Americans matched him with one of their own who was a prof at the Sorbonne. Catesby didn't understand why they were making such a fuss over the death of a very minor player. No one even knew Dieter's real name. They usually called him Herr Schwindler, Mr Cheat. In the end, both pathologists ruled out drowning or suicide. The cause of Dieter's death was a massive heart attack, but not one caused by coronary problems. Traces of cyanide were found in his nasal passages. It was agreed that Dieter had been sprayed with a jet of cyanide gas. The double-barrelled cyanide spray gun was a weapon the Russians had used before to deal with double agents and dissidents. By taking out Dieter, Spiridon – the Sov spy who ran their ops in Berlin – had got rid of one double dipper and sent out a warning message to others. As far as Catesby was concerned the matter was done and dusted and he got back to his usual routine of gathering intelligence in the spy capital of the world. When the urgent summons to London arrived, he was stumped at first – but then remembered Angleton's face staring at him over Dieter's dead body. Bastard.

Broadway Buildings, London: August 1949

The security officer at the entrance desk was a retired Black Watch NCO wearing his regimental kilt. He gave Catesby's ID a cursory look and passed over the signing-in log. The security officer then picked up an internal telephone and spoke in hushed tones. He looked up and said, 'Mr Ramsay will see you now, Captain Catesby.'

Neil Ramsay was head of personnel. In a time of post-war austerity, the department had become known as A&E, Accident and Emergency. When an officer was summoned to A&E, it meant that the next stop would be the mortuary, intensive care, rehab or – for the lucky ones – return to normal duties.

Ramsay was sitting at a desk laden with mountains of beige and grey files. Like the security officer on the entrance door, the head of personnel was a Scot. He had a pleasant welcoming manner but spoke with an accent that was both refined and unintelligible. Catesby thought the number of Scots in the SIS was out of proportion to their actual number in the UK population. Were they positioning for a Celtic *coup d'état*?

Ramsay's reading glasses were at an odd angle. It looked like the frames had been badly bent, as if someone had sat on them. Only one lens was in position, and it magnified his eyeball into a huge menacing glare. He looked like a Cyclops, but the Scotsman's voice was that of a bored bureaucrat. 'We must inform you that your personnel records have been requested by another member of SIS and passed on to that person. As is always the case, it required the agreement of the Director. It is now procedure to inform all officers when this happens. Unless, of course, it is a matter of gross misconduct or national security.'

'So I haven't been accused of murder?' Catesby immediately regretted saying his thoughts out loud. Bloody Dieter again.

'Oh, nothing as minor as a murder or two. I am sure Mr Philby wouldn't have been interested in your records if the only thing you did was go around killing people.'

'I haven't killed anyone.'

'I was, Mr Catesby, only teasing. Sassenachs don't always get our sense of humour.'

'Sorry.' Catesby forced a smile. 'A Glaswegian walks into a café and asks the waiter, "Is that a cake or a meringue?"'

'And the waiter replies, "You're not wrong, it is a cake." Very good, but you need to work on the accent before you tell that one again.'

'Can you give me lessons?'

'Ach no, I don't want to be accused of preparing you to defect to Scotland.'

'On a lighter note, have I been recalled to London just to be told that my personnel file has been passed on?'

'I would guess that there's more to it than that, but I haven't been informed. Everything is "need-to-know" nowadays.' Ramsay looked at a memo on his desk. 'You have pending appointments with both the Director and Commander Bone, but your first meeting will be this morning at the Foreign Office with Mr Philby and Mr Burgess.'

'I thought that Kim Philby was head of intelligence in Istanbul. What's he doing in London?'

Ramsay closed his eyes and looked pained. 'We never say "head of intelligence". Mr Philby's job in Turkey was "First Secretary at the British Consulate", but he is now in London pending reassignment. I'd now like to have a look at your expenses and leave arrangements. Why are you yawning?'

'Because I'm ill-mannered.'

'Try not to be when you see the Director.' Ramsay looked at his watch. 'Philby and Burgess are expecting you at eleven. If we finish up quickly, you'll have plenty of time to saunter over to the Foreign Office.'

'Has Burgess had a peek at my records too?'

'His name isn't on the access list.'

Catesby frowned. Burgess was a loudmouthed drunk and the last person he wanted perusing his personnel file.

The walk to the Foreign Office from Broadway Buildings, the ugly 1920s office block that housed SIS, took eight minutes if you stepped out briskly and didn't take the picturesque detour through St James's Park. As Catesby turned through the archway into King Charles Street he was oddly pleased by the air of shabbiness. In the era of post-war austerity, the once imperial grandeur of Whitehall was now faded and soot-stained. When Catesby entered the foyer of the FO, he was surprised there was no cop to check his ID. Standards, eh? He could have been any old Russian agent. Because Philby no longer had his own office in Whitehall, Guy Burgess's had been chosen as a meeting place. Catesby had to ask three times before he found someone who could direct him to Burgess's office. His jobs seemed to keep changing – and he had now landed on the China desk. Why the fuck, thought Catesby, would a China desk man want to see him? He shook his head and knocked on the door.

A loud voice bellowed, 'Come in, come in . . .' At first glance, Guy Burgess seemed the essence of casual chic and bonhomie – but the favourable impression didn't last long. Burgess's Eton tie was stained with food and drink – and its wearer seemed somewhere between half blotto and totally blotto even though it was only eleven in the morning. He poured Catesby a stiff whisky without asking if Catesby wanted one.

'Thank you for coming at such short notice.' Burgess eyed up Catesby as if he were a menu item, but then looked away. 'You're a welcome relief from China. Mao's won, but the Yanks don't want to admit it.' Burgess sipped his drink. 'Our current dilemma is granting Mao UK diplomatic recognition. As you know, we always recognise the government in control – even if it's led by Satan and his minions. But the Americans are different, particularly in the case of Mao.' Burgess was suddenly unsteady on his feet and spilled his drink. 'I think I'd better sit down. Had a bit of a tumble a few months ago; bad head injury – spent a few weeks in hospital.'

Catesby never found out the full truth of what had happened, but it apparently involved falling down the stairs at a Pall Mall club.

'We must humour the Yanks – and do what we can to make sure that other bits of Asia don't tip over into the communist camp. That's why we're beefing up our forces in Malaya. But the most important piece to save is French Indochina – and the dock strikes in Marseille aren't helping. The communist-controlled unions are preventing ships from being loaded with troops and supplies for Indochina.' Burgess closed his eyes as if he had decided to have a brief nap. Catesby wondered if he should shake him awake before he tumbled out of his chair. It might not be a good idea to aggravate that head injury. Another minute passed before Burgess yawned and opened his eyes. He was now staring at an open folder on his desk. 'I see you were at King's and studied under the charming Basil – and, very impressive, you were one of the daring night climbers.'

Catesby faked a smile but was furious that Philby had let someone else see his file. He was also surprised that his file was so thorough. He had never told anyone in SIS that he had been a member of the night climbers, a clandestine group of undergraduates who defied the authorities by scaling the university's numerous spires and then leaving a souvenir, such as a scarf or a hat, to show what they had done.

'Who did you climb with?'

Catesby gave three names, none of whom could be summoned by Burgess for interrogation. Two had been killed in the war and the third had emigrated to New Zealand.

'We all admired you climbers – such daring defiance.'

Despite the flattery, Catesby felt uncomfortable. He stared at his glass and realised it was a priceless Dartington crystal tumbler. His wife had inherited a set of six and they were only to be used on special occasions. Catesby sipped the whisky, and it was pretty fine too. Maybe being a drunken toff wasn't such a bad way of life.

'Top up?' said Burgess.

Catesby nodded.

'Ah, I think Kim's here.'

There wasn't a knock, the door just opened and Philby walked in. 'Greetings, Kim,' said Burgess. 'Can I get you a drink?'

'Don't get up. I'll help myself.' Philby went over to a side cabinet which contained a small fridge. 'There doesn't seem to be any gin – or ice cubes or tonic either.'

'I've had a few visits from Anthony.'

'Well, it looks like whisky then.' As Philby poured himself a generous slug, he glanced at Catesby. 'I think we've met before.'

'Yes, it was just before my first deployment to France with SOE.'

'It m-m-must have been at St Ermin's Hotel w-when I was head of D Section.'

'Yes, it was.'

'I've asked you here,' said Philby, 'to talk about your time in Occupied France.' The stutter was gone. He went over to Burgess's desk and picked up a thick file that was Catesby's life story. Philby began to skim through the paperwork and from time to time he nodded and cleared his throat.

Catesby wanted to grab the file from Philby's hands and shout, *What the fuck are you looking at!*

Philby finally put down the file and stared at Catesby. 'The Resistance group that you worked with was led by communists, several of whom are now leading the strikes in Marseille. Does the name Gaston le Mat ring a bell?'

'The other Maquisards called him that. It means Gaston the Mad in the local dialect. I don't know his real name.'

'Well, Gaston – mad or sane – is now a high-level union organiser and an influential member of the Communist Party.'

Catesby tried not to shout. 'What's that have to do with me? How was I to know that Gaston would one day be leading dock strikes in Marseille? Are you suggesting I should have slit his throat and thrown him down a ravine?'

Burgess laughed. 'Or in a canal.'

Philby gave Burgess a monitory look. His friend didn't know when to shut up. Catesby felt a chill run down his spine. The ghost of Dieter wouldn't lie still.

Philby continued. 'Part of your job as an SOE officer was writing secret reports on Resistance leaders who were likely to become powerful figures in post-war France . . .'

Catesby interrupted. 'I think we should end this session now. You are not head of counterintelligence, nor are you the Director of SIS.'

'The Director has, in fact, authorised this interview – and one of the reasons that he did so, is because of my background in counterintelligence. It was my first job in SIS. I think you need another drink.' Philby topped up Catesby's glass before he could object. 'Let's cut to the quick, you're here because the CIA's most valuable agent in Berlin was murdered – on your turf.'

'Dieter was a double-dipping spiv. Most of his intel was utter shit.'

'Don't say that to the Americans, they'll think it's part of your alibi.'

Catesby was inclined to leave but sipped the whisky instead. It was a very fine single malt.

'The Americans think that you, as a Soviet double agent, murdered Dieter to stop him from passing important Soviet secrets to the CIA.'

'I didn't kill him – the Russians did, because he was cheating them too. Have you seen the autopsy report?'

'Yes, and it certainly shows that Dieter was killed by a Russian weapon. And there lies the problem. There are some in the CIA who believe that the use of a secret Soviet spray gun proves that you are the murderer. A classic false flag op. You used a Russian weapon to deflect blame away from yourself.'

Catesby laughed. 'Obvious, innit?'

'Indeed,' said Philby. 'We have passed through the looking glass into what a poet friend of mine calls "a wilderness of mirrors".'

'Jim is a fascinating character,' said Burgess referring to the poet friend.

Philby winced. Guy Burgess just couldn't keep his mouth shut.

'James Jesus Angleton,' said Catesby, triumphantly savouring each syllable – and pronouncing Jesus the Hispanic way.

Philby raised his glass. 'To Jim – his orchids, his poetry and his penetrating intelligence.'

Catesby clinked glasses in a half-hearted way. 'You know that your friend was there when they fished Dieter's body out of the canal.'

Philby nodded.

'Maybe Angleton killed Dieter to stitch me up.'

'We have now stumbled into the land of double and triple bluffs.' Philby lifted Catesby's personnel folder. 'The CIA station chief in London asked for copies of your files. Unfortunately, C handed them over. Your reports and your time with the communist Maquis are now being pored over. They are looking for evidence that during your time in Occupied France you became a communist convert.'

'Utter bullshit.'

Philby smiled. 'And the fact that you stood as a Labour candidate in the '45 election doesn't help either. For many in Washington there isn't much difference between the Labour Party and the CP. The US is now in the grip of a Red Scare led by a senator called Joseph McCarthy. All US government employees must sign a loyalty oath – and there's something called HUAC, the House Un-American Activities Committee. Brits must walk very carefully in the corridors of Washington. Jim appreciates that and he shared with me a secret HUAC document listing suspected communist sympathisers in the UK intelligence and security services – and I'm sorry to have to tell you that your name was on that list.'

Catesby struggled not to throw the priceless Dartington tumbler against the wall. 'I've been smeared. I bet they haven't levelled the same charges at the OSS American who served with me in France – also aiding and abetting the communist Maquis.'

'You're referring to Lester Roach.'

Catesby gave a wan smile. 'In my file, of course.'

'You might be interested to know,' said Philby, 'that Lester Roach is now a CIA officer and one of Jim Angleton's favourite protégés. Roach helped mastermind the defeat of the communist coalition in Italy's general election last year – and has now moved on to Marseille.'

'Fucking hell, point proven.'

'You might be meeting Lester Roach again,' said Philby.

'Why?'

'Because you are in a very difficult position, and I suggest you take whatever is on offer. I have discussed your situation with the Director. It is clear that you can no longer continue as a serving SIS officer.' Philby paused to finish his whisky. 'You are probably totally innocent, but the world of secret intelligence is littered with the bodies of innocent victims.'

'But if you're not innocent,' laughed Burgess, 'I would suggest a cross channel ferry late on a Friday afternoon – after all the watchers have gone home for the weekend – and a flit to Moscow.'

Philby winced. 'Guy's sense of humour isn't always appropriate. Please take him with a grain of salt.' Philby poured himself another whisky. There was something about his manner that seemed inward-looking. 'You are, Mr Catesby, in a difficult position. Keep your nerve and don't act on impulse. Work out a set of answers and stick to them.'

Catesby looked at Philby and saw a man staring into a void. He realised that the words of advice weren't aimed at him; Kim Philby was talking to himself. An awkward silence descended on the office. The meeting was over.

Whitehall, London: August 1949

Catesby often had lunch in the Board of Trade canteen. You didn't have to work for the BoT, any civil servant could go there, and the canteen was considered the best in Whitehall – and a good place to sober up. Lord Woolton Pie was still served even though the war was long over. Named after the wartime Minister of Food, the pie was a concoction of non-rationed vegetables, such as swedes, cauliflower, potatoes and carrots, covered with a crisp pastry top. Catesby ordered a slice of Lord Woolton more as a show of solidarity with the principle of rationing than because he had much liking for it. He believed that rationing was one of the best things that had ever happened to Britain. No matter how rich you were, foods that were in short supply were equally shared and at the same price – and even now in 1949 it didn't look like rationing was going to end any time soon. In fact, the bacon ration had been cut just after VE day and tea was still in short supply. At home, much to his wife Frances's irritation, Catesby still echoed Lord Woolton's edict: 'One spoonful for each person and none for the pot.'

As soon as he sat down, Catesby was joined by Henry Bone. He suspected that Bone had been lying in wait, as he knew that his refined and fastidious boss was not fond of canteen food. Bone unloaded a bowl of soup and a buttered roll from his tray. 'Bon appétit,' he said with irony.

'Thank you for joining me, Commander Bone.'

'I thought it was worth risking the canteen food to have a chat. How did it go?'

'How did what go?'

'Don't try to be inscrutable, William, you can't pull it off.'

'Mr Burgess poured me a rather nice and large glass of whisky and then gave me a lecture on the state of the world.'

Bone sipped his soup and made a face. 'Absolutely ghastly.'

'Do you mean the soup or the state of the world?'

'Both. Go on.'

'Apparently, both Philby and Burgess have been reassigned to Washington. But I suppose you already knew that?'

Bone nodded.

'Then Philby arrived and there was more booze.'

'He usually handles it well. An important asset in our trade.'

Catesby looked at his Lord Woolton Pie. 'The pastry is nice. British pastry is the best in the world and worth fighting for. I wish I'd said that to them.' Catesby suddenly slammed down his knife hard. The noise of steel on crockery was loud and turned a good many heads – and evoked at least one whispered *Oh dear.*

'It is a difficult situation.'

Catesby lowered his voice to disguise his anger. 'So you know that the Americans are stitching me up as a suspected Sov agent?'

'There is a lot of paranoia in Washington – largely the result of a SIGINT breakthrough, the biggest since ULTRA.'

'If all this signals intelligence business is naming me as a double, their breakthrough is a load of rubbish.'

Bone lowered his voice to the faintest of whispers. 'So far there is only one verified name, and it isn't yours. But we don't know more than that. GCHQ say the Americans aren't keeping them fully informed.'

Catesby felt both relieved and confused. Had Philby lied and exaggerated to frighten him?

'By the way, how did you get along with Kim Philby?'

'He didn't win me over.'

'Apologies if I sound like Machiavelli, but maybe you should let him win you over – it might be beneficial for your career.'

'Why do you say that?'

'The Director will be retiring in the next year or two and Kim Philby is odds-on favourite to replace him. Which is one of the reasons I helped arrange your interview with him. I also couldn't think of anyone who could better explain your situation as a suspected double.'

Catesby flashed a wry smile.

'Meanwhile, we must think of ways to save your career. The Americans are looking for scalps and I don't want yours to be one of them. You have a valuable career ahead of you.'

'What if it's a career that I no longer want to pursue?'

Bone looked into the distance. 'Oh dear, I hope I don't sense a resignation in the offing.'

'A signed copy will be on your desk tomorrow morning.'

'The Americans will love it. You'll have handed them a scalp and they didn't even have to get blood on their tomahawk.'

'They're welcome. My wife is always nagging me to get a haircut.'

'Actually, William, I can't say I blame you. The conflicts between official duties, conscience and loyalty to friends are struggles that I also have experienced.'

Catesby looked at Bone. He knew his boss's tactics. A dash of frank personal revelation was an aperitif served before a main course of grilled manipulation.

'If,' continued Bone, 'you decide to go through with your resignation, I will personally ensure that you get a glowing reference.' Bone paused and looked at Catesby. 'You must realise, however, that you will always be bound by the Official Secrets Act – and can never reveal, not even give the most veiled hint about anything you saw, read or heard in the Secret Intelligence Service, until the day you die.'

'Thank you, Mr Bone, but I did read the document before I signed it.'

'But there could be problems even if you kept completely and utterly mum. I would not, for example, advise that you renew your ties with the Labour Party. Suppose – and I think it's very likely that you would succeed – you became a Member of Parliament, there would be those lying in wait to pounce with lies and insinuations that you would find it impossible to shake off. You would, almost certainly, be accused of being a Soviet spy who infiltrated SIS and was now aiming at an undercover role in government. As you know, there are totally innocent Labour MPs who are already being targeted and smeared with Moscow connections.'

Bone smiled. 'But that, of course, is another official secret that you dare not ever utter. Likewise, I wouldn't advise a career in journalism. Each of your written words would be subject to forensic examination.' Bone wiped his lips and pushed his soup away. 'I am sure, however, that you will easily find a post teaching foreign languages in a school in darkest East Anglia. Even if mischievous boys pass around rumours that you were once a secret agent, no one at SIS will be worried.'

'Are you trying to intimidate me?'

Bone raised an eyebrow. 'I wouldn't dare. Why are you laughing? Have I said something amusing?'

'Bleakly so.' Catesby looked at his empty plate. 'They like us to put our trays through the dirty cutlery hatch. Or on the trolley next to it.'

'I know. When you eat with the peasants you must follow the rules.'

'And I know that leaving SIS is a messy business.'

'Messier for some than others. The quick route out is a non-return ticket to Moscow . . .'

'You've read my politics wrong, Mr Bone.'

'Oh, I keep forgetting, you're a social democrat – or is it a democratic socialist? In fact, I would love to put the same question to Prime Minister Attlee.'

There was a playful note of contempt in Bone's voice which was to mystify Catesby for decades. Was Bone mocking the Labour Party from the point of view of a Tory or a Marxist? The mystery was never solved.

'Time to clear away,' said Bone as he picked up his tray.

'I'm sorry, Mr Bone, but you've forgotten something.'

Bone gave a quick glance around the table. 'I don't think so.'

'Aren't you going to leave a tip?'

'Thank you, William, a career in comedy obviously beckons. But I will give you a tip. Don't hand in your resignation before you've had your meeting with the Director. There may be some interesting developments. It's scheduled for Tuesday. Meanwhile, have a good weekend with Frances and the twins.'

Stanhope Gardens, London: August 1949

The war damage to the flat in South Kensington was still evident. The botched repairs had been carried out quickly and still needed putting right. The Regency ceiling was water-damaged from burst pipes, and loose hanging plaster was concealed with wallpaper. The house was part of a five-storey terrace and had been divided into flats overlooking the gated gardens. Catesby knew that his parents-in-law hadn't the money to carry out the renovations. They were shabby genteel idealists who had given away most of their inherited wealth – and married off their only daughter to a wharf rat from the Lowestoft docks. Catesby admired their philanthropy – even if some of it, such as handing over a castle to the Workers Educational Association, had reduced their outlays for taxes and repairs. In any case, there were few heirs for passing on property and money. Their only two sons had been killed in the war. Next to that, the war damage to Stanhope Gardens was utterly insignificant.

It was a late supper, and the four-year-old twins were already tucked up in bed. Frances had cooked a beef casserole that Catesby was washing down with Algerian red from a litre bottle – a cheap wine still available from off-licences.

'Lovely nosh,' said Catesby. 'You must be very tired.'

Frances nodded. For just over a year, she had been working part-time at MI5. She had been asked to apply for a post by a friend of her father's, who was, or had been, somewhere high up in the Security Service. Her father also thought that she needed a break from full-time childminding – although Frances later joked that being a grown-up woman at MI5 also involved a lot of childminding. Frances was much more secretive about her job than Catesby was about his. She regarded the Official Secrets Act as a religious vow. Catesby knew that her first duties had been clerical ones that included a lot of typing and taking dictation, but he had the impression that she now was more involved with covert operations – although she never breathed a word about it.

'I'll do the washing-up,' said Catesby. 'Go and have a lie-down.'

'That would be very kind indeed.'

'But before you go, I have an announcement to make.'

'Let me comport myself, Mr Catesby.' Frances put down her fork and folded her hands in her lap. 'I am now ready to receive my husband's pronouncement.'

'You would, Frances, have made a great suffragette. Emily would have been proud of you.' Catesby was referring to a distant cousin of his wife who had been knocked down and killed while trying to attach a suffragette banner to the King's horse at the Epsom Derby.

'Thank you, William. I think our sarcasms have now run their course. But it looks like you do have something important to say.'

'I think that in future I should do most of the cooking. You're now too busy with your extra hours and looking after the twins.'

'You already do your fair share.' Frances tilted her head to the side and gave Catesby a quizzical look. 'What's brought this on?'

'I might be having a lot more time on my hands.'

'Why's that?'

'It looks like my career in the Secret Intelligence Service may be coming to an abrupt end.'

'That's great news. Maybe you could also do some painting and decorating.'

'Well, actually, Frances, if you look at those walls you can see that they need replastering first' – Catesby paused – 'which, I can assure you, is a highly skilled craft. Have you ever seen a plasterer at work?'

'Well, actually, Will, I have seen plasterers at work – on numerous occasions. So don't hurl your long vanished proletarian past at me. Where did you see skilled labourers plying their craft? At Lowestoft Grammar, at King's College, in the SOE officers' mess?'

'This conversation has taken a silly turn.' Catesby held up the wine. '*Carpe vinum*?'

'No thanks, I did Latin too, you know. Apologies for my being super-cilious. I assumed your comment about having to leave SIS was a joke – an over-reaction to a minor telling-off. Can you tell me more about it?'

'It wasn't a joke. Deadly serious. A couple of toffs, both of whom have been reassigned to Washington, invited me for a chat at the FO. It turned out that they'd heard some bad news about me from their future US counterparts.' Catesby swirled his wine. 'To cut to the quick, the Americans think that I'm a Soviet double agent. Ah, you don't look as surprised as I thought you would.'

'The men who told you this, who were they?'

'Guy Burgess, a posh drunk from Eton, and a smooth charmer called Kim Philby.'

The blood seemed to drain from Frances's face.

'Are you okay?'

'I'm fine.'

'No, you're not. You turned white when I mentioned Burgess and Philby.'

'I don't really know what's happening. Just idle office gossip.'

'Your people obviously know a lot more than we do.'

'Forget I said anything. I should wash my mouth out with strong soap.'

'Have a glass of wine instead.'

Frances frowned at Catesby's bottle of Algerian red. 'I'll find something better.'

She returned with a glass of Bordeaux. 'I shouldn't have used this for the cooking. It's too good.'

'From your father's cellar?'

She nodded.

'Then it's far too good.'

'Nothing is too good for a man I love – and want to protect.'

'How does protecting me come into it?'

Frances swallowed her wine. 'There are some serious issues in the intelligence service, and I don't want you to become an innocent victim.'

'Don't tell me anything. I don't want you to get done for breaking the Official Secrets Act.'

'Be wary of Kim Philby – and that isn't based on state secrets.'

'No more.'

'Let's talk about you instead. Has SIS just left you hanging?'

'No, I've got a meeting with the Director on Tuesday.'

'Is Henry Bone involved?'

'He's always involved.'

'A fascinating man,' said Frances. 'He played the organ at my aunt's wedding in Ely Cathedral. I can't remember it, but my parents said he was magnificent.'

'And he was on the sailing team at the 1936 Olympics.'

'With a private life that one must never enquire about.'

'Indeed.'

'We live in world of shifting shadows. Be careful, William.'

Broadway Buildings, London: August 1949

Catesby had followed Bone's advice not to tender his resignation before he was summoned to 'The Seventh Floor', the hallowed location of the Director's office. He wasn't nervous as he navigated the final corridor – and had dressed a bit down by wearing his dark grey demob suit. Most of Catesby's fellow officers passed up the free civilian clothes on offer when they left the army, but he had gladly accepted his – which also included a felt trilby, shoes, shirts and a waterproof mac. The suit, a Burton, was a double-breasted pinstripe. Frances said it made him look like a low-level gangster, but Catesby was wearing it to make a point. He was a common foot soldier who did the intelligence service's dirty work. He gave C's door a hard and angry knock – and a quiet refined voice told him to come in.

Catesby wasn't surprised to see Henry Bone sitting in a corner of the office. The light from the windows was behind him, which gave his grey hair an odd hallow, as if God were sitting in to observe.

'Thank you for coming, Mr Catesby.' The Director was a man of sixty and his voice had a note of tiredness – like that of an ageing colonel who had seen too much carnage, but still had to send men to their deaths. C was a vintage upper-class Englishman. Badly wounded as a Guards officer in the First World War, he had then spent the rest of his career as an intelligence officer – a career that in many ways didn't suit his temperament and abilities. There was a long silence as the Director stared at the papers on his desk. He finally looked up. 'I am sure, Mr Catesby, that you are totally innocent of the accusations emanating from Washington. The Americans are new to the world of intelligence and are like gundog puppies that haven't been fully trained. They run ahead instead of keeping to heel. If the CIA has you in its sights, it is because they can't yet tell the difference between a loyal falcon and a cormorant predating a trout stream.'

Catesby suppressed a smile and tried not to flap his wings.

'Commander Bone and I have had a long discussion about how you can continue your career with the Secret Intelligence Service – and we have come up with a plan to which we hope you will agree. We are not so much asking for a resignation as, shall I say, a sabbatical.' C paused and looked at Bone.

'You will not be an official member of SIS – and won't be on our payroll, but you will be recompensed by other means.'

Catesby wondered if his wearing the demob suit had prompted Bone to bring up the money issue.

'You will,' continued Bone, 'be an SIS asset rather than an officer. As such, you will be operating as an NOC.'

'Non-Official Cover,' echoed Catesby.

'That's right,' said C, 'which means no diplomatic immunity if you get caught. If you take on this job, there are considerable risks involved – so, as you have a wife and children, I would fully sympathise if you turned it down.'

Catesby kept a stony face.

The Director looked past Catesby and nodded towards a painting on his office wall. 'It's by the Victorian artist John Atkinson Grimshaw. He painted it on a Saturday evening on the Glasgow docks. I love the quiet emptiness of the docks and the reflection of the gas lamps on the damp cobblestones. The workers are either home or at the pub. I chose that from the Government Art Collection because I thought it would make me feel relaxed before leaving the office late on a Friday. I was wrong.' He faced Catesby again. 'I don't want our docks and streets to become like Marseille's – and Marseille is the reason we are offering you this undercover job.'

Catesby remembered how Philby and Burgess had mentioned Marseille. It was all linking up. It sounded like C also wanted to send him to Marseille to spy on former colleagues from the Resistance who were now trade union activists on the docks.

'We are concerned,' said the Director, 'about communist-led dock strikes in France disrupting trade and preventing troops and supplies being sent to Southeast Asia.'

Bingo! thought Catesby.

'And, of course,' C continued, 'we have had our own dock strikes here. I see,' he said, looking at a file, 'that you're from Lowestoft. Was there much disruption there during the strike?'

'Not a great deal, but we are a very small port.'

'Indeed, I shouldn't be mentioning British strikes at all. They are Five's business, not ours.'

Catesby noticed Bone suppressing a yawn.

'Which brings us,' said C picking up a sheet of paper, 'to your proposed tasks as an NOC in Marseille.' He leaned over his desk and gave the sheet to Catesby. It was handwritten in the distinctive green ink that had signified a message from C since the earliest days of SIS.

MISSION OBJECTIVES FOR WILLIAM CATESBY

1 Infiltrate and report on groups organising and sympathetic to strike action in Marseille.

2 Be available as a 'dangled double' and cultivate any attempt at recruitment by a foreign intelligence agency. Use any such attempt to compile a list of individuals and methods involved.

3 Report on the role of the mafia and other organised crime groups in Marseille. Of particular interest would be any links between crime syndicates and foreign intelligence agencies.

4 Renew links with Lester Roach, who is now reported to be CIA chief of station for Marseille and the South of France. Report on the methods and successes of CIA operations in Marseille. Be prepared to assist Lester Roach if so advised by SIS.

As he finished reading, Catesby gave Henry Bone a furtive glance. The objectives might have been written with C's green pen, but the words and their hidden codes were Bone's. 'Foreign intelligence agencies' was a Bone euphemism for the CIA.

'If, Mr Catesby, you refuse to accept this job, please forget that this meeting ever took place. Should you ever mention it to anyone – especially to a prying journalist – you will be liable for prosecution under the Official Secrets Act. If, on the other hand, you decide to undertake this mission, you will not have the option of withdrawing. Any attempt to do so could lead to your being taken into custody and kept in indefinite detention. I realise these are harsh terms – and would fully understand your refusing to take it on. Would you like some time to think about it?'

Catesby smiled. There wasn't much to think about when the Secret State had your testicles in a vice. 'Of course not, sir, I'll do it.'

'Jolly good. I like officers to be decisive. Commander Bone will now brief you on some of the unpleasant things that you will have to undergo as part of your cover story.' C rose to shake hands. 'And may I convey a warm and personal thank you for having agreed to carry out this mission. You are a brave officer, and I am proud that you remain part of SIS – however remotely.'

Catesby followed Bone out of C's office and down the service stairs to the sixth floor where the deputy directors had their offices. Bone's was known as 'the jungle'. The first houseplant that greeted you was a huge Monstera whose top leaves brushed against the ceiling. As soon as the door was closed behind them, Bone gestured towards the office foliage and said, 'I think you need a drink more than the green chaps. A snifter of twenty-five-year-old VSOP?'

'How about a large glass of absinthe and an opium pipe?'

'You can still get absinthe at the Café Royal, and when you get to Marseille you will find opium aplenty. But in my office, it's brandy or Earl Grey.'

'I'll go for the brandy.'

While Catesby sipped his drink, Bone busied himself watering his jungle. There were money plants, ivies, succulents and ferns, but much of the foliage was unrecognisable to Catesby. 'I used to think,' said Bone, 'that the best agents were like the best houseplants – almost impossible to kill. But I've changed my mind, not about plants, but about agents. We don't always want them popping up year after year.'

'I didn't kill Dieter.'

'I think we can put that one to rest and move on. As C mentioned, establishing your cover story might involve some discomfort.'

'What sort of discomfort?'

'Being roughed up by Five and Special Branch. We need to make you look like a rogue agent who was sacked for gross misconduct. That will get the Americans off our backs – suspected communist sympathiser dealt with – and also make you more attractive as bait to draw in a number of interested parties.'

'Like the Sovs?' said Catesby with a sceptical smile.

'The Russians wouldn't touch you with a barge pole. They know they would get burned. You are, William, pretending to be a naïf. You know very well who we want to net.'

'You want to dangle me as a down-and-outer who is ripe to turn super-grass?'

'There are a number of possibilities, but the first stage is creating a convincing cover story.' Bone reached for a folder on his desk. 'You are about to embark on a career as a writer and you have already penned your first article. Would you like to have a read before you submit it?'

Catesby read the article with arched eyebrows. It purported to be an exposé of the Secret Intelligence Service, condemning it for dodgy practices, dirty tricks and ignoring the law. 'Fucking hell,' said Catesby, 'we're not that bad!'

'I had to exaggerate a bit to make it more of an explosive scoop. The idea is to make your cover story as a disillusioned intelligence officer turned writer even more credible.'

'I can't put my name to this.'

'It won't be your name; it will be an alias. In any case, the content of the article is irrelevant. It will never see the light of day. It would be clobbered with D-notices before it ever got to the printing presses. The news editor we've chosen is a tame one who abides by the law. He will immediately report receiving it to MI5 – who handle D-notices. The alias will be tracked back to you, and within hours Special Branch and Five will be ransacking your flat and you will be taken into custody – and then released because we don't do court cases on these sorts of things.'

'I need another drink.' As Catesby held out his glass, he looked around for a feline presence. 'Where's Elgar?'

'He's back with his owners. I was only looking after him temporarily – and they've got a new cat called Dmitri.'

Catesby began to hum the invasion theme from the *Leningrad Symphony*.

'Yes, it's that Dmitri – and we must never give up our fight against the enemies of humanity.'

'And that's why I'm going to Marseille?'

'In a convoluted way, yes. By the way, I suggest you take a few days' leave before we send in your article and the fireworks begin.'

As Catesby got up, he nodded at a small table under the greenery where Bone, a keen fly-fisherman, tied his own flies. A fly with an orange body, gold head and silver hairs was mounted in the vice. 'Is that one for me?' said Catesby.

'No, you took a deadly damsel I tied ages ago. But don't worry, you're not for the frying pan. When the job is done, I'll remove the hook and put you back in the water. Cheerio for now.'

Stanhope Gardens, London: August 1949

As Catesby recounted the meeting, Frances seemed ill at ease. 'We still call them DA-Notices, Defence Advisory Notices. The advisory part is very important. We have no legal power to stop an editor from publishing if he or she decides to ignore the notice. I hope Bone really has chosen a tame editor.'

'Are you worried about how this will affect your job?'

'I'm more worried about how it will test our marriage – but war tests marriages as well.'

'Particularly if the husband gets his balls blown off.'

'Don't be crude. I think you should pay a visit to your mother before this kicks off. You hardly ever see her.'

Lowestoft, Suffolk: August 1949

Visits home were never easy because Catesby didn't know what his mother wanted or needed. Though he had an arrangement with a coal merchant to make sure that the bunker was always full, the heat from the Rayburn and the fireplaces didn't seem to penetrate the walls and fabric of the damp house. But maybe it wasn't the damp and the cold, maybe his widowed mother was pining for her native Belgium. She had never seemed happy living in England and insisted that Catesby and his sister speak only Flemish or French within the home – and go to Mass on Sundays and holy days of obligation. As both children were now adults, there was nothing stopping her from going back to Belgium – but Catesby suspected it wouldn't be an easy move. Maybe there were problems with her Belgian family that could never be resolved. His mother was the most secretive person he had ever met. Catesby knew very little about her background in Belgium or how she had got together with his merchant sailor father. He only knew that his mother's family owned a dockside bar in Antwerp. Had his dad walked in when she was tending bar? But, as Catesby's father had died in an accident at sea when he was three years old, he had never been able to ask. As his mother got older she became a more and more devout Catholic – but didn't expect her children to follow her example. When Catesby had declared himself an atheist at the age of fifteen his mother hadn't even blinked.

Even a short spell at home meant that Catesby needed to cheer himself up by going to the pub, but the pub visits weren't always cheering. The native Suffolk side of Catesby's family had always regarded him with suspicion. Going to the grammar and then on to university had severed his working-class roots – and marrying Frances was the final straw. If he tried to get matey at the pub, they accused him of 'talking down'.

The closest thing that Catesby had to a Lowestoft drinking mate was his cousin Jack. It was a strained relationship, but Catesby was closer to Jack than the rest of his Suffolk family. Jack, who had been too young to serve in the war, looked up to his slightly older cousin for having seen action. On the other hand, as a dockworker and union organiser, he felt uneasy drinking with a cousin who was a member of the officer class. Catesby also felt uneasy. By dark coincidence, Jack was exactly the sort of person he had been asked to spy on in Marseille. Nevertheless, the evening had begun pleasantly enough, even though the crushing of the recent dock strikes still rankled with Jack.

'Are you still shuffling papers at the Foreign Office?' asked Jack. A junior job at the FO was the cover story that Catesby fed his family.

'No, I've been promoted.'

'Ohhh,' said Jack.

'I'm now cleaning the Permanent Secretary's toilet and looking after his hygiene needs.'

'Arse-kissing?'

'That's right. And how are things on the docks?'

'Membership is growing – and so is consciousness.'

'So you think the revolution might kick off in East Anglia?'

'Don't be sarcastic, Will. It's only just over a hundred years since the Swing Riots tore these counties apart.' Jack put his hand on Catesby's shoulder. 'And never forget our great kinsman.'

Catesby raised his pint. 'To Robert Kett.'

Jack had a theory that the leader of the sixteenth-century Norfolk rebellion had been a distant ancestor and that the Catesby family name was a derivation: Kett – Cat – Cates – Catesby. Kett's Rebellion had rocked the establishment. At one time he had led a force of 16,000. It was finally defeated by an army led by the Earl of Warwick. Kett was captured and hanged from the walls of Norwich Castle.

Jack looked at Catesby. 'Are you still proud of having stood as a Labour candidate in 1945?'

Catesby wanted to avoid an argument, so he didn't answer.

Jack hammered the bar with his fist. 'Can you imagine a Labour government sending in troops to break a strike?'

The government had invoked the Emergency Powers Act and sent in soldiers and sailors to unload the ships on the London docks.

'It wasn't a pretty sight,' said Catesby.

'It was fucking ugly.'

'So what are you going to do about it, Jack?'

'I've already torn up my Labour Party card and I'm thinking of joining the CP. I met Phil Piratin during the strike, and we had a long chat.' Piratin and Willie Gallacher were the last two Communist Party members elected to the House of Commons.

'What did he say?' Catesby wished that he had bitten his tongue. Did spying on communists now mean spying on your own family? He faked a laugh. 'Don't answer that. The conversation was a private one between you and Comrade Piratin.'

'Nothing much. He said it was important to work closely with left-wing Labour MPs.'

Catesby nodded. He already knew that – and he also knew that those Labour members would soon be in a lot of trouble. Power was a complex business – and he didn't want to give or receive lectures.

Jack picked up the signal that it was time to change the subject. He gave a wry smile. 'How do you think the Blues are going to do this season?'

'We're heading for promotion.'

Catesby's support for Ipswich Town was another family mystery. Jack and the rest of the family supported Norwich City. Catesby's defection was a private matter that he never discussed.

'Want to put a couple of bob on it?' Jack put his hand forward. 'No, let's make it a quid.'

'Frances won't let me gamble.'

'Quite right too. She don't want you losing all her family's money.'

Catesby smiled wanly. Going to university had been bad enough but marrying 'above himself' had permanently sealed his expatriation from the docklands of Lowestoft. Defecting to Russia couldn't have been worse. Although, as a colleague once joked, Catesby's Lowestoft was geographically closer to Moscow than anywhere else in the UK.

'Maybe I could fix you up with one of Frances's school friends. They've got even more dosh than her.'

'Hmm, I might like that idea.' Jack sipped his beer and gave another wry smile. 'Who knows? If I join the CP, they might want to set me up as a Romeo agent to infiltrate the British ruling class.'

The conversation had taken an odd turn and Catesby was a little startled. How the fuck did someone like Jack know about Romeo agents? It was suspicious, but there was no way Catesby was going to start a file on his cousin. In any case, surveillance and spying within the UK itself was not in the legal remit of the SIS – and strictly forbidden, in fact. Domestic spying on its own citizens, that was the job of the Security Service, MI5. A more conscientious SIS officer might have passed a note to Five suggesting a file on Jack – but Catesby wasn't going to do that either. Nothing, however, could have been simpler. It would just have been a matter of passing the note to the other side of their double bed.

Green Park, London: August 1949

A coded message to his office phone had summoned Catesby to the usual rendezvous bench in Green Park. It was a ten-minute walk from Broadway Buildings, but less likely to attract prying eyes than St James's – which turned into a virtual brothel after pub closing time. If Catesby had been an officer in the Guards or the Household Cavalry, he would have warned his handsome young soldiers that St James's Park was not a secure venue to top up their pay. But, alas, it was tradition. And Catesby knew that at least a few of their clients worked at SIS.

As usual, Henry Bone was impeccably turned out in bowler and brolly and reading a copy of the *Financial Times*. Not entirely a disguise, for the road between the City and the intelligence service was a busy two-way venue. Former intelligence officers were much in demand.

Bone didn't raise an eyebrow until Catesby was sitting beside him. He carefully folded away his newspaper before he spoke. 'Are you enjoying your spot of leave?'

'Not much. Would you like to help with the painting and decorating?'

'Actually, Catesby, I'm quite a dab hand at restoring Regency period cornices – of which, I am sure, the properties in Stanhope Gardens have an abundance.'

'So you will pitch in?'

'It will be a pleasure.'

'Should I stock up on Lapsang Souchong or Earl Grey?'

'Both, but I probably won't be able to get stuck in until the Marseille business is over.'

'Typical, the best builders are never there when you need them.' Catesby paused. 'And I suppose you're now going to go on about that newspaper article.'

'I decided to do a bit of a rewrite. Have a look.' Bone passed over a folder.

Catesby read the new headline out aloud: 'Why I Left MI6: Former Spy Spills the Beans on the Secret Intelligence Service.'

'And there are a few more changes.'

Catesby read the rest and handed the folder back to Bone. 'Gutter press journalism at its finest. I like the honeytrap sex scandal. It would have made the Marquis de Sade blush with envy. Any truth in it?'

'I couldn't possibly say.'

'How many people will actually see it?' said Catesby.

'The editor and maybe one or two of his assistants – and a few of the D-notice people at Five – enough, I hope, to get the rumour mills percolating.'

'I'm worried about the embarrassment it's going to cause Frances.'

'Her colleagues will rally around her; you're the bad 'un.'

'What's the next stage?'

'Even though your identity as the author of the article will be hushed up, insiders in the publishing world will know who you are – a fearless writer and secret agent gone rogue. You will be hunted down by a publisher who will give you a large advance to write a reveal-all book about the French Resistance. After which, you will head to Marseille and ensconce yourself in a writer's garret to research your work-in-prog.'

'It sounds utterly mad.'

'And so did DoubleCross, but we pulled it off.' Bone was referring to the deception operation that fed false information to Nazi Germany in the lead-up to D-Day.

'When is my faked-up article going to the newspaper?'

'Tomorrow morning. So have a good evening, it may be your last for a while.' Bone adjusted his bowler hat and strode off.

Stanhope Gardens, London: August 1949

It was Catesby's turn to cook, and he regaled Frances with Elizabeth David's *coq au vin*. Years later, Catesby's own quicker version became known in the family as 'prick au plonk', but on this occasion he went to some trouble. His efforts, however, did not mollify Frances. Unusually for her, an abstemious drinker, she had hit the gin and shouted at Catesby, 'You shouldn't have fucking gone along with this!' There was a lot more shouting to come.

Catesby felt groggy the next morning. The flat was a mess. Frances had stomped off to work without saying goodbye and the twins were being looked after by her parents. Catesby was tempted to add a slug of brandy to his tea but resisted. He had recently taken up running again – he'd been a stalwart of the cross-country team at the grammar – and too much booze didn't help. Catesby tried to imagine scenarios in which being able to run two miles in less than thirteen minutes would be useful to his career as an intelligence officer. But an East Bloc border guard wouldn't bother trying to keep up, he would just shoot the fleeing Catesby in the back.

The telephone rang. Catesby stared at the black Bakelite with disdain before he picked up the receiver. 'Chelsea 3928.'

'Good morning. May I speak to Mr Catesby?' The voice was that of the newspaper editor.

'Speaking.'

'Sorry to tell you this, Mr Catesby, but we seem to have run into a spot of bother with your article.'

Catesby was furious that the editor knew his telephone number as well as his identity. Bone had decided not to waste time in dropping him in the shit – but quick was probably best.

The editor didn't give much away, other than that Catesby's article was 'not likely to appear in the near future'.

They turned up in force one hour after the editor's phone call. The thug leading the gang was someone from MI5's A Branch whom Catesby recognised but didn't know by name. His specific section was A1A, a collection of lock pickers, bug planters, burglars, photographers and document collectors. But on this occasion, there was no need to break in or do anything covert. They were well armed with search warrants. In fact, it was more of a police operation than a Security Service sweep. The people carrying out the searches were cops from Special Branch, but they were told where to look and what to look for by the weasels from A Branch.

The search had hardly begun when Frances turned up escorted by a man in his forties. Catesby imagined that he must be someone from personnel or counterintelligence. Frances's face was livid. She turned to her colleague who was leading the searchers. 'I doubt if you will find anything, Philip. My husband never brings home any papers. He's too lazy to work evenings or weekends.'

Colleague Philip gave a knowing smile.

Frances turned to Catesby. 'You fucking bastard. You've never grown up – and now this! I hope you rot in jail and my children never see you again.'

Catesby knew that Frances's swearing and shouting at him in front of her colleagues was partly an act, but a lot of the anger was genuine too. He looked at her and spread his hands apologetically. 'I'm sorry, what I did was ill advised. I wish . . .'

'Fuck off, lying bastard.'

Catesby was concerned that one of the Special Branch constables was a woman. Was she there to search Frances herself? At the very least, it would be seemly to have a WPC there to go through his wife's underwear drawer. Catesby smiled at the WPC. 'Sorry the place is a bit of a mess. We're in the middle of painting and decorating.'

'No problem, sir, we've coped with worse.'

The most embarrassing thing about the search wasn't Frances's underwear drawer, but the bookshelves. Books were an intimate picture of the inner lives of the people who owned and read them. Catesby watched as one of the police searchers handed over each of the seven volumes of *À la recherche du temps perdu* to an MI5 officer who had expressed an interest. Catesby felt that his attempt, however fruitless, to become a person of culture was being defiled by the hands of a barbarian. The books were full of underlinings and marginalia – most were the pretentious preening of an undergraduate trying to escape the docks of Lowestoft. Hardly what one would expect of a potential Sov spy. The item of Catesby's that attracted the most interest was a pair of binoculars. He explained that they didn't belong to SIS but were his own personal pair and that he used them for birdwatching on his trips home to Suffolk – and showed the A Branch searcher his collection of bird books.

The searcher shrugged. 'Have you got a personal weapon too?'

'Yes, but it's kept locked away in the arms room at Broadway Buildings. Wouldn't want it in a flat with children.'

The MI5 officer was now thumbing through a copy of *Le Petit Prince* that Catesby hoped one day to read aloud to the twins. Something snapped in Catesby. He ripped the book from the hands of the searcher. 'Take your fucking hands off that.'

The Old Bailey, London: August 1949

The fight at Stanhope Gardens hadn't been scripted by Henry Bone, but he was pleased it had taken place and said so when he visited Catesby in his police cell beneath the Old Bailey.

Bone looked at Catesby's black and swollen eye. There were stitches above the eye and below his lip. 'You look like you came off worse.'

'He was bigger than me and had help.'

'It's lucky that your SOE unarmed combat training didn't kick in. You could have been here on a murder charge.'

'Please don't mock me, Mr Bone.'

'I am, Catesby, as you well know, totally incapable of mockery or any form of insincerity.'

'How silly of me to forget.'

'In any case, I have some very good news. They have decided not to press charges and you are free to go – but we must wait for the custody sergeant to check the paperwork.'

'Have you seen Frances?'

'Yes, we had a brief chat – but she has to keep her cards close to her chest if she wants to keep her job in Five.' Bone paused. 'And I think we know why she wants to keep her job.'

'Her brothers.'

'They gave their all – and she wants, somehow, to live up to their example. You are, William, cursed, or blessed, with a wife who will always love her country more than she loves you.'

Catesby nodded.

'By the way, she is proud of what you did. That book is something she regards as sacred too.'

'Her brothers, although they were grown up, will always be her own "little princes".' Catesby paused. It was as if he was a rock fixed in time. 'The images of those burnt bodies will never leave me.'

Bone whispered the name of the village, 'Oradour-sur-Glane.'

'I couldn't count them. There were too many to count. The poor little children were all in that incinerated church – a great pile of them behind the altar, the blackened remains of a pram and baby in front of it, the two sisters, not burned, but shot as they hid in the confessional.' There were no tears; Catesby's face had turned to stone. 'They are my little princesses – and all the others too.'

Bone had heard the story when they interviewed Catesby for SIS. It had left some doubts among the interviewing team whether he was emotionally suitable for a job as a cold-blooded SIS officer, but Bone had overcome their doubts about the applicant.

Catesby hoped Bone hadn't seen his tears. He wiped his eyes and laughed, 'It's why I punched that bastard from Five. How dare he touch that book. *Le Petit Prince* is a sacred bond between Frances and me. When we first became lovers we would lie together reading passages to each other. She was particularly drawn to near the end. The little prince has been bitten by a poisonous snake. He explains that he must leave, but if you look into the night sky you will see his star. Except, as you won't know which star is his, you will have to love all the stars. Afterwards, when the night was clear, Frances and I would go into the garden and look at the sky, she looking for her brothers' stars and me looking for the children of Oradour-sur-Glane.'

There was a jangling of keys outside the cell door. The custody sergeant had returned. Catesby was free.

Islington, London: September 1949

It was decided that Catesby should spend a few days following his release from prison in an SIS safe house in Islington. One set of neighbours were cops and on the other side was a bachelor banker who had little curiosity about the outside world. The site was well chosen. On the surface, Henry Bone's plan seemed to have worked out perfectly. If there were any doubts, it was because it was almost too perfect. There were no stories in the press and, even though Catesby's identity had been hushed up, the rumour mills were churning – embellishing. The actual story concocted by Bone, that of a disillusioned MI6 officer who resigned to expose dubious practices, was very boring compared to the gossip circulating. Catesby had been disappeared to protect a number of people in positions of power. A much more uncomfortable rumour, which later came back to haunt him, was that Catesby was part of a Soviet spy ring that had penetrated SIS and the FO at the highest level. Although the whispered gossip provided tea break entertainment, the real insiders knew that something more subtle was going on with Catesby. They didn't know who was pulling his strings – or even if there were any strings – but they wanted to find out. The jungle telegraph would soon be tapping messages to Paris and Washington. The SDECE, *Service de Documentation Extérieure et de Contre-Espionnage*, the CIA and many others would shortly be on Catesby's tail. He wouldn't be lonely when he washed up in Marseille.

On Catesby's final night in the safe house, he had a visitor, a woman dressed in black with a lace veil over her face. She looked a bit tipsy, as if she had been to a wake that had lasted long into the evening. Catesby was reluctant to answer the door and wished that he hadn't handed in his Webley revolver. He looked through the peephole but could only see the back of a black hat. Catesby decided to risk opening the door on its chain latch. His visitor had shapely legs and smelled nice. He recognised the perfume. It was a mix of plum, patchouli and vanilla. It was the fragrance of someone about to do something wicked – a perfume almost designed to mix with the smell of gun oil and burnt powder. The last time he had encountered that perfume was at a birthday party, his own, and Frances was wearing it.

He undid the latch. 'Nice to see you, assuming it is you under that disguise.'

Frances removed her hat and veil. 'I don't think I was followed. Your wrongdoing wasn't important enough to merit a watcher.'

'Thanks.'

'Let's go to bed.'

It was some of the best and most passionate lovemaking of their marriage. Frances being in disguise and Catesby being in disgrace seemed to enhance their desire. Afterwards, there were no words, only the closeness of fulfilment – but in the morning it was back to normal.

'I suppose,' said Catesby, 'you've forgiven me.'

'Not entirely. I think you should have quietly resigned and not gone along with Bone's scheme. You could easily have found a job as a modern languages teacher – and the pay wouldn't have been that much worse. Henry Bone, and maybe others in SIS, are dangling you on a string. You should have made a clean break.'

'I want to change things.'

'What things?'

'I don't know, but I'm going to find out.'

Frances smiled. 'It would be nice to have a holiday one day in the South of France with the twins.'

Stanhope Gardens, London: September 1949

The letter from the publisher came a week after Catesby had moved out of the flat. It was posted to Stanhope Gardens as Catesby found out via a note from Bone. SIS didn't like handing out safe house addresses. When Catesby arrived, the flat was a total mess. Frances had got the builders in and stripping the water-damaged plaster was the first task.

'Why don't you move out until the job is done?' he said.

'I might have to. My childminder has quit. She says she's not looking after children in the middle of a building site.'

'My mother could help.' Although they were stepchildren, the result of Frances's wartime teenage liaison with a Canadian officer, Catesby's mother regarded them as her very own grandchildren – and they loved her as their own granny.

'And so can my parents. We'll find a way through it.'

'Fine.' Catesby knew that when it came to the children, Frances always had the final word. 'I believe there's some post for me.'

Frances handed over the letter.

As soon as Catesby saw the letterhead, he could see Bone's game plan. The publisher was renowned for left-wing books, the perfect port of call for a disgruntled lefty who had been sacked from the intelligence service. Catesby read the letter. As Bone had predicted, the publisher wanted to commission him to write a book about the Special Operations Executive and the French Resistance. The letter suggested that the advance and travel expenses would be generous. Catesby was pleased that Bone understood that he needed the money.

He showed the letter to Frances. 'I wonder if your colleagues at Five would like to check out the publisher?'

'They already have.'

'And what do they think of them?'

'Well,' said Frances, 'I couldn't possibly tell you as you are no longer a fully functioning member of the Secret Intelligence Service.' She paused. 'But your publishers may not be all they seem to be.'

Bloomsbury, London: 9 September 1949

The publisher's office was in an elegant Georgian townhouse that seemed in much better post-war nick than Stanhope Gardens. The person who dealt with Catesby was a woman in her thirties who was brisk but formally polite.

'We are,' she said, 'interested in a series of books linking the experience of the war to post-war politics and social change. By the way, we tried to recruit George Orwell after *Animal Farm* was turned down by Gollancz – and one of the factors that attracted us to you as an author was your similarity to Orwell.'

'I suppose I could change my name to Blyth or Deben.'

The Suffolk rivers joke fell flat, and the woman continued. 'Your leaving the intelligence service has echoes of Orwell resigning from the Indian Imperial Police.'

'And his parents lived in Southwold.'

'Oh, did they?'

'Just down the coast from where I was born.' He could see that the woman needed help in fleshing out the Catesby/Orwell similarities.

She continued. 'The story of the French Resistance is one that is beginning to appeal to readers of all types. I believe that Violette Szabo was a colleague of yours.'

'I briefly trained with her. She was parachuted into the Limousin to become part of our *réseau* but was captured before we could rendezvous.'

'I have heard there are plans to make a film of her life.'

'She was a hero – as were many women. My story is insignificant compared to theirs.'

'But you were at the centre of things.'

It was painfully apparent that the woman was trying hard to justify offering him a large advance and taking him on as an author. The sum proposed amounted to a year's salary at SIS – and on top of that were generous travel expenses. As the woman continued to explain the financial side of things, Catesby could see that she was embarrassed. 'Of course,' she said, 'we are fully aware that you are still constrained by the Official Secrets Act.'

'And,' said Catesby, 'that any manuscript would have to be vetted by the Secret Intelligence Service before publication?' He looked at the woman. Catesby thought she was trying hard not to smile.

'By the way, if you decide to accept . . .'

'Which I would be a fool not to.' Catesby made no attempt to disguise the irony in his tone. 'I'm happy to sign now.'

'There are two copies.' The woman laid out the contracts.

As Catesby signed, he wanted to say, *This isn't a publishing contract, it's a money-laundering exercise.*

She gathered up the papers with a look of relief. 'Thank you.'

He knew the game, and he wasn't going to call her out. It was a publishing house that wouldn't survive without dosh from the Secret Intelligence Services. He suspected that passing on info about their lefty authors was also part of the deal.

As Catesby emerged from the building, he saw a stately figure striding across Russell Square as if he owned the freehold. It was Henry Bone, who was obviously keeping tabs on events.

Lowestoft, Suffolk: September 1949

Catesby managed to fit in one more visit to Lowestoft before setting off for France. Part of the reason was to test-drive the Standard 8 which he had bought on the recommendation of the head mechanic who ran the SIS motor pool in Vauxhall. The car was small, uncomplicated and non-descript – the perfect secret agent. It managed the 140 miles to Lowestoft without a grumble. The only surprise came from his mother. Cousin Jack had asked her to give him French lessons. 'Was he thinking of joining the Foreign Legion?' joked Catesby.

'He said he was thinking of getting a job on a boat.'

How odd, thought Catesby, and how unlikely.

Soho, London: September 1949

There was one more meeting with Henry Bone before Catesby departed for France – a meeting as odd as it was unexpected. It took place, at the behest of Bone, in a basement jazz club in Soho and Bone was seated with a beautiful woman. At first, she looked far too prim and proper to be in a jazz club, but later Catesby discerned a note of role-playing. Bone was dressed more casually than the woman: a cravat instead of a tie and a blue blazer. His role-playing was less convincing. They were both drinking champagne from a bottle in a silver ice bucket. Bone beckoned Catesby over with a hearty wave. It was utterly bizarre. Catesby wondered if Bone had taken to high-class pimping. The woman was a study in buttoned-up eroticism, but as soon as Catesby joined them the eroticism disappeared behind a veneer of cold primness.

'William, let me introduce you to Helen Stuart,' said Bone.

Catesby gave a silent nod.

'And let me pour you some champagne – it's on the house. Helen is an old friend of the owner.'

The woman gave a slight frown of embarrassment. 'As is my husband, who will be joining us later. He's been held up at the Foreign Office.'

'They often work late,' said Catesby.

The woman fixed him with a cold stare.

'The Stuarts,' said Bone, 'are only in London briefly. Helen's husband is head of the British consulate in Marseille and there are many loose ends that need to be tied up before they return.' Bone lowered his voice. 'And you are one of them.'

Catesby remained silent. He didn't know how to respond to being called a loose end.

'I've told Helen that you will be working undercover in Marseille and need a secure means of communicating with London. She has agreed to be your go-between. I have given her a few tips on dead drops and clandestine meetings, but don't overdo the use of tradecraft. It's best that you're just two Brits in Marseille who occasionally cross paths and say hello, nothing suspicious. A discreet chalk mark, however, to request a rendezvous may be useful.'

'I'm very fond of going for walks by the sea,' said Helen. 'There's a wall on a bridge embankment that I often pass. You seldom see other people there.' She reached into her handbag. 'Here's a map of where to find it.'

Catesby quickly folded the paper into his pocket.

'If you scrape a line on the wall, which is easy to do inconspicuously as it's only waist high, I will expect to meet you there at one p.m. on the following Friday.'

Catesby was impressed. He wondered if Bone had given her some training.

Helen sipped her champagne and smiled. 'I was hoping it would be even more cloak and dagger – a change from the dull routine of being a consul's wife.'

Bored wives in foreign postings were a big problem for any country's diplomatic corps. They were often easy pickings for Romeo agents. The intelligence service boffins maintained that the keys to being a successful Romeo were good manners, listening skills, flowers and a love of shopping; good looks and sexual athletics rarely mattered. Catesby eyed Helen. He wasn't sure those rules applied to her.

Bone looked at his watch and sighed. 'I am very sorry, Helen, but I'm going to have to drag William away as we have another appointment.'

She stared at Catesby with unblinking eyes. 'I look forward to meeting you again in Marseille, however brief our encounters.'

Bone led Catesby out of the club just as an alto sax sounded the opening notes of Duke Ellington's 'Sophisticated Lady'. The piece was a jazz standard, but Catesby thought the timing and choice were no accident.

As soon as they emerged onto the streets of Soho, Catesby turned to Bone. 'You didn't tell me we had another appointment.'

'We haven't, I wanted to get away so I could tell you more about Helen Stuart. She's not just a go-between for passing on messages, but someone we want you to watch. She looks and sounds utterly English, but she isn't. Her father is an Anglo-Irish aristo who breeds horses, and her mother is French. She speaks fluent French, and she spent the war with her mother in Lyon.' Bone smiled. 'She'll fit in with your cover story. If you're seen with her, it would look like you were interviewing her for your book on the Resistance.'

'What exactly did she do in Lyon?'

'We don't know, but we would like to find out more about what Mrs Stuart may be up to in general. A few alarm bells are ringing in the Foreign Office. There are rumours about the marriage, but her husband is close-lipped.'

Catesby decided to keep his mouth shut too. There was something about Helen that both thrilled and frightened him.

'By the way, what do you think of your publisher?'

'Your gambit, Mr Bone, was woefully transparent. The woman at the publishing house struggled to keep a straight face.'

'As you so astutely guessed, His Majesty's Government are underwriting your publishing contract, every single penny.'

'And authors don't have to pay back an advance.'

'But they do have to fulfil the conditions of the contract – which in your case is finding out what the Americans are doing in Marseille. They're getting up to some dirty tricks which, if left out of control, could affect the future of Western Europe and the United Kingdom.'

'What are these dirty tricks?'

Bone reached into his jacket pocket and handed over a document marked TOP SECRET, NOFORN and EYES ONLY.

Catesby smiled. 'Not the sort of thing you want to lose in a jazz club.'

'His name is blacked out, but it's about Lester Roach.'

It was only a summary, but a lethal summary. Catesby finished and passed the file back. 'He's either mad or evil.'

Suffolk: March 2018

Catesby stared out the window of his garden office. 'We need to get the broad beans in.'

'But, Granddad, you always say you're going to plant them in October, so they overwinter and get an early start.'

'And I never get around to it because I'm a disorganised hobbledehoy. That's why I ended up in SIS; no one else would hire me. But, as for last October, there were some beautiful autumn days and I decided on fly fishing rather than gardening.'

'Did you ever go fly fishing with Henry Bone?'

'Sadly, no. He had some aristocratic friends with splendid trout and salmon rivers running through their estates.'

'Henry Bone was an enigma.'

'Indeed.'

'I have,' said Leanna, 'asked you this question before. Was he one of the Cambridge spy ring?'

'And I've answered it before. I'm certain that Henry Bone wasn't a Sov agent, but he protected two of those who were.'

'Anthony Blunt and Kim Philby.'

'Correct. He covered for Blunt as the result of a long friendship – and also because he believed that his spying did little or no harm to the United Kingdom. It was mostly drinks-party gossip. As for Philby, I don't think Henry liked him as a person, but until his dying day he believed that Kim was a fake double who had duped the Russians.'

'Granny says she would gladly have followed Philby to Beirut and taken him out with a full clip from her Browning nine millimetre.'

'Then she would have been acting against the wishes of the Secret Intelligence Service.'

'So Henry Bone wasn't the only one protecting him from exposure.'

'It wasn't a matter of "protecting", Leanna, it was simply a matter of not believing he was guilty. C and the others could not conceive how a well-born gentleman – like themselves – could ever be a traitor. The Americans, they thought, had turned paranoid over VENONA and were rushing to a hasty judgement – and were utterly clueless about the subtle rules and refined propriety of the British upper class. If you weren't born into that elite, you couldn't possibly understand how it worked.'

'But you did, Granddad.'

'Eventually. I sometimes felt like an anthropologist studying a remote tribe – and Henry Bone was an interesting specimen. I visited him a few days before he died. He made the usual joke about me bearing the surname of one of the Gunpowder Plot conspirators – and, once again, I pointed out that the Catesbys of Suffolk were far too common. Henry nodded agreement – and suggested that the Gunpowder conspirators were the precursors of the Cambridge spy ring: "Aristocrats plotting against an establishment that was an enemy to what they regarded as the One True Faith, even though the Spanish Inquisition was in full swing." "So Soviet Communism," I said, "was the One True Faith?" I waited for an answer, but Henry just stared blankly into space. A nurse then came in to change the sheets. When he was neat and tidy again, Henry said he had asked for "In Paradisum" from Fauré's *Requiem* to be played at his funeral. "I used to play it on the organ to entertain the peasants," he said, "as it is a piece of music so easy to comprehend – but, unfortunately, I won't be able to do so on this occasion."' Catesby smiled. 'It was wonderful to see Henry Bone's characteristic sense of humour even on his deathbed.'

Leanna shuffled through the pages of her granddad's memoir. 'I hope you don't mind my saying this, but SIS seems to have been run with a lack of professionalism and management accountability.'

Catesby smiled. 'Too much secrecy creates chaos and mistrust.'

Leanna picked up a sheet of paper. 'In your interview with Philby and Burgess, they were behaving like playground bullies.'

'Bullies with charm and single malt whisky. They told me I was for the chop – and maybe worse – and I was taken in.'

'And then Henry Bone stepped in and saved your scalp.'

'The Marseille caper verged on total madness. The problem was that I was working for two bosses.'

'I had that impression, but could you clarify who they were.'

'One was the Director and the other was Henry Bone. I quickly realised that working for the Director, soon to retire, was a cover story – and that my real boss was Bone.'

'Are you sure he wasn't working for Moscow?'

Catesby stared out the window at a pair of male blackbirds who were fighting for territory. 'Absolutely sure. Henry Bone was a patriotic Englishman who thought he was outwitting the Russians.'

'Why are you laughing, Granddad?'

'Maybe Bone was outwitting me.'

'There is, however, a certain logic to Bone's actions.'

'Logic in the world of espionage often turns out to be a false flag op.'

Leanna looked at her watch. 'I think that's enough for today, Granddad – but one final question.'

'Go on.'

'Why, after so much betrayal and disillusionment, did you never leave the SIS?'

'The Secret Intelligence Service is not a club from which you can resign. It is a life sentence and I'm still serving it.'

Northern France: September 1949

Catesby was putting the Standard 8 through its paces. It was his first road trip to France – and the sense of freedom was exhilarating. He wanted to enjoy himself before getting back to work. Business was due to begin in Paris, where Catesby had a rendezvous with Paul, a former Resistance comrade – but that was still two days away. Catesby decided to follow the coastal route on his way to the French capital. After disembarking at Calais, Catesby aimed the Standard 8 down the Route Nationale towards Boulogne. His original plan had been to spend the night in Abbeville, but the thought of a detour to Étaples, a small fishing port on the River Canche, appealed to him. Catesby was already imagining a simple meal of *moules-frites* washed down with cold beer. In the summer before the war, he had been recruited by some posh friends to crew a yacht from Orford in Suffolk to Étaples. He had loved every minute of it. One of the friends had been killed in Burma at the very end of the war – and a visit to the port would also be a homage.

The post-war French roads were mostly empty. The biggest hold-ups were caused by farm carts pulled by horses or bullocks – not too different from Suffolk. The first big delay came when a farmer hauling a load of hay in a horse cart stopped to have a chat with another farmer driving an empty cart in the opposite direction – that kind of thing held up traffic in Suffolk too. Catesby wasn't bothered and was tempted to get out of the car to join them – and maybe get some info about restaurants and places to stay. It was then that he first noticed the car behind him, an impressive vehicle, a sports car with a soft top that had been folded down. Later, Catesby learned it was a Talbot Lago Grand Sport – a very exclusive and expensive piece of business. Only a handful had been built in the years following the war and you needed to be well connected as well as rich to buy one. Catesby studied the driver in his rear-view mirror. He was wearing dark glasses and a black leather jacket with a white fur collar. He didn't look happy and was tapping leather-gloved fingers on the inlaid wood steering wheel. The farmers continued chatting and the driver pressed a loud long blast on the horn. One of the farmers gave a contemptuous glance and went on talking. The driver shouted, '*Quittez la route, bande de crétins stupides!*' Catesby thought both men would have ignored him if an ancient beat-up van hadn't pulled up behind the cart in the lane opposite. The van driver seemed to be a local and, after calling out a greeting, the cart drivers moved on so the van could pass. The sports car driver then floored his accelerator and roared down the road as he made a rude sign with his right hand.

Catesby had enjoyed the confrontation and was pleased that the peasants hadn't retreated. As he set off in the wake of the sports car, he gave a fond wave to the cart drivers. A minute later, he passed the sports car parked by the side of the road. The driver was studying a map. Or pretending to? Catesby's antennae began to twitch. The twitching intensified five minutes later when he saw the sports car looming in his rear-view. Catesby wondered if he was being followed. Surely no intelligence service operative or professional gangster would use such a car to tail someone. In the French countryside, the sports car was an eye-catching display of wealth that stood out like a sore thumb. Likewise, Catesby's right-hand drive Standard 8 was conspicuous. It was, however, an easy problem to solve: just turn off the main road or make a U-turn and see what happens. A road appeared on the left, signposted to Hesdin-l'Abbé. Catesby took the turning without signalling, but it didn't trick the driver behind – who drew closer as he realised that Catesby was trying to shake him off his tail. Catesby considered slamming on the brakes and ruining the beautiful front grillework of the sports car as it ploughed into his rear, but the resulting impact might send him through his own windscreen. And, even if he held on in the driver's seat, the boot of the Standard 8 – where Catesby had packed his handgun – would be too smashed for him to retrieve the weapon. The terrible thing about this deadly situation was that Catesby was enjoying himself. He took the Boulogne turning at speed and for a moment the Standard 8 balanced on two wheels. The sports car, a much lower-slung vehicle, followed with ease. Catesby admired his pursuer's driving skill and wondered if he had racing experience. A heavily laden lorry soon appeared lumping down the road ahead. Catesby decided to overtake and immediately slow down so there would be no space between himself and the lorry for the other driver to squeeze into. With his pursuer in front, Catesby would peel off on to a side road and lose him. The driver must have read his mind, for as soon as Catesby began to overtake, he pulled up alongside Catesby to block the manoeuvre. It happened twice and then Catesby gunned his engine and managed to overtake the lorry on a blind bend – a foolish thing to do, but it worked. As soon as Catesby slowed down to put the Standard 8 bumper to bumper with the lorry, the lorry driver began to sound his horn – and no sign of the sports car overtaking. Catesby realised that the driver in pursuit had fallen back to observe his next move – and he would be easily followed if he took a turning. The lorry's horn was deafening, and Catesby decided it was time to get away. As he floored the accelerator, the exhaust gave a loud pop. It sounded like a gunshot, but Catesby was more worried about the engine blowing up. The top speed rendered by the Standard 8's 1021cc engine was just a hair over 60mph. He glanced in the rear-view and was relieved that the sports car was not behind him. A crossroads appeared and Catesby did a handbrake turn at speed. He could smell the brake pads burning. No problem. Had he lost the bastard? He looked again in the rear-view. He hadn't. While the driver smiled in seeming contempt, Catesby memorised his number plate. But if murder was on the agenda, a dead brain would be unable to pass on the information. Catesby wondered if the man would keep following until he had to stop at a railway junction or some other barrier. He could then calmly get out of his car and put a bullet in Catesby's head. A more likely outcome than an invitation to join him for supper – but you never know.

Catesby was on a long straight section of road when he spotted the tricolour flag and the sign below it: CASERNE DE GENDARMERIE NATIONALE. There were two severe barrack-like buildings behind it. What luck – assuming the gate wasn't locked. But if it was, the gendarmes would have an easy time finding his body. Catesby again did a quick turn without indicating. The tall iron gate was wide open. The only uniforms evident were those hanging on a washing line. The only person around was the woman hanging out the washing. Catesby looked behind him. The sports car had stopped on the road outside the gate. The woman put down her washing basket and began to walk over to Catesby's car. The driver then gunned his engine and drove off. He must have decided that carrying out a hit in the grounds of a Gendarmerie barracks was inadvisable.

The woman had obviously noticed that Catesby's car was British. She approached without suspicion and asked, 'Are you lost, monsieur?'

'No, I want to report a dangerous driver.'

'This is France, monsieur, all our drivers are dangerous.'

'Could I report him to an officer?'

'We are only a barracks, monsieur; no one is on duty here. If you want to report something you should go to the commissariat at Samer.'

Catesby smiled bleakly. It was obvious that the local cops weren't going to be much help; especially if no crime had been committed. He was also vaguely ashamed of trying to take the coward's way out. Catesby started his car and began to drive back to the road. He stopped, however, at the gate to do a recce. The sports car didn't appear to be in sight, but he wondered if the driver was lying hidden in the long grass. Catesby decided it was time to tool up. He got out of the car and took his Webley revolver from the boot. A lot of his colleagues in the service had ditched the ageing Webley for Browning 9mm automatics. But, as Catesby joked, how do you play Russian roulette with a clip-fed automatic? Besides, revolvers were less likely to jam in a crisis. As he reloaded, he wondered if the woman with the washing was watching him and turned to block her view. Back in the car, he found that the Standard 8's deep door compartments fitted the Webley nicely. He practised retrieving it and was ready to go.

Catesby decided to turn back towards the coast and weave his way to Étaples. Gunfight or no gunfight, he was determined to have a supper of *moules-frites*, but probably washed down with a nice white wine rather than beer. The countryside was, however, a problem. It was low, flat and very open. It would be easy for Catesby's pursuer to spot him from a distance. On the other hand, it would also be easy for Catesby to see if he was being followed. Countersurveillance techniques made the trip a long, leisurely one. Catesby doubled back several times and occasionally left the car to search the roads and countryside with binoculars. No sign of the sports car. He wondered if the driver had been frightened off by his pulling into the Gendarmerie barracks. Was he a nutcase who had enough sense left to be wary of cops? As Catesby drove along, he touched the gun in the side pocket and wondered if *he* was the nutcase: a traumatised spy suffering from paranoia. Nonetheless, when he went out to explore Étaples that evening and find a place to eat, he kept the Webley in a small rucksack slung over his shoulder.

The Étaples riverside evoked bittersweet memories in Catesby. There was a huge tidal difference and the fishing boats and yachts lay in the mud most of the day. It was only possible to get in or out of the port for one hour either side of high water. Catesby loved sailing because nature made the rules and humans had to play along with them – and if you didn't, you got wrecked and maybe drowned. The friend who had asked Catesby to crew on the sail from Suffolk to Étaples had been a little death-obsessed. On one occasion they had cycled to the churchyard in Iken, with its stunning views over the River Alde. Julian had breathed in and shouted: 'This is where I want to be buried! Don't let them bury me anywhere else!' Sadly, Catesby hadn't been much help. Julian was interred 7,000 miles away in the Taukkyan Commonwealth War Cemetery in Burma. The war had almost wiped out the family – his older brother Pen had been killed in 1941. Maybe Julian's obsession with death had been a premonition. Catesby wiped away a tear as he looked at the pier where they had moored. Why was he still alive? He wanted to wrap his arms around all his dead friends who hadn't made it to the finishing line and shout, *I should be with you!*

Catesby, replete with wine, slept very late. The hotel staff had been sympathetic and hadn't disturbed his lie-in. If they had woken him earlier, he would now be truly asleep – the Big Sleep. Catesby had packed his bags and enjoyed a leisurely breakfast of croissants and coffee. The sun was high in the sky as he made his way with his luggage to the Standard 8, which was parked by the quayside. The tide was up and the nearby fishing boats, luckily for them, were chugging out to sea. It wasn't a spectacular explosion, not at first, it even sounded a bit muffled, but the flames that followed it were truly dramatic. Catesby had filled up as soon as he reached the outskirts of Calais. The orange flames were not just dangerous; they were also beautiful and – thanks to the exchange rate – cheaper than British ones.

Amiens, France: September 1949

This time the Gendarmerie Nationale did take an interest. Catesby was taken to a large headquarters in Amiens, where he was interrogated. At times, he felt that he was the wrongdoer. The first person to interview him was a *capitaine*. Catesby described the driver and car that had been following him.

'What make of car was it?' said the *capitaine*.

'I don't know. I'm not a car expert.'

The *capitaine* sighed and returned with a book containing car photos. With the help of the gendarme officer, Catesby eventually found one that showed an exact replica.

'Are you sure? That's a Talbot Lago Grand Sport. A very rare car, few have been produced.'

'I can also give you the registration number.'

'Ah,' said the cop, 'perhaps we should have started there.'

'But,' said Catesby, 'if the driver was intent on harming me, he would have mounted a false one.'

The gendarme shrugged but wrote down Catesby's recollection of the number and disappeared to pass it on. Left alone, Catesby resisted an urge to rummage through the office. Instead, he studied the walls, which were largely hung with citations and photographs of gendarmes in dress uniforms. The Gendarmerie wasn't just a police force, it was also a branch of the military that formed La Garde Républicaine for ceremonies of state.

When the *capitaine* finally returned, he was carrying something in a canvas pouch. 'We have traced the car's registration.'

'And was it a false one?'

The gendarme didn't answer. 'You are welcome to have lunch – and dinner too – in our canteen.'

'You want me to stick around?'

'You have been involved in a very serious incident and we need to continue our enquiries.'

'Have you notified the British embassy?'

'The matter is in hand.' The *capitaine* looked at Catesby and put the canvas pouch on the desk. 'We took the liberty of going through your belongings.' He took Catesby's Webley out of the pouch. 'And we are going to have to confiscate this.' He scooped a handful of bullets out of the bag. 'As a matter of safety, we unloaded the cartridges and are confiscating them as well as ten rounds of other ammunition that we found.'

It was Catesby's turn to fall silent.

The gendarme seemed to soften. 'We will, of course, return all your other property.' He then replaced the pistol and bullets in the canvas pouch and did it up with the drawstring. 'As your life may still be in danger, we expect you to stay here this evening. I am sure you will find your accommodation comfortable and there will be further interviews tomorrow, led by a senior officer.'

The accommodation turned out to be a prison cell. It wasn't comfortable but it wasn't locked, and he was given access to toilet and shower facilities used by the gendarmes. Catesby only felt half a prisoner.

The Gendarmerie colonel who interviewed Catesby the next morning walked with a limp but was an impressive character both in stature and manner – and made it clear that he was going to do most of the talking. 'We have traced the owner of the car that you claim was following you . . .'

'So it wasn't a false registration plate?'

'I haven't finished, Monsieur Catesby . . . But we are not going to reveal his identity. There is no proof that he was involved in the explosion that destroyed your car. His following you might have been a coincidence.' The colonel paused and peered into steepled fingers as if there were a crystal ball inside. 'In fact, the other driver might have been the intended victim. Whoever carried out the attack could have got your cars confused.'

Catesby looked at the colonel with bemused disbelief. How could anyone confuse a UK reg Standard 8 with a Talbot Lago Grand Sport?

'I can see, Monsieur Catesby, that my suggestion astonishes you, but if you knew all the facts – which I cannot reveal – the possibility would have some credence.'

Catesby suppressed a smile. The senior gendarme officer was using the intelligence officer's standard dodge when caught out – the unmentionable top-secret info that would explain everything.

'I can, however, tell you that the explosive device was a very simple one that did not involve a timer or a remote control. We often encounter them in Indochina. It is simply a hand grenade with its pin removed wrapped in adhesive tape – and then dropped into a fuel tank. The petrol eventually dissolves the adhesive; the grenade lever, no longer held in place, ignites the fuse and an explosion follows.'

Catesby, as an ex-soldier, didn't appreciate a lecture on how grenades worked.

The colonel continued. 'The more layers of tape wrapped around the grenade, the longer the delay. A very crude method that guerrillas in Indochina employ against our untended military vehicles. We have instructed our soldiers to manually feel around in their fuel tanks to check for such devices.'

Catesby wasn't going to suggest locks. Soldiers lose keys even when they're not in battle.

'I have recently returned from a tour north of Hanoi. I was forced to come back owing to being wounded, but I hope to return. It is a war we must win. *La France n'est pas la France sans la grandeur.*'

Catesby understood. After the humiliation of defeat and Occupation, there were many who needed to recover *la grandeur* – and the Gendarmerie colonel was apparently one of them.

Amiens to Paris: September 1949

The remaining interview sessions at Amiens were more concerned with probing Catesby's own background than the attempt on his life. Catesby kept assiduously to his cover story: he was an ex-SOE officer who, after a spell as a civil servant, was returning to France to write a book about the Resistance. The colonel and the others on his interview team didn't seem very interested in poking holes in Catesby's dubious claims – or his reasons for packing a Webley revolver. He had the impression that he was only a minor part of a larger agenda and that they were now keen to send him on his way – which they did the next morning. The plain clothes gendarme who drove him in an unmarked car to the British embassy in Paris resisted all Catesby's attempts at small talk. Wine, fishing and film failed to elicit the slightest interest – but football got a tiny rise. The gendarme appeared to be an SC Abbeville supporter. But Catesby's mention of Ipswich Town was met with a blank silent stare.

Catesby felt a sense of relief when he spotted the Union Jack fluttering over the Rue du Faubourg Saint-Honoré. He was safe – at least temporarily. The driver stopped directly in front of the entrance where the Lion and Unicorn coat of arms, sculpted in stone, provided further assurance. A footman in a top hat greeted the car. Catesby's sense of relief began to dissipate when he saw Henry Bone standing behind him. There was then a bit of a charade as Bone addressed the gendarme driver in poor French. The driver wanted Bone to sign a receipt acknowledging the safe delivery of Catesby – and Bone's signature wasn't enough, but Bone was clueless as to what all the fuss was about. Finally, Catesby shouted, 'You need, Henry, to have the embassy's official stamp and the date next to your name.'

'Ah,' said Bone. He then sent the footman into the building to find a stamp and pad.

'Any chance of a tour of the embassy's wine cellar?' said Catesby as they waited.

'We've got more important things to do,' said Bone as the footman returned with an embassy stamp and pad. There was no more palaver as Bone duly stamped the acknowledgement. Without a word the gendarme took the document and pressed a button that unlocked the passenger door.

'Shall we go in and say hello to the ambassador?' said Catesby as he emerged from the car.

'Not today, William, we're taking you to a safe house.' A car pulled up in the space vacated by the gendarme. The driver was wearing dark glasses and the car didn't have *Corps Diplomatique* plates.

Bone nodded towards Catesby's suitcase. 'I assume you don't need a toothbrush or a change of clothes?'

'No, but the French cops confiscated my Webley revolver.'

'Good. You shouldn't carry dangerous toys.'

Paris: September 1949

The safe house was an apartment in a dilapidated building in the Latin Quarter, located next to a nunnery. The spartan rooms given to Catesby overlooked a work yard that gave off a constant sound of metal grinding.

'We chose the most suitable accommodation for you as an aspiring writer,' said Bone with a playful smile. 'Ernest Hemingway used to live here.'

'I didn't know you were a fan.'

'I'm not. Hemingway is an absolutely ghastly writer and a braggart – the product of a cultural desert.'

'But at least,' said Catesby, 'he's not a fascist like Pound and Eliot.'

'Eliot may be an awful, utterly overrated poet, but I'm not sure it's fair to call him a fascist – he's too bland to be evil.'

'Are there any American artists or writers you do like, Henry?'

'I'm rather fond of Arnold Schoenberg. I finally mastered his Suite for Piano Opus twenty-five, a complex twelve-tone piece.'

'Perhaps you could play it next time we have a Christmas do in the staff canteen.'

'Does your sense of humour ever go beyond crude sarcasm?'

'My wife often asks the same question.'

'Frances is a wonderful person; you should heed her advice more seriously.'

Catesby remained tight-lipped. Bone's praise of his wife was not reciprocated. She always advocated caution when dealing with him.

'I wouldn't mind a walk,' said Bone pointing at a light fixture as if it might be hiding a listening device. 'Perhaps a stroll along the Seine.'

Catesby nodded and followed him towards the door. As soon as they got outside, Bone turned south, away from the Seine.

'So much for a walk along the river,' said Catesby with a smile.

71

'If someone was listening in, they might send a watcher on a wild goose chase.'

'Who could have bugged the safe house?'

'Who wouldn't want to bug it? The list is very long.'

'I'd put the DST at the top of the list.' Catesby was referring to the Direction de la Surveillance du Territoire, France's equivalent of MI5, their domestic security service.

'And don't rule out the Americans,' said Bone.

'They wouldn't have liked your remarks about Hemingway.'

'That's why I made them.'

'On a more trivial note,' said Catesby, 'who tried to kill me?'

'We are not entirely sure – but why is a more important question than who. We have, however, found out the identity of the chap who was following you in the sports car.' Bone smiled. 'And he has a rather wonderful name: Xavier-Honoré-Antoine de Saint-Breuil. But that's only the short version: the full affair includes a lot more hyphens.'

'And he's the one who blew up my car?'

'I would say that he's the prime suspect. You will, however, be disappointed to know that Xavier-Honoré is not a duke, but a mere viscount.'

'Snubbed again. If you were stalked by an assassin, it would probably be a Romanov prince.'

'Jest not, William. But Xavier-Honoré is not a minor figure. He is a very rich man who owns a huge estate in the Var.'

'Not far from Marseille. Did he know I was going to be invading his turf?'

'We don't know that – or many other things. But we do know that Xavier-Honoré was openly a member of Action Française before the war – and a secret member of La Cagoule. Ring any bells?'

'A number of fascist chimes – but La Cagoule might have been too right-wing to be fascist. Both groups wanted to restore the French monarchy and the primacy of the Roman Catholic Church. They wanted to destroy the legacy of the French Revolution and return to the Middle Ages.'

Bone smiled. 'One can see the appeal.'

'I can also see where this is going.'

'Indeed. The fall of France signalled a split between Xavier-Honoré and those Action Française colleagues who justified collaboration with the Nazis as joining a war against communism. Xavier-Honoré was, however, first and foremost a French nationalist and joined the Resistance – the communists could be dealt with later. The group he led was composed of *résistants* who shared similar views to himself. They wanted a post-war France that was royalist and Catholic.' Bone paused. 'Now it's your turn to put the pieces together.'

'The Resistance could have been the beginning of a French civil war.'

'One that can still happen.'

'That sounds alarmist.'

'I'm surprised to hear you say that, since you narrowly escaped being one of the first victims of such a war. Why do you think you were targeted?'

'The obvious reason is that I was parachuted into the Limousin to advise and help supply Guingouin's communist Maquis – even though the assignment wasn't my choice.'

'There may be,' said Bone, 'a far more important reason – but we don't know all the facts.'

'What do you know?'

'The Resistant group led by Xavier-Honoré played a double game – and a very successful one. Their right-wing La Cagoule connections enabled them to maintain close contact with Vichy collaborators and the German occupiers. They used these old links to betray left-wing Resistance networks and others of whom they didn't approve. Having gained the trust of the occupying forces, they then deceived the Germans by passing on false information about allied movements – deceptions, they claim, which proved invaluable.'

Catesby stirred with anger. 'Feeble excuse. They were traitors – who betrayed many brave men and women to torture and death.'

'After the war, you went to Paris as a prosecution witness when one of them was tried for treason.'

'And he got off thanks to a clever lawyer.'

'You tried to stand witness when a second one went on trial, but you were denied permission.'

'Why, Henry? Why was I denied permission?'

'I honestly do not know.'

Catesby stared hard at Bone. 'Was it because the Americans leaned on our boss?'

Bone didn't blink.

'In any case,' said Catesby, 'Henri Déricourt walked free because one of the judges didn't vote to convict.'

'They haven't forgotten you, William – and that may be why you were targeted. Déricourt worked together with Xavier-Honoré during the war – and we think they may be working together again.'

'Do you still want me to go to Marseille?'

'Yes, of course.'

'I could be walking into a death trap. They've taken the cover story bait and they want to take me out, so I don't publish the truth about Déricourt and the other traitors.'

'I am sure there are many other reasons why they want to kill you, but it's not a death trap. There are those in Marseille who would protect you – and please invoice SIS for any expenses you incur.'

Catesby gave a wan smile.

'But,' continued Bone, 'Xavier-Honoré isn't the dangerous one, he's totally mad; it's Henri Déricourt – who also seems to be flirting with the Americans.'

Catesby nodded and smiled.

'*Capiche?*' said Bone. 'It's a lovely word you may well hear in Marseille.'

'You want me to take out Déricourt?'

'Heavens no! His Majesty's Secret Intelligence Service would never condone an assassination. How dare you suggest such a thing?'

'Silly me.'

'I believe you have one more meeting in Paris before heading for Marseille?'

'Yes, an old Resistance comrade who's promised some useful contacts in Marseille.'

'And one more thing, Catesby, your job is to cultivate, not to alienate.'

Catesby had quickly discovered that both he and Paul were outsiders. Most of the Maquisards in the remote Limousin countryside were local peasants who spoke an old Occitan dialect. Paul came from Paris and had trained as an art historian but managed to fit in better with the rural guerrillas than Catesby. He learned to speak the dialect and became the Resistance leader's most trusted lieutenant.

The Musée de l'Orangerie, where Paul worked as a curator, was an annexe of the Louvre. He met Catesby in one of the oval rooms where Monet's murals of *Water Lilies* were on display and led him into his office. It was a cramped space with shelves full of files. The only work of art was a watercolour hanging between a cabinet and a window. Judging by the sun-baked colours of ochre, brown and faded white, it seemed to be an Impressionist's image of a village in the South of France.

Paul noticed Catesby staring at the painting. 'It's one of Jean Moulin's. We lost a fine artist as well as a great hero. Marseille, of course, is the perfect place to research your book. As you know, it's where Moulin began to organise Resistance networks.'

Catesby didn't know, but nodded and said, 'That's one of the reasons.'

'And you should look up Gaston le Mat as well. He's now a trade union boss in Marseille – and still a militant communist.'

'Le Mat,' agreed Catesby, 'was always a fearless attack dog.'

Paul's face turned sombre. 'And there's someone else from our past who has also turned up in Marseille.'

'Go on, who?'

'Henri Déricourt – the double-dealing bastard who betrayed the Prosper network. My younger brother was killed in the Gestapo raid that led to Noor Inayat Khan being captured. Did you ever meet her?'

'Only once and briefly. Our SOE interviews were on the same day. She turned up early and we were together for a minute in the waiting room. She wished me "good luck" as I went in.'

'And you had it.'

'Yes – and she didn't.'

'It wasn't bad luck that killed Inayat Khan and my brother, it was treachery.' Paul looked at Catesby with a twisted smile. 'Are you going to interview Déricourt for your book?'

'I hope so. Last words always make good copy.'

'You will have my full support if you kill him,' said Paul. 'In any case, understand that Déricourt has taken up flying again – he's often seen at various airfields near Marseille.'

'How do you know so much about Déricourt and his flight plans?'

'I have a friend in Marseille who is keeping an eye on him.' Paul wrote a note and handed it to Catesby. 'When you get there, look up Serge. He's an artist who fought in the Resistance but he was arrested and deported to Buchenwald. Serge is worth a few chapters on his own – and so is his Vietnamese wife. You will find them a most interesting couple.'

Catesby folded the paper away.

'There is something else I should tell you about Déricourt,' said Paul.

'Yes?'

'He's recently renewed a friendship with an American who was with us in the Limousin.'

'Who?'

'I don't know the details.' Paul smiled. 'But maybe you will find out.'

'And I'll be sure to let you know.'

After leaving Paul's office, Catesby headed for the Louvre Métro station, where he would take Line 7 to the safe house in the Latin Quarter. But as it was a beautiful autumn afternoon, he decided he would prefer a brisk two-mile walk in the sunshine. As he did his habitual check to see if anyone was following, he berated himself for his constant paranoia – which was fed by regular SIS briefings on Moscow Centre's latest assassination devices. Some of his colleagues found the briefings a bit of a joke;

but others, like Catesby, became more cautious and paranoid. Virtually anything could fire a fatal bullet: cameras, lipstick tubes, gloves, fountain pens. You had to keep an eye out for umbrellas fitted with poison injectors in their tips. If you see a smiling chap swinging his brolly with the joys of spring, stay well clear. The Sovs, of course, loved poisoning, and atropine in restaurant saltshakers was a favourite method. It was a good reason not to accept dinner invitations from dubious characters – or, if you did, not to season your food. But, as they used to say: if the bullet has your name on it, there's nothing you can do about it. Catesby packed in his paranoia and strode happily along – but only as far as Pont Neuf. He was, in fact, being followed. An athletic-looking woman carrying a rolled-up German newspaper under her left arm on a busy Paris street is never a good sign – and she was just the sort of woman who would have interested Spiridon. When Catesby saw that the paper under her arm was a copy of *Die Berliner Zeitung*, he was ready to pounce. If she had been better trained, she would have swapped it for a copy of a French paper as soon as she got to Paris. But he wasn't going to give her a lecture on spy craft. He was going to knock her down and get the hidden weapon out of the newspaper before she had a chance to use it. A rolled-up newspaper was the ideal way to conceal the dual-barrelled gun that fired a fine spray of cyanide in your victim's face. It was the same weapon that had taken out Dieter in Berlin. Just as Catesby turned to face the woman, she disappeared into a rather tacky shop that sold postcards, trinkets and cheap scarves and ties. He followed her into the shop and listened as she bought a map and some postcards. She spoke excellent French and seemed unaware that Catesby was staring at her, ready to wrestle her to the ground. He began to have second thoughts. What if he was wrong and ended up arrested for assault? The gendarmes would love that – and Catesby, after such a mad attack in broad daylight, was more likely to end up in a psychiatric hospital than a prison. He might find himself sharing a cell with Xavier-Honoré. Catesby left the shop and continued his walk to the Left Bank, occasionally looking over his shoulder. The woman had come out of the shop and was still walking behind him but seemed more interested in studying the map than watching Catesby's back. A good ruse. He crossed over the Pont Neuf as far as the Île de la Cité and waited for her to cross. She had, however, continued on the Right Bank and seemed to be no longer following him. Was the woman an innocent bystander – and he an intelligence officer going mad? He wouldn't be the first or the last.

The walk along the Seine and through the Latin Quarter was a pleasant one. Nonetheless, Catesby gave in to his paranoia and continued to do countersurveillance checks. He was relieved when he finally got back to the safe house and bounded up the stairs. It was going to be his last evening in Paris, and he wanted to have something to drink and a good supper. Fuck everything and everybody else. But when he got to the top-floor flat something wasn't right. Someone was humming a tune. He gently turned the doorknob, it wasn't locked. Catesby pushed the door in the way they had been taught to avoid a gunshot, but there wasn't a shot – only the voice of Henry Bone saying hello.

Catesby entered and saw Bone sitting in an armchair with a file spread open on his knees. 'I wouldn't mind another walk,' said Bone pointing to the suspected listening device.

When they got outside into the Rue Mouffetard, Bone said, 'I thought I would hang around before going back to London to hear how things went with your friend Paul.'

Catesby recounted the meeting in detail as Bone nodded with considerable interest.

'How interesting that he knows about Déricourt. We seem to be on the right trail. I would also recommend that you cultivate that artist fellow Serge – but be wary of his wife Huong. She sounds dangerous.'

'And I think I've just been followed by another dangerous woman.' Catesby recounted his suspicions about the woman carrying the German newspaper.

'She sounds harmless enough – but it pays to be alert. And, by the way, we're now almost certain that your other follower, Xavier-Honoré-Antoine de Saint-Breuil, had nothing to do with blowing up your car.'

'Any clues?'

Bone gave a not very convincing shrug. 'One more thing before I go. Helen Stuart is looking more and more interesting. She is quite the athlete herself.'

Marseille: October 1949

Catesby's first night in Marseille was spent in what looked like a fleabag hotel, but happily the sheets were clean and there didn't appear to be any fleas. He assumed that the elderly woman who settled him in was the owner. She seemed very happy to have a customer, as none of the other rooms appeared to be occupied. She served Catesby coffee and cognac and plied him with questions about what had brought him to Marseille. Catesby kept to his cover story. The old woman beamed. 'We have never had a writer for a guest before.'

Catesby cringed.

'But as you are writing about the Resistance, you must visit the cathedral. It is where the Germans made their last stand before Marseille was liberated. It is only a five-minute walk – and such a beautiful place. Wait here, I have something for you.' The woman padded off and returned a minute later with a black dusty book. 'This will tell you all about it.'

The book was entitled *Basilique Notre-Dame-de-la-Garde: Une Histoire*. It proved perfect bedtime reading. It sent Catesby to sleep before he had finished the first page.

The location was as perfect for a military strongpoint as it was for a church. The cathedral was built on Marseille's highest hill, a protrusion of pure limestone that dominated the port and city. It was not, however, a piece of architecture that appealed to Catesby. As he stared at the cathedral's exterior he wondered if the architect had harboured ambitions to be a pastry chef. The church looked like a wedding cake. Bands of white limestone alternated with green sandstone. Elements of the Byzantine and the Romanesque clashed violently, but the match ended in a scoreless draw. The cathedral's crowning glory was Notre-Dame herself, the enormous gold statue of the Virgin and Child which surmounted the bell tower. As Catesby gazed at it, he remembered his days with the Night Climbers and imagined a midnight foray. You always leave a memento of your climb in place – and an Ipswich Town scarf would be perfect: Town's colours, blue and white, were also the colours of Our Lady.

The interior of the cathedral continued the wedding-cake theme. The alternating bands of colour, sandstone pink and limestone white, were a bit dizzying – and maybe that was the architect's intention. But as he wandered through the side chapels, Catesby began to warm to the place. A human side punctuated the gaudiness. There is a tradition in Mediterranean countries of making ex-voto offerings to a saint who has answered the giver's prayers. One such offering was a French soldier's helmet with a dent on one side. Presumably, the helmet had saved the soldier's life. The St Peter's chapel was full of paintings and models of ships – just what you would expect in a port city. If the ex-voto tradition had spread to England, St Margaret's church in Lowestoft would have been packed with models of drifters, trawlers, merchantmen and naval vessels. Instead, the walls of St Margaret's were covered with plaques commemorating the names of the town's boys and men lost at sea. Catesby's father was one of them.

Catesby prowled around for another five minutes before he headed for the door. He had taken in enough of the cathedral to answer any questions the old lady would ask about his visit. He was halfway down the nave when a well-dressed man of about forty stopped him. Catesby clocked the dress code insignia before the man even spoke: the Patek Philippe watch and the star-sapphire signet ring were better identity docs than a passport. The man looked at Catesby with a disarmingly warm smile. 'I believe,' he said, 'that you are a guest of Madame Albertini?'

Catesby assumed that was the old lady's name. 'Yes, I am. She is a most generous hostess and recommended that I visit the cathedral.'

'She says that you are the most interesting guest she has had since the war.'

'Madame Albertini is far too kind.'

'She says that you are an Englishman – how interesting.'

Catesby tried not to smile. He couldn't imagine anything less interesting.

'And that you have come here to write a book about the Resistance.'

'The first stage will be doing lots of research – and Marseille played such an important role.'

The man responded with a smile that was more enigmatic than warm. 'The Occupation was an interesting time for Marseille.' He reached inside his jacket pocket and handed a card to Catesby. 'As you are new to our city, may I recommend a good restaurant?'

'Thank you.'

'You may also discover it a good place to find people who will talk to you about Marseille and the Resistance.'

Catesby pocketed the card.

'It was very nice to make your acquaintance,' said the man, a hint of Italian in his accent, 'and I hope we meet again.'

Catesby was impressed. Whatever else you might say about the mafia, their intelligence network was superb. He had only been in Marseille for five minutes and they had already made contact.

Le Panier, Marseille: October 1949

Although Julot's, the *resto* recommended by the mobster, was high on Catesby's list, a visit to Serge would come first. Serge's home and studio were in the Panier district, the oldest part of Marseille and a twenty-minute walk from the hotel. Catesby immediately loved the place. It was wonderfully squalid and bohemian.

Serge's wife was a Vietnamese woman in her thirties. Her name was Huong, which translated as 'pink rose', but she was not a delicate flower. Her hands and wrists could have belonged to a bricklayer. When she saw Catesby at the door, she didn't ask his name or business, but invited him in and told him where to sit while she brewed tea. When she returned, she poured the tea without any ceremony. The tiny Vietnamese cups had no handles and Catesby had to juggle his cup from hand to hand because the tea was so hot. Huong had no such problem.

'Are you a friend of Paul?' said Huong.

'Yes, we fought together in Guingouin's Maquis.'

'Why have you come to Marseille?'

'Didn't Paul tell you?'

Huong remained silent. Catesby suspected that she had been trained to deal with interrogations as both a prisoner and a questioner.

'I recently received an advance from a publisher to write a book about the Resistance.'

'You must have been a very important figure.'

'I was an officer in the Special Operations Executive, a clandestine British organisation.'

Huong sipped her tea. 'We have friends who worked with SOE.'

Catesby decided it wasn't the time to ask who they were. Instead, he studied the wall behind Huong. It was mostly hung with drawings and paintings that he assumed were the work of Serge. The most striking was an oil painting of a worker leaning on a spade in front of a roaring power station boiler. The others were smaller and more personal, including drawings of prisoners in a concentration camp – one of which might have been a self-portrait. There were also two photographs proudly displayed on a mantelpiece. One was of Ho Chi Minh in battledress standing in a jungle clearing. The other showed Huong herself standing next to Ho Chi Minh. The similar background of thick foliage suggested the photos had been taken on the same occasion. Catesby was impressed. Paul had waved his magic wand and the hidden door to revolutionary Marseille had opened. Catesby felt Huong's eyes staring at him. They were asking a question: *Are you one of us?* Catesby looked away.

There was the sound of a door opening. A figure emerged wearing a paint-stained smock. 'You must be Monsieur Catesby.'

Catesby smiled. 'And you must be Serge.'

'I would embrace you, but I don't want to cover you in paint. Take my hand instead.'

The handshake was firm, but not quite bone-crunching.

'I'm going to make coffee,' said Serge. 'Would you like some?'

'No,' said Catesby, 'I'll be fine with tea.'

'Good. We tend to alternate between Vietnamese and French in terms of food too, but ideologically we are on the same menu.'

As soon as Serge was out of the room, Huong gave Catesby a reproving stare. 'Why did you join the British Secret Intelligence Service?'

The question unsettled Catesby. He already felt that his cover had been blown. How did she know about his SIS background? Catesby faked a laugh. 'I wasn't a spy. I was mostly a paper pusher for the Foreign Office. As I'm a bit of a linguist . . .'

'Your French is convincing.'

'Thank you – and I can do Flemish and German too. In any case, owing to my language skills I was seconded to another organisation to do some translating and help with interviews – which, I suppose, started the rumours about me being an intelligence officer. All totally false.'

Huong regarded Catesby with flinty eyes. She obviously didn't believe a single word.

'I was also young and naïve – and coming from a working-class background with a wife and two children – I needed a job.'

Huong remained stony-faced. It was clear that she didn't trust him one bit. 'The world is divided,' she said, 'into those who support imperialism and those who fight it.'

Catesby felt cornered but was rescued by Serge coming back in with the coffee.

'I see that Huong is giving you a roasting,' said Serge, 'but you must understand her perspective. She spent four years fighting in the hills and jungles of Vietnam against the Japanese occupation and is now bitter that France is trying to re-impose colonial rule.'

Catesby turned back to Huong, 'I respect you, and what you've been through, even if you don't respect me.'

For the first time, her look softened.

'I had a long talk with Paul about Comrade Catesby,' said Serge. 'He is someone we can trust.'

Catesby was embarrassed. Paul's words were far from the truth. He wanted to steer the conversation away from himself. Catesby looked at Serge. 'Paul describes you as France's leading Socialist Realist artist.'

'That is, I am sure, an exaggeration – and some would say that my work is too free to be part of mainstream Socialist Realism.'

'Revolutionaries and artists,' said Huong, 'must fight side by side.'

Suddenly, there was a knock on the outside door. As Huong went to answer, the knocking became louder and more persistent.

'I hope it isn't the cops,' said Catesby.

'In Marseille,' said Serge, 'there are worse things than cops.'

A young man with a limp followed Huong into the room.

'Hello Jojo,' said Serge extending a hand. He then nodded at Catesby. 'Let me introduce you to Guillaume.'

Catesby was sure that Serge had his reasons for giving him a French alias. Jojo's hand was small and soft. The rest of him was small and rat-like.

'The young lady,' said Jojo, 'would love to model for you – and would like to offer you a present too.' Jojo opened a brown leather attaché case and took out an object wrapped in a cloth. 'Don't worry, it isn't loaded.' He unwrapped the pistol and put it on the coffee table.

Catesby noted that it was a small calibre revolver, probably a .22, with a short barrel. It would be easy to conceal but might require more than one shot to stop someone big, strong and determined. It was unloaded; Jojo lifted a draw-string pouch containing the cartridges.

'How much does she want for it?' said Serge.

'Two thousand *balles*.'

Catesby had already noticed that few people in Marseille said francs, *balles* was the universal word for the currency.

Serge frowned. 'That's too much. I'll find another model.'

'Maybe she would accept fifteen hundred.'

'A thousand.'

'No.' Suddenly Jojo looked even more rat-like than before. 'Try twelve hundred – and don't blame me if she doesn't turn up.'

Serge sighed and left the room. Huong looked at the visitor. 'Would you like a drink?'

'No thank you, *madame*. I must be going soon.' Jojo's voice was deferential. Huong was a force that demanded respect and distance.

Serge returned and handed over the twelve hundred *balles*. Jojo took his leave.

Huong picked up the gun. 'I'm sure we can find someone who will want this.' She put the gun down and began to clear away the tea service. 'I need to start preparing dinner.'

'Let's have a pastis,' said Serge. 'You should get used to drinking pastis, it's part of Marseille culture.'

'I'd better start practising then.' As Serge got the drinks Catesby stared at the gun and tried to piece together what the transaction had been about.

Serge could see what Catesby was thinking. 'Are you trying to work out what that piece of theatre was about?'

'Is Jojo a *fourgue*?' Catesby was pleased that he knew the French slang for a fence, a dealer in stolen goods.

'Not just a *fourgue*. Jojo will do anything for the mob. We usually call him Dingo Jojo, Crazy Jojo. He's not completely right in the head. I think his mother was a prostitute who got beat up a lot when she was pregnant. Maybe that's why the mob look after him a bit.'

'What's the connection between the gun and the woman you seem to want to paint.'

'Ah, like Jojo's purported mother, she's a prostitute – a skinny wretch. She's a bargain basement sex worker who no longer cares.'

'And that's why you want to paint her?'

Serge stared at Catesby. 'She reminds me of the faces and bodies I saw at Buchenwald. Shall we go into the kitchen? I think the food will be ready soon – Huong's a quick cook. I'll bring the pastis, you bring the water.'

As Huong put the first course on the table, she said, 'If we were far from our enemies, we used dynamite to fish the rivers. But this soup is made from *rascasse* that were landed this morning at Le Vieux Port.'

Catesby looked at Huong. 'When did you leave France to fight in Vietnam?'

'After Serge was arrested in 1941. It was my first time in Vietnam. I was born in France, but my parents were Vietnamese intellectuals. I will never forget crossing the border from China into northern Vietnam. It was a moonless midnight and there were only dark shadows, but my heart leaped with joy for I knew that I had finally come home. I joined a platoon of thirty who were hiding in a cave. We kept our spirits up by singing and reciting poetry.'

'Most Vietnamese poems,' said Serge with a wry smile, 'are about love.'

'Please, Serge, do not play the cynical Frenchman.'

'I am not being cynical, but there is a line of verse in one of your country's love poems that I find very interesting.'

Huong frowned.

Serge looked at Catesby. 'If you ever want to seduce a Vietnamese you must use this line: *I love you as much as Uncle Ho loves the people of Vietnam.*'

Huong gave Serge a sharp look. 'Have I ever said that to you?'

'No.'

'Then maybe you should consider why.'

Catesby sensed a marital argument was in the offing; but Serge, instead of replying, cleared away the soup bowls and laid out the main course, sardines in a spicy tomato sauce.

'You don't have to use chopsticks,' said Huong. 'In some ways this dish is just as Mediterranean as it is Vietnamese.'

'Which,' said Serge as he poured rosé wine, 'is typical of Marseille. The city is a melting pot where cultures both conflict and merge. Look at the cathedral – it can't decide if it's Romano or Byzantine.'

'I noticed,' said Catesby. 'By the way, when I paid a visit to the cathedral someone approached me.'

'Were they shaking you down for a charity collection?'

'Well, he might have been collecting, but I don't think it was for a charity. He gave me a card for a restaurant he recommended. I believe it was called Julot's.'

Serge smiled and took a slurp of his wine. 'I'm sure the food is good, excellent, the best bouillabaisse in Marseille. And if you're the right type, they will do anything for you.'

'Am I the right type?'

'It depends on what they tell Julot.'

'Who are "they"?' said Catesby, but he had already guessed the answer.

'Mobsters. Julot's is one of the places the mafia hang out.'

'Why do you think they'd want to meet me?'

Serge shrugged, then looked at his wife. 'You recently had an interesting encounter at Julot's.'

Huong looked indignant. 'I would never go there. It is a bad place – and you never see women there. Unfortunately, I pass it when I visit a friend who lives on the same street.'

'And,' said Serge with a half-smile, 'one of the customers invited you to join him for a drink.'

'It was embarrassing. At first, I thought he had mistaken me for a prostitute, and I was about to swear at him – but then I realised who it was, an American I met in Vietnam during the war.'

Catesby's antennae were buzzing. 'I assume he was OSS, Office of Strategic Services?'

Huong nodded. 'In those days the Americans were our heroes. They were so tall and handsome, like gods.'

Catesby remembered with chagrin that many British women had felt the same but decided not to mention the joke about those in wartime jobs being issued utility knickers: *one Yank and they're off.*

'The Americans fought beside us to end the Japanese occupation. When Japan surrendered, we all celebrated together – and got very drunk. Our red flag with its gold star flew alongside the American stars and stripes.' Huong's face turned stern. 'And then it all went wrong. The Americans left and the French returned. Seeing former American comrades at Julot's brought back feelings of bitterness.'

'There was another American?' said Serge.

'Yes. He recognised me too and called out, "Villa Ferrier Saigon". I remember meeting them both. The Americans had holed up in the villa to avoid the fighting that broke out when the French struggled to regain control of the city. I was already late to meet my friend.'

'A very nice lady,' said Serge, 'who loves your massages.'

Catesby suspected that Serge's comment was drink-fuelled, but Huong ignored it and continued: 'I took my leave when a Frenchman named Henri, who was some sort of stunt pilot, joined them.'

Serge smiled. 'The sort of odd encounters that one has in Marseille.'

Catesby wanted to know more, but now wasn't the time to ask.

The rest of the evening passed pleasantly, but there was something, a transaction, that Catesby wanted to settle before he left. 'That gun you bought from Jojo, would you like to sell it?'

The deal was done, and Catesby found it easy to conceal the pistol as he got ready to leave.

'Have you found a place to live?' said Serge.

'I'm renting a flat on Rue des Frères Pecchini, not far from a beach.'

'Nice neighbourhood.'

Catesby agreed. If SIS were sending him on a dangerous mission, HM's Treasury could fork out for decent accommodation.

'When they come around,' said Serge, 'don't argue, just pay up. We all remember what happened to that butcher in St Just.'

'What happened?'

'He stopped paying – and the second time they came to collect, he refused again. They then borrowed his meat cleaver – and for the next two days the butcher's head was on display in front of his shop. They probably won't charge too much for a struggling writer. In any case, the time to worry is when they stop asking for protection money. Otherwise, they keep their side of the deal.'

La Corniche, Marseille: November 1949

The British consulate in Marseille, like most consulates in port cities, was mostly concerned with drunken sailors, tourists who had been robbed or had lost their passports and the bodies of dead expats. The Marseille consulate also had to deal with the occasional Brit who had deserted from the Foreign Legion camp at Aubagne and was trying to escape court martial and prison. The consulate's diplomatic pouch was Catesby's best way of sending and receiving secure messages from London – and the consul's wife, Helen Stuart, was the best way of getting those messages in and out of the secure pouch. Visiting the consulate would have blown Catesby's cover.

The first time they rendezvoused in Marseille was on the bridge overlooking the sea. It was the very place that Helen had suggested when she was introduced to Catesby in London. He had left a chalk mark on the bridge abutment and, as arranged, she met him on what seemed to be a casual walk the following Friday at precisely one o'clock. Helen was wearing a double-breasted trench coat with a light-blue silk scarf and a sensible dark-blue hat with turned-up brim. She looked unmistakeably English. They pretended to have met by accident, and she passed him a buff envelope. They needn't have been so clandestine, for a cold damp wind was blowing in from the sea and no one was about.

'Not a great day for a swim,' said Catesby.

'You like sea-swimming?'

'I'm from Suffolk, so I grew up loving it.'

'The North Sea must be freezing.'

Catesby had been expecting a simple brush-pass exchange, but she seemed to want to talk. 'You need to go to Walberswick on a hot calm day in August,' he said. 'Late afternoon when the tide is low. Float on your back and look at the sky. Lovely, like lying in a tepid bath.'

'We went to Aldeburgh once. The sea looked ferocious and was spitting shingle.'

'She gets like that sometimes.' Catesby opened the envelope. 'I'd better have a quick look in case they need a quick answer. Hmm, I'll have to . . .' He shook his head.

'Something wrong?'

'I don't know. Whoever sent it decided it needed to be encoded.'

'Must be important.'

'Not necessarily, sometimes they send racing tips and cricket scores that way. If the Russians ever crack the code on such a day, they'll be even more confused.'

'Any reply?'

'Not until I've decoded it. Hope I can find the current one-time pad.' Catesby guessed it was from Bone.

'Shall we schedule another rendezvous?'

'Let's place some flowers on the Drunken Boat,' said Catesby with an enigmatic smile, 'before they remove the body.'

Helen breathed a bored sigh and nodded. 'You obviously mean the Hôpital de la Conception.'

'I'm impressed. You easily unravelled my cryptic clues.'

'Not cryptic at all. Everyone knows that "The Drunken Boat" is a poem by Rimbaud and that he died in Hôpital de la Conception after having his leg amputated, as the gangrene had progressed too far. And I must bring flowers for poor Rimbaud, even if he was a silly boy.'

'And you know how to get to the hospital?'

'Of course, it's on the Boulevard Baille. I have a friend who's a patient there. She is also terminally ill – and I'm very fond of her.'

'I'm sorry. Perhaps we should change the rendezvous.'

'No, the hospital will be fine. I can combine it with a visit. How soon?'

'Would Monday at twelve be suitable?'

Helen seemed distracted by the sound of an aeroplane that was flying out to sea. She glanced in the direction of the plane and then looked back at Catesby. 'Monday would be fine.'

Rue des Frères Pecchini, Marseille: November 1949

Catesby's small flat was lacking in possible hiding places that wouldn't have been obvious to a searcher. In the end, he had decided to bury the decoding pad in the soil of a large pot of chrysanthemums. His logic was that a searcher, particularly one who wanted to leave his rummage undetected, wouldn't want to create a mess by turning out the pot. There was another reason: in England chrysanthemums were associated with joy, love and longevity, while in France, *chrysanthèmes* were the flowers of the dead. War graves were decorated with them. Thanking your French hostess for a dinner invite with a pot of chrysanthemums would be a terrible faux pas. Naturally, Catesby always advised his American contacts to do just that. In any case, if the searcher going through his flat was a Frenchman, he might just leave the *chrysanthèmes* untouched out of respect. But Catesby wasn't French, so he put the pot in the kitchen sink and dug out the codebook. As he decoded the message, Catesby felt that he had been press-ganged to crew on Rimbaud's Drunken Boat. It was turning into a voyage of violence.

The blood-soaked bodies of the hauliers appear,
Naked and nailed to brightly coloured stakes.

It was obvious why Henry Bone had encoded his message and included a warning that Catesby was to burn the note as soon as he read it. Bone was inciting Catesby to murder and was offering him a collection of weapons to do the job. The message didn't name the intended victim – or victims. Catesby wondered if it was Bone's idea of a dark joke – or a method of testing Helen as a go-between. He stared at the decoded words. No, it wasn't a joke. It was, however, a way of preparing Catesby for his real job in Marseille. The message concluded with two less lethal reminders. One, keep an eye on Helen. Two, get to know Serge and his friends better.

Part of Catesby was reluctant to destroy Bone's communication. It might come in as useful evidence if Catesby ever needed to cover his own back. This would also mean keeping the page from the one-time pad, which he had used to decode the message. Otherwise, there would be no proof that the message was real. The standard procedure was to burn OTP sheets as soon as they had been used – but not this time. Catesby ripped off the page and folded it together with the message and its decrypt. He then looked around the flat. Where the fuck was he going to hide it? But part of being a good intelligence operative was a willingness not to always cover your back. Catesby reached for a packet of matches, and soon the ashes of Henry Bone's instructions, duplicitous or not, were washed down the sink.

Le Panier, Marseille: November 1949

The instruction from Bone that Catesby found least objectionable was getting to know Serge better. In fact, he would have befriended the artist in any case. Catesby's pretext for visiting his studio in Le Panier was to give the couple wine and chocolates in return for the dinner cooked by Huong.

'You needn't have,' said Serge as he eyed the gifts with appreciation. 'Presents are so bourgeois. At least, that's what Huong would say.'

'Is she here?'

'No, she's at a meeting. She goes to lots of meetings. Would you like coffee, tea or pastis?'

'Perhaps a tiny pastis.'

As Serge fetched a bottle and a jug of water, he said, 'Have they been around yet?'

'Yes, yesterday in fact.'

'How much did they want?'

'Just under a week's rent – on a monthly basis.'

'That's about normal, but when you become a rich, famous writer they will want more. They don't charge me anything at all. A few years ago, they occasionally asked me to paint a portrait of one of the bosses, but they must not have liked my renderings.'

'Actually, the fellow who collected the money gave me the names of a few mafia chiefs who allegedly helped the Resistance and whom I might want to include in my book.'

'They played both sides.'

'It was a pleasant enough transaction, but I shouldn't have asked for a receipt.'

'They don't give receipts for protection money, but they do maintain paperwork for drug transactions – and woe betide any dealer who cheats them.'

'You seem to know a lot about their world.'

'Of course, I've lived in Marseille most of my life.'

'But you weren't born here.'

'No, I was born in Paris.'

'Please excuse me for being so inquisitive, but I would like to include you in my book.'

Serge laughed. 'My life as a member of the Resistance was insignificant. I spent most of the war in prison. The important thing for me, almost the only thing that matters, is my life as an artist – for which I am largely indebted to my mother.'

'What was she like?'

'My mother was a Ukrainian Jew whose family fled the 1905 Kiev pogrom. I don't know how she got together with my father. He was a lifelong anarchist who, after being conscripted into the army, was court-martialled and shot for his part in the 1917 mutiny. She brought me up alone in Paris. I began to paint when I was fourteen. At first, I wasn't interested in changing France or changing the world; I just loved art and wanted to paint. Painting was my drug. I began by going to museums and copying the Old Masters. I love getting lost in a different world. For my sixteenth birthday, my mother gave me a book of Goya's paintings. It changed my life. I began by trying to replicate *The Nude Maja* – which, as a sixteen-year-old, was the most erotic image I had ever seen. Goya was the first artist to paint pubic hair in a manner that was seductive.' Serge sipped his pastis and smiled. 'A reincarnated Maja would be freezing if she were posing here. This used to be a warehouse and it's the coldest place in Marseille.' He pointed to a potbellied stove. 'I light that for the models.'

'Do you prefer painting nudes?'

'Not always. The problem with clothes is that they hide who we really are – especially uniforms.' Serge refreshed their glasses with pastis. 'When you're in a bar, you always have to wait for your turn to buy even if there are ten of you.'

'I'll remember that.'

'I can't remember anything. I was telling you my life story. Where was I?'

'Copying Goya.'

'Ah, so I was. My darling mother eventually took me to Madrid so that I could visit the Prado to copy the originals of the paintings that I so admired in the book she had given me. I began with *Jupiter Devouring His Son* and then moved on to the paintings depicting the uprising against Napoleon's occupation of Spain. One shows the workers of Madrid attacking the French Imperial Guard with knives and clubs; the next was of the same rebels being executed by firing squad. I discovered that I loved painting action and conflict.' Serge paused and smiled. 'Then something very special happened – what a privilege!'

Catesby felt a wave of shame. This was exactly the type of conversation that he was supposed to transcribe for the Secret Intelligence Service. He hated being a two-faced bastard. Was it possible to be a good spy and a decent human being?

'One of the Prado's curators had begun to take an interest in my copy studies. Once a day, he stopped for a brief conversation. Then, early one afternoon, he locked the door of the gallery where I was working and said, "Your things will be safe here." "You want me to leave?" I said. "Only for a little while, the others are at lunch, so we won't get caught." Serge laughed. 'Well, I wasn't a foolish young man, but I felt I could trust him. More pastis?'

'Please.'

'He then said to me, "I want to show you a collection of drawings that aren't open to public view – but you must swear never to tell anyone that I showed them to you or I will lose my job." "Maybe you shouldn't take such a risk," I said. "No," he said, "it is a risk worth taking for someone who loves and understands Goya as much as you do."'

Catesby smiled. 'But now you've told me.'

'It's too late for the curator to lose his job. He was killed in the civil war. You mustn't keep interrupting, Monsieur Catesby.'

'Apologies.'

'As soon as I saw Goya's drawings, I understood why they were hidden from public view. More raw and disturbing than Jupiter biting the head off his son. That was only based on a Greek myth. The drawings were of things that Goya had witnessed with his own eyes. They were not part of the 1808 uprising in Madrid, but scenes that took place in a remote village where the rebellion had spread. The events focused on a *jefe de policia*, a police chief who had ruled the village with brutality and sadism. But the tables have now turned. The policeman has been sewn inside the carcass of a recently disembowelled horse. The guts of the horse are scattered around, and the village dogs are fighting over them – except for the dogs who are biting the face and feet of the chief of police. The cop's head is sticking out of the horse's anus and his feet are protruding from the dead animal's throat. So different from Goya's rendering of the second of May rebellion. In contrast to the drawings of the tortured policeman, there was something noble and heroic about the workers standing up against the charge of the Mamelukes.'

Catesby remained silent. Revenge is a drug with ugly side effects.

'There were two more drawings of the policeman. In one, he has been stripped naked by the village women, who are trying to stick some sort of plunger up his arse. It's a plunger, as thick as a man's leg. Why are they doing it? Had the police chief used his power and authority to demand sexual favours – and is this an apt revenge? Pathetically and poignantly, the cop tries to fend off penetration with a hand over his bottom. The third drawing of the cop shows him hanging upside down from a tree – naked and still alive with his legs spread wide apart. There is no indication of the order in which these events took place – nor any drawing of the policeman's final fate.'

As Serge spoke, Catesby noticed that a darkened wall behind him was entirely covered in pencil drawings – not a single hint of colour. There was little light in that part of the studio, but Catesby could discern lean figures wearing the striped uniforms of concentration camp inmates – and one of them was Serge himself.

'Paul mentioned that you were in Buchenwald,' said Catesby.

'I was lucky to survive. My mother, already an elderly woman, died on the way to Auschwitz. She was taken prisoner during the July 1942 raids in Paris. They crammed thirteen thousand of them into the Winter Velodrome that had been built for the 1924 Olympics. All the toilets were blocked off because they had windows and the Gestapo didn't want anyone to escape. There was only one water tap for all of them. My poor darling mother.' Serge picked up a book. It was the Goya paintings. 'This is all I have left of her.' He paused. 'When the curator showed me the secret Goya drawings, I had the faintest pang of compassion for the policeman being tortured. Now I have none.'

Huong had silently drifted into the studio. 'Serge should tell you that he had been arrested the year before and could do nothing to protect his mother.'

'I was conscripted into the army in '39 and captured by the Germans in June 1940. I managed to escape and made my way to the Limousin, where I joined the Resistance. My job wasn't fighting but designing pamphlets. I was arrested in November 1941 and sentenced to two years for producing drawings that were communist propaganda. One drawing that particularly annoyed them was my rendering of a hostage being put to death in retaliation for the killing of a German officer. He was one of twenty-seven hostages who were executed in reprisal. In any case, as promised, I was released after I served my sentence.' Serge smiled. 'And immediately rearrested. I was subject to what was called "an administrative internment measure". The Vichy traitors were always careful to use official-sounding language. They couldn't just say, "Lock the fucker up". Likewise, the Vichy government prison was not called a concentration camp, but a "supervised residence centre". My fellow inmates were the usual lot: communists, anarchists, artists, poets. I was allowed to paint, and the poets were allowed to make up poems – but not to write them down. The nightmare began the very last day of July 1944. Just as France was being liberated, we were handed over to the Germans. The women were sent to Ravensbrück; me and the rest of the men were sent to Buchenwald.' Serge turned and gestured to the wall behind him. 'And there it is.' He then laughed. 'Have another pastis. One must never forget the horror – but one must celebrate life too.'

Catesby held out his glass and looked at one of Serge's Buchenwald self-portraits. 'You look different from the others.'

'It wasn't the food; it was the drawing that kept me alive. As soon as I arrived at Buchenwald, I knew that I had to record those faces. A guard gave me pencils, but the paper was stolen for me by some other inmates. In return, I had to give them an existence while death awaited them. They had grown so accustomed to cold, hunger and hopelessness that death was just another passing banality. I could never have used colour to paint those faces. A pencil and rough paper were all that was needed – oil paint and canvas could never have told the story. My stay there was a period of gestation, just under nine months.'

'And afterwards?'

'I was free and full of passion. By the way, you must stay with us for dinner.'

'I would love to. I need something to soak up the pastis.'

'But first, let me show you my work in progress.'

It was a huge canvas which depicted an enormous punch-up. The dockworkers slightly outnumbered the police, but the police had guns and dogs. There were women among the strikers. One was being viciously attacked by a snarling police dog with bare teeth. Another woman was hoisting the French tricolour with echoes of Delacroix's *Liberty Leading the People*. The hull of a ship formed the background. All the police were faceless – except for one who resembled Hitler and was being well and truly thumped by a burly striker. It wasn't a subtle painting, but Catesby loved it – and wished that he could have a copy to give to his cousin Jack.

Hôpital de la Conception, Marseille: November 1949

Catesby composed and encoded his reply to Henry Bone only an hour before he was due to meet Helen at the Hôpital de la Conception. He mentioned that a conventional murder weapon, such as a gun or a knife, would be very easy to obtain in Marseille, but that he would appreciate any poisons or biological agents that were on offer. He also queried the wisdom of sending such items via Helen. Catesby confirmed that he had contacted Serge and gave a brief biographical sketch of the artist. As for Helen Stuart, he still hadn't noticed anything suspicious about her but would keep London informed.

The rendezvous time, twelve noon, was also the beginning of visiting hours at Hôpital de la Conception. Perhaps the staff thought it would be useful to have family and friends on hand to help with lunchtime feeding. Catesby was five minutes late. Helen Stuart didn't look particularly pleased – and she was carrying a bouquet of chrysanthemums that didn't look very happy either.

'Are you planning to kill me?' said Catesby, nodding at the funeral flowers.

Helen gave him a withering look. 'No, they're for my friend. She died this morning.'

Catesby writhed with embarrassment. He had forgotten her saying that she had a friend who was a patient.

'Her family told me to leave the flowers in the mortuary chapel. They might collect them later.'

'I am so sorry,' said Catesby. 'I know my insensitivity is unforgiveable, but please accept my sincere condolences.'

She sighed and looked at him as if he were a child who wasn't worth correcting.

The chapel was empty except for a nun replacing candles who gave a polite nod to Catesby and the consul's wife and left them alone. Helen placed the flowers next to other bouquets of chrysanthemums on a table next to the altar. Catesby noticed that there was a card inscribed, *To Vitalie, with fond memories, Helen.* The name Vitalie struck a bell in the back of Catesby's head that chimed somehow with Hôpital de la Conception. He looked at Helen. Her head was bowed in silent prayer.

After they left the hospital, Helen checked her handbag to make sure she had the envelope with Catesby's encoded message. 'I'll put it in the diplomatic pouch this afternoon.'

'Thank you.'

'When a new message arrives from London, I'll put a chalk mark on the bridge.'

'And I'll meet you there the following Friday at one,' said Catesby.

'On the dot,' said Helen.

He watched her stride away. Her thighs and calves were as firm and athletic as they were desire-inducing.

As Catesby made his way back to his flat, a lecture from university kept bubbling up in his mind. The prof was a renowned authority on Rimbaud and Baudelaire – and he seemed to regard the long dead poets as his lost lovers. But who was Vitalie? Catesby made a detour to a library, where he found a biography of Rimbaud. Yes, the words of the lecture flooded back. Vitalie Rimbaud, née Marie Catherine Vitalie Cuif, le 10 mars 1825, à Roche, was the poet's much loved and influential mother. And no, she hadn't been with Arthur when he died at the Hôpital de la Conception, but her spirit was.

Catesby returned the book and left the library with a smile of satisfaction. There was no dead friend named Vitalie. Helen had fabricated the story as a clever ruse. A simple lie wasn't enough. The elaborately constructed falsehood wasn't just intended to deceive, it was meant to humiliate as well. Helen had a dark side which made her all the more alluring.

7th arrondissement, Marseille: November 1949

Lester's apartment had a terrace with a sea view. He had invited Kit
Fournier for drinks and to explain the job they had in hand. It wasn't an
assignment that you could put down in writing – or one that you could
write a report on once it was over. Lester had known Kit since 1945. They
had first met in Vietnam. As Kit Fournier spoke pretty good French, he
had been plucked from the ranks and sent to OSS. Like many in the unit,
Fournier came from an old money East Coast family and had been pri-
vately educated – but Lester thought there were problems. He wondered
if Kit was a thoroughbred who had turned jittery through inbreeding.
He was in quite a state after Peter Dewey had got his head blown off
– which was perhaps understandable. Kit had to run back to the Villa
Ferrier dodging bullets, and when he arrived his tunic was stained with
blood and fragments of Peter's brain. Lester remembered the horrified
look on Kit's face when he spotted something grey on his shirt sleeve and
flicked it off with his middle finger as if it were a noxious insect.

'Would you like some bourbon, Kit? Or some French rotgut?'

'Bourbon would be fine.'

'Good. I stock up on it whenever I can get to the PX in Orly. You
ought to visit when you pass through Paris. Just flash your ID and the
gates open to a little America.' Lester smiled. 'But don't flog the stuff to
the frogs. A couple of airmen tried it and they got busted bad. If you do
crime, do it big and don't leave a trail.'

Kit sipped his bourbon and stared out over the sea. 'You have a nice
view of the Château d'If.'

'Pity it's no longer a prison. An inmate could send me Morse messages
with a mirror to tell me where to find the treasure at Monte Cristo.'

'A beautiful novel. My mother read it to me when I was ill.'

Lester shrugged. 'I think the so-called count turned a bit soft in the end.'

'Or wiser.'

'It's easy to be wise when you have enough money to choose to forgive, forget or take revenge. But we're getting too philosophical. How does Marseille compare to Nice?'

Fournier gave a grim smile. 'Nice turned out badly. I was in the wrong place at the wrong time.'

Lester knew the story and didn't ask Kit to repeat it. Unlike Lester, who had gone straight from the army to the CIA, Kit had taken a detour. After leaving the military, he had joined the State Department and been trained as a foreign service officer. His first assignment had been as US consul in Nice. With no other staff, his job had been dealing with tourists who had lost their passports and drunk US sailors who had ended up in French jails. But the worst part of a consul's job was repatriating the bodies of dead Americans. His training had taught him to always follow procedure – even if the corpse was the daughter of Joe Kennedy, a man of enormous wealth and influence. She had been on her way to a kinky weekend in the South of France with a married lover in his private plane. Disorientated by an unseasonable storm, the pilot had flown into a mountain. Consul Fournier had closely followed procedure and was making an inventory of the dead woman's possessions – including items of underwear, various playthings and contraceptive devices – when her father walked through the door of the mortuary. An enraged Joe Kennedy shouted, 'Who the fuck are you and what the fuck are you doing?' He then called Kit a necrophile pervert and ordered him out of the room.

Fournier was summoned to Paris where the ambassador told him it might be an idea to consider some time 'in the shadows'. His career in the US Diplomatic Corps was clearly over, but a recently spawned secret organisation known as CIA would welcome Kit, as a former OSS officer, with open arms.

'I think,' said Lester, pouring himself another bourbon, 'you will find Marseille a lot more fun – and a lot friendlier too. They like us here.'

Kit didn't need to ask who 'they' were. Instead, he looked around at the apartment, which seemed very luxurious. American bucks bought things that most Europeans couldn't afford, but Lester's lodgings were certainly far beyond his generous CIA accommodation allowance. There wasn't just a sea-view terrace, but a swimming pool; not just an office, but a music room – and a bathroom big enough to have a party in.

'What do you think of China going communist?' The bourbon seemed to be having an effect on Lester.

'It means we've lost a fifth of the world's population to communism.'

'No, Kit, one quarter of the world's population. There are now four Chinese commies for every American.' Lester smiled. 'But we've got better guns – and the atom bomb too.'

Kit looked out to sea and wished that he was on a boat with someone he loved – or just by himself.

'You don't seem upset by it,' said Lester.

'It's too big and too devastating to take in.'

'A lot of people in Washington are like deer trapped in a truck's headlights – but there are some, including one of our bosses, who have their heads screwed on right. Our primary job in Marseille isn't just saving France from communism but saving Southeast Asia from communism. If you want to see the Viet Minh in action you don't need to go to Vietnam, you only need to go down to the docks of Marseille. You won't see wiry little men in black pyjamas, but beefy stevedores in boots and boiler suits. Compared to most frogs, they're big guys and they need taking down.' Lester topped up Kit's bourbon. 'Do you know the history?'

'It's a confused one.'

'Explicate.'

'The leader of the French Communist Party, Maurice Thorez is a totally committed Stalinist who always follows Moscow's party line. When Thorez was part of the French government . . .'

'Deputy fucking premier in '46 and '47. Really scary that such a piece of shit could rise so high – well, turds float. Carry on.'

'Well, oddly, during his time in office, Thorez supported the French government re-establishing colonial rule in Vietnam and the rest of Indochina.'

'Not odd at all. Thorez was following Stalin's direct orders. Uncle Joe, after too much vodka, decided that France was about to become communist and, if all her colonial possessions were still under French rule, they would have to become commie countries too. Go on, Kit, you've read the file. Tell me what happened next.'

The bourbon was getting to Fournier. 'I'm not a school kid.'

'Mea culpa.'

'The communist deputies in the National Assembly voted against the government because they were opposed to a colonial war in Vietnam – and the premier sacked Thorez.'

'Bravo. Even Thorez's fellow commies hate him. But Stalin himself has now reversed the party line and turned against French rule in Indochina. So, Kit, what lessons can we learn from this?'

'We should seek to foment and exploit divisions within the French Communist Party – and the left in general.'

Lester smiled. 'They seem to be able to do that without our help. On the other hand, commies are shapeshifters. They divide and then merge again, but they always want to destroy us and our way of life – which I would call freedom. In any case, there is one thing on which all the lefties in France agree: Vietnam and the rest of Indochina must be handed over to the communists. Our job in Marseille is to stop that happening by any means possible – and by any alliance. If Satan wants to join our cause, he's welcome.' Lester paused. 'Do you know much about art?'

'A little bit.'

'What do you know about Socialist Realism?'

'I believe it's a form of art that originated in the Soviet Union and glorifies the struggle of the workers. I don't think the images are particularly subtle.'

'Indeed.' Lester cradled his bourbon. 'We have our very own Socialist Realist painter right here in Marseille. His most recent works are of dockworkers beating up policemen and stopping ships from being loaded with arms, supplies and troops intended for Vietnam. Not real art, but rabble-rousing propaganda posters. He also likes painting nudes of syphilitic whores ridden with tuberculosis. Don't you see why? They're victims of capitalism – but I wonder if he gets his own pecker out and asks them for a blowjob. Incidentally, his wife, common law or otherwise, is a Vietnamese communist who hangs around with Ho Chi Minh. She is a dangerous fucking woman, who needs taking down a peg or two.'

Kit noticed a look in Lester's eye that was even more sinister than usual.

'But don't you try anything on with her. An East Coast preppie like you would end up in a dark alleyway with your cock cut off and stuck down your throat. But you can help keep an eye on her and her whore-monger husband.' Lester smiled. 'Oh, there's a recent development. I love it! And I've checked him out. What, Kit, do you think of the British?'

'I think they're cold and duplicitous – and have awful teeth.'

'Not bad. Perfidious Albion has tooth decay and mouth ulcers too. Now, does the name William Catesby ring a bell?'

'Not the slightest tinkle.'

'Well, for some reason Catesby has turned up here in Marseille. Our friends in the mob, who keep an eye on everyone, spotted him in the cathedral – maybe he was going to confession. I can't wait to introduce you. Catesby and I go back a little way. He was the first person I met when I was parachuted into Occupied France. It took me less than a minute to realise that he was one supercilious limey bastard. Fortunately, I only had to deal with him for a couple of months. After the liberation of Limoges – which was the centre of our Area of Operations – I was sent back to the States for redeployment to Vietnam, where you and I had such a good time. In any case, Catesby spent most of his time in France sucking up to the commie bastards who ran the Maquis Rouge. After he left the army, no one else would employ him, so he joined the British Secret Intelligence Service – who spend most of their time sucking up to Moscow.' Lester gave Kit a close look. 'Have you ever heard of the VENONA project?'

'No.'

'Good. It would be a serious breach of security if you had. But, Kit, you're becoming an important player so I'm going to try to get you access. It will change your view of the world. Back to Catesby, whose own world isn't a million miles away from VENONA. He seems to have left the Secret Intelligence Service – and thereby hangs a mystery that could explain why he has ended up here in Marseille.'

The bourbon had emboldened Fournier. 'Maybe he's following you.'

'I need to know more about what Catesby is doing in Marseille. The gangster who cornered him in the cathedral says he's writing a book about the Resistance – so I got our guy in London to check it out. Catesby did, in fact, resign under a cloud and has been taken on by a publisher with a reputation for recruiting left-wing writers. Part of me thinks the whole thing is bullshit. But, on the other hand, he is a bit of a lefty.' Lester laughed. 'But if Catesby were a commie spy, something I haven't ruled out, Moscow would have told him to remain in SIS undercover – like the VENONA traitors.'

'Maybe it's not a cover story,' said Fournier. 'Many former intelligence officers became writers: Somerset Maugham, Erskine Childers . . .'

Lester slapped the table. 'Who got shot by a firing squad! You know something, if a publisher wanted a book about the Resistance, they should have come to me instead of fucking Catesby. If I hadn't gone into this business, I could have become a goddamned good novelist. The stories I could tell about my youth in Chicago would sell a million copies – a lot more than Hemingway, who brags about shit he's never done.'

Fournier responded with a nervous smile. Lester had begun to sound really drunk.

'You know, I met Hemingway a couple of times and I know some of his family. They're from a boring suburb called Oak Park. His father was a doctor who got a bit depressed and blew his brains out. I think the whole family are a bit nuts – and I don't think Hemingway knows who he really is.'

Kit nodded. 'I don't like his obsession with guns.'

Lester gave a giddy laugh. 'Hey, hey, then you're in for some action you're not gonna like.' His voice dropped to a whisper. 'We've got some very special visitors arriving. And one of the reasons I wanted you here is because your French is so much better than mine – especially after I've had a few drinks.'

Kit laughed. 'I find German just the opposite; the more you drink the better you sound.'

'Our visitors don't speak the French we learned in the classroom.' At that moment there was a knock at the door. Lester shouted, 'Entrez!' Then realised the door was locked and went to let them in.

The older one was wearing a dark suit with an open-necked white shirt. The younger one had a moustache and was wearing dark glasses. He was also dark-suited but wearing a gold-coloured tie and gold cuf-flinks. Both men wore large pinkie rings set with blood-red stones. They gave Lester kisses on both cheeks and shook hands with Kit. Lester offered them drinks and they accepted.

Lester started in fairly good French. 'Thank you for coming. I remem-ber our conversation from last time when you told me how much you were looking forward to deer hunting when the season begins in September.'

The older one said something to his companion that neither American understood. Kit whispered to Lester, 'I think they're speaking Corsican.'

The older man smiled and began speaking English. 'How impolite of me to speak a language you not understand. My English is not good, but I learn a little when I lived in America. My Italian is much better, but when I tried to speak Italian to Lucky, he always answer me in English.'

'How is Lucky?'

'We often talk, but as he now lives in Napoli, we speak Italian.'

'I would love to meet Lucky.'

'Who know, maybe we arrange something.'

'I must show you your hunting present.' Lester suddenly sounded a lot more sober. 'Follow me.'

Kit had noticed that part of the music room was covered by a dust-sheet. He assumed that some painting and decorating had been in progress, but when Lester drew the sheet back he saw stacks of wooden boxes. Lester chose a long narrow one and opened it. The older visitor nodded approvingly.

'It's a Karabiner 98k, but not an ordinary one. It's the sniper variant.' Lester reached into the case and took out a telescopic sight. 'This is a 6x. You can use this for an easy headshot on one of your deer up to a range of five hundred metres. With luck and practice you can nail one at a thousand metres.' Lester presented the box with the rifle to the older man. 'Happy birthday.'

'It isn't my birthday.'

'Well, happy hunting then.'

The older man smiled.

'Before you go,' said Lester, 'I've got some other things to show you – but sadly they're not for you. At least, not yet.' Lester drew a pine packing crate towards him. 'These are for deer with really thick hides. Our friends in Southeast Asia might find them useful. We got them, as well as your rifle, at a closing-down sale in Germany in 1945.' Lester opened the pine box. The four Panzerfaust 30s were in pristine condition. 'They're easy to use. Eleven-year-old kids were taking out Soviet tanks with them as they rolled into Berlin. But be careful.' Lester pointed to a notice stencilled on the firing end of the Panzerfaust with a warning arrow pointing backwards: *Achtung! Feuerstrahl!* 'You don't want to get another hunter caught in the backblast.' Lester closed the crate. 'Once again, let me reassure you. No one is going to touch us.'

The older visitor handed the box with the rifle to his companion. 'Ciao, we must go now – but thank you very much.'

'Tell Lucky I look forward to meeting him.'

After the two men left, Lester turned to Kit. '*Capiche?*'

Kit nodded. '*Capiche.*'

Lester suddenly looked very relaxed and poured himself another bourbon. He looked at Kit. 'Help yourself.'

Fournier poured himself a small one.

'We have a mole or two inside the British intelligence service – but not as many as the Russians.' Lester laughed. 'Why do they all have second jobs? Maybe their pay is really shit. Ergo, William Catesby leaving to take up a different line of work.'

'You said earlier that Catesby becoming a writer was nonsense.'

'I didn't say nonsense, I said bullshit, a cover story – and it might be. One of our moles in SIS says that the real reason Catesby has come to Marseille is to work for the Russians. But who can trust a limey? They are either lying – disinfo – or don't know they're lying – misinfo. Ergo, we haven't a clue what Catesby's really up to.' Lester looked out to sea and pointed at a ship. 'That one's to Porto Vecchio. I love the ferries to Corsica. They're always full of legionnaires and gangsters – and the food is great. But now, how do we handle Catesby?'

Fournier stuck out his index finger and pulled the trigger with his thumb. 'Bang.'

'One option, but it could be a wasted opportunity. We might be able to use Catesby to uncover whole nests of commies.' Lester paused and looked thoughtful. 'One of the things that I learned in Occupied France is that nine people out of ten can be turned. The one in ten who can't be turned are usually stupid or suicidal fanatics.'

'Or heroes?'

Lester slapped his thigh and gave a loud barking laugh. 'You still believe in that shit!'

Kit remained silent.

'Long before OSS, when I was still at Officer Candidate School, one of my instructors took me aside and said, "You're going to go far, cadet, because when it comes to people you are one perceptive motherfucker. You know which dumb fucks to use to shine your boots and polish your brass." He laughed. "They're so stupid they think you're gonna help them get through the course. Now, which guys in your platoon do you think are gonna wash out?" I gave him seven names and they all failed. Then he said, "Which cadets do you think are going to get shot in the back by their own men?" I gave him four names – but I will never know if I got it right because combat is one foggy motherfucker.' Lester smiled. He sounded even more drunk than before. 'But all four of the fuckers were listed as killed in action one way or the other. So, Kit, as I was telling you, I am one fucking good judge of human character – and I know that we can manipulate William-the-limey-Catesby.' Lester stopped swaying and gave Fournier a searching look. 'Tell me, Kit, what is the most valuable type of agent if he's working for you or the most damaging if he's working for the other side?'

'A double agent.'

'No, you're wrong. It's a triple agent: a fake double who's still working for his original side. Hey, remember the guy who met us for a drink at Julot's?'

'Very charming. I believe his name is Henri something? The pilot?'

'You don't know Henri's full story. He was a triple agent who was being run by an officer high up in the British SOE – a rare Brit who wasn't duplicitous, but used those who were. During the 1930s, Henri made his living as a stunt pilot and was based in Paris. At the same time, the British officer who was to recruit Henri, was a journalist there. They became close friends. And Henri was a good contact for a journalist. He was a charmer with a wide social network. Henri became a drinking buddy with the head of security at the German embassy – who passed on titbits that Henri then gave to his Brit journalist pal. In 1941 the embassy security guy was back in Paris: this time as head of the Gestapo. Meanwhile, Henri was becoming a valuable and trusted air operations officer for the Resistance. Well, Kit, I think you can see where this is going?'

'Henri renewed contact with his former German friend who recruited him as a double agent.'

'Exactly.'

'Did he make that contact on the advice of his British friend who was now a high-ranking officer in SOE?'

A dark look crossed Lester's face. 'You are, Kit, being a bit forensic. I'm not sure of the exact timetable, but sometimes an agent must take risks and act on intuition.'

'Sure.'

'It wasn't long before Henri was being used to feed false information to the Germans – the most important disinfo being that the allied invasion was going to take place in the Pas-de-Calais. Can you imagine how many lives that saved? In fact, if the Germans had been waiting for us on the beaches at Normandy the invasion might have failed. And then what? It would have taken the Soviet Army a couple more years to beat Hitler, but the dividing line between free Europe and communist Europe would now be the English Channel. It was a race to Berlin. We weren't just fighting the Germans; we were trying to save Europe from Soviet domination.'

It was a line Kit had heard before. He gave a perfunctory nod.

Lester's glass was now empty, and he pushed it away. 'But I'm going off on a tangent. Let's get back to Henri Déricourt. He had to pay a price to convince the Germans that he was a genuine double agent – and that price was a Resistance network called Prosper. The Gestapo wouldn't have settled for chicken-feed intel, they wanted real meat – and Prosper was that meat. Paris-based, it was the largest and most important Resistance network in France – and Henri had to betray them to keep the trust of the Germans. Hundreds of agents were sacrificed, they were expendable, a price worth paying.'

Kit felt uncomfortable. He poured himself another drink.

Lester sighed and sat back. 'Oh, what a web we weave when we practise to deceive. In any case, Henri knew he was playing a dangerous game – and almost went to the guillotine – or in his case, I suppose, the firing squad. A lot of people in the Resistance refused to believe that Henri was a triple agent. In 1946 he was arrested for treason. If his SOE officer friend hadn't turned up to testify in his defence, Henri would have been shot as a traitor.' Lester paused. 'But his acquittal wasn't the end of it. A lot of people still hate Henri Déricourt and would like to see him hung, drawn and quartered – and one of them is William Catesby. Part of our job is to persuade Catesby to be a friend of Henri's and . . .' – Lester smiled – 'wean him away from Moscow and turn him into a triple agent.'

Kit found that the best way to deal with a drunken Lester was to just let him rant. The more he drank, the more certain he became that his conspiracy theories were rock solid. Kit stared at the dark mystery of Château d'If and wondered how many shadows of the dead were whispering of complex plots in its prison walls. 'Isn't there a possibility that Catesby could turn into a quadruple agent?'

'Jesus wept, Kit. Why not a quintuple or a sextuple agent? It ain't gonna happen. Meanwhile, I'm going to send a report to Washington on Catesby hanging around with commies – which, of course, they will pass on to SIS in London. Stirring the shit always helps – even if you don't know how it will help.'

La Corniche, Marseille: November 1949

Catesby had been pleased to see the chalk mark, which looked as wobbly as a child's scrawl – good spy craft deception – on the bridge abutment. He wasn't looking forward so much to hearing from Henry Bone as he was to seeing Helen. It was already a week since their meeting at the hospital. When Helen finally hove into view, she was nearly ten minutes late and tottering on high heels. She was also dressed in black and looked as if she had been to a funeral. For a second, Catesby wondered if her tale of the dead Vitalie had been a true story. As Helen approached, she steadied herself on the bridge abutment. He extended a helping hand, but she ignored it.

'I'm fucking late,' she said. There was no apology in her voice. It was just a statement. She looked a bit untidy: there was a run in one of her stockings and her slip was showing. Her breath smelled of strong drink, but it had the pleasant scent of good cognac.

'Have you been to a funeral?' said Catesby.

'No, I just like dressing in black.' She pivoted around to give him a full view. 'Don't you think it makes me look sexy?'

Catesby decided to stick to the funeral theme. 'Was it a good wake?'

She ignored his question and reached into her handbag. She handed over an envelope. 'London calling.'

He was about to ask her if she would like to go to a café. He didn't want to leave her tottering around Marseille alone, and he had other reasons. But before he could say anything, she had turned around and was striding back the way she had come. In normal circumstances, Catesby would never have surreptitiously followed a woman. It was unacceptable behaviour, but the duties required of a spy were not always compatible with the manners of a gentleman – and Catesby remembered that Henry Bone had instructed him to keep an eye on Helen Stuart. When she was about fifty yards ahead, he began to tail her. There were no shadows or trees or anything to hide behind on La Corniche, but she never looked back. After another hundred yards, she suddenly crossed to the other side – causing at least one car to screech to a halt. She then set off up a road leading to an area of grand houses and parks but didn't go far. The Talbot Lago Grand Sport was waiting for her with the passenger door open. Although Catesby could only see the driver from behind, he knew it wasn't Xavier-Honoré-Antoine de Saint-Breuil – but it was his car. With a roar it sped up the hill, Helen's head on the driver's shoulder.

Rue des Frères Pecchini, Marseille: November 1949

When Catesby got back to the flat, he was dying for a drink. He had been intoxicated by Helen's breath and now he wanted a real drink. He opened a bottle of cheap brandy and poured himself a small measure. He needed at least a little help in working out the what-the-flying-fuck-is-going-on scenario. He began by lifting his glass in a toast to Henry Bone. His hunch that Helen needed watching was a splendid piece of intelligence officer's intuition. Meanwhile, Catesby's excitement was dulled by a thought working its way from the memory part of his frontal lobe to the problem-solving complex section of his cortex. That part of his brain now seemed out of action. The problems weren't being solved and alarm bells were ringing. Helen was pally with a guy who was driving a car that belonged to an aristo who had tried to kill him. Catesby poured himself a larger brandy and decoded Bone's message.

THE DIRECTOR IS DISAPPOINTED THAT YOU STILL HAVE NOT PROVIDED ANY INTELLIGENCE ON THE DOCK STRIKES. DO SO ASAP.

'Give me a fucking chance,' shouted Catesby. 'I've just got my feet on the ground.'

THE ITEMS THAT YOU REQUIRE TO CARRY OUT YOUR ASSIGNED TASK WILL NOT BE DELIVERED BY DIPLOMATIC POUCH. THEY WILL BE HANDED OVER TO YOU PERSONALLY AT A TIME WHEN THEIR EMPLOYMENT IS IMMINENT.

Catesby shook his head. Bone wouldn't use the words 'murder weapons' even in a coded message.

CONTINUE TO OBSERVE AND REPORT ON HS. HER USE AS A
GO-BETWEEN IS MOSTLY A DEVICE TO ENABLE YOU TO INVESTIGATE
HER ACTIVITIES AND ASSOCIATES. IF HS BECOMES UNTENABLE AS A
MEANS OF COMMUNICATING, PLEASE USE THE FOLLOWING METHODS
IN AS DISCREET A MANNER AS POSSIBLE.

The next part of the message was a list of telephone numbers and addresses that Catesby could use to convey encoded messages. In an extreme situation, he would be allowed to send messages in the clear. The final line wasn't particularly reassuring.

IF YOUR LIFE IS CLEARLY IN DANGER YOU ARE PERMITTED TO LEAVE
YOUR AREA OF OPERATIONS UNDER COVER. YOU WILL FIND
EMERGENCY CONSULAR ASSISTANCE IN THE CANADIAN EMBASSY IN
BERN. UNDER NO CIRCUMSTANCES MAKE CONTACT WITH A BRITISH
EMBASSY.

It was kind of funny. Catesby raised his glass. 'Thank you, Canada!'

Le Panier, Marseille: November 1949

Catesby had never known anyone braver in battle than Gaston le Mat. During the Battle of Mont Gargan, Catesby had seen him run up to a German armoured car and drop a hand grenade down its hatch. The Germans in the car behind opened up on le Mat, but miraculously he escaped off the road and into the trees. But le Mat hadn't finished. He picked up a Sten gun and a bazooka and led a group of Maquisards to attack the rest of the column. The stunned Germans had retreated up the road. Later, le Mat had to be physically restrained from launching what would have been a suicidal one-man attack through the concentrated fire of the now regrouped German column.

'Yes,' said le Mat to Catesby, 'that would have been a stupid thing to do – thank you for stopping me.'

'It was mostly the others. I only managed to pull off one of your boots.'

Catesby had used Serge to get in contact with le Mat. The painter would have made an excellent agent: he knew everyone. Serge had told le Mat that an old comrade of his had turned up in Marseille to research a book about the Resistance and wanted to interview him. Le Mat had been wary at first, but his ego had won out and he'd agreed to meet Catesby at Serge's studio.

Le Mat stared at his pastis with a smug smile. 'But since those days I've learned that brains and cunning are just as important as bravery.'

'Serge says you're now involved in trade union work?'

'*Involved*,' said le Mat with a touch of indignation. 'I'm the CGT's chief of region for Marseille and the Bouches du Rhône.'

Catesby already knew that but didn't want to let on that he had been researching his former colleague. The CGT, the Confédération Générale du Travail, was France's biggest union, and le Mat was a very important player in an organisation that had strong links with the French Communist Party.

'And things are kicking off on the docks,' said Catesby.

'They are indeed,' said le Mat. 'And the action isn't going to stop in Marseille.'

'You have, I believe, local connections.'

'I was born and brought up in Marseille – but that doesn't mean that I love all the people who live here. I went to work on the docks when I was twelve years old – and it wasn't long before I met strike-breakers who had infiltrated the workforce with false papers certifying them as trained dockers. They were vermin recruited by the mafia. I continued to work and organise on the docks until I went to fight in Spain.' Le Mat smiled and showed Catesby the title of a book he had been conspicuously cradling: *Pour qui sonne le glas*. 'You know Hemingway?'

'Not personally, but I've read some of his writing.'

'This is his book about the Spanish Civil War.' Le Mat smiled. 'So your literary efforts, Comrade Catesby, will not be the first time that I've been mentioned in print.' He opened the book and pointed to a page with an underlined passage. 'Hemingway calls this character "Comrade Crazy" and he's obviously based on me. When I fought in Spain, the Spanish used to always say *está loco* – "is crazy" – when I turned up. Hemingway noticed and put me in his book. His picture of me is far from the truth, just the kind of backstabbing you would expect from a bourgeois writer – which I'm sure, Comrade Catesby, you're not going to be.' There was a note of threat in le Mat's voice.

'I think it's unfair that Hemingway didn't let you see a copy of the manuscript before he sent it off.'

Le Mat slapped the table and gave a loud laugh. 'As a fellow writer, maybe you could approach Hemingway on my behalf and tell him what needs to be amended in the next edition.'

Catesby smiled. He could also tell Hemingway that his former flat in Paris had been turned into a safe house for British spies – and ask for some signed copies that the Secret Intelligence Service could leave around as reading matter.

Le Mat looked at his watch. 'I can't stay much longer. I've got a strike meeting to go to. As you said, things are kicking off. There's been a serious development. Six of our members have been arrested for taking part in a demonstration against the Indochina war and are being held in cells at the Palais de Justice. No one else was arrested, just our members. They were targeted for their politics. The Resistance didn't end in 1945. If you want to write about the ongoing Resistance, meet me at the Café de L'Industrie at eight tomorrow morning. Come prepared to fight.'

As le Mat left the studio, Catesby looked up at Serge who was standing behind an easel. He had been painting them. 'You're just a shadowy figure. I concentrated on le Mat, but I don't think I've done a much better job than Hemingway.'

Palais de Justice, Marseille: November 1949

The Café de L'Industrie was near the basin of La Joliette, where large numbers of ships took on and unloaded cargoes. The customers were mostly men in working clothes. Catesby arrived early for the rendezvous with le Mat and indulged himself with a café crème and a brandy chaser. He wanted to continue the pleasure of a good night's sleep. He always slept well the night before a day of action – and the more dangerous the anticipated action, the better the sleep.

When le Mat entered the café, he was accompanied by two dock-workers who looked very big, very tough and were carrying crowbars. They were speaking rapidly in Provençal dialect and Catesby struggled to understand a word. Le Mat finally spotted Catesby and came over to his table. As he sat down, he looked at the empty brandy glass. 'You're preparing for battle?'

'If I get arrested or have my skull fractured, it might be a long time before I can have another drink.'

'By all means, write about what you see, but stay on the sidelines. Let the workers lead the line. Today isn't going to be a battle like Mont Gargan with peasants dashing in and out of the woods. Today is going to be an uprising of the urban proletariat. There won't be any work done on the docks today. The CGT are downing tools and marching on the Palais de Justice. There will be at least eight thousand of us. If they don't free our members from their prison cells, we'll tear the building down and free them ourselves.' Le Mat quickly stood up. 'I must be off. There is much to do.'

Catesby found himself swept up in a massive crowd of angry workers. He was underneath a long banner demanding *Le pain, la paix, la liberté*. There were shouts demanding the immediate release of the prisoners.

They were all pushing towards the courthouse, which was a hundred yards away from Catesby's part of the crowd. The Palais de Justice was a neo-classical building bleached white by the morning sun. Catesby thought it looked very noble and calm as it towered over the disorder below – which, he thought, was probably just the effect the architect had intended. Catesby stood on his tiptoes trying to look over the heads of the striking dockers, who, for the most part, were big and burly. If there was a fight, he wouldn't mind being on their side – but the *flics* had guns. Catesby's best view of the cops were of those standing on the steps of the courthouse. Wearing helmets and jackboots and carrying rifles, they looked more like soldiers than police. And there were a lot of them. He could make out lines and lines of helmets and the tops of rifle barrels above the heads of the demonstrators. There were no orders, but suddenly the crowd of strikers surged forward. It was an unstoppable mass of bodies, and Catesby couldn't have pushed back out of the crowd even if he had wanted to. Shots were fired, but it didn't seem to make any difference. The strikers carrying the banner had now furled it and were brandishing the polls like weapons.

'What's happening?' said Catesby to a striker who was shouting instructions.

'The police are giving way. They always do when they're outnumbered.'

Catesby watched someone who must have been a senior cop – he was wearing a kepi rather than a helmet – mount the steps of the Palais de Justice and enter the grand brass doors. Meanwhile some of the strikers had begun to sing 'The International'. The striker next to Catesby joined in – and so did Catesby for the chorus. If his former colleagues at SIS could see him now.

As the singing finished, Catesby overheard messages being passed back. The authorities had begun to negotiate. The strikers were now close to the police lines and the tension seemed to be rising. Several of the cops had un-shouldered their rifles and were using them as clubs to push back the crowd. One of the protestors had blood streaming from a head wound, and there was a clang as the helmets of two policemen clattered on the cobbles. One cop had been knocked to the ground and was being kicked. A phalanx of police pushed forward to rescue him. Voices on both sides were pleading for calm. Meanwhile, Catesby noticed that other members of the crowd were talking and laughing with some of the cops as if they were old pals. A moment later, all talking stopped as cheers went up from the crowd nearest the Palais de Justice. It was good news: the prisoners had been released and all charges dropped. There was another rendition of 'The International' as the demonstrators linked arms. A dockworker next to Catesby said, 'If you show enough force, they always give in.'

'Is that it? Is it all over?' said Catesby. He was a bit disappointed that the demo seemed to have ended. He had been enjoying the excitement. But before the docker could answer, voices started shouting, *à la mairie*! Something was up at the town hall. As he followed the crowd, Catesby learned there was an ongoing punch-up between Communist Party councillors and other elected members. Some demonstrators were shouting: *Burn down the mairie and hang the bastards!*

The town hall was a splendid seventeenth-century building that overlooked Le Vieux Port. In fact, it was so close to the harbour that a team of battling officials could – with a good heave-ho – have tossed an opponent into the water from the first-floor balcony. Catesby was surprised to see that the only police present were CRS, Compagnies Républicaines de Sécurité. The CRS were supposed to be elite riot police, but they didn't seem to be doing much at all. They had arrived on bicycles which they were still wheeling around. If they were going to bash rioters over the head, they needed to stack the bikes somewhere so they could wade in unencumbered and freely swing their truncheons. Catesby was amazed to see that a few of the CRS had lent their bikes to strikers, who were gleefully wheeling around Le Vieux Port. It got even weirder. One of the CRS had removed his revolver from its holster and handed it to a demonstrator as if showing off a toy. The demonstrator laughed and handed the gun back. It looked like the CRS were going to do nothing to stop the striking dockworkers from attacking the town hall. On the other hand, it might have been a clever bit of policing, as the mood of the demonstrators had become calm.

Catesby turned to a dockworker who, a few minutes before, had been bellowing for blood. 'Can you tell me what's happening . . . comrade?'

'I believe, comrade, that we are about to hear an announcement – from our mayor and the right-wing bastard who claims to have replaced him.'

A minute later two men appeared on the balcony. The first to speak was the communist who had been Marseille's mayor until ousted in a recent power struggle. There was a hush as he began to speak.

'Thank you, comrades, for your loyal support. An agreement has been reached and I will let . . .' He extended his hand towards an older man with glasses standing next to him. He must have been the new mayor, for the crowd immediately burst into a chorus of boos. 'Please let him speak, comrades. He has something very important to say.'

The mayor seemed ill at ease addressing a crowd that was baying for his blood. He took out a piece of paper and began to read in a monotone voice. 'I have tendered my resignation as mayor of Marseille. The peace of our city is more important than my remaining in office.' His announcement was greeted by laughter and a fresh chorus of boos. The now ex-mayor turned and quickly left the balcony. There was loud cheering followed by yet another triumphal rendering of 'The International'.

As the crowd dispersed, Catesby made his way back to the Café de L'Industrie. He was hoping to find out more about what had happened. When he arrived, the staff had moved the tables together and were setting them for a late lunch. Eating in a workers' bar or café was like dining *en famille*. There wasn't any menu, you just sat down with the others and paid a standard charge regardless of what you ate or drank. Le Mat spotted Catesby and swapped seats with one of the strikers sitting next to him. The meal began with a simple fish soup that the diners mopped up with baguette.

'Today seems to have gone well,' said Catesby.

'Not as well as it looks. The mayor's resignation was a cheap trick to avoid the town hall being ransacked. The bastard will be back within days – and so will we.'

The waiters began to clear away the soup bowls and the pastis glasses to make room for platters of cassoulet and litres of red table wine.

'By the way,' said le Mat, 'if you want the best of Marseille cuisine you need to wear dark glasses and an expensive suit.'

'Why's that?'

'To make sure they give you a good table at Julot's. It's not the only restaurant where the mob hang out, but it is the best.'

'Have you ever eaten there?'

'Once, at the very end of the war when the Calenzana gang wanted to prove they had been loyal members of the Resistance.'

'Had they been?'

'Only out of opportunism. They saw which way the wind was blowing. Until the war, their core business had been prostitution. Marseille's mafia bosses were happy to let them run that sector as long as they didn't branch out. But after the big boss was killed in a Resistance attack, the Calenzana gang took over the other rackets too – gambling, nightclubs, drugs and smuggling. They played a clever game.' Le Mat shook his head and stared into the distance.

'What's the matter?'

'As I said before, don't think today was a big victory. Just because the cops didn't put up a fight, don't think we've won. The police aren't the ones who wield the power in Marseille.'

'I know what you're saying.'

'Good – and don't forget it.'

It was a long lunch that went on until late in the afternoon. When Catesby left the café, the sky was overcast and darkening – and he could see that things were revving up again. Groups of demonstrators, mainly younger ones, were re-forming and seemed to be looking for trouble. An older man with a sketch pad was sitting on a bench observing them. It was Serge. Catesby went over to him. 'Were you at the demonstration?'

'Of course,' said Serge as he continued to sketch, 'but there wasn't much to draw in terms of action. On the other hand, the dockworkers are always good subjects: powerful figures and totally unselfconscious.' He gestured towards the young men who were milling around. 'These lads are interesting too – young and looking for trouble. Most of them are apprentices or students – and all of them are militant Communist Party members. I find the combination of anger, youth and recklessness fascinating. It reminded me of the street fighting in 1941 before I was arrested. When the young lads got shot, their faces were so amazed and confused – and the arms and legs always go funny.'

'What are this lot up to?'

'I think they want to ransack a few bars and nightclubs – the ones owned by the mafia.'

'Foolish?'

Serge shook his head. 'Just because something is dangerous, doesn't mean it is foolish. No, not foolish, they're aiming at the right target. By the way, what did you think of the police today?'

'They didn't do much.'

'Indeed – and from an artist's point of view they were even more useless. I was tempted to bribe a cop or two to use their truncheons.'

'That sounds a bit counter-revolutionary.'

'I was, Monsieur Catesby, only joking – but there are those who would say that art comes first. In any case, the battle for who controls Marseille isn't going to be with police or soldiers; it's going to be between the mafia and the unions.' Serge closed his sketchbook. 'Look, they're moving off.'

'Where to?'

'The area around the Opéra. It's where the mob have a lot of clubs and pimps.'

'Shall we follow them?'

'Have you got that gun you bought from me?'

'No, it's only for personal protection.'

Serge gave a worried smile. Meanwhile, there was a lot of shouting. The crowd of demonstrators moving on to the Opéra district was growing. 'I think,' said Serge, 'they're preparing to have some fun. Let's follow them.'

There is, Catesby thought, as he heard the first shattering crashes, no other noise like the sound of breaking glass. Gunfire is loud and frightening, but it is the well-worn and predictable soundtrack that accompanies war. Breaking glass, on the other hand, is the sound of anarchy. It signalled an end to dull social convention – and gave permission to loot and riot. The first broken glass was the result of an iron chair being thrown through the window of a gangster bar. The rioters then pushed their way into the premises and soon cleared the shelves of bottles and glasses. The destruction created an intriguing cocktail smell as pastis flowed into crème de menthe, Scotch whisky, rum, vermouth and various brandies. The Temperance Movement would have loved it, but Catesby wondered if he could secret away a still-intact bottle of VSOP cognac to share with Henry Bone.

There was no physical violence. The bar staff simply stepped back and shrugged. They weren't the owners, and they weren't going to get beaten up on their behalf. The first ransacking emboldened the rioters and they decided to move on to one of the bigger nightclubs. The pimps saw what was happening and quickly abandoned the streets. There was, however, a wonderfully top-of-the-range pimp car parked in front of the nightclub. The Delahaye 135 MS Cabriolet still had its top rolled down. Catesby was sure that the ignition wouldn't respond unless the hand turning it was wearing a star-sapphire pinkie ring. The rioters began kicking the sleek sports car with glee until one of them told the others to step back while he lit the wick of a Molotov cocktail. The petrol bomb landed in the driver's seat and exploded a second later. Serge was sketching with undisguised glee. When the petrol tank went up, reminding Catesby of the explosion that took out his Standard 8, the rioters gave a great cheer.

The nightclub had been locked and barred in advance, but the demonstrators managed to break a dozen or so windows before moving on to a less defended club. This time there was some fighting. Catesby couldn't see what was actually happening, but he heard a lot of angry shouting and swearing – and saw two demonstrators being led away with bleeding heads. The fighting raised the temperature, and this club was well and truly smashed. The rioters moved on with confidence to their next target. They now passed close to the Opéra de Marseille itself. It was an imposing white building with stone columns. It seemed to be looking down on the scenes of chaos below with lofty indifference. Despite the calm radiated by the opera building, a self-preservation bell started ringing in Catesby's brain, triggered by animal instinct rather than any warning signs that you could see or hear. It was a bell that had saved Catesby more than once during the war. He dived for cover even before the first shots rang out.

At first Catesby wondered if the shots had been fired by a sniper hidden on the top floor of the opera house, but then he recognised them as pistol shots that were coming from close range. He decided it was best to stay curled up on the ground. Pretending to be one of those hit made it less likely that a gunman would want to take aim at him. Catesby wondered if Serge was still sketching. He tried not to laugh at the absurd thought. In times of danger, he often saw the funny side. Maybe it was a survival technique – but it didn't always last long. The humour had turned to horror. Catesby was terrified that he would soon feel a hand reaching down to drag him upright – and then the bullet to the side of the head. He needed to see if anyone was near him. He opened one eye and looked over his right forearm. There were three of them and they were a good distance away – about fifty feet – and only one of them was brandishing a gun. He was a lot taller than the other two and had begun to reload his pistol. Catesby could hear people crying out for help. As the gunman fed new cartridges into the revolver, one of the others made a gesture with his head. They were finished; it was time to go. As the three strode away, Catesby looked at the smallest of them – who seemed to be the one in charge. His coat pocket bulged as if he too was carrying a weapon. Afterwards, opinion was divided on how many shooters had taken part.

It turned out that four demonstrators had been shot. Two had leg wounds and were in a lot of pain, but their lives were not in danger. One of the other two, having been shot through an eye, was clearly dead. Serge was trying to help the remaining casualty, who had been shot in the chest and was saying, 'I can't breathe, I can't breathe, please loosen my belt.'

Catesby was about to tell Serge to put his hand over the bullet hole as that would help him breathe, but Serge had already done so. The welcome klaxon of an ambulance pierced the night air, and a moment later it screeched to a halt a few feet away from the victim. The badly wounded demonstrator was still breathing and talking when they stretchered him into the ambulance. He'll make it, thought Catesby, he's young and fit and he will make it. Catesby was wrong.

7th arrondissement, Marseille: November 1949

'Good score at yesterday's match,' said Lester as he passed a drink to Kit Fournier. 'Our mafia chums, two; the commies, zero. Pity it's more of a soccer score than a basketball score, but these are early days.'

Fournier frowned and nodded.

'By the way, Kit, I keep hearing this term, *beaux voyous*, when people are talking about what seem to be tough guys. How would you translate it? The literal version, "handsome thugs", doesn't ring true. After all, many of them – including one of the guys who pulled the trigger – are not what you would call handsome.'

Fournier smiled. 'If they were operating anywhere else, my translation would be "real bad asses", but in Marseille the term *beaux voyous* only has one meaning.'

'Which is?'

'Mafia mobsters.'

'I like it – and they managed to take out the commie filth with their own guns.' Lester paused. 'What's the matter, Kit? You look down in the dumps. We should be celebrating.'

Fournier stared at his drink before he finally spoke. 'Unfortunately, the earlier demonstrations easily succeeded in getting six war protesters released from prison and secured the resignation of Marseille's mayor. We can't ignore that – and the mafia only got involved because their own property was attacked.'

It was now Lester's turn to stare into his drink. 'Has anyone, Kit, ever compared you to a ray of sunshine?'

'I try to be objective and rational.'

'Okay, sunshine boy, give me some more rationality.'

'The news of the killings has resulted in calls for a general strike, not just in Marseille, but all across France.'

'That's even better. It will give our pals a chance to take out more commies. We're gonna win, Kit, we're always gonna win because we're capitalists – and capitalism is the most powerful system that human history has ever produced. People want wealth and pleasure, and capitalism gives it to them. Let's get back to the mafia. The Calenzana gang are the best capitalists in Marseille. They know, for example, that men need pussy, and their first racket was providing pussy to anyone who had the cash. When the Calenzana began the business, the Carbone mob were ruling Marseille. Pimping wasn't a big part of Carbone's portfolio; so, as long as the Calenzana didn't challenge the mob's authority, they could run their whorehouses without interference. Well, you know what happened after Carbone got killed?'

Fournier nodded. 'Carbone's successor as mob chief had to clear off to South America to avoid getting lynched by the Resistance as a collaborator.'

'Exactly. And, hey presto, the Calenzana take over all of Carbone's rackets. And, of course, they're on good terms with the Resistance because a lot of their whores have been sleeping with German officers and picking up the priceless intelligence they pass on. Don't worry; the mafia will do our bidding. They appreciate the rationality of profit.' Lester poured them both more bourbon. 'By the way, I've got a date tonight.'

'Anyone interesting?'

Lester smiled. 'We'll see. Back to capitalism, the problem with a lot of lawmakers is that they're joyless assholes who want to stamp out human pleasure and the free trade that goes with it.' Lester raised his glass. 'Look at prohibition.' Lester lowered his voice. 'But there are two sides to that story. Some of my family made a lot of money out of bootlegging. They were pissed off when congress repealed the law – they had to go out and find jobs. And I'll tell you something else, the Calenzana would be fucking devastated if there were no drug laws. If drugs were legal, you would pay less for a hit of heroin than a cup of coffee. The stuff is dirt

cheap to grow and produce. Booze and whores and drugs are victim-
less crimes. Nothing to have a bad conscience about. The laws are about
taking away people's free will.'

Fournier laughed. 'Next time there's a Supreme Court vacancy I hope
Truman puts your name forward.'

'I hope you're not being sarcastic, Kit, I'd make a fucking fantastic
judge. And, in any case, I'm sure that what we're doing here has the
White House's complete blessing. Speaking of which, we need to hand
out more guns and money. The gang may seem very willing and generous at the moment but it's not going to last unless we grease more palms.'
Lester looked at his watch. 'Drink up, Kit, I've got an appointment.'

'I thought you said you had a date.'

'Same thing.'

A moment later there was a knock on the door. At first, Fournier
thought they were real nuns, but the high heels, rouge and revealing
breast cleavages suggested otherwise.

'I didn't know you were Catholic,' said Kit.

'Of course, I am. I come from South Chicago which is full of wops
and micks.' Lester looked at the nuns. 'I wanted identical twins, but I
shouldn't complain. They're a free gift.'

Fournier finished his bourbon and got up to leave. 'See you at the
basilica for Mass on Sunday.'

Le Panier, Marseille: November 1949

Catesby was drinking Vietnamese tea in Serge's studio as he watched the artist paint an impression of the dying demonstrator. 'The good thing about memory,' said Serge, 'is that only the most important images remain in your mind.'

Catesby remained silent. His own memory echoed with the words of the dying man: *I can't breathe, I can't breathe.* Serge's version of the young man was of a gaping mouth gasping for air and of eyes staring blankly at the sky. The harsh lines seemed to shake with pain and rage.

'The guy,' said Serge, 'that pulled the trigger on this lad was the one they call The Boot, a big stupid bastard that's killed before for the gang.'

'Wasn't there more than one shooter?'

'The boss fired some shots too, but he'll get away with it – particularly since he told the cops that The Boot was the only one who opened fire.'

'But on the boss's orders.'

'Oh no, they'll say that The Boot is a known psycho who just pulled out his gun. The boss will admit that they were there to threaten and intimidate the demonstrators – the nightclub was, after all, their most lucrative brothel – but didn't want things to go any further.'

'So they sacrifice The Boot to keep themselves out of jail?'

'Not at all. He's now on his way to South America, where he'll have a very happy life carrying out hits for the gang and lending a hand with the drugs. The Calenzana aren't just a local mob, they're a global business. There are national governments that depend on their support. Hold your nose when you visit the boardrooms and the presidential palaces. The corridors of power are perched over a cesspit of violence and corruption.'

Catesby looked at the portrait of the dying demonstrator. 'If his killer were a prisoner here in your studio, what would you do to him?'

'I wouldn't do anything to him. I'm an artist, not an executioner.' For a second Serge looked pensive. 'But I might call in someone else to deal with him. The Harkis in Algeria had their own way of carrying out revenge. Their victim's testicles and penis were amputated, then shoved down his throat to muffle his screams. And while all that's going on, I would be painting it. Why are you smiling?' said Serge. 'Have I said something amusing?'

'No, I often smile when I'm feeling bitter and twisted.'

'And there is a lot to be bitter and twisted about. Sometimes I wonder if the war and Buchenwald turned me into a monster too.' With rough brush strokes, Serge began to darken the background of his painting. 'There's going to be a general strike on the day of his funeral. Marseille will grind to a halt.'

'What about the other victim?'

'The family are not from Marseille. They are heartbroken and want a simple, private burial. We will respect their wishes.'

Catesby nodded at the portrait. 'When will his funeral take place?'

'On Thursday. The cortège will depart from the Labour Exchange. I believe there are plans for his body to lie there for two days before.'

Le Canet, Marseille: November 1949

It was the evening before the funeral. Catesby hadn't known the young man but felt that he had to pay his respects. It required a long wait to do so. Catesby had been queuing for two hours before he finally passed into the main hall of the Labour Exchange. There were candles and photographs of the young man from his early childhood. He had obviously loved football and swimming. His coffin was covered in a red flag. As he left the building, Catesby saw a notice saying that the cortège would leave at three the next day.

It was the largest funeral that Catesby had ever attended. The streets were packed. He later discovered that more than a hundred and fifty thousand mourners had turned out. Catesby had set off from Le Panier with Serge and Huong, but it was impossible to get anywhere near the Labour Exchange. It was mostly a matter of standing around and waiting. Huong was dressed in Western clothes impeccably chosen for a funeral, from her black veil to her gleaming black shoes. Serge was wearing a suit and black tie and hadn't brought a sketch pad. Respect was the order of the day.

Serge looked at his watch. 'You're on time, but I don't think the coffin will get here soon. Marseille is a city in shutdown.'

It was another half an hour before the organisers cleared a route through the surging crowd, but everyone was eager to cooperate and help. The coffin was on an open carriage drawn by four bay horses with red plumes. The family followed immediately behind. The next in line were two young members of the metal workers' union carrying a huge portrait of the deceased. Following them were workers carrying the flags of the CGT and all the other unions represented in Marseille. There were also flags belonging to Resistance groups, notably the Forces Françaises de l'Intérieur and the Maquis Rouge. Oddly, it reminded Catesby of a Pathé film of George V's funeral that he had seen when he was twelve. The whole school had been taken to the Lowestoft cinema to see it – and what a sensation it was! Afterwards, Catesby and all the other boys wanted to join the Royal Navy so they could pull the gun carriage bearing the coffin at the next state funeral.

After the flags had passed, it was now the turn of the throng to follow the cortège. It was only a two-mile walk to the Cimetière du Canet, but it took more than an hour. The neighbourhoods through which the cortège passed were mostly working-class ones. Many of the homes and buildings were hung with black, and all the shops and businesses were closed. The longest stretch was the Rue Belle de Mai. There were blocks of flats as well as factory buildings. Catesby pointed at one of them. 'What do they make there?'

'Cigars and cigarettes. Belle de Mai is the heart of the French tobacco industry.'

'Most of the workers are women,' said Huong. 'And they are exploited. The work is terrible drudgery.'

How ironic, thought Catesby, that the district was called Belle de Mai. What a pretty name for such a depressing place.

'One of my models worked in that factory,' said Serge. 'She got fed up with rolling cigars for ten hours a day and became a prostitute instead.'

'Is she the one who made you fence the pistol?'

'That's the one. She contracted tuberculosis from one or more of her many clients – and has other lung problems from inhaling tobacco dust. It's even money to see which job kills her first.'

Just as Catesby was wishing that he'd brought a hipflask along, Serge took one out of his pocket and passed it over. 'Have some rat poison.'

Catesby sipped a slug of the brandy and passed it back. 'That's one less rat gnawing between my ears.'

The procession passed on to the Boulevard de la Révolution, which was overlooked by some very poor-looking blocks of flats. The only people who came on to the balconies to watch the cortège were women and children.

Most looked as if they were of North African origin. One little boy of about eight shouted something in a language Catesby didn't understand.

'The kid wants to know who's dead,' said Serge.

'You know the language?'

'Only a few words. It's the Arabic of the Maghreb. If you live in Marseille, you pick some of it up. If you want to know what's going on, say *wesh*. If someone says *chouf*, they want you to have a look around.' Serge smiled. 'And if someone mentions *le kif*, they're talking about drugs.'

The boy on the balcony seemed to be shouting another question, but a veiled woman came out and ushered him back inside the flat. Catesby looked at Serge and joked, 'She must have heard you say something about *le kif*.'

'Always be careful what you say when children are around.'

They had now turned on to the Boulevard de Plombières. The rundown houses on both sides of the road suggested they needed plumbers as much as they needed a revolution.

Serge gestured a hand towards the state of urban decay. 'The living conditions are squalid, child poverty – and the government doesn't care.'

'But,' said Huong, 'there's still enough money to send bombers and Legionnaires to kill my people in Vietnam.'

Catesby folded his hands and walked on in silence – and reminded himself that he wasn't there as a genuine mourner, but as a spy. Part of him wanted to tell Bone and the London gang to get stuffed. Catesby's thoughts were cut short as the procession ground to a halt. They had arrived at the Canet Cemetery. Catesby could see the whitewashed entrance arch above the heads of the crowd. It looked far too small to funnel in the enormous throng that had followed the coffin.

'I believe that most of us are going to have to wait outside,' said Serge. 'The authorities don't want us trampling the graves and flowers of the other dead.'

Catesby was relieved. French cemeteries gave him the creeps. They were close-packed cities of the dead with too much statuary and ornamentation. He also didn't like the custom of photographs of the deceased being attached to the tombstones, sarcophagi and mausoleums. That was creepy. Catesby preferred English churchyards with widely scattered graves, inscriptions that soon faded and blackbirds singing – and no wretched photos.

The crowd was spreading out around the cemetery walls. The procession had begun at half-past three and it was now nearly six o'clock. Catesby was dying for a drink and hoped it wouldn't be long before he was sitting in a bar. The singing was a welcome relief: it signalled the end of the funeral. It began with the 'Marseillaise', a combination of the revolutionary and the patriotic, and ended with 'The International'. Catesby only knew the choruses, but mimed the bits he didn't know – like an English Secretary of State for Wales pretending to sing 'Hen Wlad Fy Nhadau' at a conference.

The crowd began slowly to disperse. 'Some of us,' said Serge, 'are meeting up at L'Industrie. You're welcome to join us.'

'I might see you later,' said Catesby as he waved them off. He wanted a drink, but he didn't want to socialise. His own place would be better, even though it was more than an hour's walk as the tram drivers were on strike. And though the thought filled him with self-loathing, he also needed to start compiling a long-overdue report for London. Would it have to include intel that would help his bosses? Or could he pad it with disinfo? As a sly smile crossed Catesby's face, he felt something hard prodding into the centre of his back. Catesby put his hands up. It would be useless to run. Had a psychic SIS gunman read his traitorous thoughts? A voice behind him did indeed speak in English – but with a Suffolk accent. It wasn't a gun. It was a strong workman's finger and the finger belonged to his cousin Jack.

'You can't run, Will, and you can't hide. They'll always know where you are.'

'Who are "they"?'

'Your mum and your wife.'

'I suppose,' said Catesby, 'that the obvious question is, what the fuck are you doing here?'

'And the obvious answer is, helping with the revolution.'

'Why aren't you doing it from the docks of Lowestoft?'

'I know, Will, that you're trying to be sarcastic – and I'm not going to rise to the bait. Yes, the revolution is well on its way to Lowestoft, but Marseille is where it's happening now. I'm impatient and want to be at the centre of things – and learn lessons that I can take back home.'

'How were my mother's French lessons?'

'She told you about that, did she?' Jack smiled. 'I asked her not to.'

'As there's so little interesting in Mum's life, she couldn't resist.'

'She enjoyed it and was very patient – and refused to accept any money. She taught me the basics, but I'm learning a lot more on the docks – and at CGT meetings.'

'How did you get a job and union membership?'

'I've got connections,' Jack said with a wry smile.

'I bet you became a Party member.'

Jack looked straight ahead and didn't answer.

'I apologise,' said Catesby, 'if it sounds like I'm interrogating you.'

'Well, Will, wasn't that your job at the, uh, Foreign Office?'

'It's a good thing I resigned then, because I'm not very good at it.'

'I was surprised to see you at our comrade's funeral.'

'"Our comrade,"' echoed Catesby. 'So the Party did fund you coming to Marseille?'

'Your sense of humour can be grating, Will.'

Catesby had been trying to wind Jack up, but it wasn't just a joke. The Communist Party was a bit of a travel agency. If a young member wanted to go anywhere in the world to organise, recruit or support a revolution, the Party would help plan and finance the trip. At a time when travel was difficult and expensive, it provided a means to get around and learn about other cultures. On the other hand, the trip could prove a dangerous affair that ended in front of a firing squad – and sunny Marseille was already turning into an ideological battleground where the bullets were flying.

'I won't ask you where you're staying,' said Catesby, 'as you would regard that as further interrogation, but I'll tell you where I am.'

'I already know. You've got a flat in the Rue des Frères Pecchini, not far from the beach. Your wife told me.' Jack paused and gave Catesby a searching look. 'She also told me that you got sacked from the Foreign Office because you're a security risk and that's why she threw you out of the house.'

Catesby began to stir uneasily.

'And then, just as I was about to leave, she got a bit flirty. She said I should come back to the flat for a drink and a chat after she'd put the kids to bed.'

'By the way, what were you doing in London?'

Jack broke into a broad smile. 'I really had you going, didn't I?'

'I didn't believe a word.'

'You ought to have seen your face, Will. Don't worry, I would never go anywhere near your precious Frances – especially after she got that job working for the police.'

'Who told you that?'

'Your mum, she also gave me your address.'

The lies and cover stories began to click into place. Frances was telling people that she had a part-time job doing typing at Scotland Yard. It was a good excuse for not being able to see people when she was at work.

'How's the book going?' Jack said with a smile that seemed tinged with irony.

'Very well. Would you like me to read you a chapter or two?'

'No thanks.'

Catesby had indeed managed to finish a few chapters. He had started writing to pass the time and cut down on his drinking. It was entirely to come to terms with his own troubled memories, and he would never attempt to get it published.

'I'm lodging with a dockworker and his family,' said Jack. 'I'll give you the address. Have you got some paper?'

Catesby gave him a pencil and the back of the Julot's restaurant card that the mobster in the cathedral had passed to him.

Jack scribbled an address. 'It's Rue de Montevideo if you can't read my handwriting. I hope you pop round. I could use help with translating. Things sometimes get confusing.'

'Don't worry, Jack, it's probably just your pal's wife getting flirty.'

'Touché.'

'Your French is coming along fine.'

La Corniche, Marseille: November 1949

In the end, the accounts that Catesby wrote and encoded were frank and honest evaluations. Nothing that he could report to London would bring the dead demonstrators back to life or aid the French government's Indochina war. Catesby was sure that the Director would be pleased with his eyewitness descriptions of the French dock strikes and his assessment of where they were going. He also hoped that his accounts of the mafia killings would sound alarm bells in Whitehall. But, in a way, his reports were irrelevant bullshit. The strikes were Henry Bone's pretext for sending him to Marseille. His real mission was to kill someone Bone wanted removed – and to keep an eye on Helen. Could the two tasks be related?

As was the usual plan, Catesby scrawled a chalk mark on the bridge abutment and then returned the following Friday afternoon to rendezvous with Helen as she strode out on her walk beside the sea. But this time she wasn't walking, she was driving a fancy sports car – a Talbot Lago Grand Sport. She was wearing dark glasses and a white headscarf. She looked like someone modelling for an advert in a car magazine.

'Hop in,' she said.

'This is a pretty smart motor. Does it belong to your husband?' said Catesby feigning ignorance.

'No, it belongs to a friend of a friend of mine. Fancy a trip to a bistro?'

'Sounds like fun.'

'You look like someone who needs to have more fun.'

'Off we go then.'

She put down her foot and the car roared up La Corniche. She drove fast and confidently, but Catesby thought she came too close to the cyclists.

The place she had chosen was a bistro bar called La Floriane. It was the smartest place that Catesby had seen in Marseille; exactly the sort of bar for someone who drove a Talbot Lago Grand Sport. He had the impression that the clientele was mostly highly paid professionals in journalism, acting or academia – and maybe a filmmaker or two.

'This,' said Helen, 'is the type of place where someone like you should be seen.'

Catesby was worried about her loud voice. He wondered if she had already been drinking. 'Can we move into a quiet corner?' he said.

'You dirty dog – you mean more romantic. Okay, let's go.'

The new seats were in an alcove which seemed far enough from eavesdropping ears – and was a bit romantic. A waiter came over and Helen ordered a gin and Suze, the French equivalent of a G&T, and asked the waiter to add a dash of Amaro. Catesby thought pastis would be a bit infra dig for La Floriane, so he ordered Dubonnet and gin.

'How's your book going?' she asked with an ironic smile.

'There are number of new chapters I'd like to send to the editor,' said Catesby tapping the envelope in his breast pocket.

'And you want to send it by diplomatic bag to prevent other writers from stealing your ideas.'

'Naturally.'

She removed the orange peel garnish from her drink and bit off the fruit, leaving the rind. There was a flash of white teeth and pink tongue. 'I don't see much of my husband, but I could get someone to drop your message off at the consulate.'

Catesby tried to look nonchalant. 'Don't worry.'

She sipped her drink and smiled. 'I used to be an acrobat, you know. In Ireland, one of my tricks involved drinking a pint of Guinness while standing on my head.'

The Irish connection added another complication to her story, but Catesby wasn't going to pursue it. It was best to let her talk and reveal all at her own pace.

'My husband was dragging me into a world where I felt more and more like a total stranger. I certainly could play the role and follow the script – better than most – but it wasn't me.'

'I know the feeling.'

'I'm sure you do.'

'Be careful who you pretend to be. If you do it long enough, you risk becoming that person in reality.'

She gave Catesby a smile that was almost flirtatious. 'Indeed.'

Catesby nodded and sipped his Dubonnet. He was pleased with himself. He was much more convincing at uttering bullshit than saying what he truly felt. A good spy became his cover story.

'I'm not sure,' said Helen, 'that I could have finally made the break if it hadn't been for Henri.'

Catesby raised an eyebrow. 'Although I don't want to intrude into personal matters . . .'

'Henri's a good fuck and does things I like, but that's not the only reason I went off with him.'

The conversation began to remind Catesby of his drunken forays into the bohemian corners of Fitzrovia during the war. The Blitz destroyed rules of behaviour as well as buildings.

'It sounds like Henri is a Frenchman.'

'Indeed. He was a big hero in the Resistance – a daredevil pilot who organised air movements of people and supplies that outwitted the Germans.'

Catesby hoped she couldn't see the flashbulbs going off in his head.

She sipped her drink and closed her eyes in what looked like a moment of blissful recollection. 'Before the war he was part of an aerial circus that toured Europe. It was something we had in common. I ran away from home when I was seventeen to join an aerial circus. Of course, I wasn't a pilot at that age, but I used to do acrobatic acts hanging from aeroplanes or strutting across the top wing of a biplane. Henri says he'll help me get back into it – we'd be a team.'

'Henri sounds a fascinating person.'

Helen smiled. 'You have, in fact, met him – and Henri speaks very fondly of you. He says you were one of the bravest and most competent SOE agents he ever met.' She gave a slight frown as she stirred her drink. 'I wouldn't mind another one of these.'

Catesby signalled for the waiter and ordered another gin and Suze.

'Thank you. Henri says that there were differences between you – but he respects you having doubts about him. Resistance operations created nightmares of suspicion – and sometimes you had to talk to the enemy.'

Catesby nodded and whispered, 'Of course.' He knew it was a time for lying and hoped his inner revulsion didn't show. It wasn't necessary to mention that Henri Déricourt had been recalled from France in 1944, arrested for treason in 1946 and acquitted in 1948. She already knew these things, but they were the sort of unpleasant facts that friends left unsaid when having a pleasant drink.

'By the way, Henri says that he would love to meet you again.'

'I am sure we can arrange something. It would be good to see him.' Catesby put his hand on hers and wondered if he was laying it on too thick. He then looked at his watch, 'Oh dear, sorry but I must be going.'

'Despite everything, I am sure my husband can pass on your report to the consulate.'

Catesby took the envelope out of his pocket and pretended to be ready to hand it over – and then stopped. 'Ah, but on reflection, I think I need to make some changes – and, as this is going by dip bag, add a bit more confidential stuff. I'll pass it on when we next meet.'

'As you please.'

Catesby hoped that the expression on her face didn't reveal a slight hint of suspicion. He leaned over and whispered, 'What do you wear when you do your acrobatic acts?'

'You'll have to come and see, you naughty boy.'

'I can't wait.'

Le Vieux Port, Marseille: November 1949

It was an ugly incident, but one that was an education too. Catesby had decided to try Henry Bone's idea of a telephone rendezvous to send his encoded reports, rather than relying on Helen. The problem was that he didn't have a telephone – and France was a country that had a shortage of phones in general. If you didn't have your own, the best way to make calls was to find a café that did and would let you use it for a small charge. Catesby had found a rather seedy café near Le Vieux Port and struck up a friendly rapport with the proprietor based around horse racing – both agreed that the only races worth betting on were those that were rigged. The owner didn't enquire into Catesby's background but thought that he was a Belgian with an English father rather than an Englishman with a Belgian mother. He sympathised with Catesby as someone down on his uppers who had seen better days and sometimes served him a pastis on the house. The proprietor showed no curiosity about Catesby's long telephone messages, which didn't consist of words, but long lists of phonetic alphabet letters. The problem was that the café was located in a quiet cul-de-sac.

The woman had dyed her hair blond and was no longer carrying a German newspaper under her arm. Her eyes were deadly and her shoulders broad and powerful – the figure of a champion gymnast. She lunged at Catesby as soon as he left the café. Her dual-barrelled gun began to fire a fine spray of deadly cyanide at Catesby's mouth and nose, but not before Catesby raised the folder containing his encrypted message over his face. He felt the damp cyanide on his fingers and there was a slight smell of almonds. It was going to be a rugby tackle followed by a wrestling match. Catesby put his head down and launched himself at the woman's legs, but she didn't go down – at least, not at first. He wrapped his arms around her thighs and finally managed to tilt her over – but she was still fighting. He felt a fist crash into his testicles – and then an elbow smash into his face. Catesby was in pain but tried to get an arm around her neck. She rolled away and he put a knee into her stomach. She flinched, but still had the spray gun in her hand and was trying to aim it at Catesby's face. He twisted so her back was turned towards him and tried to put his shoulder into the arm that was holding the spray gun. It was then that a real rugby player joined the scrum. A very solid man of about thirty who thought he was witnessing a woman fighting off a rapist.

Catesby shouted, 'She's trying to kill me.'

But the man didn't seem to believe him. He got an arm around Catesby's neck and started dragging him away.

At this point, the café owner came out brandishing a chair and shouting, 'Stop it!'

'Help me!' screamed Catesby. 'Get that spray gun off her.'

The proprietor didn't pick up what Catesby was talking about and brought the chair down on the rugby player's head – which did more damage to the chair than to the player. Others joined in and the cul-de-sac was soon full of men and women who either wanted to get stuck into the fight or see what was going on. Catesby could see that his attacker had concealed the cyanide weapon and was trying to escape.

There was a sudden hush. Catesby looked towards the entrance of the cul-de-sac and saw two men in smart suits wearing dark glasses. One of them said, 'Police.' The other was brandishing a gun. Catesby recognised it as an American Browning 9mm automatic. He suppressed a smile. They were not police.

The man who had spoken said, 'All of you, faces against the wall and hands above your heads.' He walked up behind the woman. 'You need to come with us, *madame*, to lodge a complaint.' For a second, she looked confused and indecisive – as if she were considering kneeing him in the groin and making a run for it. Another man arrived, not in a suit, but clearly a street thug under contract. The woman complied.

The man with the gun grabbed Catesby's elbow with a firm grip. 'And you come with me.' They followed the other man and the woman out of the cul-de-sac and the street thug brought up the rear. There was a black Citroën Traction Avant parked on the quay of Le Vieux Port. The woman was hustled into the back seat. Catesby's minder let go of his elbow and said, 'You can clear off.' He then got into the back seat of the car with his pal and the woman. They clearly weren't going to let her get away. Catesby watched them drive off but didn't wave.

Rue des Frères Pecchini, Marseille: November 1949

They knew where he lived and came once a month to collect the cash. No cheques, just pure *espèces*. Catesby couldn't complain. He now knew that the 'protection' they offered was real – but maybe there was more to the deal than met the naked eye. He wasn't surprised when a visitor turned up. It wasn't the usual one who collected the cash, but someone who looked a lot more important. He was older and wore a gold diamond-studded tie pin. He was carrying a small leather pouch, which he offered to Catesby. 'A present for you, monsieur.'

Catesby took the pouch and said, 'Can I offer you something, monsieur?'

The man mentioned a sum that was about the equivalent of a month's salary for someone like Catesby. It wasn't a huge amount, but not something that Catesby – or London – would want to hand over on a regular basis.

'I'll have it for you in a week.' Catesby did, in fact, have quite a lot of cash hidden in the flat, but he didn't want to advertise the fact.

'Not more than a week, monsieur.'

'How is the lady who was involved?' Catesby knew it wasn't the sort of question you ask a gangster with a diamond-studded tie pin, but he didn't like the thought of her dead body in a watery grave.

'She is well and has returned to her home country.' The man turned on his heel and strode towards a waiting car.

Catesby closed the door and emptied the pouch onto the flat's only table. The contents were surprising. He wondered what the mafia were trying to convey by handing over such items. One was the spray gun, fortunately emptied of cyanide. The back of Catesby's hand had blistered as the result of his contact with the poison. The next two items were pure gold dust. One was an identity card confirming the woman as a member of the newly formed Ministerium für Staatssicherheit, the East German security service. The other was a love letter from Spiridon, her Soviet controller and Catesby's former rival in Berlin. The love letter was brief and banal – an attempt to keep a girlfriend sweet. Catesby was astounded that she had brought such items to Marseille, a flagrant breach of security. On the other hand, if she had ended up on the run, the ID card, at least, would have guaranteed her a safe refuge in any Soviet embassy. Other pieces of the puzzle began to link together. Spiridon's ordering Catesby's assassination wasn't ideological or an espionage ploy, it was purely personal. The two men's animosity was mutual, but in Spiridon's case the hatred had become toxic. Catesby had grown too fond of ridiculing his Sov counterpart at drinking sessions with other members of the intelligence community in Berlin. The breaking point was mocking Spiridon's manhood – and Catesby had the proof to support it, a report from a honeytrap agent who had seduced Spiridon at Catesby's behest. The honeytrap had been unable to inveigle any useful intel out of Spiridon, but her report of his lovemaking had not been flattering. It was very unprofessional of Catesby to leak the details – and it had nearly cost him his life. 'But that,' Catesby said aloud, 'is all water under the bridge.' He picked up the woman's East German ID card and stared at it. He worked out what was happening. Someone was paying the mafia to take out communists. Who was it? Catesby smiled. When you do a deal with the devil, bring American dollars.

Rue de Montevideo, Marseille: November 1949

Catesby needed time to recover and reflect, and it wasn't until the weekend that he paid a visit to his cousin Jack. Visitors to the flat announced their arrival by hammering a cast-iron knocker on a huge wooden door in an ancient stone wall. Catesby thought that the setting looked a bit grand for a humble worker's residence. He finally heard the sound of bolts being drawn, and the wooden door creaked open.

'Hello Jack,' said Catesby. 'Thank you for inviting me to the château. I assume, as it's Saturday, they've given the servants the day off.'

'Marcel and his family need a secure place. As you know from the funeral, there have been attacks on senior members.'

They were in a tidy enclosed garden. It was planted mostly with lavender and herbs. There were also three racing bikes carefully covered by tarpaulins.

'Marcel's passion is cycling,' said Jack, 'and I sometimes train with him.'

'I hope it's a safer sport than leading a workers' revolution.'

'Please, Will, will you cut the cynicism – especially when you're talking to Marcel.'

'Sorry.'

It was a large flat and the walls were covered with posters – two of which had been designed by Serge. Catesby was surprised by Marcel's voice and manners. He sounded more like a university professor than someone working on the docks. Catesby nodded at the posters. 'Do you know Serge?'

'My father was with him in Buchenwald but didn't survive. Jack, by the way, tells me that you're in Marseille to research a book on the Resistance.'

'Yes, but I'm struggling. What was your father's role?'

'He was a doctor who used our home and his surgery as safe houses to shelter Jews, escaped prisoners and downed airmen. It got very crowded at times.'

'And what,' said Catesby, 'was your role?'

'Nothing much. After my father was arrested, I helped organise escape routes into Spain.'

Catesby warmed to Marcel's modesty. 'And now you work on the docks?'

'Well, yes, but I don't operate a crane or carry sacks of grain on my back, I carry a clipboard. I'm an administrator. My job is, in fact, a useful one, because I can warn the comrades about which ships will be carrying arms to Vietnam and where and when they will be docking. My bosses don't like it, but' – Marcel smiled – 'if they dismissed me there would even be more strike action.'

At that moment, a woman entered the room carrying a baby. She looked a bit older than Marcel.

'This is my wife, Teresa. She helped smuggle people into Spain.' Marcel gave her and the baby a warm hug. 'During the Civil War, Teresa was a member of the Mujeres Libres, the women's anarchist militia – but we now form a united front.'

Catesby looked at Jack and spoke in English: 'Would you form a united front with the Labour Party?'

Jack's lips moved as if he was practising something. He then spoke in his Lowestoft-accented French, 'I'm in favour of forming a united front with anyone who opposes the imperialist war in Indochina.'

However tortured the French, Jack's pronouncement was greeted with applause by Marcel and Teresa. 'I think,' said Marcel, 'that calls for some pastis.'

For the first time since arriving in Marseille, Catesby felt comfortable and sort of happy. He liked being with Marcel, his family and Jack – and wished there was something he could do to protect them. Catesby wasn't going to report meeting them to Henry Bone, but he was going to carry out his mission to find out what the fuck the Americans were up to in Marseille. Catesby remembered Bone's instruction when they met in Paris: *cultivate, don't alienate*. It was time to have a drink at Julot's.

153

Julot's Restaurant, Marseille: November 1949

The restaurant was located near the Opéra quarter, where the rioters had gone on their rampage. Catesby felt he had crossed enemy lines – and by the time he was on his second pastis he could almost hear the jungle telegraph sending out messages. Catesby felt particularly privileged when Julot himself emerged from the kitchen, sat down with him and ordered another round of pastis on the house. 'I have heard,' said Julot, 'that you are an Englishman who is writing a book – but you speak French like a Frenchman.'

Catesby smiled. 'But not a Frenchman from Marseille.'

Julot spread his hands. 'We are a city of many voices: Corsican, Provençal, Italian, Catalan, Spanish, Arabic. A grand mixture – like a good bouillabaisse.'

'And I understand that yours is the best in Marseille.'

Julot looked a little hurt. 'No, no, no – not the best in Marseille, but the best in the world!' He laughed and gave Catesby a friendly slap on the shoulder. 'But sadly, we are not offering bouillabaisse this evening. It is a speciality that we serve, at most, once a week. It depends on the catch.'

'How do I find out when bouillabaisse is on the menu?'

'You must come here and ask – and book a table as soon as possible.'

'I must remember that. But as there is no bouillabaisse, what are you serving this evening?'

'We can do tuna carpaccio or oysters followed by *magret de canard*. Shall we lay a table for you?'

'Yes, and I will start with the tuna.'

'Follow me, monsieur.'

Catesby's table was in a corner of the restaurant near a potted palm. He was apart from the other clients but had a good view of what was going on. One man with slicked-back hair was counting out two equal piles of banknotes. His gold pinkie ring flashed as he laid out each note. The man sitting next to him watched carefully with an expressionless face. When Catesby carried out such transactions, he always met the agent in a backroom where there were no prying eyes.

Julot's, thought Catesby, was the perfect place to offer a fly. The spy-craft expression was a 'dangled double', but Catesby preferred to think of himself in fly-fishing terms. He was a Gold-Ribbed Hare's Ear fished just below the surface on a slow retrieve. As soon as he saw Julot heading back towards his table, he wondered if a trout had begun to stir. 'It is,' said Julot wringing his hands, 'a terrible imposition, but another diner would like to join you.' He paused. 'The gentleman is an American and says that he met you during the war.'

It was time to set the hook. 'Tell the gentleman that I would be hon-oured – and I'll have another pastis.'

Julot nodded and withdrew. A moment later, two immaculately uni-formed waiters appeared. The staff at Julot's were the best dressed that Catesby had ever seen. The chefs wore double-breasted jackets with silver buttons, black piping and French cuffs. The waiters wore bow ties, white shirts and waistcoats with velvet backing – and white-cotton serving gloves. Bare flesh would never touch your cutlery or glasses. One of the waiters laid a place for Catesby's dining companion; the other poured a pastis for Catesby with his left arm tucked respectfully behind his back. It was like watching a ballet. The two bowed in unison and backed away to the shadows of the nearby potted palm.

Catesby sipped his pastis and began to look forward to an evening funded by His Majesty's Secret Intelligence Service. He was certain that the American who wanted to join him was Lester Roach, but when he saw the head waiter leading a man in a white tropical suit towards his table, he wasn't sure. He looked like a film actor dressed by a costume department that didn't know the difference between flashy and refined. When, however, Catesby clocked the broad toothy smile he knew it was Lester.

'Hey,' said Lester, extending his hand, 'great to see you again.'

As Catesby got up to shake hands, the American crushed him in a bear hug. Lester reeked of expensive 'aftershave'.

'You're looking good. You haven't changed a bit, Captain Catesby.'

'Please call me William. The only people who call me Captain Catesby are the workers on my country estate.'

'Wow, so you've gone up in the world. Maybe I should call you Sir William.' Lester's eyes gleamed. 'This country estate of yours, I bet your primary crop is irony – with maybe a few acres of crude sarcasm that you can export to America.'

'Sincere apologies, Lester. I deserved the telling-off.' Catesby sniffed. 'And I love your perfume; I must get some for my wife.'

'God, you haven't changed at all. Just like old times. When did we last meet?'

'I think it was September '44. We were both waiting to be redeployed after the liberation of Limoges.'

'You were sent back to England – and I was sent to Vietnam to finish off the fucking Japs.' Lester laughed. 'Remember how you used to tease me about not turning up in France until the war was almost over. Well, after Limoges, the war may have been over for you, but it wasn't for me.'

Lester pointed at Catesby's glass of pastis. 'I think I'll have one of those.'

On cue, a waiter emerged from the shadows with a bottle.

'Are you sure you wouldn't rather have a bourbon?' said Catesby.

'No, when in Rome, you always drink their stuff.'

A waiter arrived with the port's traditional *amuse-bouche*, a tapenade with strips of golden toast. 'I bet,' said Lester with a grin, 'that you're bursting to suggest that we have white wine with the appetiser and the main course, but you're holding back because you don't want to sound patronising to an uncouth American.'

'I wouldn't have dreamed of it – but I might have considered a Provençe rosé as well.'

'I'll order.' Lester snapped his fingers and shouted, '*Garçon!*'

The waiter, having guessed what was being discussed, came over with the wine list. Lester made a quick perusal and chose a Bandol white. The waiter beamed with approval. 'An excellent choice, monsieur.'

'Bandol,' said Lester, 'is a fishing village to the east of here – the other side of Cassis.'

The waiter arrived with the uncorked Bandol white in a silver ice bucket. He offered the cork to Lester who smelled the cork and nodded. The waiter then poured a sample into Lester's glass who swirled, studied and sniffed before tasting. He closed his eyes and nodded again. The waiter returned the bottle to the bucket and departed. Meanwhile, another waiter arrived with the smoked tuna carpaccio salad.

Lester poured Catesby a glass of the Bandol. 'You'll find it does have a slight eucalyptus nose, but one that is not overwhelming, and it adds a distinct character to the usual Provençal herbiness – of which rosemary is the strongest scent. It should go well with the smokiness of the tuna.'

Catesby looked on with a wry smile and wondered if Lester had rehearsed the wine comments.

Lester tucked in, and after a few bites said, 'So, William, what have you been doing since the war?'

'I am sure you already know.'

Lester laughed. 'We would never spy on our British colleagues.'

'Oh, that's a relief – so you won't know that I was sacked for being a suspected Soviet agent.'

For a second, Lester looked disconcerted, but he quickly recovered. 'That's a double bluff.'

'Or a triple bluff.'

'I know you're not a Sov agent because your socialist beliefs are too obvious. For example, your standing as a Labour Party candidate in the '45 election. The Russians wouldn't have someone like you. When they recruit Brits, they go for upper-class snobs who vote Tory and go to garden parties at Buckingham Palace.' Lester laughed and put his hand over his mouth. 'Oops, I've said too much.'

Catesby knew that Lester's comment was more than a tease; he was taunting him about the VENONA decrypts. Catesby didn't rise to the bait and kept a straight face.

Lester laughed. 'Maybe the real reason the Secret Intelligence Service sacked you was because you weren't a Soviet agent who went fox hunting with the King. You were the odd one out.'

Catesby lifted his glass and took a long swig. 'Nice wine.'

Lester wore a smug smile. 'Didn't they even let you have a tiny peek at the transcripts?'

'What transcripts?'

Lester stared hard at Catesby and spoke in a low voice. 'You're pretending not to know because the fact that you guys know is top fucking secret.' Lester shook his head. 'But part of me half believes you. In any case, I'd better shut my big mouth. If counterintelligence heard what I was saying, they'd cut my balls off. What wine should we have with the duck?'

'As your choice of the Bandol for the entrée was so perfect, you should pick the next one too.'

'No, William, it's your turn.'

Catesby smiled. 'I will choose with humility and trepidation. If we were having beef or venison, I would stick to the Bandol region and go for a Mourvèdre, but that would have too much power and tannin for duck breast. May I suggest a Cinsault from Languedoc-Roussillon?'

The wine waiter soon arrived with the list. Catesby chose a Cinsault from a château in Faugères. He was clueless about its reputation, but it was reassuringly expensive. A few minutes later, the waiter returned with the bottle. Catesby quickly went through the tasting routine but asked for the wine to be decanted. 'I think,' he said, 'this one needs to breathe.' The image of the dying demonstrator, who had been shot through the chest and couldn't breathe, suddenly flashed pulsating onto his brain. Catesby had to blink twice before it disappeared, and Lester wasn't much help.

'Did you see those awful fucking riots?' said the American.

In case one of Lester's watchers had spotted him, Catesby gave a cagey answer. 'Curiosity got the better of me, so I went to see what was going on.'

'The commie strikers were bad enough, but the kids ransacking and robbing the bars were unspeakable filth.'

Catesby could see that Lester was testing him. Too quick a conversion to the anti-communist cause would make his motives suspect – and too strong a defence of the rioters would put him beyond the pale. He weighed his words. 'There has always been a strong feeling of resistance in Marseille – that's why the French national anthem is called "La Marseillaise".'

'Yeah, but back in those old days, the guys singing it were fighting for an independent France, not a France that was becoming part of the Soviet Bloc.'

Catesby answered with an enigmatic smile – and the arrival of the duck spared him having to add words.

'And I'll tell you another thing,' said Lester. 'You wouldn't find food and wine like this in a commie France. The château owners would be executed, and the vineyards ploughed up and turned into collective farms. Let's tuck in.'

They had nearly finished eating when a man in a dark suit wearing dark glasses and the obligatory star-sapphire signet ring approached their table. He bent over and whispered something in Lester's ear. Lester nodded vigorously and said, 'Okay, okay.' The man then padded off with a slight limp.

Catesby finished off the wine and pretended to have noticed nothing unusual.

'That was René la Patte.'

'*La patte* in what sense: foot, hand or leg?'

'I think in his case, it must be leg – he only has one. In any case, René reminded me that I've got a meeting later. Only boring business stuff, but it means I won't be able to hang around after the brandy and coffee.'

Catesby suspected la Patte's message was less reminder than urgent summons.

'I suppose, William, that I owe you an apology for not telling you what I'm doing in Marseille.'

'Well, it's none of my business.' Catesby tried to fake an engaging smile. 'But I would love to know.'

Lester laughed aloud. 'And so would I! Tell me if you find out.' He then gave the table a hard slap, which Catesby remembered as one of Lester's trademark gestures from the war. 'I'm serious, William, I might need your help.' Lester looked at his watch. 'Shit, I don't think I have time for brandy and coffee, after all.' The American gave Catesby a warm handshake and was gone. His white suit gave him a ghostly air as he left the restaurant – and Catesby suddenly realised that His Majesty's Secret Intelligence Service had been left to pay the bill. 'What the fuck,' said Catesby as he summoned the waiter over to order a double Fine Champagne cognac – but no coffee.

Catesby closed his eyes as he savoured what was probably the world's most expensive cognac. He did feel a slight shiver of guilt but was also curious as to how much it was all costing HM's Treasury. He then motioned to the head waiter to ask for *l'addition*, but the man smiled and replied, 'There is nothing for you to pay, *monsieur*. Your friend asked me to put it all on his account – including a generous service charge. Would you like another cognac?'

Catesby was tempted, but said, 'No, thank you.' He relished the rest of the Fine Champagne as the waiter disappeared. It tasted even better with Washington paying for it.

Avenue de la Canebière, Marseille: November 1949

The boss's office was located on the fourth floor of a grand Second Empire building on the Canebière, a street that Lester referred to as 'Marseille's Fifth Avenue'. The building dated from the same time as the cathedral of Notre-Dame de la Garde – and, in a way, was also a place of worship that involved paying homage, confessing sins and asking for favours.

'As I told you before,' said the boss, drawing on his Havana cigar, 'we can't do the job without more money and equipment.'

Lester nodded. He knew that 'equipment' was a euphemism for weapons, that wasn't a problem, but the money aspect was. You had to drive hard bargains with the mob; otherwise, you just kept pouring cash into a bottomless pit. Lester remembered the advice of a retired cop who had specialised in mafia matters. *You can't buy the mob's loyalty, you can only rent it.*

The boss looked at the ceiling and exhaled fragrant cigar smoke. 'Have you ever been to Cuba?'

'Briefly.'

'It is a wonderful place, but the current president needs more back-bone. I'm a friend of Fulgencio Batista. I would love to see him back in power.'

Lester tried not to smile. He knew that his CIA colleagues were already plotting a coup in Cuba to put Batista back in power, largely with the support of mafia mobsters in the US.

'But,' said the boss, 'you haven't come here to discuss Cuba; you want to talk about Port-de-Bouc.'

'We want to make sure that ship gets loaded – and there aren't any problems on the docks.' Lester was referring to the French government's secret plan to divert a ship, originally scheduled to pick up armoured vehicles from Marseille, to Port-de-Bouc, a harbour forty miles to the west. The tanks, personnel carriers and self-propelled artillery were all part of an American military aid programme. Lester was under pressure from Washington to make sure that the heavy weapons were embarked to Indochina.

'And how,' said the boss, 'are you going to help us?'

Lester could see that the mob chief was driving for a hard, expensive bargain, and he wasn't going to give in – at least not too soon. 'We need to have another meeting after I've consulted some colleagues.'

'Is one of those colleagues Monsieur Benedictine?'

Lester was a bit nonplussed to hear the name mentioned. Sam Benedictine was a rival with fingers in many pies. 'I think,' said Lester, 'I will have a word with him too.'

'Good,' said the boss. 'He's a friend of Pierre's.'

Lester wasn't quite sure to which Pierre the boss was referring. He simply said, 'Monsieur Benedictine has lots of friends.'

After he left the office and found himself back out on the Canebière, the boss's words about Sam Benedictine began to reverberate and disturb Lester. Benedictine was a smooth operator who was highly regarded by many in Washington – and Lester suspected that one of his jobs in France was looking over his shoulder. He and Sam had different ideas on how to gain control of European trade unions.

7th arrondissement, Marseille: 7 December 1949

Lester found the lack of telephones in France a real pain. In a population of 750,000, Marseille had only 17,000 subscribers. Lester's preferred way of doing business was lounging around in his luxury apartment in a silk dressing gown, enjoying the view over the sea with a glass of bourbon in one hand and a telephone in the other. It took a long time for the PTT, Postes Télégraphes et Téléphones, to get around to installing a phone in Lester's apartment – and then longer still to get a specialist from the US embassy to put in anti-bugging devices. But now Lester had a secure phone on which he was dialling Sam Benedictine's equally secure phone in Paris. Lester listened to the distinct French dial tone for five minutes before he hung up. Sam was probably out causing trouble for communist-led trade unions. That was his job in Europe.

Lester first met Sam Benedictine while training with the Office of Strategic Services. Although Sam was a dozen years older, they were both still second lieutenants. Despite his unusual name – which Lester made fun of as soon as they met, 'Are you a liqueur or a monk?' – Benedictine was a tough guy from the Bronx, but he didn't have a Bronx accent in English or French. Lester wondered if Sam had lost it when he studied at Harvard – or if he had ever had a Bronx accent. Once, after a few beers in the officers' club, Lester had teased Benedictine about his well-spoken transatlantic voice: 'Did Eleanor Roosevelt give you elocution lessons?'

'No, she gave me boxing lessons.'

'Is that how her husband ended up in a wheelchair?'

One of the other officers remarked that Lester's joke about the polio-stricken president was a bit tasteless. Sam finished his drink and looked at Lester. 'Shall we go a few rounds in the ring?'

The impromptu match lasted less than four minutes. Sam totally slaughtered Lester. It wasn't just the power of his punches, but his quickness on his feet. Sam had it all: he could bob and weave and was impossible to hit, but when he closed in with jabs, crosses and hooks he was lethal. Lester later found out, too late for his bruised face, that Benedictine had been a professional boxer before he became a trade union organiser.

After their OSS training, Lester and Sam parted ways. Lester, dropped into France as the Occupation was drawing to a close, was soon sent back to the States and redeployed to Southeast Asia. Sam had been sent to Italy but remained in Europe after the German withdrawal. Now in civilian clothes, Benedictine was working undercover as an anti-communist trade union organiser – and France was his main turf.

Lester had a sip of bourbon before he began to dial the number again. Benedictine was often out during the day organising Force Ouvrière, the French union he was setting up to oppose the communist-led ones. Lester wondered what made Sam work so hard. Fanatics slogged their guts out for ideological reasons; greedy bastards did it for money. So why did Benedictine do it? Lester poured himself another bourbon and savoured the sun-dappled sea view to the Île d'If. Sure, Benedictine wanted a secure life for his wife and two kids – and he got that through his salary as a senior official in the AFL, the American Federation of Labour. It was something else that made him tick. Benedictine wanted to be a player, a big player: he wanted to shape the post-war world, especially Europe, in a way that fitted with his ideals. Sam Benedictine was a committed trade unionist to the very marrow of his bones. As a young man, he had flirted with communism – and even wrote articles for the Party's newspaper. Lester wasn't sure why Sam had broken with the Party – but he did know that ex-communists often became the fiercest fighters against communism. The cunning and passion of the heretic often outfoxed the plodding true believers. And no one could ever say that Sam Benedictine was anything less than a totally committed trade unionist. He was okay with capitalists making a profit, but they had to pay fair wages and provide good conditions for the workers. Sam had a great advantage over undercover CIA officers who were trying to turn European unions against Moscow.

Benedictine spoke the language of the workers and their union officials, and they knew, despite any disagreements, that he was one of them. There were those in Washington who regarded Sam Benedictine as the most lethal weapon in the anti-communist arsenal. Lester realised that he and Sam were in competition – and there would only be one winner. He put down his bourbon. It was time to try Sam's number again.

After two rings, a voice answered, '*Capitole: neuf, quatre, six, huit.*'

'May I speak to Monsieur Benedictine?'

'It's me, Lester.'

'Gosh, Sam, I thought there was a real Frenchman in your office.'

'Gosh, Lester, I was thinking there might be a real asshole in yours.'

'Once again, Sam, your refined Ivy League charm has won me over.'

'What can I do for you?'

'I recently had a meeting with the local scoutmaster. We discussed the various merit badges he wants to put his scouts up for: Citizenship in the Community, Crime Prevention and Rifle Shooting – but the most important appears to be Coin Collecting.'

'I know – and I deal with them separately and in my own fashion.'

The answer confirmed what Lester feared. The mafia was trying to touch both of them for cash and playing them off against each other. Lester listened to the clink of ice cubes as he swirled his bourbon. It was a better sound than Benedictine's self-assured voice. He was a rival who needed taking down a peg or two.

'It's nice talking to you, Lester, but I've got a very busy schedule. Why exactly have you phoned me?'

Lester wanted to shout *fuck you asshole*, but stayed calm. 'I understand there's going to be some trouble down on the docks tomorrow.'

'There's always trouble on the Marseille docks.'

'I'm not talking about Marseille, Sam, and you know it. I'm talking about Port-de-Bouc.'

Benedictine laughed loudly. 'There are no flies on you, Lester. You've discovered some highly classified top-secret information.'

'Top secret, my ass. Every sailor, bartender, whore, cop and stevedore

165

in Marseille – and especially every commie – knows about that ship diversion. So tell me, Sam, what are you going to do about it?'

'Tomorrow is a big day for my boys.'

'Which boys?' said Lester.

'FO, Force Ouvrière.'

'Workers Force.'

'I prefer the French original – and so do the members. A lot of them are former members of the CGT who left because they didn't like being bossed around by the communists in charge. FO is a rapidly growing union.'

'Are they going to take charge of the docks in Port-de-Bouc?'

There was a pause on Benedictine's end of the line – and, when he finally spoke, Lester detected a note of uncertainty. 'We'll see. Tomorrow is an important test.'

'Now you've got me a bit worried about your Force Ouvrière boys.'

'Why?'

'They've been infiltrated by the commies.'

'You're talking through your ass,' said Benedictine.

'Okay, Sam, I'm now taking the phone away from my sphincter. So tell me, what are your Force Ouvrière boys going to do when the commie-led CGT gangs from Marseille turn up?'

'I hope they beat the shit out of them and load the ship,' said Sam.

'So all the stevedores on duty at Port-de-Bouc are Force Ouvrière strike-breakers?'

'Not all of them. Members of other unions will be among the work-force. It's a test.'

Once again Lester noted uncertainty in Benedictine's voice. Did he fear that his FO strike-breakers wouldn't be able to handle the communist thugs from Marseille?

'Anything else?' said Sam.

'I'll keep an eye out for your boys and let you know how they get on.'

'Thanks.'

As Lester put the phone down, he knew which side he wanted to win.

Rue des Frères Pecchini, Marseille: 7 December 1949

As often happened, Catesby hadn't a fucking clue as to what role he should be playing the next day. He was supposed to be reporting back to London on all aspects of the French dock strikes, but how was he going to do that? As a neutral observer, or as a friend – or false friend – of the striking dockworkers and anti-war demonstrators. As an active participant, agent-provocateur – or spy? Personally, he regarded the Indochina war as a vainglorious attempt to regain control of a lost colony. Not a view that he could shout loudly in the Director's office – but one quietly shared by many in SIS. But he did know there was going to be a hell of a punch-up on the Port-de-Bouc docks the next morning – and he had to be there.

Port-de-Bouc was sixty-five kilometres from Marseille – too far to walk, but a brisk two-hour cycle ride. He knew that the dock battle was not one that Serge and Huong would miss for anything. When Catesby visited Serge's studio in Le Panier, the artist was already making preparations: sketch pads, camera, first aid kit and a hip flask of brandy.

'How are you getting there?' said Catesby.

'We're getting a lift in a works van. Huong is going disguised as a pregnant woman with a pair of petrol bombs hidden under her maternity smock. They're the twins she's always wanted. I wish I could offer you a lift with us, but I'm not sure there'll be room.'

'I'm sure I can find a way there.'

'It won't be difficult. Most of Marseille's buses are going to be hijacked – with, of course, the enthusiastic cooperation of the drivers. But the heavy squads are setting off very early in trucks and vans.' Serge smiled and raised an eyebrow. 'By the way, I've now met your cousin Jack. He's already quite popular on the docks – and he and his comrades enjoy

167

swapping swearwords in French and English. Jack's obviously a fighter and he wants to be in the thick of it. He describes you as the big brother he never had.'

Catesby was moved. Jack would never say that to his face.

'And you've met Marcel, the union official he's lodging with,' said Serge.

'Yes – and his wife and child.'

'Family and fighting against oppression is a difficult balancing act, but Marcel's father managed it. We were at Buchenwald together.'

'And he didn't survive.'

'But his family did and so did his memory. Some of us must pay a price.' Serge smiled. 'And speaking of price, you paid too much for that gun you bought from me. Have you still got it?'

'I'll be taking it with me tomorrow.' Catesby wasn't sure why he was taking the gun. He didn't like leaving it in the flat in case a searcher or burglar found it. Port-de-Bouc might be a good place to throw it in the sea.

'By the way,' said Serge, 'Marcel is an extraordinary young man: a great leader in the workplace, an intellectual – and a very fine cyclist. If he wasn't so committed to the struggle, he could have become a Tour de France professional.'

Port-de-Bouc: 8 December 1949

Serge was right. It wasn't difficult to find transport. Every municipal bus, hijacked or not, seemed to be heading there. In fact, there was even a traffic jam en route to Port-de-Bouc. Not everyone on Catesby's bus was a dockworker heading for a punch-up; many were ordinary citizens who wanted to protest against the war in Indochina. In the crush of the bus, Catesby was squashed against a grey-haired woman who looked about sixty. The fact that she was wearing a red earring in the shape of a hammer on one ear and a sickle on the other suggested she was a Party member. From overhearing a conversation that Catesby was having with another passenger, she realised he was an Englishman. The woman nudged Catesby just above the pocket where he was carrying the gun and put on a creditable Mae West voice, 'Is that a pistol in your pocket or are you just glad to see me?'

Catesby answered, 'Both.'

The woman continued speaking in an American accent, 'But I won't ask you to come up and see me somctime because you look too young and innocent.'

'You speak very good English.'

'I learned it in Hollywood.'

'Are you an actress?'

'No, I'm a photographer.'

More people got on the bus at a stop near Saint-Antoine and Catesby was pushed further back. He regretted not being able to continue the conversation. The woman was an example of why people in power hate the art world. You can't control artists. Just when you think you've got them on your side, they turn. When they got to Port-de-Bouc, Catesby looked for the woman, but her diminutive grey head had been lost in the crowd.

Instead of immediately heading to the docks, Catesby turned the opposite way and followed the road to a railway siding that was heavily guarded by both police and soldiers. There was a long line of flatbed wagons with vehicles covered in tarpaulins – the largest of which had the silhouette of tanks. The smaller profiles suggested trucks, jeeps, halftracks and artillery pieces. On many wagons, the canvas flapping in the wind revealed the five-pointed white star markings that designated US military vehicles. It was obvious to Catesby that the trucks and weapons being sent to Indochina were almost entirely of American origin. A grizzled-looking soldier waved at Catesby with a threatening look and shouted, '*Hétoi, va-t'en!*' – Hey you, fuck off! Catesby shrugged and decided it was time to find Jack.

He finally spotted his cousin among a group of a dozen CGT strikers who were engaged in a heated argument with a much larger group of Force Ouvrière scabs. One of the FO was shouting, 'We just want to feed our families.' Another shouted, 'That lot don't need the money, they get paid by Moscow.' There still wasn't any physical confrontation, not even a little pushing – but the mood was changing. Catesby decided it was time to stand beside Jack. Blood was thicker than orders from London. He started running towards his cousin, but he wasn't quick enough to help. The punches had started to rain down and the FO were winning. Catesby looked on in horror at what happened next. They must have picked out Jack because he was so obviously *un rosbif*. Two of the scabs grabbed his arms and two more managed to pick up his kicking feet. The choreography was perfect: *un, deux, trois, quatre* – and with the final heave-ho Jack's body was over the guard rail and into the dark cold November waters of the harbour. One of the scabs shouted, 'Now you can fucking swim back to England.'

There are worse places to be tossed into the water than a harbour surrounded by dockworkers. They all knew the drill. Life rings and ropes rained down. Workers from both sides joined in, and Jack was soon being hauled up a ladder built into the harbour wall. The mood momentarily lightened and there was a lot of laughter. Catesby walked Jack to a van that had been set aside as a first-aid station. His cousin was wet and humiliated, but unhurt. Jack was left in the hands of a capable nurse who joked that, despite his quick rescue, there were much better places to go swimming. He was the day's first casualty, but far worse were to come.

When Catesby rejoined the demo, the mood was turning violent. There were now a lot of cops swinging truncheons and trying to separate the two groups. Someone on a megaphone was calling out for the Force Ouvrière dockers to cross the lines and join the *anti-colonialiste* struggle. The soft power persuasion of the megaphone caller was joined by the hard power of well-muscled CGT members wielding chains, metal spikes and bludgeons. The FO scabs who had thrown Jack in the water were now targeted and retreating. Meanwhile, police reinforcements in riot gear were arriving. The cops were no longer trying to keep the two sides separated but were wading in to aid Force Ouvrière. Catesby noticed that several of the strikers were carrying pickaxes. At first, he thought they were going to be used as lethal weapons, but then he saw their real purpose. The pickaxe bearers had begun to dig up the tarmac, and paving stones, bricks and all manner of hardcore were being grabbed by the crowd as ammunition. Many were cradling armfuls of broken brick and concrete ready to be hurled. Someone blew a whistle, and the crowd began to stone the police. Meanwhile, the pickaxe men continued to feed the strikers with more broken tarmac and paving. The arc of missiles framed against the grey December clouds reminded Catesby of the scene in Olivier's *Henry V* where the longbow men at Agincourt fill the sky with arrows. He could also hear the hail of stones and bricks thudding on the helmets and riot shields of the cops. It was an epic sight. Five minutes later a whole host of whistles were blown in a sustained blast. The stoning suddenly stopped. The signal to attack had been sounded. Catesby struggled not to be swept up in the surge of CGT strikers who were rushing forward to confront the police. There was shouting and then cheering as the battered and outnumbered police began to retreat to regroup. There was then a loud pop followed by flames and smoke as a petrol bomb exploded. Catesby, to his shame, was beginning to enjoy the chaos and violence. It reminded him of a guilty secret from his SOE days: if you were personally out of danger, watching a battle was riveting. No wonder the Romans built coliseums and sold tickets to watch the gladiators. Catesby's enjoyment, however, waned as wounded strikers were passed back through the throng. Most had head wounds, and a few seemed barely conscious. One of those helping a bloodstained casualty was Serge, who had a camera slung around his neck and a backpack with sketch pads. Catesby followed to try to help, but the injured docker was soon picked up by a man and a woman in nurses' uniforms. He noticed that the male nurse spoke French with a strong German accent and walked with a slight limp. Catesby addressed him in German and asked where he had learned to be a *Krankenpfleger*, a nurse.

The German half-smiled and said, 'In the Foreign Legion. I was a medic in Vietnam and had my leg blown off by a mine. I now want to stop this fucking war.' Meanwhile, Serge was standing to the side sketching the one-legged ex-legionnaire *Krankenpfleger* as he staunched the flow of blood and wrapped a dressing around the casualty's head.

The fighting on the docks was continuing. Someone was beating a drum, and the demonstrators were chanting anti-colonialist slogans. The police had given up keeping the two groups apart. It was now obvious that the Force Ouvrière were outnumbered. Catesby could see that some FO were giving up the struggle. He overheard an FO docker talking to a CGT docker. 'Loading this fucking ship isn't worth getting my head bashed in.' The FO man then laughed. 'But we'll still get paid even if we don't load it – and your lot won't get paid regardless.' The CGT comrade answered. 'I'd rather starve than be a fucking scab – and, in the end, the bosses will shit you lot out their fat backsides.' The FO type shrugged and looked slightly ashamed. 'I agree – it's a stupid fucking war. But if the government is stupid enough to pay us to load up – or not load up – a pile of military shit for Indochina, I'll gladly take the money to feed my family.'

The battle for the Port-de-Bouc docks was becoming a standoff, but there was a still lot of angry pushing and shoving. The Force Ouvrière dockers began to realise that they hadn't the numbers to break through the CGT picket lines to load the ship, but the hired goons among them still wanted to continue the battle. Catesby could see that there was a big difference between the ordinary workers and the thugs armed with steel clubs and chains. The goons made a final charge to try to regain lost ground, but many CGT fighters had come wearing helmets, with dustbin lids for shields. They formed a protective barricade while others went for the shins and legs of the FO goons with their steel-capped work boots. The tactic was to get them on the ground, where the kicking and stomping would begin. It wasn't a pretty sight to see a burly thug curled up in the foetal position trying to protect his face and genitals. Serge, of course, was there with his sketch pad.

The CGT strikers and the more determined of the demonstrators, sensing that victory was in the offing, surged forward. Catesby could see that the Force Ouvrière dockers were abandoning any attempt to load the ship. The violence began to die away and before long most on both sides were just standing around and waiting. Two hours later the demonstration started to break up. The dock strikers had won. Catesby joined up with Serge. He had become reunited with Huong who looked very pleased with herself.

'Let's have a look at Huong's handiwork,' said Serge.

They walked to the dock entrance, where two police cars were still smouldering. A couple of bored-looking cops were standing guard over the burnt-out vehicles. Catesby thought it was a bit reckless of Serge and his wife to revisit the scene of her crime. As Serge snapped photos of the scene, one of the policemen posed with his hand gesturing towards the wreckage.

'He must think that you're a journalist,' said Catesby.

'He's right. I am a journalist, recording a victory for posterity.'

7th arrondissement, Marseille: 9 December 1949

Lester often felt smug, it was his normal emotional state, but the sudden arrival of Sam the-union-fixer Benedictine from Paris had made him more smug than usual. The Port-de-Bouc debacle had led Benedictine to request an urgent meeting. It took place in Lester's own apartment – and he taunted Sam with its lovely views of the sea. 'Well,' said Lester cradling a morning bourbon, 'your Force Ouvrière boys completely fucked up. You didn't put enough fire in their bellies.'

Sam stirred his coffee. His face bore an enigmatic smile. He never rose to the bait with words. When he did bite, he sometimes replied with his fists or a kick in the groin or a headbutt to rearrange a nose – or a bureaucratic stab in the back. The last was bloodless, but often the most devastating – and Sam knew that he could easily destroy Lester with a written report or a few words in the right ears. But destroying someone as useful as Lester would be pure incompetence; he was too valuable a player – and already well established as an anti-communist crusader.

Lester sipped his bourbon and shook his head. 'Force Ouvrière don't give a fuck about fighting communism, they only want to line their pockets with easy money. At the end of the day, they're typical trade union workers, lazy as hell. It's a fucking disgrace that they still got a full day's pay for not loading that ship at Port-de-Bouc. The rule should be: you don't finish the job, you don't get paid.'

When Sam finally spoke, it was in a quiet calm voice. 'It was a test of strength, sometimes you have to probe the enemy's lines to see where the weaknesses are.'

'And which weaknesses did your useless boys find?'

'Overconfidence – and a tendency to celebrate too soon. The communist leaders of the CGT think that winning one battle means they've won the war. They have been deluded into thinking that strikes and demos are always going to prevail.' Sam paused. 'And that they can win without taking casualties. When they find this isn't true, my guess is they will crumple. Port-de-Bouc might have been a useful defeat.'

Lester laughed. 'So you wanted your guys to lose?'

'No, I wanted to test the waters.'

'And what would have happened if your Force Ouvrière pussies had won?'

'Then, Lester, I might not have needed you.'

'But now you do?'

Sam finished his coffee and stood up.

'Are you leaving?'

Sam smiled. 'I can't leave. I was never here, and this conversation never took place.'

'How much money have you got to offer?'

'A lot.'

'It will have to be. Those guys don't come cheap.'

'The usual channels,' said Sam. 'And no fingerprints.'

Les Calanques between Marseille and Cassis: December 1949

Marcel's training circuit was from Marseille to Cassis via Aubagne and then back home along the coastal road through the rocky calanques. It was the most stunning and precipitous countryside that Catesby had ever seen. The landscape reminded him of Edward Lear's poem about two old bachelors climbing a lofty pinnacle to the home of 'an ancient Sage' addicted to books and learning. The old bachelors are hungry and intend to chop the Sage into 'endless little bits' that they will mix with onion. The interaction of sunlight, sea reflection and rocky crags had created a landscape that was truly 'purpledicular'.

Marseille to Aubagne was a bit of a warm-up. The first serious climb began after the legionnaire camp and continued for about five miles. Marcel waited for Catesby and Jack at the village of Roquefort-la-Bédoule, which marked the summit of his route. He pointed to a castle. 'That's where Napoleon kept one of his mistresses.'

'Power and sex are squalid companions,' said Jack.

'But a pretty place for a bike ride,' said Catesby.

'And this is where it gets interesting,' added Marcel.

The next section was a steep downhill all the way to Cassis. The previous evening Marcel had talked about the importance of descents in bicycle racing. 'Climbing,' he said, 'is just a matter of sweat and physical effort. Any donkey can do it – but steep descents are where you win races, where you trim off valuable seconds. They're not about muscle, they're about skill and risk-taking. There are no limits.' Descents were also where the deaths of most racing cyclists occurred. The speeds sometimes exceeded seventy miles per hour. The thought chilled Catesby – and he hoped that Edward Lear's two old bachelors weren't waiting to turn Marcel into a steak and kidney pie.

It wasn't long before Marcel was well ahead. Jack was a bit more daring, but Catesby was using his brakes and taking care around the bends – particularly where there were oily patches. He was impressed by the way that Marcel positioned himself to ensure the least wind resistance. His body was parallel to the road surface and his chin was nearly resting on the handlebars. Catesby was terrified on Marcel's behalf as he watched him take the steep sharp corners at speed with, at most, a light feather touch on the brakes. A skid would send him over the guard rails – in the rare places where they existed – and into 'purpledicular' oblivion. Catesby felt relieved when he was finally out of sight.

Cassis was a stunningly beautiful small town. It was dominated by an ancient, fortified château which overlooked the harbour. Behind the château, the sheer cliffs of the calanques scoured the sky. The town quay was lined with double-ended clinker-built boats from which fishermen were unloading their catches. If Catesby's bike had been outfitted with panniers, he would have bought ingredients for a bouillabaisse. The only thing missing from the picture was Marcel: he was nowhere to be seen. Catesby feared the worst and wondered if he'd bought it taking a corner too fast. Then Catesby spotted Jack, who had arrived before him, leaning on his bike and practising his awful French on a fisherman who answered in Provençal dialect. Catesby wheeled his bike over and asked the fisherman if he had seen another cyclist. The man hefted a dripping basket filled with a single conger eel – still alive – onto the quay and nodded. He pointed to a café and said, '*Lou boun ami.*'

'It took you long enough to get here,' said Jack. 'Marcel's having a coffee.'

'I wasn't that far behind.'

They joined Marcel at an outside table. The December weather was like spring in Suffolk. The drinks before them were character studies: Marcel's espresso, Jack's beer and Catesby's red wine.

Catesby regarded Marcel with a look that combined admiration with a suspicion of madness. 'Is the next descent as terrifying?'

'The descents aren't so frightening when you get to know them. I've committed every metre of this route to memory; I've done it dozens of times and I don't take too many risks.' Marcel smiled. 'After all, I have a family and comrades to support.'

Catesby sipped his wine. Fear comes in different ways for different people. Catesby was terrified of going fast downhill on a bike – or anything else – but had no fear of parachuting or sailing at sea in stormy weather. He loved the water and the sky and could not see how either could do any harm.

'Would you like another wine?' said Marcel.

'What's the next bit like?'

'It's a steady climb of eight kilometres to the Col de la Gineste.'

'Good – just as you said earlier, a matter of muscle and sweat.' Catesby summoned the waiter. 'In that case, I will have another wine to oil the sinews.'

'It isn't easy,' said Marcel. 'The maximum slope is ten per cent and the hardest bit is near the beginning.'

'And the other side?'

'All downhill into Marseille, but not as steep or twisty as the descent into Cassis.'

'I'll try to be braver this time.'

They drank up and started off in a small peloton of three. As Marcel had warned, the first bit of the route was the steepest. Finding it a slow hard grind, Catesby and Jack put their bikes in low gear. It was obvious that Marcel was hanging back with them out of politeness. Catesby glanced over and said, 'Don't wait for us – you're not getting any exercise.'

'I don't mind. I like being with friends.'

'But you're making us feel guilty. In any case, if you take off, it will encourage us to up the pace.'

'Okay,' said Marcel, 'but I'll wait for you at the top.'

'You might be there a while.'

'I don't think so. You and Jack are very fit athletes.'

'We need you as a trainer.'

'There's a short flat bit up ahead. When you get there, put your bike in higher gear to pick up some pace for the final climb.'

'Thanks.'

Marcel powered ahead. It was a move, when a rider or group of riders separate from the peloton, that racing cyclists call an 'escape'. Catesby watched as Marcel's calf muscles tensed under the strain. He didn't have any hair on his legs. Like all serious cyclists, Marcel shaved them, because, when you come off, the wounds are cleaner and faster to heal if hairs don't contaminate the scrapes and cuts. The leg-shaving was a grim acknowledgement that accidents were inevitable.

'He could've qualified for the Tour de France,' panted Jack.

'And you could've played for Lowestoft Town. Go on ahead.'

Marcel was right. The first two kilometres of the climb to the Col de la Gineste were difficult – very difficult. Catesby had to put his bike in the lowest gear and stand up on the pedals – but the views compensated for the pain. It was a spectacular landscape of peaks, sheer cliffs and sparkling sea. Despite the arid climate, the sun-baked rocks were far from barren. Evergreen shrubs – sage, juniper, rosemary – forced their way out of stony cracks to scent the air. Catesby felt exhilarated when the road suddenly turned less steep. The route certainly wasn't level, but the lesser gradient enabled him to slip his bike into a higher gear. Catesby smiled as he gained on Jack and overtook him. Jack responded by pushing harder. They continued neck and neck, often trading the lead, for the next three kilometres. Each time Catesby inched ahead he victoriously shouted, 'Ipswich Town!' When Jack powered back into the lead, he shouted, 'Norwich City!' Jack increased his lead as the gradient became steeper and shouted: 'Canaries fly high while your lot spread manure on their lordships' fields.' The football rivalry had turned ideological. A lot of Ipswich fans were indeed farm workers, but Catesby didn't think it likely that the Canaries were going to lead a proletarian revolution either. Jack had already reached the summit. Catesby swore that he must do more training, but the race had exhilarated him.

Marcel was waiting for them at the Col de la Gineste, looking fresh and totally recovered from the climb. 'The pair of you did very well, you would have beaten a lot of club riders. You seemed to be shouting encouragement at each other.'

'Local football rivalries: I support Ipswich Town and Jack is a Norwich City fan. I suppose you support Olympique de Marseille?'

Marcel vigorously shook his head. 'No, I support Red Star.'

'They're a long way from Marseille,' said Catesby.

Marcel shrugged. 'That is true, but I always go to a match if they're playing when I'm in Paris.'

'Several of their players were executed by the Nazis,' said Jack. 'You ought to put that in your book, Will.'

'That is a slight exaggeration,' said Marcel. 'One of their players, Rino Della Negra, a member of the Resistance, was captured and shot by firing squad.'

'I've never understood,' said Catesby, 'why they have an English name.'

'An interesting story,' said Marcel. 'Red Star's founder had an English governess called Miss Jenny. One clear evening Miss Jenny took him out to look at the night sky. She pointed to Mars and called it the Red Star. The name stuck with the future owner, and he chose it for the team he founded.'

'The twists and turns of history,' said Catesby. 'A wealthy man names a football team in fond memory of his governess and the team's name makes it a magnet for socialist fans.'

Catesby looked along the coast towards Marseille. The view was breathtaking, but for some reason he felt a chill of fear run down his spine.

Marcel mounted his bike and pushed off. 'We're nearly finished. Six kilometres and all downhill.'

'Don't wait for us,' shouted Catesby.

'Lunch will be on the table when you arrive.' Marcel waved as he powered into the descent.

The first part was straight and less scary than the downhill run into Cassis. Jack was three lengths in front when they encountered a peloton coming in the opposite direction. Most of the riders gave Catesby and

Jack a fraternal salute. There had been little motor traffic, but Catesby now heard a car closing up behind him – too close. The driver couldn't overtake immediately because of the bikes coming in the opposite direction. Catesby sensed impatience from the vehicle behind, which only seemed a couple of metres from his rear wheel. He didn't like it: usually French drivers had more respect for cyclists. After football, it was their national sport – maybe even before football. When the last of the peloton had passed the driver gunned his engine, but instead of racing past Catesby, the car pulled up level with him. It was a black Citroën Traction Avant. He remembered those black Citroëns well from the war. It was the Gestapo's motor of choice. They had quickly ditched their German cars for requisitioned Traction Avants. It was a sinister car, but a tough and reliable vehicle – and the sight of one still sent a shiver down the spine. As the driver stayed level, the man in the front passenger seat, wearing a suit and dark glasses, gave Catesby a close look which chilled him to the marrow. The man said something to the driver who braked to keep level with Catesby. The passenger then rolled the window down and there was a gun pointing at Catesby's head. He needed to take evasive action, but the bike was wedged into a narrow gap between the car and a wall of rock. The only solution was to brake hard, get behind the Avant and start cycling back the other way. It would take the driver a while to make a U-turn, and Catesby would have time to get off the road and run for cover through the rocky scrubland that ran down to the sea on the other side of the road. The quick braking left the bike lying on its side between Catesby's legs. The car stopped and the gunman got out and took aim at Catesby, who ducked and started running, but the expected gunshots never came. The only sounds were the gunman's laughter and the car speeding away. Catesby flung himself behind a rock and peeped out to see if the gunman had stayed behind, but the road was empty. He then looked down the twisting descent and saw with horror that the car had pulled up alongside Jack. He shouted, 'Run! Get off the road!' Jack didn't seem to hear him, but it didn't matter. After giving him a close look, the mobsters in the Traction Avant raced on with a loud engine roar. Jack wasn't the one they were looking for either. It was obvious who they were after – and Catesby knew there was nothing they could do to help. Marcel was too far ahead to hear a shouted warning. He was doomed.

Catesby didn't see the impact, but he saw the riderless bike somersaulting down the road. It happened on a sharp hairpin bend where the road had been carved and blasted out of the rock of the calanque. Marcel had been catapulted hard into the rockface next to the bike lane – a messier death than being knocked over the safety barrier on the opposite side. In that case, his last earthly vision would have been a bird's-eye view of sea, limestone cliffs and turquoise inlets – a few seconds of rare beauty – before he crunched to a quick death. Instead, Marcel was smeared into a rock wall – from which blood and scraped flesh were still dripping when Catesby and Jack found his body.

Jack reached out and felt Marcel's wrist for a pulse. 'None,' he said.

Catesby made the sign of the cross. It was an ingrained childhood habit that outlasted actual belief.

'What do we do now?' said Jack.

'Let's move him off the road.'

They carried Marcel across the road and placed him on the other side of the safety barrier.

'Now what?' said Jack.

'We flag down a car to get you a lift into Marseille. I'll ask them to drop you off at a police station. I'm going to stay here with Marcel.'

Before Jack could argue the case, a rather beat-up old Peugeot panel van pulled up, loaded with building materials and chickens. Catesby bundled his cousin in and explained the situation to the driver, a man of about sixty who must have seen worse in his time. Catesby waved them off and sat down on the safety barrier. It had all happened so quickly. It was still less than ten minutes since the car had first appeared. Catesby's decision to stay with Marcel's body was half instinct and half a desire to protect Jack. He was afraid they were going to come back – and he was right. As soon as Catesby saw the black Traction Avant appear around the bend, he was over the safety barrier and scrambling downhill through the rocky shrub land – and this time shots were fired.

The steep stony slope from the road was almost as dangerous as the bullets cracking overhead. The safest way to make a quick descent was to slide down on his bottom. It also made him a smaller target. He wondered if the gunman in his smart Italian suit would copy him. The important thing was to increase the distance between himself and the killers. Picking someone off with a revolver was almost impossible at a range of over 100 yards – and very unlikely at half that distance. If you're a target, the important thing is to keep weaving and bobbing.

Suddenly, all was quiet. At first, Catesby thought the gangster might be reloading, but then he heard the car engine start. He continued down through the scree – and then he saw it. There was another road – and that's why the killers had gone back to the car. They were going to cut him off as he descended the slope. Catesby felt totally fucked when he saw the Traction Avant come to a halt on the road below him. If he tried to crawl back up, they would turn around and be waiting for him by Marcel's body. He was caught in a cage. Suddenly, a story that he had heard in the war came into his mind. It was about the Italian invasion of Ethiopia. A group of mountain tribesmen had managed to disable a Fiat tank by throwing rocks at it. The hillside around Catesby was strewn with cricket ball-sized rocks – and the downward angle to the gangsters' car was perfect. The first rock smashed the driver's side window. The second and third rocks nearly took out the gunman as he got out of the car; he quickly decided it was safer back inside the Traction Avant. The driver gunned the engine just before a lobbed rock took out the wind-screen. As Catesby rained down a hail of rocks on the car, the driver decided to move the car out of range.

Catesby had to make a quick decision. Continue playing the angry caveman – or try escape and evasion? He decided on the E&E option because there was a fast-flowing mountain rivulet to his right which poured down the steep slope. He low-crawled towards it, keeping an eye out for the killers. The water was clear and cool, and vegetation provided some cover. He continued crawling down the stream towards the road. But would the gangsters see him as he dashed across? No, they wouldn't – for there was a culvert running beneath it. Catesby smiled. Every army obstacle course that he had been put through during his training involved at least one culvert. Sadistic army instructors loved putting trainees through damp, dark and narrow passages – and now here was one for a real-life E&E.

As Catesby crawled through the tunnel there was the sound of disturbed wildlife. He elbowed past a nest of baby rats and continued towards the light at the end. He stuck his head out to make sure the coast was clear – and then dropped out of the culvert into a pool of dirty water. The stream continued through heavy vegetation and, as long as one of the rat kids didn't grass him up, he was sure he could escape the killers – if, after being stoned, they were still in the mood for killing.

Catesby made it back to Marseille along the rocky coastal calanques, but the recurring image of Marcel's crumpled body took the beauty away. He tried to piece together what had happened. He assumed the Traction Avant gangsters had been instructed to take out Marcel during one of his training runs – and to make it look like a car accident rather than a murder, hence they didn't use guns. They would have assumed that, as normal, Marcel would be cycling alone and there would be no witnesses. But the presence of himself and Jack fucked up that plan – and the killers were then ordered to return to take them out. But who knows how such monsters think? If murderers had more brains, there would be far fewer convictions.

Avenue de la Canebière, Marseille: December 1949

'Good job,' said Lester cradling his drink. 'The cops are classifying it as a hit-and-run accident – even if any *flic* with half a brain knows it was a planned murder.'

The man sitting opposite him remained silent and stared at Lester with an expressionless face. After a minute had passed, he tapped the desk between them with his star-sapphire pinkie ring.

Lester responded by putting a briefcase on the desk. He opened it and began to divide banknotes into three piles: one for US currency, one for French francs and a third for Swiss francs. The American dollars were neatly bound in currency straps. Each bundle contained a hundred notes: a yellow strap for five-dollar bills, red for tens and green for twenties. The French and Swiss currencies were all used notes bound by rubber bands and divided into bundles of a hundred. 'We agreed the price in American dollars, and I made sure that the amount in francs was calculated at a good exchange rate.' Lester smiled. 'Better than you would get at any bank – and no commission.'

The other man remained stony-faced. He looked vaguely bored.

'To reiterate,' said Lester, 'you wanted one third paid in each of these currencies.'

The man gave a nearly imperceptible nod, then spoke in a loud voice that was almost a shout. Lester didn't understand any of the words, and they weren't aimed at him. The man was speaking a Corsican dialect that sounded more Italian than French. A moment later, a dark thin man with a perfect pimp's moustache came into the room and gathered all the money into a cloth bag. Lester assumed the newcomer was taking the cash off to count it. What, he thought, would stop him from hiding a few thousand and saying that they had been short-changed? 'Shouldn't we count it together?' said Lester.

'Don't you trust us?' The man stood up. 'Come with me. We will all count it together – every centime.'

'No, that's fine. I do trust you.' Lester laughed. 'And why should I want to count it? It isn't my money; it comes from the American taxpayer. But I wouldn't mind another drink.'

The man topped up Lester's glass with Fine Champagne cognac. 'You are totally safe, my friend – your American passport is a bulletproof vest.'

Lester gave a slight smile. It wasn't his US passport, which was in fact a black diplomatic one, that made him invulnerable, it was his status as a CIA officer. When it came to getting rid of communists, there were no laws you couldn't break.

'But it is we,' said the man, 'who have to take risks.' He took off his suit jacket, rolled up his shirt and revealed the scars from where the surgeons had fished out the bullets. 'For you it ended in 1945, but for us, Marseille will always be a city at war.'

'Who did that to you?'

'It doesn't matter.' The man tucked in his shirt. 'It was a long time ago and we are now friends.' He smiled. 'Or, I should say, the ones we didn't kill now pretend to be our friends.'

'How can we make things better for you?'

'Keep the money coming – and don't interfere with our businesses.'

'Maybe,' said Lester, 'we could help with some of your business interests.'

The man gave Lester a piercing look.

Lester replied with a sly smile and sipped his cognac. 'I have a lot of connections in Southeast Asia.'

'We don't like interference.'

'Even if it would open up new supply routes – as well as better-quality opium and lower prices. We're pals with the best warlords in the Golden Triangle.'

The man didn't reply.

Commissariat de police, Marseille: December 1949

The police inspector who took statements from Catesby and Jack seemed resigned to finding nothing useful. They both identified the car as a black Traction Avant – and Catesby could even remember part of the car's number plate, which he gave to the cop.

'Are you sure about the letters LG?' said the policeman.

'Totally sure,' said Catesby.

'LG is the geographical code for a car registered in Brittany.' The cop shook his head. 'I don't think the people who ran over your friend were Bretons. The number plate was either stolen or fake – probably the latter. But we will check in any case.'

'So you regard this as a murder enquiry?'

'I cannot say.'

Catesby suddenly found the manner of the police inspector very annoying. He may not have been under the thumb of the mafia, but he wasn't going to go out of his way to hunt them down.

The policeman looked at Catesby. 'I would advise you, monsieur, not to question police procedures. I appreciate the fact that you served as a British officer with the Resistance – and congratulate your bravery. But Marseille is a very different place from the remote hills of Limousin.'

Catesby was tempted to reply that while the Maquis fighters in the Limousin had got rid of fascists and criminals, Marseille chose to protect theirs. But he decided it was better to keep his mouth shut.

Cimetière du Canet, Marseille: December 1949

Marcel's funeral was just as much a protest march as it was a memorial service. It echoed the funeral that had been held for the student shot by the mafia during the rioting in the Opéra district – except, thought Catesby, that there didn't seem to be as many people. Was it the result perhaps of Marcel's killing being widely reported as a hit-and-run accident rather than a targeted murder? A lie that seemed to have traction. Or because the weather was unusually wet and miserable? Or owing to a general sense of weariness? Like the murdered student, Marcel was interred at the Cimetière du Canet. The cortège had set off in the December drizzle, but when the coffin reached the graveside, the cloud cover dispersed. The sun seemed to be saluting a fallen hero, and as the rays fell on the cemetery, the mourners began to sing 'The Internationale'. Catesby joined in – and so did Jack in his poor, but improving, French:

> *C'est la lutte finale*
> *Groupons-nous, et demain,*
> *L'Internationale,*
> *Sera le genre humain.*

Well, thought Catesby, it had certainly been the *lutte finale* for Marcel.

As the crowd began to disperse, Catesby saw Serge and Huong talking to Marcel's widow Teresa. The baby was in a pushchair. Although she was far too young to retain a memory of her father's funeral, Catesby could understand why Teresa had brought the infant there. Teresa was crying, and Huong had her arm around her. The baby started to cry too – and Catesby was surprised to see Jack lift the child out of the pushchair to comfort her.

Serge came over to Catesby. 'Some of us are going back with Teresa, to her place. I hope you will join us.'

Catesby nodded. 'What can I do to help?'

'Give history a kick up the backside instead of watching others do it.'

'I'll try my best,' said Catesby with a wan smile. 'And what can I do to help Teresa?'

'Encourage your cousin Jack to be close to her when she needs him.'

Catesby didn't answer. He didn't like complicated emotional situations – especially when they mixed bereavement and love.

The wake at Teresa's was well attended. The garden was full, and the crowd of mourning friends overflowed into the road. There were bouquets of chrysanthemums and cases of champagne had been donated by the unions to toast Marcel's life.

Catesby found Gaston le Mat, 'the mad one', standing next to him with a bottle of champagne. He gestured at Catesby's half-full glass, 'Drink up, Comrade Guillaume.'

Catesby emptied his glass with a guilty slurp. 'This is awfully good champagne.'

'Of course, it is. Nothing is too good for the working class. Have you come here to research your book?'

'No, I've come here as a homage to Marcel.'

'I believe you were with him when he was murdered.'

'And my cousin Jack.'

'He's the Englishman who is consoling Marcel's widow?'

Catesby didn't like le Mat's tone, but he nodded and held out his glass for more champagne.

'Marcel's killing,' said le Mat, 'is a lesson that we knew was coming. He shouldn't have made himself an easy target by cycling on lonely roads.'

It was obvious that le Mat had no truck with such bourgeois conventions as only speaking kindly of the recently deceased. 'I suppose,' said Catesby, 'that training for long-distance bike-racing wasn't a good pastime for someone organising anti-government strikes and protests.'

'Indeed. But now we've got to regroup and look forward.'

'How soon will Marcel be replaced?'

'Soon.'

'Could you be the new leader?'

'That's for the comrades to decide.'

Catesby could tell from le Mat's expression and tone that he knew he wasn't in the running. Maybe the comrades felt that he was too much of a tough guy and not enough of an organiser.

'What we need,' said le Mat, 'is guns.'

'I bet there are big caches of Resistance weapons that were never turned in,' suggested Catesby.

'Not as many as there should be. The decommissioning was a big mistake. Too many people thought the fighting was over.'

'Maybe you could ask Moscow for airdrops.' Catesby hoped the irony in his voice wasn't too obvious. But it didn't matter, for le Mat already knew the harsh truth. The Russians hadn't supplied a single bullet to the Maquis during the war – and wouldn't dare supply arms to striking workers in post-war France. Stalin had to perform a tightrope balancing act, just as he had done with the Berlin blockade. Direct Soviet military action, such as shooting down US planes airlifting supplies to Berlin – or providing weapons to striking workers in France – risked provoking an American response that could escalate into nuclear strikes to which Moscow could not retaliate.

Le Mat had a face of thunder. 'If they kill us, we kill them. We need to move from protests to revolutionary violence.'

Catesby remained silent. He didn't want to tell le Mat that that was exactly what the French government and their American backers wanted – a chance to unleash the military and shoot down communists in the street.

'I'd better circulate,' said le Mat. For the moment he was less worried about guns than refilling champagne flutes in homage to Marcel.

Dunwich, Suffolk: December 1949

Catesby was pleased to be spending Christmas in Suffolk – far from prying eyes that might be suspicious about what appeared to be a reconciliation with Frances. They were staying at her family's remote home between Dunwich and Walberswick. The twins, no longer toddlers, enjoyed the freedom of running wild, swinging from tree ropes and digging dens. Catesby feared they might be prepping for careers in the Commandos or the Parachute Regiment. He tried to add a gentler dimension to their untamed derring-do by teaching them songs and nursery rhymes before bedtime – but with little success.

'They need to get used to you again,' said Frances.

'Or maybe I'm just useless.'

'Being good with children doesn't always mean you're a good person. Kids can be easily deceived.'

'Have you any particular monster in mind?'

Frances stared into her glass. 'A friend of mine says that he's absolutely wonderful with children.'

'The Big Bad Wolf?'

'No, the one I have in mind is a bit more subtle. His name is Kim Philby.'

'What makes him a monster?'

'I didn't say he was a monster. It's still only an investigation.' Frances paused and shook her head. 'I shouldn't be telling you this, William, I'm breaking the Official Secrets Act.'

'Don't say another word.'

'My love for you is more important than keeping state secrets. And if you don't take your fingers out of your ears, I'm going to pour this glass of wine over your head – and if you put that cushion over my mouth I will scream for help.'

191

'What's love have to do with this?'

'I want to protect you – and I think you may be in danger from Philby.'

'What's your role?'

'They've asked me to help compile a top-secret file on Kim Philby for the head of counterintelligence.'

'Including the VENONA decrypts?'

Frances nodded.

'Why hasn't he been dismissed and arrested?'

'Because there are those who think the whole thing is a conspiracy to stop Philby from becoming head of SIS.'

'And the chickens don't want to annoy the fox who will be taking over the henhouse?'

'Exactly. He is also a wily fox that pretends to be friends with both sides. In the 1930s he cosied up to right-wing groups including Franco's fascists and Action Française.'

'He's a chameleon with a smooth smile.'

'Indeed.'

Catesby stared into his wine glass for a long time and then looked up at his wife. 'You've seen undeniable evidence that Philby is a communist double agent. Haven't you?'

She didn't answer.

'You still haven't explained why I'm personally in danger from Philby?'

'He's desperate to stitch you up as a VENONA file Sov agent to deflect attention from himself – and he realises that you know what he's up to.'

Le Panier, Marseille: 12 January 1950

'Marcel's murder was indeed a bitter blow,' said Serge as he poured glasses of pastis, 'but the dockworkers are regrouping under new leaders – and things are looking very promising.'

Catesby trusted Serge's judgement and he now feared that the reports he had been sending back to London had got it wrong. He had written that strike action was ultimately doomed to fail owing to a lack of popular support and the death of Marcel, one of its leading lights. Maybe, thought Catesby, he had been unconsciously singing a tune that would please the Director and ease fears in Whitehall.

'The present tactic,' continued Serge, 'is not to refer to industrial actions taken on the docks as strikes, but boycotts. The dockworkers turn up for work but refuse to load US weapons and supplies bound for Indochina. It's a popular move and the CGT union has endorsed it. The boycotts have already spread to other ports and industrial sectors, and American military cargoes are starting to be shunned as if they were carrying the plague.'

'In practice, how are these boycotts different from strikes?'

'Not very different, but more streamlined and focused. And the French public find the word boycott more acceptable than strike.'

Catesby nodded. During the war the technique was known as white propaganda. The term had been coined by a shadowy organisation called the Political Warfare Executive. The French trade unions were finally catching up.

Huong had been sitting silently in the background staring into space. She finally spoke up. 'I am not sure you should be sharing this information with Monsieur Catesby.'

An awkward silence filled the room. After a few seconds, Serge picked up the bottle of pastis. 'I think we need another drink.'

Catesby looked at Huong. 'Why don't you trust me?'

'Because you behave like a spy who has been sent to infiltrate our movement.'

Catesby smiled. 'If I am a spy, I'm sure that my bosses would have given me a better cover story than pretending to research a book about the Resistance.' The words came easy, for Catesby had been tempted to shout the same ones at Bone and the Director. The paranoia kicked in again: *Had he been set up to be taken out?*

Serge looked at his wife and then at Catesby. 'We are a movement, a dangerous revolutionary party, which is under attack from the ruling class. It is understandable that we are suspicious of others.'

'And especially me as an outsider.'

'We are suspicious of each other as well. As you know, during the Resistance, family members and close friends often turned traitor. It created a toxic atmosphere. I can't reveal who warned Huong about your activities – but it was from a highly placed source that we normally trust.'

Catesby was tempted to say, 'Her controller from Moscow Central', but decided it was best to keep quiet. He had detected, however, a note of scepticism in Serge's voice.

Serge looked at Catesby. 'Would you like to comment, William?'

'What can I say? I would just as strongly repudiate the accusation if I was innocent or guilty. I suggest that you judge me by my actions and not by what other people say about me.'

Serge raised his glass in toast.

Catesby looked at Huong. He remembered that his car had been blown up by a device often used by Viet Minh guerrillas – for all Henry Bone thought the assassination attempt had been carried out by a mad right-wing viscount.

Suffolk: May 2018

Catesby had been looking through a seed catalogue when Leanna strode into the garden office with tea and biscuits, followed by Frances. 'Granny was just telling me there was a bit of excitement here last week.'

'Well, planting out courgettes is not normally exciting, but the arrival of a Royal Signal Corps motorcycle despatch rider did rather make things more interesting. I asked if the Met Office had sent him to warn me of an early frost.'

'No, William,' said Frances, 'you asked him if he was bearing the offer of a knighthood in the Birthday Honours.'

'I was, my dear, being ironic.'

'The expression on your face suggested otherwise.'

'In any case,' said Catesby, 'it wasn't even a lesser gong, but a copy of a Secret Intelligence Service document that had recently been declassified.'

'The latest release on Kim Philby,' said Frances. 'His shadow keeps getting longer.'

'I was touched that someone in SIS knew that I was still alive and would want to see the report.'

'And it was dynamite,' said Frances.

'Not exactly dynamite, but the doc shed light on what would have been a fiery death in my Standard 8. The document seemed part of a plea bargain deal, probably from just before he did his flit from Beirut to Moscow. Philby confessed that he told his Sov controller I had uncovered the identities of everyone in SIS who had ever worked for the Russians – an impossible task – and that I had been heading to Paris to sell those names to the highest bidder. Consequently, I should be liquidated as soon as possible. Moscow passed the job on to Huong.'

'And when she failed?' said Frances.

'I suppose that Philby's disinfo on me may have helped Spiridon get backing from Moscow Central to send the Stasi woman after me with a cyanide spray gun, but who knows?'

'If, Granddad, you didn't know the identities of all the spies in SIS, why was Philby so intent on having you murdered?'

'Because I did know the name of one of them. His.'

7th arrondissement, Marseille: January 1950

Lester was standing in the immense bay window of his apartment, looking out over the sea to the islands of Frioul. 'You know something, Kit, this place grows on you. I'd like to buy one of those islands – and maybe Château d'If itself. We could have some wild parties, and no cops or neighbours to complain.'

At first, Kit Fournier had regarded his colleague as a mad eccentric living in a fantasy world, but he now realised that Lester wielded a magic wand that was transforming fantasies into reality. Of course, the wand wasn't really magic at all: it was the genuine transformative force of American money and power in a world still reeling from war.

'What,' said Lester, 'do you think of the way Sam Benedictine is handling things?'

'He doesn't want to get his hands dirty – but he wants to take the credit when you do.'

'Exactly. Sam would never have handed over cash in person to pay for a hit. He would have used a dozen go-betweens to make sure there were no fingerprints – but every time you do that, a big slice of money and control disappears. In any case, turning Comrade Marcel into a dead fucking commie was an important stroke, but now we've got to keep whacking off any heads that appear out of the corpse.' Lester paused and sipped his bourbon. 'You know what I mean, that Greek story about a monster that keeps sprouting new heads?'

'The Hydra. Each time you cut one off, two more reappear – each breathing poisonous fumes.'

Lester laughed. 'Damned clever those ancient Greeks: they were predicting the spread of communism. How did they get rid of the Hydra?'

'They called in Hercules . . .'

'That's me.'

'And his nephew . . .'

'That will have to be you, Kit.'

'They covered their mouths and noses with cloths, then Hercules quickly cut off all the monster's heads and his nephew cauterised the severed necks with a firebrand before any more could grow back.'

'And that's just what we're going to do.'

'Is that all for today?' said Kit as he picked up his file.

Le Vieux Port, Marseille: February 1950

The punch-ups on the docks were becoming more vicious and more tar-geted. Catesby didn't want to get involved, but he needed to see what was happening. He attached himself to Serge as a sort of artist's assistant. On what was to prove the most violent day of fighting, Catesby went along clad in a paint-stained smock and a beret. His job was setting up Serge's easel and cleaning his paintbrushes. Serge wasn't content with mere pencil sketches; he was painting in watercolours to catch the light and the changing colours. No one, on either side of the coming confron-tation, seemed interested in what he was doing.

'It is a bit humiliating,' Serge complained. 'I've become an insignifi-cant fly not even worth swatting away.'

Catesby despised himself for being on the sidelines. He looked with admiration and envy at the lines of dockworkers who were block-ing access to the ships awaiting war materials. Jack was among them. Catesby noticed that Jack and the other dockers were armed with the tools of their trade: shovels, cargo hooks, hammers, grappling hooks and weighted slings. They weren't the best of weapons in a pitched battle for control of the docks – and this became painfully apparent when the thugs hired by the mafia began to turn up. They were carrying clubs, crowbars, pipes, chains and leather straps with lead-filled pockets. Their objective was to break through the lines of dockers so that scab workers could load the boycotted war equipment, which had begun to clog up the wharves. Catesby sensed that this confrontation wasn't going to end like the one at Port-de-Bouc, where the Force Ouvrière scabs had been sent packing. They were pussycats compared to the mafia hirelings.

Catesby heard one of the dockers cry out, *'No pasarán!'* – and the fighting began. The dockworkers were up for a battle, but the mob descending on them with clubs and chains were professional enforcers and seasoned fighters. Yet the battle wasn't one-sided. Catesby cheered as a well-muscled dockworker took out a mob hireling with a grappling hook. When the man tried to clobber another thug, his hook was parried by a crowbar, splintering the handle in two, leaving the docker with a mere piece of wood in his hands. Another swipe of the crowbar caught his legs, and he was on the ground being kicked and stomped on.

Serge put down his paintbrush and stood up. The final straw for Catesby was a mafia thug calling out, *'Prends ce connard d'anglais!'* Jack was in trouble. Catesby ran towards the voice and saw Jack curled up on the tarmac trying to ward off kicks and blows. The thug with the crowbar pointed at Catesby, who was still carrying a jar of turpentine containing a paintbrush, and laughed.

'Un artiste!'

Catesby threw the turpentine in the thug's face, who screamed as he tried to scrape the burning liquid from his face and eyes. Catesby hurled the empty jar at his head and then kicked him in the balls. The mobster hireling bent double and dropped his crowbar – which Catesby quickly retrieved. He shouted, 'Fuck you!' and aimed the metal bar at the hoodlum's head. The thug, seeing the lethal iron descending, raised an arm to protect himself. Catesby felt a bit sick when he screamed in agony – and he realised he had just fractured a human arm. But that one, at least, was out of action.

Jack was back on his feet, but blood was streaming down one side of his face. A couple of mob enforcers were now approaching to rescue and avenge their fallen colleague. One of them was whirling a chain around his head with a spiked metal ball on the end.

Catesby raised his crowbar to catch the whirling chain. The ensnared crowbar was yanked out of Catesby's hands, landing with a loud clang ten feet away. In the same moment, Jack launched into a two-footed sideways tackle at the mobster's legs. The thug went down in a heap. But taking out the thug was an isolated victory. Their picket lines had been broken and the mafia enforcers had cleared the docks. The scab workers were now free to load American tanks and artillery pieces for shipment to Indochina.

Meanwhile, the dockers were trying to get their wounded comrades to a safe place where they could be looked after. Many were badly injured. Several had suffered severe testicular injuries, having been repeatedly kicked in the balls with steel toe-capped boots. Another had an eye gouged out.

With the fighting over, Catesby and Jack accompanied Serge back to his studio. There was now a new bond between the cousins. They had fought for the same cause – and probably saved each other from death or serious injury. Serge had joined in too, not so much to fight, but to look after badly injured dockers.

'I didn't get much of a chance to paint,' said Serge. 'But the images are still there.'

'How do you paint evil?' said Catesby.

'It isn't easy. Their faces are empty and blank – and they want us to be like them.'

Saint-Charles Station, Marseille: February 1950

The letter had a Paris postmark. Catesby regarded it with suspicion and made a mental list of the people who knew his address in Marseille. No one. The envelope was too flimsy and lightweight to contain poison or a lethal device, so he opened it. The message, like his address, had been typed. The sender didn't want his or her handwriting as an identity giveaway. It was brief and to the point:

```
Spring is sprung,
Duh grass is riz
I wonder where dem boidies is.
Duh little boids is on duh wing —
But dat's absoid:
Duh little wing is on de boid.
```

As Catesby ascended the monumental grand staircase to the station and made his way to Platform K, he wondered if he should greet 'the poet' with a line or two of verse. Maybe something from Lewis Carroll: *Just the place for a <u>Snark!</u>* But as soon as he saw the man waiting for him, he knew he wouldn't like being called a Snark. He was a well-muscled gent with a boxer's face. The dark-grey fedora hat was as unmistakeably American as the poem he had sent. As he walked towards him, Catesby presumed he was meeting a gangster – but, as soon as the man spoke, he knew he was wrong. His accent was American, but transatlantic and refined – not unlike that of the late President Franklin Roosevelt. 'Thank you for coming to meet me – and coming alone.'

'I liked your poem.'

'It's not mine. I could have done a better Bronx accent.'

'Are you from New York?'

'You're asking too many questions. I see you have come unarmed, but could you fold back the lapel of your jacket – the side where your buttonhole is.'

Catesby did so.

'Good. No camera either.'

'Your message said you had more poetry to recite.'

'It's free verse. If you want to make it rhyme or follow a metre, that's up to you.'

'Sadly, I'm not a poet.'

'Then maybe you should pass on this line to someone who is. Lester Roach paid the mafia to kill your friend Marcel.'

'Why are you telling me this?'

'I haven't told you anything and we've never met.'

'Then how can I verify that what you didn't tell me is true?'

The American smiled. 'Say a little boidie told you. I think you'd better skedaddle – and don't try to find out who I am. This meeting never happened.'

Catesby kept a blank face as he turned and walked away. He didn't want the 'little boidie' to read his thoughts. It was obvious that someone in a very high place – possibly in the US government itself – wanted to stitch up Lester. Could the story that Lester had paid the mafia to take out Marcel be disinfo? A lie calculated to get someone on the left to avenge Marcel's murder? The American was playing a clever game.

Rue de Montevideo, Marseille: February 1950

Jack's head wound required twenty-five stitches. It was deep and ran from his temple to the top of his eyebrow. 'How,' said Catesby, 'did you manage to carry on fighting with your head bashed in?'

'My blood was up – and the wound looks worse than it is. It was a deflected blow with a sharp piece of metal. In any case, they didn't want to kill me with a metal bar. They wanted to get me on the ground and kick me to death because they knew I was a Brit.' Jack smiled. 'And then you waded in and saved my life.'

'Lowestoft boys have to stick together.'

Jack laughed. 'I bet you would have done it even if I came from Yarmouth.'

'There are limits, Jack.'

There were tears in Jack's eyes. 'We'll always be mates, Will. Always.'

Catesby wanted to wipe out the last ten years of his life. He wished he'd never gone to Cambridge, never become an officer – and wished that he had told the SIS recruitment panel to get fucked. He wanted the solid integrity of being someone like Jack. Not speaking fake posh, but standing shoulder to shoulder on the docks and in the pub. But it wasn't to be – for when you cut off your roots they never grow back.

'It looks like you need a glass of wine,' said Jack.

'Or maybe three.'

'Good. We need to empty a few bottles to make Molotov cocktails. We also need guns.'

'You'll also need tanks and aircraft. Guerrillas can't win a war against a modern well-equipped army by themselves. We learned that in the Resistance. If it hadn't been for D-Day, we'd have eventually been wiped out.'

'What if the army and the police came over to our side?'

Catesby gave a low whistle.

'You seem doubtful.'

'Soldiers and cops only change sides at the last minute – and, even then, only the brighter ones.'

'I'm going to get the wine.'

'Fetch the cheapest you've got.'

Jack returned with a litre bottle of table wine. 'This is what the workers drink.'

'Thank you, comrade.'

'I'll join you later. I'm going to help Teresa give Dolores a bath and put her to bed.'

'It sounds like she's named after Dolores Ibarruri, better known as La Pasionaria?'

'Well spotted, Will. You know your stuff.'

'Of course.' Catesby could have added that SIS provided a postgrad course on revolution and radical politics. La Pasionaria was the Spanish communist who coined the *¡No Pasarán!* battle cry in the darkest days of the civil war.

'But our Dolores needs bathing and putting to bed before she sees off the fascists.'

As his cousin left, Catesby poured himself a glass of wine. He noticed that Jack had said *our Dolores*. He was now a stepdad as well as a lover. Catesby stared into lonely space. He realised that his cousin, nearly five years younger, had evolved into a more responsible adult than himself. Catesby tried to be good with his step-kids and tried to make Frances happy, but felt he never succeeded. Was he good at anything? Catesby sipped his wine and finally smiled. The still-fresh memory of the fight on the docks warmed him. He was good at kicking evil bastards in the balls.

Bath time seemed to be finished. As Catesby helped himself to more wine, he could hear Teresa reciting a bedtime story to Dolores in Spanish. He wasn't fluent in the language, but knew it was a bad idea for

Caperucita Roja to tell *el lobo* that her grandmother lived alone at the end of the path. Catesby began to doze off.

'Wakey, wakey,' said Jack as he lifted the wine bottle. 'This one will soon be ready for the Molotov mixture. By the way, you were snoring.'

'Sorry. How are things?'

Jack poured himself a big slug of wine. 'It isn't easy for her. She's deeply grieving for a man that she loved and finds herself having to look after a child alone.' Jack smiled. 'And when I ask, "What can I do to help?", she says, "Carry on Marcel's struggle for a socialist revolution. That's how you will honour his memory."'

'How do you feel about that?'

'I will try to do what Marcel would have done.'

'Which is?'

Jack smiled. 'Who knows? But the leaders that he worked with most closely are now saying we should shift from massive protests to sabotage and clandestine activities – that we become a guerrilla army of the night.' Jack paused. 'And that's another reason we need guns.'

Catesby looked at Jack. He wondered if he should tell his cousin about his encounter at Saint-Charles Station? The answer was a firm no. If Jack believed the line that Lester had paid the mob to kill Marcel, the consequences could be dire. If Jack went after Lester to get revenge, he would end up just as dead as Marcel – and so would Catesby or any other man. There were other less perilous options open to Jack.

During the next few weeks Catesby coached Jack in the art of sabotage. The important thing was to leave no fingerprints for the police to chase up. In the end, the destruction wreaked proved a mere irritant: the saboteurs derailed a few trains carrying military supplies to the docks, they slashed the tyres and put sugar in the fuel tanks of unguarded lorries. The authorities responded by increasing police overtime and deploying soldiers as security guards.

Meanwhile, the mafia remained active. One trade unionist was found floating in the harbour – the oddest of suicides, since, according to the pathologist, he had managed to crush his windpipe and choke himself unconscious before he jumped into the water. Two more were found dead as the result of muggings, and another union activist, who had done military service in Algeria, was found with horrible mutilations. A note, written in bad Arabic, claimed that his killing was revenge for his part in the Sétif massacre of May 1945 – even though the former soldier hadn't been sent to Algeria until a year later. Another union leader was simply shot – one bullet through the eye and two more to the back of the head. There was no attempt to disguise it as anything other than what it was – and rumours had begun to swirl. During the November riots, it had been logical as well as barbaric for the mafia to gun down demonstrators who were torching their bars and nightclubs in the centre of Marseille. They were protecting their turf. But why was the mob murdering trade union activists and communists now? All the street gossip said the mafia were being paid to do it. But by whom? Some rumours suggested it was the French government itself; others pointed to a coalition of the far-right who were planning a coup – and, of course, the Americans got a big mention too. And, Catesby reasoned, the Yanks had the deepest pockets. He reconsidered the message from the 'little boidie' who flew into Saint-Charles Station. It wasn't just Marcel who needed avenging. There were now many more.

Le Panier, Marseille: March 1950

Catesby's next visit to Serge's place was a difficult and tense one. Huong was withdrawn and sullen – and seemed annoyed that he had turned up. Serge nodded towards his studio, a silent suggestion that Catesby should follow him. As they entered, they had to sidestep a pile of paintings that were wrapped up in packing paper. Serge picked up a bottle of cognac and two glasses. 'Some of my paintings have just been shown at a big exhibition in Paris.'

'Congratulations.'

Serge laughed and poured the cognac. 'They were on show for one day before the police ordered them removed.'

'That's fucking awful.'

'In a way, it was a bigger compliment than any critic has ever given me.'

'Which paintings were they?'

'Mostly the ones of the dock strikes and the weapons boycott – with a few from the Spanish Civil War and Buchenwald mixed in. But the *collabo* cops removed those too.'

Catesby swirled the cognac in his glass and took in its fine aroma. When everything is turning to shit, little pleasures matter.

Serge turned to his easel, which held a work-in-progress showing a man with one eye. The empty socket was purple and ugly. 'You might have rescued your cousin Jack from a similar fate. Bruno's eye was gouged out by a mafia enforcer the same day.'

'Could we have helped him?'

'No, he was on the other side of the docks – part of the first group attacked by the mobsters. Totally outnumbered.'

'But he survived?'

'Just about. He's in a lot of pain. He had a hand and leg smashed up too. But he still comes to sit for me – and lets me give him pastis. If this painting had been in the exhibition, they would certainly have removed it as well.'

'What does Bruno think of the situation?'

'He wants to keep fighting.'

'And you?'

'History is on our side even when we get our heads kicked in.' Serge sipped his cognac. 'And I've just had my head kicked in – not physically, but emotionally.'

'What happened?'

'Huong is packing her bags. She's leaving me.'

'I'm very surprised to hear that.'

'I wasn't.'

'I didn't realise things were going that badly.'

'They weren't. Huong isn't leaving me for another man, she's leaving me for another country. She loves Vietnam more than me.'

A voice echoed in Catesby's mind. It was Henry Bone explaining why Frances had joined MI5. After losing two brothers in the war, she needed to show that she loved her country too. It may not have been entirely rational, but it was an emotional commitment that he couldn't argue with.

'She has decided to join the Viet Minh,' Serge continued. 'I expect they'll give her dangerous undercover jobs and there is a good chance she'll be captured or killed. I offered to come with her, but she refused.'

'It must be very upsetting for you.'

'It will pass. Revolutionary struggles involve personal estrangements. It turned out much worse for Teresa.'

'You know my cousin Jack is . . .'

'He is being a great support – both emotionally and ideologically.'

'I'm glad.'

'I first met Teresa in Spain – still in her teens at the time, but a very brave fighter and organiser. I recently went to see her, and we had a long chat about my dilemma.' Serge gave a wry smile. 'Teresa, of course, fully understands and supports Huong's decision to fight in Vietnam. Relationships as well as lives are casualties of conflict and war.'

'Indeed,' said Catesby sipping his cognac.

Serge walked over to the easel and started to darken the background behind the injured Bruno, as if it were a stormy sky.

'Any chance,' said Catesby, 'that my cousin Jack could have a chat with Huong?'

The meeting with Jack took place in Serge's flat. Catesby immediately saw that his cousin's youth and naïve charm were a winning combination. His accounts of the brutal dockside battle at Le Vieux Port and the wounds the workers received were factual and totally unemotional – and all the more moving as a result.

Huong looked a bit uneasy. 'Unfortunately, I wasn't there – I had an important meeting.'

Catesby wondered if the meeting had been with a representative of the Viet Minh or her Soviet controller – or both.

'But,' said Jack, 'you were at Port de Bouc – and your petrol bombs lit up the sky.'

Huong smiled. 'That was a battle the workers won – and I was pleased to play a part.'

'We're going to win again,' said Jack. He then gave an account of the sabotage recently carried out.

Huong looked on with a sceptical frown. Catesby guessed that she thought the workers' battle for France was a lost cause and that's why she was going to Vietnam.

Serge poured everyone pastis – and on this occasion Huong joined in. She looked at Jack. 'I am pleased that you are being such a support to Teresa – I am very fond of her.'

'I try to help around the flat and with Dolores – but she always says that the most important thing is that I follow Marcel's commitment to a socialist revolution.'

'And,' said Serge, 'to avenge his death.'

There was an awkward silence until Catesby pitched in. 'Someone paid the mafia to murder Marcel.'

Huong gave him a cross look. 'Any fool can see that.' She finished her pastis and left the room.

'See you later,' said Serge as he followed her.

Catesby poured more pastis. 'Well done, cousin.'

'I think I pissed her off.'

'No, I did. She's a complex person whose loyalties pull her in different directions.'

'And brave as hell. I wouldn't want to be one of the bastards who murdered Marcel if Huong is on their tail. Teresa tells me she's taken up karate lessons.'

Catesby smiled at the image of Huong delivering a lethal roundhouse kick. The pieces were falling into position.

Ten minutes later Serge came back into the room and made straight for the pastis bottle. 'I'm glad you haven't finished it, I need a drink.'

'How's Huong?' said Catesby.

'She's decided to put off going to Vietnam. She thinks there's still work to be done in Marseille.'

Marseille: March 1950

Catesby had waited a long time for Bone to answer his enquiry about the identity of the American he had met at Saint-Charles Station. He wondered if it had been difficult to track him down – or if Bone was being cagey. Communications with London were now by telephone – either encoded or in the clear. Not an ideal situation, but Helen, having left her diplomat husband, was no longer a viable go-between. He missed using her.

Catesby had already decrypted the long-awaited answer from Henry Bone – and burned it and washed the ashes down the sink. It was potential dynamite. The mystery man on Platform K was Sam Benedictine, Washington's chief union-fixer in Europe. Unfortunately for him, his Force Ouvrière scabs had needed the help of the mafia to clear the docks. But, it seemed, instead of being grateful to Lester Roach for enlisting the mob, Benedictine now wanted someone to take him out. Was it a matter of personal pride – or US government policy?

The annoying thing about Bone's reply was that it hadn't confirmed nor denied Benedictine's claim that Lester Roach had paid the mob to kill Marcel. It was clear that Bone was playing his own game. A waiting game or a keeping-his-options-open game? Catesby was about to draft a message back asking for clarification when there was a knock on the door. It was unexpected, for no one ever came to Catesby's flat on the Rue des Frères Pecchini – not even the Pecchinis. He wasn't in the mood to receive a visitor. He had just been for a run along the seafront and needed a shower. The hope was that long-distance running would compensate for his late-night drinking. Drunks that got exercise were generally healthier than drunks who didn't – but he wasn't a drunk. Not like Philby and many of his colleagues at SIS. He was an idealist and long-distance runner who had fallen in with a bad lot. At least, that was his excuse. The knocking continued. Sweaty or not, he decided to answer it – and immediately wished that he hadn't. The combination of beauty and pure eroticism took his breath away. The consul's estranged wife had dressed for the occasion.

'May I come in?'

'If you like, but I'm all hot and sweaty.'

'Thank you, my husband used to say I often have that effect on men.'

'In my case, I've just been for a run.'

'What a charmer you are.'

'But please come in' – Catesby removed a pile of books and papers from the flat's only armchair – 'and take a seat.'

She sat down, and as she crossed her legs she revealed an inch of bare pale skin above her stocking top. She adjusted her dress to hide the flesh. Catesby could see that each gesture was a practised one. 'Would you like a cup of tea?' he said.

'I suppose it is a bit early for a G&T, but could you make some coffee?'

'I'll have to grind the beans.'

'You are a domestic hero.'

'Do you want it strong?'

'Of course.'

'I don't normally drink coffee . . .'

'My name is Helen. Have you forgotten?'

'I don't, Helen, normally drink coffee.' Catesby smiled. 'It makes me overexcited.'

'How interesting.'

'And then I can't sleep at night.'

'Caffeine is a drug,' said Helen, 'and I've recently taken an interest in drugs.'

'They can be lethal.'

'Did you take amphetamines when you did all those daring things during the war?'

'Only twice – and I didn't do any daring things. I only tagged along with the Maquisards.'

'That's not what Henri says. He speaks highly of you as one of SOE's bravest members.'

Catesby busied himself with transferring the ground coffee into the percolator.

'Are you going to join me – or will it make you too excited.'

'I'll risk a tiny cup.'

'Good. I suppose you're wondering why I turned up out of the blue.'

'I suppose you think I have a report that I need to pass on to the consulate, but I still haven't written one.'

'No, that wasn't the reason. And, in any case, I am sure you have other means of communicating with London.'

A note of suspicion began to gnaw at Catesby. She was a sleek feline, and he was a mouse she was tossing from claw to claw. 'Would you like milk with your coffee? I haven't got any cream.'

'Milk would be fine.'

'It will take a while to percolate.'

'I can understand why you don't want me to pass on your messages for London.'

She was good at the game. She was prompting Catesby to ask a question for which she already had prepared an answer. He decided to play along. 'What makes you think that I don't want you as an intermediary?'

'Because you think that I'm a tart – and that I'd share your messages with Henri.'

Catesby kept a stony face. She was half right. 'I certainly don't think you're a tart – how unkind that you suppose I would think that. You're a beautiful and fascinating woman – and, like most fascinating people, a little unconventional.'

'That is a polite way of putting it.' The whistle of the percolator began to pierce the room. 'Even the coffee thinks so.'

Catesby poured. 'I imagine that being the wife of a diplomat can be very boring.'

'Indeed – and that's why many of them go in for adultery as a diverting pastime. We are, of course, sent to foreign places and surrounded by glamorous and interesting people. Temptation is within easy reach. I wonder if the Foreign Office realises how much unfaithfulness there is among diplomatic couples.'

Catesby smiled. 'If you write a report, I'll pass it on.'

'Or perhaps I'm exaggerating to justify my own behaviour.'

Catesby was taken aback by her frankness. In a mollifying tone he said, 'Did you know that Lady Mountbatten and Nehru had an affair?'

'We were told not to talk about it. By the way, their relationship is still ongoing, but may never have been consummated.'

'I wonder why.'

'Maybe Lady Mountbatten doesn't know how to arouse his passions.'

Perhaps, thought Catesby, you could give her a lesson or two.

'This coffee is delightful.'

'Thank you, Helen.'

'And I still haven't told you why I came to see you.'

'You said you like hot, sweaty men.'

'In addition to that, Henri and I would like you to join us for lunch.'

'Well, I suppose I'd better have a shower and change.'

'Would you like me to soap your back?'

There was no polite way to turn the offer down – and Catesby didn't want to, either. 'That would be lovely.'

She dropped her skirt a second before Catesby undid his running shorts. It wasn't exactly a striptease, but Helen knew how to undo each item of underwear in the most tantalising way. Catesby tried to keep his back to her so that she wouldn't see his throbbing erection but could still see that her pubic hair had been trimmed into the neatest of triangles. He preceded her down a short corridor to the shower room. The sound of her bare feet on the stone floor behind him was far more erotic than Wagner's *Liebestod*. Catesby was breathless with a desire that he knew he must contain.

He got into the shower first, still keeping his back to her, and began to soap himself. She had found a flannel and began to scrub his back – and his buttock cleavage and between his legs. She was good at hygiene. 'You

215

have,' she said, 'a slim waist and very well-toned muscles. You remind me of a gymnast I knew when I was in the circus.' Catesby was in a heaven that would not last. After a few minutes she reached around his waist and wrapped a hand around his stiff penis. 'I see what you mean,' she said, 'about coffee making you excited. Another time, I must give Monsieur Zizi a nice kiss – but not now, we must get ready for lunch.'

Catesby gave a sigh that combined both disappointment and relief as she exited the shower stall. She could do an expert tease that would put the best-trained honeytrap agents to shame. His training in both SOE and SIS had emphasised the need to avoid falling into such situations – and he had prided himself on never doing so. But after what had just happened, he would never again condemn an agent who fell into a honeytrap. As with its opposite, torture, there was a limit to what a human being could withstand.

He watched her putting her underwear and clothes back on; it was a slow, erotic ritual in which the re-fastening of each button and hook was designed to torment. The message was clear: *You missed all of this and you may never get another chance.* Catesby, however, was regaining strength and clarity of mind.

The restaurant was a ten-minute walk from Catesby's flat. He felt a bit awkward with Helen's hand resting in the crook of his elbow as they walked along. He was too mousy to be with someone as glamorous as her – but, as his SIS instructors had frequently pointed out, mousy non-descript men like him made the best spies. No one noticed them – and, if they did, there were few clues to identify them: medium height, brown hair, normal build, one head, two legs, answers to the name of Fido. Catesby had, however, tried to smarten himself for the occasion. He was wearing a pair of Oxford bags that his roommate at Cambridge had lent him. Strachan had always looked after him; pity his tank had brewed up at Normandy. It was still a little chilly and Catesby had on a tweed jacket – but no tie. As he was supposed to be writing a book, he wanted to look more bohemian – and the old-fashioned Oxford bags certainly contributed to the image. Poor Strachan – too late to return the bags. He turned to Helen with a question you were never supposed to ask. 'What did your husband do in the war?'

'Nothing much, he was captured at Singapore a week after his unit landed.'

Nothing much, just three and a half years as a Japanese prisoner of war. And now this. But no one should expect pity.

'I hope you like fish,' she said.

'Of course, I'm from Lowestoft.'

'I don't know East Anglia very well, but I have been to Aldeburgh.'

'You mentioned that before.' Catesby wondered if Helen's memory lapses had to do with drink or drugs. 'Aldeburgh has the music; we have the fish.'

'Both are good.'

'Thank you.'

'Henri says the place we're going is a good restaurant, but we'll be too early for the full bouillabaisse.'

'We'll save that for a special occasion.'

'By the way,' said Helen, 'I've recently met a friend of yours. We're taking lessons from the same karate master.'

For some reason, Catesby wasn't surprised by the news. 'A certain Vietnamese friend?'

'The very same. She's a superb athlete – soon she'll be a brown belt.'

'I bet you're both lethal.'

'I'm rather taken by her. You ought to see her in the shower.'

For the first time, Catesby realised that Huong was a beautiful woman – and it had taken another woman to point out the obvious.

'Look.' Helen pointed across a small harbour to a building with glass terraces that was clinging to a rocky outcrop. 'There it is.' She was wearing a short-sleeved chemise and her fully stretched bare arm was elegant but firmly muscled. Catesby imagined that beautiful arm choking the life out of someone.

The harbour was called Vallon des Auffes and was packed with fishing boats. Almost all were *pointu* design, double enders with sharply pointed bows and sterns. They were gracefully curved, elegant craft. Many were still rigged with lateen sails, but the smoky put-put of diesel engines echoed across the port. Catesby noticed that most of the boats had deep wells where their catches were kept alive until they reached the pot.

'Does it remind you of Lowestoft?' said Helen.

'No. Our catches are still mostly herring, tons and tons of them, we used to feed Britain. There are also cod and whiting in quantity.' Catesby smiled. 'But our favourite treat was Cromer crab. For special occasions, my mother would manage to buy them live.' He pointed to the boats in the harbour. 'And that's how the fishermen here sell their seafood catches. Cooking them poses an interesting problem. How do you kill a crab? If you whack them with a hammer, you splinter the shell into the meat.'

'How did your mother do it?'

'She just threw them live into a big pot of boiling water. For a couple of minutes, you would hear them trying to crawl out of the pot – and, occasionally, you would see a claw push its way past the lid.'

'Did it upset you?'

'Not as much as it should have.'

'I don't have any children,' said Helen.

'Would you like to?'

'I don't think that I would be a very good mother.' She smiled. 'I certainly wouldn't have any qualms about boiling crabs or other crustaceans alive in front of the kids. In any case, I'm sure they don't feel pain in the same way that humans do.' She paused. 'And what if they did? We paid for them and they're our food. If you keep trying to sidestep cruelty, you're never going to have much pleasure.'

For a second Catesby was consumed by a dark desire to pull up her skirt and have her right there in the open air. Her evil was contagious.

'What are you thinking?' she said.

'I'm wondering what's going to be on the menu.'

Her strong acrobatic arm pulled Catesby close to her. 'Let's go and see.'

It was the first time that Catesby had seen Henri Déricourt since early 1944 – and, once again, he was outclassed by the debonair glamour of the stunt pilot. Catesby's pride at cutting a bit of a dash in his Oxford bags and tweed jacket was immediately crushed. Déricourt was wearing jodhpurs, elegant brown leather riding boots and a beige turtleneck jumper. He looked like a model who had stepped straight out of *Horse and Hound* – but in an outfit that was not particularly appropriate for the centre of Marseille.

'Captain Catesby,' exclaimed Déricourt. 'What an honour to have you join us.' He extracted a bottle of champagne from an ice bucket and filled a glass for Helen. 'And yourself?'

'Thank you,' said Catesby.

'I sense that you think my attire is a bit odd.'

'You don't look as if you've been flying.'

'Only over a few jumps. I have been riding with a friend at Borély Racecourse. He breeds thoroughbreds, but now wants to get into harness racing.'

'Is that where the horse pulls a two-wheeled cart with a driver?'

'That's the one.' Déricourt smiled. 'My friend wants to know if I would like to train to be a harness-racing driver. The idea is tempting.'

'I certainly would like to,' said Helen. 'Other countries allow women to compete as drivers, but not France. I might be able to dress up as a man as I have small tits.'

Catesby sipped his champagne and savoured the thought of transcribing this conversation, and the day's earlier events, for a report to Henry Bone. The ladies in the typing pool would need to be reminded that gossiping about the document would be a violation of the Official Secrets Act.

'You would make a superb harness driver even if you had enormous tits,' said Déricourt, 'but I love them the way they are, firm scrumptious apples.'

'What do you think of them, Captain Catesby?' said Helen.

'I was thinking of ordering lunch.'

For some reason, his reply provoked a burst of laughter from the couple.

Their table was in a private dining room. The decor was minimal and tasteful. The designer wanted nothing to detract from the views. Its glass walls overlooked the harbour. The chef himself came in to announce the day's menu options. He wore a light-beige silk scarf over a dark-blue tunic. The scarf complemented Déricourt's jumper. 'If you're not having shellfish,' said the chef, 'may I recommend the turbot? One of our fishermen caught one last night that weighed twenty kilos, a beauty and so fresh.'

'Are we agreed?' said Déricourt.

They were – and it wasn't a mistake. The thick slices of turbot were perfectly cooked, the skin lightly seared, and served with pancetta, artichokes and emulsified bouillon. When asked about the wine, Catesby suggested a bottle of Château La Coste Rosé and the chef vigorously nodded his approval. You didn't need to be Master of Wine to work that one out. The La Coste was the obvious accompaniment to such a fish dish.

It was the perfect lunch – not only as a gourmet meal, but also in allowing Catesby to forget temporarily the situation he had been landed in. As he washed down the last of the turbot with a slug of the excellent rosé, reality returned. He was sharing the table with a dangerous femme fatale and a man who, Catesby was almost certain, had betrayed members of the Resistance to the Gestapo. And the whole thing was taking place in a glass box in the full light of day. So different from the clandestine *treffs* of divided Berlin. Catesby imagined that photographs of himself dining with the traitor Déricourt – and his dangerous honeytrap woman – would soon be winging their way to Washington, Moscow and, worst of all, his wife's MI5 desk in London. He wondered if that was why Déricourt had chosen a restaurant with glass walls overlooking a busy harbour.

'Would you like coffee and brandy?' said Déricourt.

'Just brandy.'

'Otherwise,' laughed Helen, 'we know what will happen.'

Déricourt began speaking English. 'It's great to see you again, Guillaume – I mean William.' He pronounced it 'Ouiyum', but his accent was a lot better than it had been in 1944 – even if it sounded slightly American.

'I suppose I should apologise,' said Catesby, pleased that the lie came so easily to his lips. It didn't matter if Déricourt knew he was lying, it was all part of the game.

'I think that we should get the rhinoceros out of the room.'

Catesby didn't bother to correct the mangled metaphor.

'I don't blame you for what you said about me in 1948 – and I accept your apology.'

'Are you sure you know what my apology is for?'

'My lawyer had a copy of your statement.'

Catesby smiled. They were exchanging lies, but the lies didn't much change the truth. Catesby had never hidden the fact that he thought Déricourt a traitor, but he had made no official statement. When Déricourt was put on trial for treason, Catesby had offered to go to France as a witness for the prosecution, but his offer was turned down. He sensed that some in SIS were not happy about his being refused permission to give evidence – and that a lot of shit was flying around in places far above his pay grade. Catesby later learned that a former high-ranking SOE officer had testified at Déricourt's trial. His testimony, *in camera*, had cleared Déricourt. The former officer claimed that London had learned of Déricourt's meetings with the Germans and had encouraged them. Catesby suspected that the officer in question had also mentioned Catesby's suspicions – and rubbished them.

A waiter arrived with the coffee and brandy and rescued Catesby from having to comment about a statement that he had never made. Déricourt regarded Catesby with the look of an older brother, one full of fond concern for an inexperienced sibling who had been led down the wrong path. 'She was,' said Déricourt, 'a very beautiful and persuasive woman. She led many other men astray, men who were older,

221

experienced and worldly wise.' He was talking about Marie, Catesby's French radio operator turned lover.

Catesby knew that he had to play along with Déricourt's act – and that there was some truth in his comments about Marie. For some reason she had hated Déricourt with a mad passion – and would have disembowelled him gladly with a Fairbairn–Sykes commando knife and then paraded his heart on the point of the blade. Did he know something about her that she never wanted revealed? But that aside, Marie's case against Déricourt was convincing. She knew that in the 1930s he had formed a close friendship with a French-speaking German. Later, when that German became head of the Gestapo in Paris, Déricourt renewed the association. In Catesby's view, reinforced by Marie, Déricourt then duped his SOE controller into believing that he was using his Gestapo pal – and other Germans – to pass on false information. Catesby despised the senior SOE officer who had been taken in by Déricourt – and then went to Paris to rescue him from being executed for treason. Déricourt's line was that you needed to pass on some true information to the Germans to keep their confidence. Sure, that info would lead to a Resistance network or two being betrayed and its members executed – but they were pawns being sacrificed for the greater good. Déricourt's drug of choice wasn't alcohol or sex or opium – it was the thrill of pure evil.

After the long awkward silence that followed Catesby's sham apology, Déricourt returned to speaking French. 'I wouldn't blame you if you never forgave me. I don't think I will ever forgive myself.'

Catesby's first impulse was to throw his brandy in Déricourt's face, but something in the Frenchman's voice gave him pause. It was hard to fake such sincerity. He drank the brandy instead.

'We did trick the Germans into thinking the allied invasion was going to be in the Pas-de-Calais,' continued Déricourt. 'How many tens of thousands of lives did that save?'

Catesby now wanted to puke up the brandy. Déricourt had trumpeted the Pas-de-Calais line for far too long. It was his theme tune.

'I can see,' said the Frenchman, 'that talking about it makes you uncomfortable. I think I should order another round of brandies.'

'I'll do it,' said Helen.

Catesby intuited that she was looking for an excuse to leave the two of them alone.

'I am someone,' began Déricourt, 'who lives only to take risks. Otherwise, I could not endure the sheer boredom of life.'

For the first time, Catesby believed what he was saying.

'I think that you, William, are a bit the same – but you won't admit it. You were very brave in the war, don't deny it. But you could only justify the thrill you felt in battle or jumping out of planes, by telling yourself that it was for a noble purpose. I do not need a noble purpose to enjoy risk.'

Catesby laughed. 'Thank you for looking into both our souls.'

'Ah, there is something else that I must never forget. Despite your Belgian mother, you are an Englishman. Your policemen don't carry guns, but why do you need policemen at all? Every Englishman has a policeman inside his head.'

'I could show you a number of English heads totally lacking a member of the constabulary.'

'I fear that once again I am talking out of my buttocks.'

'But we do form queues.'

'Indeed, you even did that at Dunkirk waiting to board the ships.'

'How do you know?'

'I flew over the beaches.'

'Did you?'

'You always doubt me, William. True, I wasn't in the air force. I was flying as a civilian pilot dropping supplies to French soldiers.'

'Apologies again, Henri.'

'I would love to take you on a flying trip. In fact, I would love to teach you to fly.'

'Is that why you invited me to lunch?'

'Not entirely, there are other reasons.'

'Helen is taking her time.'

'Maybe she's gone to powder her nose. You never let me finish what I'm saying.'

Catesby suppressed a self-satisfied smile. He loved winding Déricourt up. 'It's a bad habit. Please go on.'

'Helen has told me all about you. She knows that writing a book about the Resistance is a cover story and that you are still working for British intelligence. She does not, however, know what your real mission is. I would speculate that it may have something to do with the communist-led dock strikes. I am sure that London would like some warning if France is about to become part of the Soviet Bloc. If so, may I pass on a piece of intelligence for your bosses?'

'Please do.'

'There is no fucking chance of France going communist.'

'My bosses will be relieved.'

'As you know from your experiences in the Limousin, the French Communist Party can't even decide whether to have croissants or brioche for breakfast.'

Catesby wanted to add that the communist-led Maquis were the most effective fighters in the Resistance, but he didn't want to stop Déricourt's flow.

'But who knows? There might be other items on your agenda – and, if so, I should be able to provide some interesting intelligence.'

'Why would you want to help us?'

'Because Britain helped me – and trusted me too. When I escaped to England in 1942, I was recruited by the Secret Intelligence Service – the very same organisation of which you are still a serving officer.' Déricourt laughed. 'But they took me on first.'

Catesby was tempted to add that SIS had also played a role in saving Déricourt from being executed for treason.

'And, of course William, I love and respect you as a person even if the feeling isn't completely reciprocal.' Déricourt gave Catesby a searching look. 'We were once colleagues in battle – and the time may soon come when we will again be on the same side. There are strange patterns emerging. Navigating the world of secrets is like flying in a thick fog. You must always trust your instruments more than your instincts.'

'What if your instruments aren't working?'

'That is where we are now – but my last compass reading suggested we are heading for a landing field on which we can replenish ourselves with the fuel of mutual advantage.'

Helen returned, followed by a waiter bearing more coffee and brandy. He looked back at Déricourt and his mission in Marseille became clear. Thank you, Henry Bone.

Stanhope Gardens, London: March 1950

Catesby's recall to England was shorter than he would have liked, but it was still most welcome. The journey to London began at Marseille Saint-Charles railway station and lasted twenty-four hours. From Paris, Henry Bone and most other SIS gents usually booked a sleeping car on the Night Ferry, whose first-class carriages were loaded onto a train ferry. The journey from Gare du Nord to London Victoria took eleven hours and you arrived in London at nine in the morning, well rested and fit for the new day. But Catesby preferred travelling as a foot passenger on an ordinary ferry from Calais. If it was fine, he loved to see the morning sun slanting across the chalk cliffs of Dover. Crossing the Channel was an emotional experience. On his second deployment to France in 1943, Catesby had been placed in a rear-facing seat in an RAF Lysander. He had cried as he'd watched the English coast receding, knowing it was a sight he might never see again. He still felt ashamed that Marie had seen his tears.

It was late morning when Catesby found the key to the Stanhope Garden flat in its far-too-obvious hiding place. Anyone who knew that the two adult residents were intelligence officers who often dealt with top-secret files would have been appalled. Catesby let himself in. As he shut the door behind him and put his bag down, he closed his eyes with a sense of bliss. He was home and safe – but he wasn't alone. The sound was coming from the sitting room. Who was it? He knew Frances was at work. Had she hired a cleaner? The door into the entrance hall opened. It was Frances.

'You gave me a start,' he said. 'I thought you'd be at work.'

'I wanted to be here to welcome you back.'

'You are looking lovely. Is that a new dress?'

'No.'

'Are the twins home?'

'No, they're at nursery.'

A second later, the dress was up and around Frances's hips. Catesby was breathless with desire. He leaned into her while she undid his belt and pushed his trousers down. Her tongue was deep inside his mouth. He was soon inside her, and they didn't stop making love even when the letter box rattled with new post. Afterwards, still entwined, they stumbled onto a sofa.

'You didn't even take your hat off,' said Frances.

He flung it into a corner. 'I've missed you.'

'And you found me.'

'And I'll find you again this evening.'

'Why not this afternoon?'

'Of course, I love you so much.'

'And now the postman knows too.'

'Do you think he was peeping through the flap?'

'You can't see past the box. I've checked.'

'So you were planning this?'

'You started it – I was going to make a cup of tea.'

Catesby licked her thigh. 'You are delicious.'

They finally made their way into the kitchen, and Frances put the kettle on. Mad passion had given way to the soothing rituals of domesticity. Catesby loved it all. 'I really am going to quit this time. I'll stay home and look after the kids so you can concentrate on becoming head of MI5.'

'Your girlfriend has lovely legs.'

The statement came like a bolt into Catesby's newly tranquil sky. He suspected that Frances had seen a photograph of their having lunch in the glass-walled restaurant overlooking the harbour. 'The other man is her boyfriend. He's a Frenchman I met during the war.'

'There's no one else in the photo. It's of her entering your flat on the Rue des Frères Pecchini.'

227

It was the last thing that Catesby wanted – both professionally and personally.

'She came to my place, on behest of her boyfriend – a former member of the Resistance – to invite me to lunch with the pair of them. It was a great restaurant, and I would love to take you there some time.'

Frances replied with a knowing smile.

'How much more do you know – or how much more can you tell me?'

Frances poured the tea. 'Would you like a biscuit?'

'No thanks.'

'I suspect that my boss, who would love to get in my knickers, passed the photos on to stir up trouble between us. I haven't seen the file on the lady in question, but she seems to be a person of some interest to the Secret Intelligence Service as well as ourselves. She is, I believe, the errant wife of a rising diplomat.'

'I keep no secrets from you, Frances – official or otherwise – so I will spill all the beans.' Catesby recounted the whole story – with the exception of the scene in the shower, which he hoped to re-enact with her. 'Any idea, by the way, who snapped the photos and passed them on?'

'No one told me, but I suspect they were DST.'

Catesby knew that the DST, Direction de la Surveillance du Territoire, the French equivalent of MI5, disliked MI6 poking its nose around in France. 'They probably put a tail on the consul's wife – and a photo of her visiting me was a trouble-making diamond too good not to pass on.' Catesby paused. 'Shit – and they're probably keeping me under surveillance as well.'

'You need to convince them they're wasting their time.'

'Have you got any friends in DST?'

'Only Raymond – whom we both met at the *Quatorze Juillet* party.'

'You hit it off.'

'He struck me as very nice and innocent.'

'A bit naïve for an intelligence officer.'

'He visited me last time he was in London – with a present.'

'Underwear?'

'No, he's too innocent for that. It was a box of *À la Mère de Famille* chocolates – which I've already finished.'

'I hope he's innocent enough to tell me what DST is up to in Marseille.'

'Raymond won't be with them much longer. He's leaving the service to become a ski instructor in the winter and a diving instructor in the summer.'

'It sounds like sweet, innocent Raymond is a risktaker who doesn't find life in DST exciting enough.' Catesby wanted to introduce him to Helen and Déricourt.

Broadway Buildings, London: March 1950

The disguise and wardrobe people had provided Catesby with a naval officer's uniform and a fake beard so that he could go to the SIS HQ without compromising his cover as a disgraced officer turned writer. He removed the beard as soon as he entered the Director's office and was immediately subjected to what sounded like a dressing-down.

'A number of issues,' began C, 'have arisen out of your undercover deployment in Marseille. And at least one allied intelligence service believes you are a card-carrying communist inciting the Marseille dockworkers to revolution.'

Something in C's demeanour suggested to Catesby that he might believe it too.

'Would you like to comment?'

'The job of an undercover intelligence officer,' said Catesby, 'is not just to observe from the sidelines, but to infiltrate the groups he is observing. On no occasion did I incite.'

The Director took a piece of paper out of a folder. 'But you seem to have formed some very close friendships – and to have taken part in a number of demonstrations that turned violent.' C saw that Catesby was about to speak and put his hand up. 'I appreciate that an undercover officer's role often involves showing sympathy for the target group that he is infiltrating – but there are reports that you went beyond that. Apparently, you encouraged a member of your family to follow you to Marseille and join the French Communist Party.'

'My cousin, Jack Catesby, did so without any encouragement from myself.'

C glanced at the paper from the file. 'And your cousin is now living with the widow of the union leader who led the dock strikes.'

'I would, sir, like to point out that the union leader in question was murdered by the mafia – which brings up some alarming issues.'

'I don't believe there is any evidence of that.' C shuffled the papers again. 'He was killed in a hit-and-run – and, despite an ongoing investigation, the police have not been able to track down the driver in question.'

'If I may say so, sir, you do not seem to be referring to any of the reports I sent from Marseille.'

The Director frowned and sorted through a file. 'Yes, here they are.'

'Marseille, as I pointed out,' said Catesby, 'is not Tunbridge Wells. The hit-and-run was not the first killing of a union activist attributable to the mafia – and nor was it the last.'

'May I,' said Henry Bone, 'intervene?'

For a few seconds C remained stony-faced; then he gave a reluctant nod.

'I think,' said Bone, 'it would be both enlightening and useful for Mr Catesby to know the provenance of the report you were quoting from at the beginning of this interview.'

The Director suddenly looked very weary, as if longing for retirement and a rough shoot with his favourite gundog. He finally sighed, 'Bloody Washington, of course.'

Bone looked at Catesby. 'And who is CIA head of station in Marseille?'

'Lester Roach.'

'And why,' continued Bone, 'would Mr Roach be painting such a picture of you for his bosses in Washington?'

C interrupted. 'I think, Commander Bone, that we have now passed into the world of pure surmise and speculation. An American colleague, a rather learned one, would say that you've been "looking-glassed" – a rather nice expression.'

'May I ask, sir,' said Bone, 'if you would consider Lester Roach a valuable ally in our struggle to preserve what we hold dearest?'

The Director looked past Catesby towards the John Atkinson Grimshaw painting of the Glasgow docks that was still hanging on his office wall. 'I love my country – and I don't want gangsters gunning down trade unionists and protestors on the streets of Britain.'

Bone shot Catesby a look of relief. They had gained an important ally, albeit a reluctant one. The next stage could begin.

The Director breathed a weary sigh. The meeting was over.

As they walked down the corridor, Bone spoke to Catesby in a low voice. 'If you haven't already twigged, William, Benedictine's hint that Lester Roach paid the mafia to take out your friend Marcel was a hundred per cent true gen.'

'And what should I do about it?'

'Revenge is a dish best served cold – and without fingerprints.'

Scotland Yard, London: March 1950

Catesby had forsaken his naval uniform for his visit to the cop shop. If anyone saw him summoned for a little chat with the police, it would reinforce his cover story rather than cast doubt on it. And, as soon as he was led into the interview room, he felt that he himself was a suspect. The two uniformed senior police officers seated at the table regarded him as something the cat had dragged in. The Chief Constable sat with his hands folded on a chair in the corner. As Catesby took the suspect's chair, one of the policemen on the opposite side of the table laid out a notepad and the other started quizzing him on the Marseille mafia. The cops didn't seem particularly interested in how the mobsters had put down the dock strikes, rather they wanted information about their rackets and their identities. Catesby related what he knew about their Corsican and Italian connections and the bars and nightclubs where they hung out. One of the cops asked, 'Have you seen any drug dealing?'

'No, but I've heard about it. By the way, Marseille slang for drugs is *le kif*.'

'I'll keep that in mind.'

Catesby looked from one policeman to the other. 'Would that I could tell you more.'

The Chief Constable spoke for the first time. 'I can sum up our concern about Marseille in one word: heroin. Mafia-manufactured heroin from Marseille has been flowing into Britain since the 1930s, but in the last year the amount seized was five times what it was before the war. It's not just a matter of creating new addicts, but of funding crime in general. It is the most alarming development I have seen during my thirty years in the police service.'

Catesby felt compelled to nod. The top cop was a powerful figure.

'I visited Marseille last November to express our concerns about French heroin on the streets of London. While I was there I had a meeting with a municipal police director – who I later discovered, much to my annoyance, was not the highest-ranking officer in Marseille.' The Chief Constable looked at Catesby. 'I wish that I had known you were there at the time. I could have used your knowledge of the city. Our Paris embassy provided me with an interpreter–translator – who confided that I was being given the run-around by the Marseille coppers. When I started talking tough, the so-called municipal police director came back with an English copy of the ICPO Charter.'

Catesby looked blank.

'The ICPO is a bullshit talking shop called the International Criminal Police Organisation – we and the French are members. The Marseille cop waved a page at me entitled Article 3 that prohibits foreign police intervention in political matters.' The Chief Constable laughed. 'I'm sure my French colleague didn't need an interpreter to translate my response: *What the fuck has heroin smuggling to do with political matters!*'

The Chief Constable's two junior colleagues were vigorously nodding. Catesby guessed they were not Francophiles.

'Well, to be fair, my French colleague did take me to a very posh lunch in a restaurant overlooking a harbour full of fishing boats – and, although I'm normally a beer drinker, we had some very nice wine.' The Chief Constable gave Catesby a penetrating stare. 'I haven't been fully briefed about your role in Marseille – and I can understand the need for secrecy – but your help could be very valuable to Scotland Yard. There's something big going on – and I think it might involve the Yanks.' The Chief Constable gave a sly smile. 'And that's why, when the Marseille police director came up with that line about "political matters", he wasn't telling a complete porky.'

Broadway Buildings, London: March 1950

As Catesby strode towards the Broadway Buildings HQ, he was once again a bearded naval officer. In case he was confronted by a drunk ex-sailor who wanted a sing-along, he had memorised the chorus of the Royal Navy marching song:

Heart of Oak are our ships,
Jolly Tars are our men,
We always are ready: Steady, boys, Steady!

Steady indeed, thought Catesby. Bone had summoned him to a meeting at which a cabinet minister would be present.

When Catesby entered the Director's office he was still in character. Henry Bone mimed a disguise-removing gesture and Catesby unhooked the thick black beard. He then plumped it up on his forearm, stroked it and said, 'Miaow.' The cabinet minister was the only one who laughed.

C began the meeting with a brief summary of what had been happening in Marseille and of Catesby's role as intelligence officer operating under deep cover. Catesby noticed there were no files or pads for taking notes. There would be no minutes, this was an off-the-record meeting – totally deniable. As the Director finished his introductory remarks, he nodded at Catesby, who in turn looked at a stony-faced Henry Bone. After a few seconds, Bone gave a barely perceptible wink. It was a signal to hold nothing back.

'The dock strikes in Marseille,' said Catesby, 'were not broken up by the French police or by strike-breaking unions. They were put down by murderous thugs hired by the mafia – and by actual murders carried out by the mafia itself.'

'Is there any truth,' said the cabinet minister, 'to rumours of American involvement?'

'It is a matter of public record that Force Ouvrière, the union that tried unsuccessfully to break the strikes, is in receipt of American funding.'

'But what about American collusion with the Marseille mafia?'

Catesby looked at the minister. Part of him wanted to shout, *Why the fuck don't you ask your American counterpart?* But instead, he smiled and said, 'I can't provide you with a copy of a signed cheque from the US Treasury made out to the head of the mafia – but collusion would be in the interests of both parties.'

'Being in government means having to make difficult decisions – and weighing advantages against disadvantages. Accepting the American loan in 1945 was not an easy decision – and there were strings attached. But without borrowed American money, we would never have been able to establish the National Health Service.'

Catesby knew that the minister had carefully weighed his words. The underlying message was, *You're walking a tightrope, sunshine – and don't blame HM's government if it all goes pear-shaped.*

'But what happened on the docks of Marseille was a disgrace.' The minister's voice was loud as he hammered the table. 'And it will never happen here.'

Catesby waited for more, but there wasn't any more. The signal, however, had been given.

As the meeting broke up, the Labour minister took Catesby aside. 'I remember you from the '45 election. The seat you were contesting was totally unwinnable, but I'm sure you haven't lost your values.' The minister was a big man who spoke with a working-class accent. 'We need more people like you in the security services. Things are looking grim: in the February election, our majority was reduced to five. I can't see how we can hold on.' The minister put a big avuncular hand on Catesby's shoulder. 'But the legacy we leave behind must be protected, *till we have . . .*'

'*Built Jerusalem.*'

The minister laughed. 'You ought to hear me belting it out at confer-ence. Look after yourself, lad.'

The word reverberated in Catesby's mind as he hummed the tune.

Bring me my Chariot of fire!
I will not cease from Mental Fight,
Nor shall my Sword sleep in my hand.
Till we have built Jerusalem,
In England's green and pleasant Land.

As Catesby was about to leave Broadway Buildings, once more bearded and impeccably naval, he heard someone shout, 'William.' It was Henry Bone. This time the use of his first name sounded more parental than friendly.

'How are you feeling?' said Bone.

'I wish I'd stayed in Berlin handing out D-Marks to double-dipping spivs like everyone else on my pay grade, but you tricked me into spying on people fighting against war and injustice. Can I have my soul back now?'

'Not quite yet, but I think you will find your future duties in Marseille more compatible with your conscience.'

'By which you mean murdering someone?'

'Murder is a harsh word – particularly on a nice spring day when the daffodils are out. Fancy a walk through St James's?'

Catesby nodded and, remembering that Bone had been a naval officer and Olympic yachtsman, began to hum 'Heart of Oak'.

In a barely audible voice, Bone sang back. '*We still make them fear and we still make them flee, And drub them ashore as we drub them at sea.*'

'To what extent does the cabinet minister agree?'

'Totally. The message was just do it and keep us out of it.'

'And C?'

'He's going to retire next year – and he's more worried about his per-sonal life than deniable ops.'

There were rumours that the Director was having an affair with his secretary and that his wife was an invalid. Catesby felt sorry for everyone concerned and dismissed the rumours whenever he heard them. 'It sounds,' said Catesby, 'that we are all alone in this business.'

'Not quite all alone. In a few days we'll be meeting an old admirer of yours from SOE.'

'I don't have any old admirers.'

'On the contrary, Vera was very fond of you.'

Catesby's face lit up. 'Vera Atkins?'

'None other.'

Catesby, like everyone else in SOE, had been in awe of Vera Atkins. She had been in charge of recruiting agents and deploying them to Occupied France. Vera was tall and elegant and, although Romanian-born, spoke English without a trace of an accent. 'She's in London?' said Catesby.

'No, we'll be meeting her in Paris the day after tomorrow.'

Paris: March 1950

Catesby's final night in Stanhope Gardens was a passionate one. After the twins were bathed and put to bed, the wine and kisses began. He wondered if Frances's passion was partly because she knew he would be seeing Vera Atkins the next day in Paris. Was his wife competing? Catesby had reassured her – with some honesty – that he regarded Vera as a big sister and that he wouldn't venture beyond a brief peck on the cheek. He had, however, noticed that other women were often envious of Vera's effortless sophistication and beauty. She had been SOE's film star in residence. To prove that she wasn't jealous, Frances had insisted that Catesby dress smartly for the Paris rendezvous. She got out the stylish French suit Catesby had worn when travelling undercover in Occupied France. The suits had, in fact, been Vera's idea – and although they had French designer labels, they were fakes cut by an East End tailor.

The meeting with Vera Atkins and Henry Bone took place in the Latin Quarter safe house. As soon as Catesby entered the room, Vera embraced him – then stepped back and said, 'And I am so pleased that you are wearing your French suit.'

'Would you like to check the turn-ups to make sure I haven't dropped any incriminating British coins or ticket stubs into them?'

'I'll do a full security check after Commander Bone has finished his briefing.'

'By the way,' said Bone, 'we can talk freely here. Since our last meeting, the room has been submitted to thorough debugging.'

Catesby frowned. He didn't trust debugging procedures.

'Please sit down,' said Bone as he hovered over a small stove. 'Coffee, tea – brandy?'

'I'll have tea,' said Atkins.

'I'd better stick to tea too,' said Catesby with reluctance.

As Bone was making the tea, he looked at Catesby. 'I was just telling Vera that your old friend Lester may be a harbinger of the future. The CIA's crusade against communism recognises no limits. They do deals and form alliances with drug dealers, mafia and criminals of all description. Nothing or no one is more evil than communism.' Bone began to pour the tea. 'I hope you don't mind Earl Grey. It's the only one I've got.' He looked at Vera. 'Would you like it with a slice of lemon? One never serves Earl Grey with milk.'

'That would be lovely,' she said. 'Only the English drink tea with milk.'

'Miss Atkins,' said Catesby, 'always warned of that giveaway prior to deployment.'

'Before we imported tea from the colonies,' said Bone, 'we only drank beer – gallons of it. You can see proof of it in medieval architecture. Gargoyles spreading their buttocks to defecate on the faithful as they enter the church for Mass.'

Bone seemed to be in a bit of a strange mood. Catesby wondered if he'd been drinking.

'Back to the American fight against communism,' said Bone. 'There is a lot of money to be made in that global battle.' Bone looked at Vera. 'And you have something to report on that.'

'It all began nine months ago when I received a package in the post – which had been sent from Monte Carlo. When I opened it, I discovered a jade pendant necklace – and a note written in English. Of course, I was more suspicious than flattered. It was a very elegant necklace, tasteful and understated – the sort of jewellery I would have chosen for myself. I still hadn't read the note but suspected that it was a present from someone who knew my tastes – which made me even more suspicious and a little frightened. I wondered if the necklace had been treated with nerve gas or some other chemical weapon. I carried it to a sink with a pair of tongs and covered it with hot water. And now, for the note. I held it up to a bright light with the still-wet tongs, which made some of the ink run. The paper looked normal – and I couldn't recall a case of anyone being poisoned by notepaper even if they had to swallow it.'

'Your precautions,' said Henry Bone, 'are to be admired.'

'Thank you.' Vera reached in her handbag. 'I have, by the way, brought the note with me. So, if it has been treated with a slow-acting chemical-biological agent and I end up collapsing, please do not come anywhere near my body.'

'If,' said Bone, 'we follow your instructions, it will not be because we lack care and compassion.'

'Thank you. By the way, the actual words of the note did make me want to vomit, but that was an emotional rather than a physical response. Bear with me, I will read them now. *My most darling respected Vera, the enclosed is a token of my high esteem for you. Jade is the perfect jewel for you. Jade represents virtue, wisdom, justice, sincerity and truth. You are all those things. It breaks my heart that you hate and despise me. I know that you accused me of treason and that you wanted to testify against me. Had I been found guilty, I am sure that you would have volunteered to have been a member of the firing squad . . .'* Vera paused and smiled at Catesby and Bone. 'Those words,' she said, 'were more perceptive than he realised. But I must go on . . . *As they put me against the wall, I would have refused a blindfold and my eyes would have regarded you with love and longing as you pulled the trigger. I was never a traitor – to you, to France, to the brave men and women who fought beside me. Sadly, I doubt that I can ever make you think otherwise. But I hope that, regardless of what you believe about my past, I can prove to you that I am a good man now. Evil is still with us, and I want you to help me fight and defeat it. My ways of fighting evil were not straightforward in the war, and they are not straightforward now – but I will keep no secrets from you, I will reveal everything. I want you to trust me. I hope that you will contact me – and I would love to see you again. You can write to me at the following post restante address or leave a message at one of the telephone numbers.'* Vera folded the note and put it back in her handbag. 'I wasn't sure why Henri Déricourt wanted to re-establish contact – but it wasn't an opportunity to be missed.'

'And,' said Henry Bone, 'you didn't inform anyone that you were going to France to meet him?'

'Of course not. I was embarking on a secret mission.' She reached into her handbag again and took out a dark object the size of a person's palm. 'It was remiss of me not to have handed in the .25 calibre Beretta that I was issued during the war. The arms instructor who taught me how to use it said it was ideal for concealed carry and self-defence, but that to kill someone with it you needed to get up close and put at least two rounds in their head.' She smiled and looked at Catesby and Bone. 'And I was more than confident that I would be able to do so.'

'Why did you want to kill him?' said Bone.

'I wanted to avenge those he betrayed – particularly Noor, Diana Rowden and the other women. They were all so beautiful, so young and so brave.'

For a minute, silence engulfed the room.

'But I didn't do it. I didn't pull the trigger when I had the chance, because I realised that a live Déricourt could be a useful tool for leading us to others – all my instincts as an intelligence officer were humming. You don't kill a traitor who can still be useful.'

Bone steepled his fingers and nodded sagely. Catesby still wasn't sure what was going on.

'But,' said Vera, 'there were still a few things I wanted to check out before I went to France. By the way,' – she went back into her handbag – 'the jade necklace still hasn't proved lethal.' She lifted it up for the others to see. 'I wasn't going to wear it, but I wanted to find out more about it, so I paid a visit to Albert. Remember him?'

Bone looked at Catesby. 'Albert was the jeweller that SOE commissioned to design necklaces and bracelets with hidden compartments for cyanide pills. There were cufflink equivalents. Were you issued a set?'

'No.'

'Albert,' Vera continued, 'confirmed there were no suicide pills hidden in the necklace, but he did find it an interesting piece of jewellery and asked if he could pass it on to a friend who specialised in jade. I agreed.

A few days later, I went back to Albert, who reported that his friend had been utterly fascinated by it. He said that it was both rare and valuable – worth around three hundred pounds, about half my annual salary when I was in SOE – and that the jade was from Laos and seemed to have been crafted by a tribal artisan rather than a jeweller with modern tools.' Vera smiled. 'Now, I really wanted to find out what Déricourt was up to.'

Bone looked at Catesby. 'How does this tie in with your own recent meeting with him?'

'All that nonsense about loving us and wanting to convince us of his innocence is just an excuse to make contact – and I don't think he's so dim-witted he expects us to buy it. He wants to use us, and he thinks he can get our help by offering a tempting prize.'

'If you don't mind, Commander Bone,' said Vera, 'I would like to report on *my* meeting with Henri Déricourt.'

'Apologies for the interruption.'

'Knowing Henri's tastes, and after his expensive gift, I assumed that our rendezvous would be a very flash and expensive restaurant – probably in Paris. And afterwards, he would invite me into bed – and I would agree and, when he was naked, I would stick my gun between his eyes and tell him to reveal what he was up to or I'd pull the trigger. And then I would shoot him, regardless of what he revealed. But it didn't turn out that way. Our meeting place was in Tulette, the sleepiest of towns in *la France profonde*. It's about eighty miles north of Marseille, but I got off the train at Orange, only fourteen miles away, and completed the journey by taxi.' Vera smiled. 'I am sure the taxi driver was utterly confused as to why someone like me was going to Tulette. In any case, I met up with Déricourt in a clean and modest hotel restaurant in the middle of the village. Most of the clientele appeared to be herders or farmers or retired herders and farmers. Not the most romantic of venues, nor was romance on the agenda, as Déricourt had turned up with a woman. And actually, I felt a sense of relief. I wouldn't have got away with killing Déricourt, after disgusting foreplay, in a hotel room in Paris or anywhere else. I would have been tracked down and arrested

– and he isn't worth it. If I ever kill him . . .' – she glanced at Catesby – 'or get someone else to kill him, it will have to be an undercover job with no fingerprints.'

'Was this woman,' said Catesby, 'Helen, the estranged wife of the Marseille consul?'

'Indeed. She wasn't just open about her misdeeds, she bragged about them. I got the impression that Déricourt wanted to rein her in. After a simple supper with house wine, she seemed to pick up a signal that Déricourt wanted to have a word with me alone over the coffee and brandy. As soon as she was gone, he said, "She has her uses, but I'm still not sure what they are." It was an awful thing to say about any woman, even a bitch from hell, but I felt he was trying to distance himself from her to get closer to me. I didn't know then – and I still don't know now – what game he was playing. I asked him what he was doing for a living. He said that he was still flying – and that was the only thing he could do for a living. Then he added, "But I'm flying some difficult routes – which is why I need help from people like you and William Catesby." "Why us?" I said, and he answered, "Because you have influence in very high places in the world of British intelligence – and you can help get my flights the cover and free passage that they need."' Vera went silent and sipped her Earl Grey.

Catesby was tempted to ask for a brandy, but it was only eleven in the morning.

'You seem,' said Bone, 'to have gone reticent, Miss Atkins.'

'I was thinking that I should have shot him the next day. We were driving alone down a lonely country road. I could have said I was dying for a pee and then shot him as soon as he stopped the car. I could have hidden the body somehow and made my way back to England – but I took the bait.'

'Can you explicate?'

'Of course. I had asked Déricourt the obvious question the previous evening: "If we help you with your flights, what are you going to give us in return." He then put on a smug smile and handed me the photographs.

I didn't have a chance to have a close look at them, because Helen the acrobat swung back in. The timing was probably choreographed because it gave Déricourt an excuse to gather up the photos, denying me a closer examination. I was furious and he knew it – so he selected one to give me as a present.' She reached into her handbag, took out a photo the size of a playing card and handed it to Bone. It was faded monochrome with frayed edges. The only Westerner in the snap was dressed in US Army field clothing. He was surrounded by tribesmen in native dress, all of whom were a head shorter.

Bone passed the photo to Catesby, who nodded.

'A rather nice snap of Lester Roach,' he said. 'I don't know the area very well, so I can't identify his local friends.'

'I've checked with an ethnologist,' said Vera. 'They are Hmong tribesmen. The Hmong are a fairly widespread ethnic group, but the dress of the ones in the photo suggests they are *Hmong Daw* – a group that settled in central Laos in the seventeenth century. They are, apparently, fierce warriors.'

'And from the look of your jade necklace,' said Catesby, 'skilled artisans.'

'And textile designers too,' said Vera. 'But I believe the Laotian Hmong have other means to support themselves.'

'Déricourt,' said Catesby, 'is an entrepreneur too. He reckons that intelligence on Lester is a commodity he can sell.'

'Can you recount what happened next?' said Bone.

'At breakfast the next morning, Déricourt offered me a lift and I accepted. When I got into his car, which looked like the same Traction Avant that he drove around in during the war – without, of course, ever being stopped by the Gestapo or the *collabo* police – he started off in what seemed to be the wrong direction. "Aren't you taking me to the train station in Orange?" I said. "No," he replied. "I'm taking you to Calais." "That's a very long drive," I said. "We're not driving," he said. What we shortly arrived at wasn't an airfield, just a pasture with some grazing goats. The plane was a stubby one with two engines. Déricourt described it as a "Twin Beech" that could go "anywhere that had a flat bit the length of two football fields". We boarded the plane. It was a very bumpy take-off, the goats scattered and then we were flying. "This," said Déricourt, "is how I make a living." "But not by flying from Tulette to Calais?" "Usually not," he said. "Flying to Southeast Asia is much longer and more complicated. Sometimes I have to make five or six stops to refuel." "Is it dangerous?" I said. "Very much so – but I love danger. It keeps me alive." I laughed and said, "But sometimes danger has the opposite result." "Indeed," he smirked, "but it is usually the fools who die." If I had known how to land a plane, I would have taken out my gun and put an end to him then and there. Instead, I asked, "Is Lester Roach a fool?" "That," he said, "remains to be seen." The entire flight lasted just over two hours. At one point, he let me take over the steering. I was reluctant to play around and just kept on a steady course. Meanwhile, Déricourt took out a camera and began taking snaps of me at the controls. I was livid, but in no position to grab the camera and take out the film. I wondered if he – duplicitous shit that he is – was going to pass on the photos of me to Lester or anyone else. In the end, he didn't fly me all the way to Calais, but landed in a water meadow near Étaples. We were met by a driver in a van who refuelled the plane before giving me a lift to Calais – but, before we set off, he helped Déricourt transfer a number of boxes from the plane to the van.' Vera gave a grim smile. 'I also noticed that the van contained several boxes overflowing with soft toys.'

Catesby frowned with disgust as he recited: '*Baa, baa, black sheep, have you any drugs? Yes, sir, yes, sir, Three bags full . . .*'.

Vera smiled and continued. 'It was a brief drive to Calais for me and the teddy bear drug mules, and the driver remained silent for the most part. He was a dark man in his twenties who looked Arabic or Turkish. His few words of French were heavily accented – but he did wish me a fond and charming *Bon Voyage*. And that is all that I have to report on the ongoing mystery of Henri Déricourt.'

Bone spoke in a quiet voice. 'I was recently asked to deputise for the Director at an important and confidential meeting at the Treasury. The

Chief Secretary was very concerned about the effect of organised crime on the world economy. He read out some startling statistics. Criminal profits laundered through the banking system each year amount to between four and five per cent of annual global economic production – enough to fully fund the NHS for the next twenty-five years. But the amount of money actually laundered may be only a small percentage of illegal earnings. Gangsters don't pay taxes and money from crime corrupts an entire society. Politicians and bankers are bought; the police are paid to turn their backs on criminal activities – and the legitimate economy suffers from underinvestment and the need to pay out protection money. Afterwards, the Chief Secretary had a brief quiet word with me. "What is the CIA up to?" he said. "They seem to be recruiting gangsters from all over Asia, Latin America – and they now have a foothold in France. Too close to home." Then he strode off without saying more.' Bone looked at Vera and Catesby. 'You two need to get down and dirty.'

Marseille: April 1950

The first step in getting down and dirty was contacting Raymond – who Catesby regarded as one of the least down and dirty types he had ever met. But appearances can be deceiving. Raymond had been recruited into the DST because of his heroism and skill as a member of the Resistance. He had blown up railway lines, helped allied airmen escape over the Pyrenees – and used his skills as a diver to blow up German vessels in Marseille harbour. As Frances had mentioned, Raymond had recently resigned from the DST and relocated to Marseille to set up a diving school. It was easy for Catesby to track him down when he returned to the city. On Bone's advice, Vera Atkins had accompanied Catesby back to Marseille as his minder. Catesby would need someone to help him out of the gutter when he got too down and dirty to look after himself.

As soon as they met, Catesby could see that Raymond was utterly charmed by Vera – and it wasn't just his background as an intelligence officer that made him want to know more about her. As Vera recounted her gilded youth on a Romanian country estate, her passion for skiing, her time studying at the Sorbonne, her daring rescue of Polish code-breakers and their replica Enigma machines at the beginning of the war, her own narrow escape from the Netherlands and her heartbreaking love affair with a British pilot who was killed in the Battle of Crete, Catesby could see that Raymond was falling head over heels in love. He was becoming Vera's lapdog.

The besotted Frenchman looked at Catesby. 'You seem always, my friend, to be in the company of elegant and fascinating women. How is your beautiful wife Frances? We worked briefly together.'

'She is well and still speaks fondly of you.'

'You must give her my fondest regards.' Raymond then looked at Vera and back to Catesby. 'I have heard, Monsieur Catesby, that you have left the intelligence service and are now in Marseille to research a book on the Resistance.'

'It is,' interrupted Vera, 'a complicated situation.'

Raymond no longer looked the naïve innocent that Catesby thought him to be. 'I am sure it is. Can you tell me more?'

'Mr Catesby has come to Marseille on a secret mission.'

'How interesting,' said Raymond, new love brimming in his eyes. 'I promise that I won't breathe a word about it.'

'We have come to you,' implored Vera, 'because we need your help.' She decided to test the water before going further. 'Are you familiar with Henri Déricourt?'

'You mean the traitor? He should have been executed.'

Vera reached forward and touched Raymond's hand. 'I fully agree. After the war, I interviewed two captured German intelligence officers who admitted that Déricourt had been working for them – and there was other evidence too.'

'And now,' said Raymond, 'the traitor is in Marseille. There were those of us in DST who wanted to investigate Déricourt and find out what he was up to, but we were told that it would not be in France's national interest.' Raymond looked at Catesby. 'If, Monsieur Catesby, your mission in Marseille has anything to do with bringing Déricourt to justice, you will have my full support.'

Vera smiled at Raymond. 'Your help would be warmly appreciated.'

'I am at your service.'

Marseille: April 1950

Something had snapped in Catesby, and he no longer gave a fuck about his undercover job in Marseille. He was having a breakdown and it wasn't a fake one. His memories of the war had begun to haunt him more and more. Not just the atrocities and the horrors of close battle, but the stolen moments of intense pleasure as well. His most erotic experience ever was sex with Marie just hours after she had killed a German soldier with a deep downward stab through his throat. Her stockings and underwear – on which she had wiped her hands – were stained with the soldier's blood. Catesby still desired her – or any woman – and no longer wanted to be a faithful husband as the lonely hell of being an undercover spy began to suffocate him. He was drinking too much and had started frequenting nightclubs.

Afterwards, Catesby said it was Albert Camus's fault he got beaten up. He hadn't really been chatting up the beautiful young Algerian girl, even if it looked that way. They had been talking about Camus's latest novel, *The Plague* – as it turned out that the girl was from Oran, the Algerian port city where the novel was set. Catesby tried to show off by quoting passages from Camus. The girl kept clapping her hands and shouting, 'More, more!' Catesby was too drunk to realise she was being sarcastic. The boyfriend finally decided enough was enough – and his punches were not at all sarcastic. Catesby used his usual barroom-brawl tactic to avoid punches and take down his opponent. He dived for a leg tackle. The idea was to get the other person on the ground and in a leg scissors so he could pummel his face and choke him. But on this occasion, his opponent had very strong legs and didn't go down when tackled. The boyfriend was a professional football player.

Catesby's face ended up a bloody mess that required a number of stitches, and he suffered a broken wrist when he fell awkwardly to the floor. The football player had a lot of friends in the nightclub, all of whom told the police that the drunken Catesby had started the brawl. Consequently, he spent the night in a police cell, but was released in the morning and no charges were pressed. Normally, a nightclub punch-up would have received zero or very little press coverage, but the fact that one of those involved was a sacked British secret intelligence officer going to seed in Marseille was too good to resist. There was even a mention in a national newspaper.

Two days later, Vera Atkins turned up at Catesby's flat. At first, he wouldn't let her in, but she refused to go away.

'I'm going through a bad phase,' said Catesby. 'I don't want you to see me like this.'

'I'll make some coffee, if you don't mind.'

'Not for me, thanks.'

'You do look the worse for wear.'

Catesby smiled. 'You should see the other guy.'

'I have – and there's not a mark on him. By coincidence, he's been taking diving lessons from Raymond. Don't be ashamed of coming off second best. He's a very fit and fine athlete.' Vera continued making the coffee. 'Are you sure you wouldn't like a cup?'

'No, it makes me too excited.'

Vera looked at Catesby's bruised face and smiled. 'So I've heard. Tea?'

'Yes please – but don't look at me.'

'What, William, do you really want?'

'I've had enough. I want out – and, if I become a complete degenerate and drink myself to death, it's my choice. I don't want anyone to interfere.'

'But, William, I will always be there to support you because you are one of mine.'

Marseille: April 1950

Things got ugly – very ugly – a week later. The football player who had beaten up Catesby turned up dead in the street outside his home. Two bullets to the head. Catesby, of course, was an immediate suspect. The police searched his flat and confiscated his pistol – which, fortunately, was a much smaller calibre than the murder weapon. The cops didn't arrest him, but he was called in for some heavy questioning. Ironically, having a gun in his flat probably helped save Catesby from arrest. If he had been the killer, he would surely have got rid of it – even if it was the wrong calibre. Or were the police concentrating on convincing suspects, with no time to waste on a drunken Brit.

Rumours were rife in Marseille. Was there a connection between Catesby and the mafia? Had the hit been carried out in revenge for his being thumped in the nightclub – a nightclub, of course, that was part of the mafia's turf? The press refrained from speculating, but Catesby was now a toxic presence on the streets of Marseille. If he went into a bar or café, the place emptied. Jack alone wanted to help, but when he approached his cousin, Catesby told him to fuck off. And then things got even worse. Raymond was found dead in the lagoon where he gave his diving lessons. He had been drowned. The two students he had been instructing had disappeared.

Catesby was full of self-contempt for ever having taken on the Marseille job. He wanted to go back to 1945, when he could have kissed war and violence goodbye and become a modern languages teacher – or a Lowestoft trawler man or a tractor driver or a bin man. He longed for the earth and sea of Suffolk.

The evening after Raymond's death, Vera turned up at Catesby's flat again. She sat in an armchair by an open window with a worn lace curtain. The setting sun cast a lacy pattern of shadows across her face. As Catesby regarded Vera, the fine shadows seemed to form a veil of remembrance. She looked far older, and her face was deeply etched with lines of sorrow. 'It isn't the first time,' she said, 'that I've made a mistake and sent people to their death.' Her voice was choked by tears and grief.

'Why are you blaming yourself?' said Catesby.

'Because their deaths are my fault. I decided that your cover story needed considerable enhancement. I wanted to portray you as a former intelligence officer who had gone completely off the rails – and was ripe for rescuing, dare I say, by the Forces of Darkness. I didn't realise that you really, sincerely, wanted out.'

Catesby reached out and touched her hand. 'It's not your fault. Don't blame yourself.'

Vera shook her head. 'I went to Raymond and explained my plan. He arranged the fight in the nightclub.' She gave a forlorn smile. 'If you hadn't started talking to the football player's girlfriend, she would have flirted with you. It was a piece of theatre that I was arranging – and now two lovely men are dead.'

Catesby's face had turned hard. 'Their deaths need avenging. I want back in – we must carry on.' He fetched a bottle and poured them both a glass of brandy. He raised his glass. 'I will always be one of yours.'

Vera sipped her brandy, then spoke in a voice that was heavy with grief. 'Can I stay with you tonight?'

'Yes.'

They lay together, like spoons, fully clothed on the bed. Catesby put his uninjured arm around Vera. She took his hand in hers and held it tight. Catesby felt the damp of tears falling on his hand and arm. His own tears were falling on her shoulder. They lay entwined in silence and sorrow until sleep, and its temporary healing, overcame them. The morning was another day – and Catesby's breakdown was a thing of the past.

Marseille: May 1950

Catesby had frequent clandestine meetings with Vera, who was choreographing his decline and fall in such a way that it would attract a rescue from the right quarters. A degenerate and desperate former intelligence officer was a fine bait to dangle – and one that soon attracted takers. One of the first was an Eastern European agent, probably from Bulgaria, who offered him money and a holiday in a Black Sea resort. Catesby swore at the agent and tried to headbutt him, but the man ducked and ran off. There were no further approaches from the East Bloc. The next offer of help came from a Jesuit priest who was looking after down-and-outs. Catesby saw him off more gently. But still no bites from the big fish.

The next chapter in Catesby's decline into degeneracy was eviction from his flat in the Rue des Frères Pecchini for non-payment of rent and keeping the neighbours awake by singing *J'attendrai* at the top of his lungs when drunk at three in the morning. Catesby had, however, insisted that Vera reimburse his former landlady for the outstanding rent. It was, he explained, part of his inherent working-class decency.

Catesby's new flat was in the rundown Panier district, rented from a slum landlord with mafia connections. The previous resident, a prostitute, had recently died of tuberculosis. Catesby wondered if the woman had been Serge's model. The flat was, in fact, not far from Serge's studio – which was very convenient for he needed an excuse to see Serge and Huong and just turning up would have looked too suspicious. Having seen Catesby stumbling around the neighbourhood, it wasn't long before the artist invited him round for a drink. Serge's note explained that he had seen an article about Catesby in *La Marseillaise* and that he was very welcome to pop by, 'Provided,' he wrote, 'you don't start a fight.'

Catesby turned up half-drunk – and was soon totally drunk, which made his act more convincing. Huong regarded him with disgust. Meanwhile, Catesby prepared to unload his bombshell – but the preliminaries came first. He picked up his glass of pastis and looked back at Huong. 'The problem with socialism, Madame Huong, is there's no money in it for a poor kid like me from the Lowestoft docks. When I was at Cambridge, all the Communist Party members were toffs rolling in inherited wealth.'

Huong looked at him with utter contempt. Catesby feared a lethal karate chop was on the way.

Serge tried to defuse things with a calming smile. 'William is going through a rough patch – and he's a victim of the very capitalism that he seems to be defending.'

'I'm not defending it for everyone, I'm defending it for *me*!' shouted Catesby. He was letting the alcohol take control. 'I need money to get me out of the gutter.' He cradled his drink and laughed. 'And I think I know where to find it.'

'What about your book?' said Serge.

'Fuck the book! I'm never going to finish it and I've already spent the advance. I think I'm going to be sick.'

'Let's get you to a toilet.'

'No, it's starting to go away. Wait a second.'

'Would you like to lie down?'

Catesby shook his head. 'No, I want to find my old pal Lester.' He looked at Huong. 'You remember him, Lester Roach, you met him in Vietnam in '45 after he was parachuted in with an OSS team.' Catesby grinned. 'I think he fancies you.'

Huong's face was a blank.

'Perhaps you'll have the chance to be reacquainted,' Catesby went on. 'He's doing some big shit here in Marseille – splashing a lot of money around.' He suppressed a smile. He could tell he had hooked his audience. 'I was hoping Lester might offer me a job. We served together in France before he redeployed to Southeast Asia. I showed him the ropes, so he owes me a favour.'

'What exactly is he doing in Marseille?' said Serge.

Catesby shook his head so hard he spilled his drink. 'That's top secret, Serge – but I'm surprised you haven't guessed?'

'Guessed what?'

'It's fucking obvious, isn't it?' Catesby grinned at Serge. 'Stop playing the naïf.'

Serge gave a slight nod.

'You know exactly who paid the mafia to take out those dockworkers.' Catesby suddenly leaned forward.

Huong quickly left the room and returned with a bowl.

It was a well-needed vomit. Catesby looked at the milky green in the bowl. *What a waste of pastis.* He wiped his lips, looked at Huong and said, 'Thank you – and apologies for being a drunken bore. I'd better be going.' Catesby stood up. He was unsteady on his feet and nearly fell over.

'I'll help you get back,' said Serge.

'No thanks, I can manage.' Catesby turned when he got to the door. 'You know, the funny thing about my old pal Lester . . .' He lowered his voice. 'Who do you think Jack's got to thank for his little tableau of domestic bliss? It's not just the Lord who works in mysterious ways.'

The fresh air revived Catesby somewhat as he walked back to his flat. He suddenly felt much less drunk. The bait had been laid. 'Maybe I should take up acting.'

La Corniche, Marseille: May 1950

Catesby kept up his cover by walking the seafront promenades with a half-empty litre bottle of red wine in his hand and singing 'La Mer':

La mer
Les a bercés
Le long des golfes clairs
Et d'une chanson d'amour . . .

He now had a beard and his hair had grown long and untidy. Catesby began to fear he was turning into a local figure of fun. He also began to fear that Lester wasn't going to take the bait – in fact, he was on the verge of letting London know that the plan had failed. But would they even reply? Had SIS decided to abandon Catesby and let him spend the rest of his days singing *chanson* classics on the Marseille seafront and drinking himself to death on cheap red wine? He felt very lonely. There was no contact with Frances, and Vera had gone back to England.

The fact that it was a beautiful warm afternoon made Catesby even more depressed. The Mediterranean was still a bit cold, and he wondered if a swim would cheer him up – if it didn't, he could keep on swimming and swimming. There were worse ways to go, but Catesby took another swig of wine instead. At first, when he saw the black Traction Avant pull up next to him, he wondered if some well-wisher had stopped to give the singer-tramp a few francs – but then he saw Déricourt at the steering wheel and Helen beside him. 'Get in, Captain Catesby,' said Déricourt. Catesby tumbled into the rear seat behind Helen. 'Poor William,' she said. 'You do look the worse for wear.'

'Don't worry, my darling,' said Déricourt. 'Our dear Guillaume is putting on an act – and he is an excellent actor.'

Catesby rolled his eyes. Had his cover story been blown? Or did acting out a false cover make him more attractive bait than the story itself? He lived in a wilderness of mirrors.

'I think,' said Helen, 'we should take him back to ours so he can have a wash and a tidy-up.'

Catesby wondered if she wanted to soap his back again.

'No, Helen, I think it's best we take him to see Lester just as he is.'

The half-empty bottle wasn't a prop, it contained real wine. Catesby put the bottle to his lips and took a long slug.

Déricourt glanced at him in the rear-view mirror. 'I am pleased that you are still playing your role.'

Catesby wanted to whack him over the head with the now-empty bottle.

Déricourt must have noticed. 'Don't let Lester know you're pretending. If you do, the whole thing will be off.'

Catesby threw the bottle out of the car window.

7th arrondissement, Marseille: May 1950

'It appears,' said Lester as he scrutinised the scruffy Catesby, 'that the Russians are no longer looking after you. Or are you spending all your Soviet emoluments on booze?'

'Sadly, the Russians have never paid me a single rouble.'

'What a sly answer, Captain Catesby. As a former intelligence officer, you know perfectly well that the Sovs never pay spies – even stupid ones – with the worthless rouble.'

Catesby smiled. 'I was just testing you, Lester.'

'I'm pleased we're still on first-name terms. Do you prefer Bill or Willy?'

'William would be fine.'

'I greatly admired you during the war. You did a fantastic job running around with those guerrillas in the hills of Limousin – pity most of them were commies. I often wondered if you'd gone native and become one of them.'

'I struggled with the local dialect, as you may have noticed.'

'But what about their politics?'

'It wasn't my concern. My business was supplying and advising them.'

'But you reported back to London on their communist allegiances – and the implications for moulding the Resistance into a united movement.'

'You've caught me out, Lester.' Catesby still wore a smile, but the comment suggested that someone in London had passed on information about him to the Americans. Or maybe Lester was just making it up.

'And you must have been a sympathiser, because you stood as a Communist Party candidate when you returned to England for the 1945 election.'

'I was a Labour Party candidate.'

'I didn't know there was a difference.'

Lester's tedious right-wing American humour was grinding on Catesby's nerves, but he didn't want to get drawn into an argument. The situation reminded Catesby of the words of another American who had been a colleague of Lester's: 'Never get in a wrestling match with a hog. You both get covered in shit and the hog loves it.' But the hog wasn't going to give up.

'Come on, William,' said Lester, 'give us a lecture on the hidden differences between Democratic Socialism and Soviet Communism.'

Catesby remained silent.

'What's the matter? Cat got your tongue?' Lester smiled. 'Don't worry. I couldn't answer that question either.'

Catesby stared out the bay window across the sparkling sea to the Isles of Frioul and Château d'If. 'Stunning view – and what a nice place you've got here.'

'Unfortunately, the US taxpayer isn't footing the whole bill.' Lester studied Catesby again. 'And what gutter are you living in at the moment?'

'A wet one in Le Panier, but it should be dry in the summer.'

'A slum full of commies, artists and whores. All good customers.'

Catesby noticed that Lester's conversation was seeded with clues, probably intentional – and that he was playing to an audience. The others present were Déricourt, Helen and Kit Fournier – all obediently listening to the saloon bar bore grill his victim.

'I think,' said Lester, 'it is time to toast our being reunited with William Catesby. He certainly looks thirsty – and I am too. We need a magnum, not an ordinary bottle.'

Catesby was left alone with Déricourt while the others got the champagne and glasses. Catesby was thinking of asking what Lester might be planning, but Déricourt put a finger to his lips and pointed to a light fixture before Catesby could speak. The room was bugged.

Lester returned with the champagne and handed the magnum bottle to Déricourt. 'Popping the cork requires a genuine Frenchman.' A second later the cork took flight and hit the ceiling next to the hidden microphone. Lester was amused: 'You are a devil, Henri.' Lester flourished the magnum around the room. 'Our friend William, like the others, went to Cambridge – so he must be a champagne socialist.'

'What others?' said Catesby with a teasing note in his voice.

'Hasn't your wife told you about the VENONA tapes?'

Catesby wasn't going to reply in a bugged room – or mention Frances at all.

'We've been warning British intelligence for over four years,' said Lester as he poured the champagne. 'Sov double agents aside, SIS is also the last chance saloon for stumbling drunks, cock-gobblers and crackpots having nervous breakdowns. Congratulations, William, for having legged it.' Lester tapped his glass and looked around the room. 'May I now propose a toast to William Catesby and whatever new future he chooses.'

There was a 'hear, hear' from Helen and a clinking of glasses followed by the guzzling of Bollinger.

'My first present for you, William, is a little vacation in a thirteenth-century French château with a genuine viscount to look after you.'

A bell labelled Xavier-Honoré rang in Catesby's brain. Another piece of the puzzle was slotting into place.

'The viscount looks forward to giving you fencing lessons – and there will be a quality lady barber to give you a good haircut and, to use the polite term, a back massage. I think a few days away from Marseille would be a good idea.'

Catesby decided to be a bit cagey. 'It sounds like you're trying to bribe me.'

Lester shrugged. 'We bribe everyone – but in your case it's also a gesture of appreciation for a comrade in arms. Shoulder to shoulder, we fought the good fight – and now Lady Freedom beckons that we fight for her again. But the choice is up to you, William. I don't want to have to ask Henri to drop you off back in the gutter – but, if that's what you want, have some more Bollinger before you go.' Lester refilled his glass.

'Look at me,' said Catesby holding out his torn and tattered jacket. 'I'm a victim of the capitalist system.'

The others laughed.

'I didn't mean that as a joke. I was born into a working-class family in Lowestoft. By sucking up to the system, I got into Cambridge – but left to fight in the War against Fascism. Not having any money or prospects, I was then herded into the Secret Intelligence Service.' Catesby gave a furtive glance at the hidden microphone. Washington would love it and then pass it on to London, but he had rehearsed his act and wasn't going to stop. 'I put up with it for a couple of years, but there's a limit: I wasn't going to spy on my fellow socialists and betray them to the State.'

Lester laughed. 'The best place to spy on your fellow socialists would have been within the SIS itself.'

Catesby suspected there was some truth to that, but he wasn't going to comment or suggest names under the looming hidden microphone.

'I'll give you a list later,' said Lester, 'the same list we've already sent to London, but which your bosses ignored.' Lester laughed again. 'Maybe because some of their own names are on it.'

Catesby knew that Lester was looking for ammunition to pass on to Washington to help justify his own activities.

'What have you got to say, William?' Lester wasn't letting up.

'At the moment, my life is shit and I want something better. When you're born into poverty, money and wealth has a strong appeal. That's why a lot of us turn to crime.'

'And the biggest crime of all is communism.'

Catesby felt that Lester was a talking puppet. When you pull a string, the same lines come out. But he had a job to do, so he wasn't going to counter by mentioning the slave trade, Indian famines – or Wall Street bankrolling the Nazis.

Lester gave a sly smile. 'What constitutes crime, by the way, is relative. Britain's wealth in the nineteenth century was largely based on exporting India-grown opium to China. If it hadn't been for the British Empire's drug dealing, the Industrial Revolution and global capitalism may never have taken off.' He raised his glass. 'Here's to the opium poppy!' Déricourt seconded the toast with enthusiasm and clinked glasses.

Catesby could see where things were going, but he had to play a subtle game. Too quick a conversion wouldn't be credible. 'I seem to be getting through this champagne.'

'Let me give you a refill. Are you with us, William?'

'I'm still a socialist . . . but I could use some money.'

'Let's have a chat.' Lester put an arm around Catesby and led him on to a terrace that was cool in the night air. The lights of ships entering and leaving the port punctuated the sea with red, green and white dots.

'How can I be of use?' said Catesby, trying to sound drunker than he was.

'It's what you Brits call the old boy network. You may deny being an old boy until the cows come to roost, but anyone with your background at Cambridge, in SOE and in SIS remains part of that network – even if you hand over secrets to Moscow. It may be regrettable, but it's true. You are one of the untouchables.'

Catesby now understood why Lester had led him onto the terrace. He was about to say things he didn't want picked up by the secret microphone.

'If you don't already know – but I expect you do – Guy Burgess, Donald Maclean, Anthony Blunt and, last but by far not least, Kim Philby are commie double agents.' Lester laughed. 'But you ought to stay in with Philby, he's well on his way to becoming Director of SIS. And Blunt is Princess Elizabeth's cousin. What a bunch you are! The names I've mentioned are not the only ones in SIS working for Moscow, but the more serious problem is that almost everyone will cover up for them.'

Catesby felt that he was being sucked under in a whirlpool full of shit, with currents coming from both sides of the Atlantic. 'You still haven't told me how I can be of use.'

'I want you to help Henri Déricourt. He needs an assistant who is cunning, ruthless – and also British.'

Catesby smiled. 'You could have just said British.'

'Perfidious Albion? You guys ought to take that as a compliment.'

'Thank you.'

'Do you speak Arabic, Persian, Pashto, Hindi or Burmese?'

'Hardly a word.'

'Doesn't matter. Just shout at the natives in an officer-class English accent. Déricourt's flight path passes over ten different countries – most of which were at one time ruled by the British. But if you're blown off course and you have to land in a communist country, just say you're a friend of Kim Philby. The only local words you need to know are those for aviation fuel – but Henri says that normal gasoline works fine. How do you feel about this?'

'I'll feel even better about it after more champagne.'

'We'll open up another magnum. Henri's girlfriend really puts it back too. Any moral compunctions?'

'About champagne?'

'Don't be an asshole, William. I mean about trafficking heroin.'

'I'll try not to think about the implications.'

'Well, here's one implication. If it wasn't for harvesting opium, a lot of Hmong villagers in Laos would die of starvation. It's their main – and sometimes only – source of income. It's a very valuable crop. That's why they call the region the Golden Triangle and not the Shit Circle. We pay them well – and give them guns too. The Hmong are fierce warriors. We're training a guerrilla army to fight the Pathet Lao, who have sided with Ho Chi Minh.' Lester smiled. 'You'll love it, William. It's just like fighting with the Resistance in Occupied France all over again.'

There were differences, but Catesby wasn't going to argue the point.

'Are you going to join us, William?'

'Fuck you.'

'Fine, I'll get Henri to give you a lift back to the gutter.'

Catesby stared hard into the night. He was tempted to fake a few tears, but that would be going too far.

'I'll get Henri now.'

'Wait,' said Catesby. 'It's only a few plane rides?'

'Not much more.'

'And I can get out at any time I want?'

Lester shook his head. 'That might be asking too much.'

'I need some money up front.'

'How much?'

Catesby named a sum that was just over a month's salary for an SIS officer.

Lester gave a low whistle. 'You drive a hard bargain, partner – but you'll have it in the morning.'

'Okay then, I'm on board – where's the champagne?'

'You've made the right choice, William – and the champagne is on the way. After we clean you up a bit, you'll be flying to Laos in a week's time to start picking up this year's harvest – and it's a big one.'

When they got back to the main room, things were kicking off. Helen was standing on her head. Her skirt was all askew, revealing her thighs and knickers, and, for modesty's sake, Déricourt was trying to cover her up – and she wasn't happy about it. 'Don't do that, Henri, you're making me lose my balance.'

At first, Catesby couldn't work out why Helen was doing upside down acrobatics. Was it to show off her athleticism and her perfect legs? But then he remembered that drinking a pint of beer while standing on her head was her party trick. There wasn't any beer, but she was managing it with a large glass of champagne. As she finally drained the glass, beautiful thighs revealed, there was clapping and a cheer of *bravo*.

'The important thing,' she said, looking at Catesby, 'is to suck and swallow every drop.'

It was two o'clock in the morning when Déricourt gave Catesby a lift back to his hovel in Le Panier. As they drove along the empty streets, Helen put a hand behind the passenger seat and stroked Catesby's calf. The angle made it impossible for her to reach higher up. When they arrived at Catesby's place, Déricourt said, 'I'll be driving you to the Château de Saint-Breuil. Can you be ready to clear off the day after tomorrow?'

'No problem.'

As Déricourt motored away, Catesby noticed that Helen was staring in the opposite direction. No fond goodbye smile. He was off the agenda.

Sainte-Baume, Provençe: May 1950

The slum landlord demanded an extra month's rent for Catesby moving out without notice. He was surprised when Catesby paid up without a quibble. Likewise, the neighbours were surprised when they saw the down-and-out English drunkard load his belongings into a gleaming car with the help of the suave and smart-suited Déricourt. The local rumour mills would be churning.

Catesby knew it was going to be a long drive, but the countryside was stunningly beautiful and, kissed by the Mediterranean, greener than the land further inland. 'I love it here,' said Déricourt. 'The Sainte-Baume massif is like a lush oasis in the heart of Provençe.'

'How far is the château?'

'About two hours. Helen is already there. She loves the place, and I dropped her there yesterday.'

An hour later, Déricourt drove past a sheer rock wall that reached hundreds of feet into the sky. There were religious-looking buildings at the base of the cliff and much decor around what seemed to be the entrance to a cave. 'This is where Mary Magdalene came to do penance for the last forty years of her life.'

'What was she doing penance for?'

'They say she committed sexual sins.'

'If she were still alive, I'd ask you to drop me off.'

'But Helen's alive. Would you like her to join you?'

Catesby didn't answer.

'Helen loves sex – and nothing is out of bounds – but you must be careful around her; she can turn violent and kill.'

And wouldn't it be lovely, thought Catesby, if you were her victim. He pictured Helen sticking a dagger through one of Déricourt's deceitful eyes and into the back of his brain – and then twisting it.

Château de Saint-Breuil, Côte d'Azur: May 1950

It was a no-nonsense château. It hadn't been built for comfort, but for war. It was a fortress. Two enormous towers guarded the entrance gate, and the castle walls were protected by turrets with arrow slits. Considering the martial nature of the building, it was apt that Viscount Xavier-Honoré-Antoine de Saint-Breuil greeted Catesby with a sabre in his hand. The Viscount raised the sword in front of his face, before tilting it forward in salute. He then extended his free hand to shake hands with Catesby.

'I must apologise for my pursuit of you in the Pas-de-Calais,' said Xavier-Honoré. 'You must have wondered what was going on.'

'Indeed – but your driving skills were excellent.'

'Thank you. Driving is one of my talents. I was hoping to put you in a position where you would have had to bring your own car to a stop – and would not be able to escape.' The Viscount was smiling.

'Did you want to kill me?'

'No, absolutely not, I wanted to challenge you to duel – but the result would have been the same. My plan was to lead you at sword point to a secluded place where we could have duelled. I would, of course, have given you the choice of weapon: foil, épée or sabre.' The Viscount hefted the sword in his hand. 'I prefer the sabre because death is quicker. A puncture wound delivered by foil or épée can lead to a long painful death.'

Catesby stared at the weapon. 'Excuse my curiosity, but why did you want to challenge me to a duel to the death?'

'For the glory of France, of course.' Xavier-Honoré regarded Catesby with a cagey smile. 'My whole life has been devoted to the glory of France. In the 1930s I was a member of an organisation that was devoted to restoring France to her long-lost grandeur and majesty. Our goal was so important that, if necessary, we would resort to violence and underhand methods. During the Occupation there was a parting of the ways. Some of us wanted to form an alliance with the occupier to fight communism. Others, like me, wanted to do so from a France freed from foreign occupation. I became the leader of a Resistance group that was royalist and Roman Catholic.'

Catesby glanced at a looming guard tower and wondered if a crossbowman in a red-cross tunic was aiming at his heart.

'Shortly before your arrival in France,' continued the Viscount, 'I was contacted by a member of the secret organisation with which I had once been associated, who identified you as a danger to France. I have since discovered that that person had passed on false information either wittingly or unwittingly.'

Catesby remembered Frances telling him that Kim Philby was a chameleon who had posed as a friend of the far-right during the 1930s. He wondered if he had used an old *Action Française* contact to pass on info to the Viscount.

Xavier-Honoré touched the blade of his sabre. 'I was hoping to give you fencing lessons, but we have a dinner guest we would love you to meet. A royal princess.'

Pre-dinner drinks were served on a terrace, which turned out to be the roof of the château's dungeon. The princess would have been recognisable as a princess without introduction. She was wearing Lao traditional dress which also seemed to have a hint of fashion-house Paris – especially the high-heeled shoes – but the jewellery was definitely Lao. Catesby thought of the jade necklace that Déricourt had given to Vera. It was difficult not to take his eyes off the princess. Her gold blouse gleamed of real gold, and its red sash was a badge of royal office. Helen looked at her with an envy which seemed tinged with longing. He could see that she wanted to touch her, run her hands over her jewellery and unwind her hair.

When Catesby was introduced to the princess, she didn't extend her hand in greeting, but held her champagne flute against her midriff as if it were a shield against contact with a lesser being. Her French was as perfect and refined as her appearance. 'I believe,' she said, 'that you served in the war with Messieurs Déricourt and Roach.'

'That is true,' – Catesby hesitated over whether to address her as *madame* or *votre Altesse*, before choosing the latter – 'Your Highness.'

Xavier-Honoré sidled up to them and topped up their champagne flutes with Taittinger. 'Monsieur Catesby,' he said, 'will soon be visiting the Kingdom of Laos.'

'We need entrepreneurs,' said the princess, 'as much as we need soldiers. We are going through a difficult time – and it is important to help the mountain tribes who have so few resources to live on.'

Noblesse oblige, thought Catesby with a half-smile.

The meal began with lightly fried foie gras before moving on to braised sea bass. The Viscount kept apologising for serving a simple country meal. The main course was Limousin beef filet and garden vegetables. Catesby only had nibbles from the vast cheese board – and he was stuffed by the time the *vacherin glacé* arrived, trying just a mouthful of the rich creamy dessert. He was amazed by the women. They were slim and beautiful but shoved the food down with abandon. Helen seemed to get livelier with every mouthful. As she finished off the *vacherin glacé*, she asked Xavier-Honoré if he could put some swing music on the phonograph so that they could have a bit of a jive. The Viscount replied that his only records were classical music and patriotic songs. Just then the coffee and brandy were rolled out and he said they were welcome to listen to music in the sitting room.

As people began to leave the table, Helen came over to Catesby. She seemed a bit tiddly and confided in a whisper, 'What an utterly fascinating woman. I believe I'm falling in love.'

Catesby wanted to know more but felt Déricourt's hand on his elbow. 'Can you follow me into the library? We must look at some maps.'

It was an enormous room with towering shelves of books that needed dusting. As Déricourt laid out the maps, Catesby perused a shelf devoted to books in English. There weren't many, but they included Thomas De

Quincey's *Confessions of an English Opium-Eater*. Catesby wondered if it had been left behind by one of Déricourt's previous helpers. Another was a dog-eared copy of Dale Carnegie's *How to Win Friends and Influence People*. Catesby flipped to the title page and found an inscription: *Happy Birthday, Lester. Love, Mom.* Catesby repressed a smile and put the book back – and wondered why Lester had given it to Xavier-Honoré.

Meanwhile, Déricourt had finished laying out the maps. 'The shortest route between Marseille and Laos is ten thousand kilometres. The problem is that we would have to fly over three Soviet republics as well as Bulgaria and Yugoslavia. Lester says it's a pity you're not a Soviet double agent. You could have arranged refuelling stops in Armenia and Turkmenistan.'

'Maybe Washington would pay us to test Soviet air defences.' Catesby meant it as a joke, but he knew the Americans were probing them all the time, sometimes quite recklessly.

'The maximum range of the Beechcraft 18 is two thousand kilometres; that means at least four refuelling stops.'

'Have you ever managed the trip?' said Catesby.

'Not the direct route. That's why we need your help. The last time we tried it we were turned back by British fighter planes based at RAF Dhibban in Iraq. They escorted us back to the Turkish border – the Turks are friendlier.'

Catesby bent over the map and studied possible routes to Laos – and where London could help. The Marseille to Laos flight paths were littered with the remains of Britain's empire: Afghanistan, Pakistan, India, Nepal and Burma. It was a lot to pile on Henry Bone's plate, but he was sure that he had the cunning and diplomacy to deal with it.

'How soon can you arrange things?' said Déricourt.

'Two or three days.'

Marseille to Laos: June 1950

Catesby's telephone call to Henry Bone had been in the clear as encoding it would have been pointless. It was mostly a list of places where he hoped that help from His Majesty's Diplomatic Service would be forthcoming. Catesby then returned to the posh hotel where he was spending his final night in Marseille. He laid out everything he needed on the bed. He had managed to buy tropical gear including a sunhat and a mosquito net. Déricourt had given him a Smith and Wesson .32, which he placed next to the sunhat.

The following morning Catesby took a taxi to the airport, which stretched out next to the sea. He was surprised that Déricourt was flying so openly from a commercial airport. No covert take-off from a lumpy pasture for this part of the trip. A member of the runway staff escorted Catesby to the waiting plane. 'We can't just let the public walk around where planes are landing and taking off – even if they are sober.'

'Thank you for noticing.'

Catesby was surprised to see that Déricourt was not alone. Lester was with him, as well as three men in dark suits and dark glasses.

'The first leg,' said Lester, 'is a business trip to Italy. I'm going to be the co-pilot; you'll have to sit in the back with the gentlemen.'

As Catesby got in the passenger section, there was no exchange of smiles. Two of the men were chatting rapidly in Corsican, and Catesby could barely pick up a word. After a while, they shifted to Italian for the benefit of the third man, who didn't seem to be a Corsican-speaker. They seemed oblivious of Catesby – who, in turn, kept his eyes averted. He noticed, however, that all three men wore gold pinkie rings – one of which seemed set with a jade stone. So much for the virtue, justice and truth of jade.

'By the way,' called Lester from the cockpit, 'our destination in Italy is Matera, a beautiful city near the heel of the boot.'

'Flying time is about two and a half hours,' added Déricourt.

Lester turned to look at Catesby. 'You'll love Matera. It's an ancient hill town carved out of stone. The original inhabitants lived in caves – and some still do.'

The thought of meeting cavemen didn't particularly appeal to Catesby, but they would probably prove more agreeable than his present company. Meanwhile, he tried to eavesdrop on his fellow passengers' conversation. He struggled with Corsican but could pick up a few words of Italian. He twigged that they were talking about shared acquaintances, places and dates. The Italian sounded a bit on the defensive. After a while Catesby got bored and began to doze off. He found flying soporific. When he was fully awake again, they were over Italy and Lester was talking. 'I've asked Henri to do a few low-level passes of the town so you can have a look.'

Catesby had to admit that it was a spectacular sight. Beige stone bleached for centuries in the Mediterranean sun. Twisting pathways and ravines. The people moved slowly and surefooted – and none of them looked up at the noisy aircraft that was disturbing their late-morning peace.

'People have been living there for three thousand years,' said Lester.

'I bet they've got to know their neighbours.'

Lester was saying something to Déricourt in a low voice, which Catesby didn't pick up. Lester turned around again. 'We're going to land soon, not particularly near the town because there aren't many places flat enough. You'd better do up your seat belt because it's going to be a bumpy one.'

Three minutes later Déricourt began a rapid descent towards a landing strip which looked like an abandoned road. There was a decrepit lorry with an open cab towing a fuel bowser waiting for them. It was a very bumpy landing indeed, and Catesby feared the plane was going to somersault into a flaming wreck. Déricourt laughed and howled as he taxied the Beechcraft 18 to a halt. The lorry followed, and two leathery old men began refuelling the plane. Meanwhile, the two Corsicans and the Italian left the plane and began walking towards an approaching cloud of dust. A shiny black limousine emerged and stopped next to the disembarked passengers. Catesby watched with interest from the plane window. The only people in the limousine were the driver and a passenger in the back. Catesby wondered if they were disembarking a passenger or picking up a new one. The man in the back of the limousine got out and approached the other three. He was bald, fierce-looking and had the build of a light-heavyweight boxer. Like the others, he was wearing dark glasses and a black suit. An animated conversation began, mostly between the boxer type and the Italian plane passenger. The Corsicans were nodding. The bowser men had finished and were reeling up their hoses. For a few seconds Catesby could hear shouting from the men in suits. The shouting then died down and the Italian from the plane bent his head. One of the Corsicans took out a pistol and shot him in the back of the head – and then delivered a *coup de grâce* while his victim was lying twitching on the sun-scorched earth. One of the bowser men stopped curling up the hose, closed his eyes and made the sign of the cross.

Lester turned to Catesby. 'He was taking more than his share.'

The one that looked like a boxer then called out to the two bowser men. They went over to him, then picked up the body and carried it to the plane. Catesby guessed that the killer and the others were reluctant to get blood on their fine suits. And Déricourt didn't want to get blood in the passenger section of his plane. He told Catesby where to find a supply of towels. When the dead man's head was suitably wrapped, he was laid out on the floor between the seats. The bowser lorry was now a cloud of dust disappearing into the distance. The limousine followed in its wake.

The Beechcraft's twin engines rumbled into life and Déricourt aimed his plane down the dusty road, a road so straight it must, reasoned Catesby, be a Roman relic.

Lester turned around and called out, 'Has Montale got his seat belt on? We wouldn't want him to get beat up any worse than he is.'

One of the Corsicans laughed and replied in English, 'He's fine.'

When they were well out to sea, Déricourt cut the plane's speed and dropped to a low altitude. Following his instructions, Catesby and the Corsicans dropped open the passenger door-ramp behind the port wing. They then managed to slide Montale's body onto the ramp – the Corsicans careful not to get blood on their trousers. Déricourt banked the plane to the left and Montale became part of the sea. Catesby threw the bloodied towels out after him and they pulled the door-ramp back up into a closed position.

'Mission accomplished,' said Lester.

The next leg of the flight was much longer. When they reached land, the countryside looked reddish brown and very craggy. Catesby didn't find the landscape inviting and wondered how the peasants scraped a living. The plane finally descended onto a flat brown plateau – a much easier landing than the one near Matera.

'Great country,' said Lester. 'Big and empty.'

A tanker lorry, with what looked like military markings, was there to greet them. The men tending it were young and looked like soldiers. The other vehicle was big with a sky-blue body and a white roof – obviously American. 'That's a Buick,' said Lester. 'My mother's boyfriend has one.'

For a second, Catesby wondered what planet he had landed on. The fact that Lester had a mother was in itself astonishing – but one with a boyfriend was beyond comprehension.

Two men got out of the Buick. One was in Western clothes, a light-grey summer suit, and the other, a man with fabulous moustaches, was wearing baggy traditional-looking clothes. Catesby guessed they were in Turkey. The Corsicans had gathered up their bags and were greeted warmly and driven off in the Buick. When the refuelling was finished, the plane was readied for take-off. 'That's the easy part,' said Lester, 'they love us.'

The next refuelling stop was in the middle of fucking nowhere. It wasn't difficult to find a place to land. The desert countryside was firm and totally flat as far as the eye could see. It was a place that Catesby had chosen.

Lester looked around and shook his head. 'It looks, William, like we are totally fucked – and it's your fault.'

'Don't worry. They'll be here soon.'

'Soon enough, I hope, to identify our bodies before the vultures have picked them clean. The sun is already going down. I think your fellow Brits realise that you've been kicked out of the club in disgrace. The only ones your guys look after are the commies.'

Part of Catesby feared there may be some truth in Lester's words. Had Henry Bone's confidential whispers that Catesby was on a hush-hush mission and needed assistance been ignored? At least, thought Catesby with a grim smile, if worse comes to worst and no one turns up, it will convince Lester that my cover story as a sacked and disgraced intelligence officer was true.

Half an hour later, Lester turned to Déricourt. 'Have we got enough fuel to get someplace decent?'

'Just about.'

'I've got the cash for bribes if we need to deal with fucking officials. It's probably what we should have done in the first place.'

Just as Déricourt was about to start the engines, a speck of dust appeared on the horizon. The leading vehicle turned out to be a Bedford MW driven by a British officer wearing a red-and-white checked keffiyeh turban-style. It was followed by a Bedford OY tanker lorry. The officer, who wore the rank insignia of a major, greeted Catesby and the others: 'Welcome to the cradle of civilisation. It might not look like that here but wait until you fly over Baghdad and the rivers.' The major walked over to the Beechcraft 18, which he regarded fondly. 'Lovely aircraft,' he said. 'They can go anywhere. And so can this chap.' He thumped the bonnet of the Bedford MW. 'He doesn't have four-wheel drive, but he handles like a sportscar. It's an insult to call this brave fellow a "general purpose lorry". I had one that hauled my anti-tank gun all over the Western Desert.' He then said something in Arabic to the two men in the tanker lorry and they began to fill up the plane. When the job was finished, the major turned to Catesby. 'Sorry we were late. Had a spot of bother with the locals. I don't think we are going to be welcome in Iraq for much longer. And, by the way, this refuelling never happened.'

As the British officer and the tanker lorry drove off there was a conversation between Lester and Déricourt. Lester came over to Catesby. 'Henri says he's not doing a long night flight even on amphetamines. Let's get out the sleeping bags and the Jim Beam.'

The next refuelling stop was much easier and not at all covert – and dead simple to find. Déricourt just had to guide his Beechcraft towards the tall distillation towers of an enormous oil refinery on the Persian Gulf. As the aircraft descended, Catesby could see that all the tanker ships taking on newly refined oil were British flagged. The airfield was right next to the refinery, which looked like a medium-sized industrial city. As soon as they landed, Catesby was greeted by a 'former' SIS colleague with whom he had trained and a big fuel lorry with ANGLO-IRANIAN OIL COMPANY written on the side. The SIS officer shook hands with Lester and said, 'I hope the money's in the bank.'

'The Anglo-Iranian account?'

'That's the one – but it might not be for long. There's talk, as I'm sure you know, about Iran nationalising the oil industry.'

'I've heard rumours about that,' said Lester, 'from Kermit.'

Catesby felt uncomfortable about his colleague treating Lester as a fellow intelligence insider – and Lester, in turn, dropping the name of Kermit. Kermit Roosevelt was the grandson of US President Theodore Roosevelt and was regarded by many in the intelligence sector as a loose cannon eager to plot *coup d'états* to install any leader who was pro-American. Catesby hoped that his colleague's friendliness towards Lester was fabricated.

The first few hours of the next flight were passed in silence. Twenty-five hours of flying broken only by one night's poor sleep was taking its toll. Lester was the first to speak. 'The great thing about India is its long history of being a smuggling route – and since it got independence from you guys, the tradition has been revived. But the most dangerous bit is near the coast – which is why Henri is flying so low. We need to avoid getting picked up on radar.'

'Maybe,' said Catesby, 'he hasn't been flying low enough.' He was looking out the window, where two fighters with Indian Air Force markings were coming up fast behind them.

'Don't worry,' said Déricourt as he banked the plane sharply to the left, 'the only way to force an aircraft to land is to shoot it down. The other alternative is to follow it until it runs out of fuel – which will soon be a problem in our case. Fortunately, we're near the border. I am sure the pilots must be under orders not to create an international incident that could lead to war.'

The Indian Air Force planes became increasingly aggressive as Déricourt flew nearer and nearer the Pakistan border. One of them let off a burst of tracer fire across the Beechcraft's nose. The other played chicken with Déricourt, peeling off just seconds before a mutually fatal headbutt. And then, finally, it was all over. The Indian fighters wriggled their wings goodbye and flew off as Déricourt guided his plane into Pakistani airspace.

'Good riddance,' said Lester.

'We're running low on fuel,' said Déricourt.

'Can we make it to the next airfield?' said Lester.

'The next one is Jinnah International in Karachi – and, even if we could make it that far, it will be crawling with police and officials who'll want to know why we don't have a flight plan and clearance.'

'It sounds like we're fucked,' said Catesby.

'*Complètement foutus*,' echoed Déricourt.

'There must be a place where we can land down there,' said Lester.

There was little solid land below them. They were flying over the River Indus delta. There were no villages or towns to be seen. Just a pattern of islands covered in mangrove forests.

'The beaches look good,' said Déricourt. 'Probably our only hope since we're flying on empty.'

'Let's try it,' said Lester.

'It'll be a tricky landing. If the beach is too soft, we might end up with our nose in the sand and our rear end sticking upright. Not the worst thing imaginable provided we don't bend the prop blades. Fasten your seat belts and put your heads between your knees.'

'And kiss our asses goodbye,' laughed Lester.

Afterwards, even though both Lester and Catesby were patting his back, Déricourt still refused to call it a 'miracle landing'. 'I don't believe in miracles,' he said. 'Luck is a factor, but after that, it's sheer skill.' They were now out of the plane and walking along the beach. 'It is only a little firmer than I expected, but long and straight. On full power, we should be able to take off. No danger of a wreck if we don't, we just end up stranded.'

'But we haven't any fuel,' said Catesby.

'There is always fuel,' said Déricourt, pointing to a fishing boat in the offing. He took his shirt off and began waving madly.

Ten minutes later the fisherman, clad in a spotless white shalwar kameez, beached his boat and dropped an anchor in the sand. He didn't speak any English and was totally illiterate, but via sign language – and his own common sense and knowledge of engines – he quickly understood that the plane had run out of fuel and made an emergency landing. Likewise, the fisherman soon perceived that they wanted him to bring fuel to the beach. Just as Catesby said, 'Petrol,' Lester shouted, 'Gasoline.' To make sure the message got through, they wrote notes in both English and French that the fisherman could pass on. Lester also gave him a handful of dollars to show that he was being rewarded. The fisherman stared at the banknotes. He didn't know their value or from where they came, but he tucked them along with the handwritten messages into a slit in his shalwar kameez. They helped him relaunch his boat and waved him off.

'What a damned nice guy,' said Lester as the fisherman headed up the coast.

The next day a police launch arrived – and the fisherman was with them. The police were wearing blue berets and carrying guns. The one in charge spoke perfect English but didn't ask any questions. He ordered Catesby and the others onto the launch. Two other policemen, carrying submachine guns, were left behind to guard the plane. It was a very fast launch, and they were soon making bow waves to Karachi.

They weren't put in prison cells but weren't free to walk around either. They were interrogated individually and kept separate from each other both before and after. The person interviewing Catesby was wearing civilian clothes and gave the impression of being a high-ranking civil servant rather than a police officer. Catesby's passport lay open on the desk in front of him. He could almost make out the iconic words: *His Britannic Majesty's Secretary of State Requests and requires in the Name of His Majesty all those whom it may concern to allow the bearer to pass freely without let or hindrance, and to afford the bearer such assistance and protection as may be necessary.* He knew they represented a wish list rather than a requirement but hoped that a name check might open a pathway.

'You are Mr William Catesby?' said the interviewer, flicking through the passport.

'Yes, I am.'

'Your passport seems lacking in recent visas or entry stamps.'

'I was travelling with friends in a private plane.'

'For what purpose?'

'As a former British officer in the Special Operations Executive,' – Catesby tried to put a bit of pride and arrogance into his voice – 'I was recently commissioned to write a book about the French Resistance. Both my companions are former colleagues from my time in Occupied France. They invited me on a jaunt, a bit of a holiday adventure. I wasn't particularly keen to go, but I thought the long flights would provide a good opportunity to talk about their memories of the war for my book.'

The interviewer listened to Catesby's words with all the disdain of a cricket umpire dismissing a shout for LBW. He slowly closed the passport as he said, 'You are under arrest, Mr Catesby, for having entered Pakistan illegally. You are also suspected of being involved in smuggling. Your aircraft is currently being searched.' The interviewer then opened a desk drawer and took out a gun with a label attached to it. 'This pistol was found in your luggage.'

Catesby stared at the revolver. It was the one Déricourt had given him before the trip to Laos – and a far better pistol than the one the police had confiscated when they searched his flat after the murder of the football player. Catesby had bought that pistol from Serge via one of his models. The model, a prostitute with a battered and sagging body, had forced a deal with the artist: 'You want to paint me, you buy this gun.' Catesby had relieved Serge of his unwanted purchase from the poor woman. Her decline had been hastened by heroin addiction – and now he was helping to fly the shit into Marseille.

'I've never seen it before,' lied Catesby. 'Someone must have put it there.' He wished that he had used the confiscated gun to put a bullet in Lester's head and one in Déricourt's too – then it would have all been done and dusted.

'It will be confiscated and retained as an illegal firearm. That is all for now.'

Catesby spent the night on a cot in a small room. The door wasn't locked, but there was a guard outside who kindly escorted Catesby to a toilet when he needed to pee or have a shit. He was clearly getting VIP treatment. Late the next morning a British consul arrived. Catesby was pleased that he had been granted consular access and that no Pakistani officials were present at the meeting.

'I am sorry to report, Mr Catesby, that we have made little progress. The Pakistani authorities refuse to grant your release or the return of your passport, even under the condition that you immediately leave the country under escort. I am awaiting advice and instructions from London.'

Catesby was tempted to ask the consul, who looked barely out of the sixth form, *Do you know who the fuck I am?* Instead, he said, 'Have the others been granted consular access?'

'I couldn't possibly comment. Their cases are confidential to them and representatives from their countries of origin.'

Catesby asked because he thought he had heard an American voice, loud and brassy, in the corridor while he was being escorted for a piss. He decided not to press the matter. The young consul seemed terrified of blotting his copybook so soon in his career. When Catesby was taken back to his room, he lay on his cot and stared into space. Was London going to ditch him? It was all part of the spy trade. When you signed up you ceased to be an innocent civilian worthy of humanitarian rescue, but a player who accepted the risks without complaint. A colleague from the rough streets of Belfast had warned that a career in SIS meant 'big boys' rules'. And years in a Pakistani prison was just another playground penalty.

The next morning Catesby was summoned from his room by an unsmiling policeman. This is it, he thought. He followed the policeman down a corridor. He was let into a conference room where the man who had interviewed him was sitting at the table surrounded by uniformed officers. Lester and Déricourt were standing in front of the table. Another Westerner, with a plump face and wire-framed glasses that seemed embedded in his face like old barbed wire set in the bark of an oak tree, was standing beside Lester. He was wearing a seersucker suit with sweat-stained armpits and whispering to Lester in an American accent. Catesby was certain they were there to be sentenced.

The Pakistani official at the head of the table silently read a document and signed it with a frown. He then handed the document to a colleague who appeared to be the highest-ranking officer and looked at Catesby and the others with utter contempt. 'You are all free to go,' he said.

They were driven away in a van without windows. Lester leaned over to Catesby from a seat opposite. 'It's just like World War Two; Uncle Sam stepped in and saved your ass.'

'What happened?'

'I'll tell you later. Your guy was fucking useless.'

When they were dropped off, Catesby was surprised to see water rather than an airport. The police launch that had brought them to Karachi was moored along the harbour wall directly in front of them. Sailors were offloading jerry-cans from a lorry onto the launch.

'They're going to help us refuel,' said Déricourt.

They boarded the police launch, and as they roared off in a spume of white spray, Catesby felt that he was trapped in a nightmare that kept repeating itself. The wretched Beechcraft 18 was on the beach just as they had left her.

Their flight from Pakistan into Indian airspace was cautious and below radar level. They had been flying for five hours when Déricourt descended to treetop level. Catesby assumed he was looking for a place to land – but hadn't expected to be greeted by dancers. One of the persons signalling the plane was waving a red sari, the other a green sari. The countryside was green and hilly, but not mountainous. The landing strip was next to a fast-flowing stream. Catesby searched the land below for a tanker lorry – and noticed there were no roads at all. Was it, he thought, a good idea to land in a place where there was no chance of refuelling? Then he saw the elephants. All four of them were heavily laden with jerry-cans that were now being unloaded. 'Attention aux éléphants,' he shouted to Déricourt.

The pilot smiled and nodded as if the beautiful beasts were an everyday sight.

They landed just as the sun was setting. It was a stunning location and Catesby wished that he was sharing it with someone other than Lester and Déricourt. Lester was warmly greeted by a man wearing a turban and loose traditional dress. The man spoke perfectly fluent English with an American accent. Catesby was summoned to join them, but instead of seeing the white face of someone who had gone native, he found the American-speaking man distinctly Indian and bearded.

'Let me introduce you to Chuck,' said Lester. 'He went to Yale.'

'I've got other names too,' said Chuck, shaking hands.

'And he played baseball for Yale.'

'Rounders,' said Chuck, recognising Catesby as British. 'Excuse me for now, I've got things to organise.'

Catesby noticed that there were now two more elephants on the scene and that Chuck was giving instructions in the local language. 'You can tell when someone's been to Yale,' said Catesby.

'You like being sarcastic, don't you?' said Lester.

'I'd like to know what the fuck is going on.'

'You flunked the test in Pakistan.'

Catesby didn't want to continue the discussion. He had begun to walk away when Déricourt joined them and said, 'Is something wrong?'

'Lester has just sacked me.'

Déricourt looked at the American. 'I don't understand. What's happening?'

'Our friend William isn't pulling his weight or showing much influence. During our stay in Pakistan, Washington was forced to make a choice – a choice I didn't want to put to them. At least not yet.'

Déricourt and Catesby stared at Lester in silence.

'You guys don't know what's going on.'

'But I do know,' said Déricourt, 'that William got us two secure and easy stopovers in Iraq and Iran.'

'We could have done it without him.'

'But the British connection always provides extra options.'

'We'll see.' Lester walked away.

The last two elephants were burdened with tents, food and belly dancers. The refuelling stop was turning into a party. They washed down various curries with a locally made beer called *sura*. Chuck, the Yale-educated Indian, sat cross-legged between Catesby and Lester. 'Be careful not to spill your beer,' he said. 'The elephants have acquired a taste for it and spillages can provoke a stampede.'

'Then they must like it a lot better than I do,' said Lester.

'Have you tried the palm wine?'

'It looks and tastes like sour milk.'

'What about the belly dancers?' said Catesby.

Lester frowned. 'I'd rather not comment.'

'You're a hard man to please,' said Déricourt. 'I remember that from taking you to a wine-tasting.'

'I did like that white Burgundy,' said Lester. 'The Montrachet. I bought a case of it.'

'You could have bought another Beechcraft 18 for about the same price.'

'I know – and I have.'

Catesby gave a furtive smile. Lester's offhand remarks were often gold dust. The business was expanding. Catesby helped himself to more *sura*. Like the elephants, he was acquiring a taste for the beer and getting a little tipsy. He turned to Chuck. 'What do you do when you're not organising refuelling stops, elephant caravans and dancing girls?'

'I work for the Indian government.'

'Do your bosses know about this sideline?'

'I understand, Mr Catesby, that you used to work for the British government.'

'We all make mistakes when we're young.'

'I don't suppose your job ever brought you into contact with Krishna Menon at the Indian High Commission in London?' Chuck had just thrown a live hand grenade into the conversation, and he knew it. Menon was a militant anti-imperialist who had been a leader in the fight for Indian independence and had strong links with the Communist Party of Great Britain. If you mentioned his name at MI5, the office lights began to flicker, and faces turned pale with concern or red with rage. In some ways, Catesby admired Menon's idealism – but it was an admiration that he could express neither at work nor at home.

'My position,' said Catesby, 'was far too humble to involve coming into contact with someone like Krishna Menon.'

'Or to discuss how to deal with him?'

'Indeed.' Catesby had to be cautious. He wasn't sure what side Chuck was on regarding Menon – who was a controversial figure in India as well as outside.

'I am sure, Mr Catesby, that you are far too modest.'

Catesby noticed that Chuck was now speaking British English with a slight Indian accent. He was a chameleon.

Chuck looked at Lester, who was attentively eavesdropping on the conversation. 'One of the advantages of being part of the non-aligned movement is that you are free to make friends with both sides. In fact, it is imperative that you do so. What a pleasure to make your acquaintance, Mr Catesby. At some point, we must have a long talk.'

Catesby wished that he could have taken a picture of Lester's face. He imagined a speech bubble coming out saying, *Perfidious Albion has turned you guys into Perfidious India*. But he knew that Lester couldn't say that because he needed Chuck's help. In fact, Chuck was the sort of non-aligned nation insider that all of Washington needed to cultivate – and Chuck knew it.

'I suppose, partner,' said Lester, looking at Catesby, 'that you'd better stick around a bit longer.' As the fires dwindled, and they made their way to their tents, Lester took Catesby aside. 'We don't need any Brits in Laos, it's just between us, the Frenchies and the natives, but it looks like we might need your help getting there and back.'

Xieng Khouang Plateau, Laos: June 1950

It was love at first sight, but the problem with love at first sight is that it overlooks the difficulties – and the vices. At first, Catesby was won over by the natural grace and ready smiles of the Hmong people. As they weaved their way backwards through the opium fields, they looked like a ballet troupe clearing the stage for more dancers. A great variety of bright colours and patterns were woven into their tribal dress. The handweavers seemed to take pride in their originality. Most of those harvesting opium were women. Several were still breastfeeding, their babies swathed close to them by folds of cloth, as they scored incisions into the mature opium pods. There was an art to getting the incisions perfect. If the cut is too deep, the opium will flow too quickly and fall wastefully to the ground. If too shallow, the opium will stop flowing after a few drips, solidify in the pod and become impossible to harvest. It was a valuable crop, and not a single drop of the milky sap must be squandered.

The person showing Catesby around wasn't a Hmong tribesman, but a Lao named Phoumi, who spoke perfect French. 'You don't have to call me *altesse*,' said Phoumi when they were first introduced. 'I am only the younger son of a very minor prince.' Catesby had been impressed by his modesty and self-effacing good manners. Had Phoumi been born in Britain, he would soon have found himself a trusted adviser at a Prime Minister's elbow – or Private Secretary to the King. He was someone born, not to wield power himself, but to control those who did. His ethnic group, the Lao, comprised more than half the country's population and inhabited the more prosperous lowlands.

'What happens next?' said Catesby as they walked by the field of opium poppies.

'I am not sure,' said Phoumi. 'Monsieur Lester has not yet made a schedule – or, at least, not confided such a schedule to me.'

Catesby gave a furtive smile. Phoumi had misunderstood his question. 'I meant,' he said, pointing to the Hmong cutting slits into the opium pods, 'what is the next stage in the harvest?'

'They all come back early in the morning – and the men farmers will be among them. The raw opium slowly oozes out of the pods overnight. It is a matter of scraping the opium off the surface of the pods before the late-morning sun causes it to congeal. The opium is collected in metal tins that the farmers wear around their necks. The best pods will continue to ooze for five or six days, but you must scrape all the opium off each morning to keep them flowing.'

'Have you ever smoked it?'

'On a few occasions. It tastes faintly of almonds – and the effect is very pleasant. Many of the older Hmong farmers smoke it regularly – which is why you don't always see them in the fields.' Phoumi stared at Catesby. It was the look of a high-level civil servant telling a cabinet minister a home truth. 'If it wasn't for opium, the highland Hmong would starve to death.' He scraped the ground with his sandal-clad foot. 'You can't grow anything else here. These mountains are a wasteland – but the opium poppy will flourish in the most unlikely places. The mountain tribes are the only people in Laos who cultivate opium poppies. The money they earn from selling opium enables them to buy food and survive. An acre of poppies will provide enough opium to satisfy five heavy users for an entire year. A year's supply is called a *choi* and weighs exactly 1.6 kilograms – and the money from five *choi* of opium will feed a family of seven or eight for a year.'

Catesby was impressed by the exactitude of the figures. 'It sounds like a well-thought-out business model.'

'The Hmong are capitalists who don't exploit their workers.'

Catesby was tempted to suggest that maybe the person who did the exploiting was 'Monsieur' Lester. He bought the opium from mountain tribesmen faced with starvation at rock-bottom prices and then sold the drug on at ten or a hundred times what he paid for it. As the picture grew clearer, it became apparent that the Lao Royal Family were also doing it.

The thatched wooden house that Catesby shared with Lester and Déricourt was simple and primitive, but they were well looked after by their Hmong hosts. The house had no windows. The Hmong were animists and believed that window openings would allow evil spirits to get into the house and cause havoc. Catesby regarded his two companions and wanted to tell his Hmong hosts that the evil spirits had walked in through the door. There were no cooking facilities, but generous quantities of food were brought to them three times a day. Catesby was surprised – and relieved – to find the dishes weren't very exotic: white rice, vegetables, fish and chicken – and sometimes a bit of goat's head. The drink was a wine called *cher hue xue*.

'You have to be careful with that,' said Déricourt as they ate their midday meal. 'Sometimes it's only lightly alcoholic – and sometimes it will blow your head off. The fermentation process is variable.' Déricourt took a mouthful from his cup. 'I think this one is a bit stronger than table wine, maybe like vermouth or well-watered pastis.'

Lester was drinking bottled French beer with the number 33 on its label. He lifted the bottle. 'The Vietnamese call it *ba mười ba*, their word for thirty-three. If they think you're getting horny, they say you're *ba mười ba*.'

Catesby remembered that Lester had been parachuted into Vietnam towards the end of the war with the US Office of Strategic Services. His mission at the time was helping Ho Chi Minh fight the Japanese occupation. How things had changed.

'Lester,' said Déricourt, 'has a big cache of *ba mười ba*.'

'You guys can guzzle that tribal poison – I like to know what I'm drinking.'

Déricourt sipped his drink again. 'This one isn't too bad.' He turned to Catesby. 'You ought to see the Hmong drink it during a ceremonial occasion, especially a wedding. You're not allowed to touch the bowl with your hands. You have to put it between your teeth and drink the whole contents in one go. If you spill any or accidentally touch the bowl, you have to do it again until you get it right.'

'After which,' said Catesby, 'the groom is totally legless.'

'The Hmong think it's great fun, all part of the celebration.'

'I bet Helen could manage it.'

Déricourt gave a smile that had a hint of unease. 'I'd love to bring her here. I bet I'd get a fantastic bride price.'

'They wouldn't mind marrying a Westerner?'

'Not at all. The Hmong are completely exogamous. They are divided into eighteen different clans, and it is forbidden to marry someone from your own clan.'

'It prevents inbreeding,' said Lester, 'and it's good for the biological stock. That's why the Hmong look so healthy.'

The Hmong, thought Catesby, would find Norfolk a bit strange – or, to be fair, most European royal families. He had already begun to fall in love with them. So-called primitive people faced with a daily struggle for survival often turned out more robust than so-called civilised people. Catesby sipped the milky wine out of a bowl that looked like it had been fashioned from a hollowed-out animal bone – a very big animal. He looked closely at the bowl. Was it shaped from a water buffalo's hip? No, it was too perfectly round. The penny dropped. He was drinking wine from a human skull. At that moment there was the sound of explosions and small arms fire in the distance.

Lester slammed down his beer with a splash. 'I bet it's the fucking KMT again – and I bet they've ambushed our mule train from Kan-chanaburi. Twelve fucking tons of opium. They're worse than the commies.' He turned to Déricourt. 'Are you fuelled up?'

'As always.'

'Then let's get moving.'

They needed help from a couple of Hmong tribesmen to manoeuvre the 55-gallon drum onto the plane. 'Don't touch the detonator,' Lester said with a wry smile.

Catesby could see that an explosive device with a timer had been attached to the top of the oil drum.

'We're going to teach those sons-of-bitches a lesson once and for all. They lost to the fucking commies despite us giving them weapons and millions of bucks – and now this!'

The plane took off and they were soon over thickly wooded country-side from which smoke was rising. Catesby could make out a rough road that was wending its way through the trees. He saw men in uniform with guns running and crouching along the track.

'Can you make radio contact?' said Lester.

Catesby couldn't make out what was being said because the ramp-door was still open and the engine roar was deafening. Finally, he heard Déricourt say, 'One hundred fifty metres north of white smoke.' Through the open door, Catesby could see a thick billow of white emerging from a smoke grenade.

'Give me a hand,' said Lester.

Catesby helped roll the gallon drum onto the ramp.

'Set it for twelve seconds and push now!' shouted Déricourt.

Lester fixed the dial and a second later the oil drum was falling towards the troops in uniform. As the plane banked away, Catesby saw a widening circle of dark orange flames and smoke blot out the trees. It was the first time he had seen a napalm attack. Twenty minutes later they were back in their hut, sitting on woven mats and finishing their interrupted meal. The Hmong cook had warmed up the food, but Catesby had lost his appetite.

'Was Junior with the mule train?' said Lester, looking at Déricourt.

'Yes, but he wasn't the one who called in the attack.'

'He won't be very happy about it.'

Catesby wasn't happy either. Blowing up people was bad enough, but deep-frying them in burning oil was barbaric.

'Junior doesn't like talking on the radio,' said Lester. 'He acts like a fucking native – and he doesn't like watches or clocks. We need to send a Hmong with a message in a cleft stick.' He looked at Déricourt. 'Can you arrange it?'

'I think a verbal message would be better.' The pilot called over the Hmong tribesman who had brought their food. The Hmong seemed to understand a little French and Déricourt could manage a few words in Hmong. The tribesman disappeared. 'I hope he finds someone fleet of foot. Junior always responds better if you ask him in a local language.'

'Who is Junior?' said Catesby.

Lester laughed. 'That's a goddamn good question – and I keep asking it myself. When you look at Junior, you think you see a clean-cut American boy who plays baseball, goes to church and wouldn't dream of putting his hand up your sister's skirt. But that's just the cover story he puts on when someone from Washington turns up. The real Junior is a Southeast Asian tribesman – who doesn't belong to just one tribe, but five or six. He speaks fluent Thai, Hmong, Lao, Khmu, Shan and Katang – and can get by in Yunnan Mandarin.' Lester waved his chopsticks. 'But beneath all that, Junior's a hundred per cent patriotic American who would gladly give his life for the Stars and Stripes – and he's also a devout Christian.'

'I smell a missionary,' said Catesby.

'Missionaries don't smell. They are washed in the Blood of the Lamb.' Lester laughed. 'Personally, I'd rather wash in soap and water followed by a splash of Old Spice and a martini. No, Junior is no missionary, but he was born into a family of evangelical missionaries and brought up in Thailand. Junior still wants to convert Asians, maybe not to Christianity, but belief in American freedom. That's why he became an intelligence officer – and, second to myself, he is our best in Southeast Asia.'

Catesby poured a big slug of *cher hue xue* into his bowl. He needed a drink. He looked again at the bowl. It was definitely a human skull. So what? When in Rome.

Junior arrived late that evening. He was handsome and athletic-looking – and utterly charming and personable. At first, Catesby was taken by him, and would have introduced him to his sister. He was also surprised to see that Lester treated Junior with more than a little deference. There was no sarcasm or shouting and hardly any swearing. 'Thank you for coming,' said Lester. 'It sounds like you had a difficult afternoon.'

'We were ambushed by elements of the Kuomintang's Third Army.' Junior gave Catesby a winning smile. 'I am sure, Captain Catesby, that you know this part of Laos is plagued by rogue elements of Chiang Kai-shek's defeated nationalist armies. They have turned to drug smuggling.'

Catesby nodded. He was starting to piece things together. The Thailand-born Junior still had connections in that country. He had been leading a mule train laden with raw opium from northern Thailand to Lester's base in the hills. Junior wasn't just a missionary turned CIA agent, but an evangelical Christian drug smuggler as well. Maybe he wouldn't introduce him to his sister after all.

'Casualties?' said Lester.

'We lost over half the opium, and five Thai muleteers were killed in the ambush. We managed to bring back ten wounded. Eight mules are dead or disappeared. Your napalm bomb caused a lot of panic on both sides. Two of our mule teams ran off and we don't know what's happened to them.'

'But it stopped the ambush?'

'Yes, but at a cost. Our mule teams need to be better armed in the future. The Kuomintang attacked with sixty-millimetre mortars and recoilless rifles.'

'It's a pity Mao didn't finish them off.' Lester looked at Catesby. 'Chiang Kai-shek's soldiers were more interested in extortion and crime than fighting the communists. After Mao's victory in 1949, tens of thousands of defeated Kuomintang soldiers poured over the border from Yunnan into Burma and Laos.' Lester shifted his glance to Junior. 'We need to arm and train your tribesmen friends to finish them off. It'll be good practice for taking on the communists.'

'It looks,' said Déricourt, 'like the ambush will delay our return run to Marseille. We don't want to set off with a plane that isn't fully loaded.'

'And,' said Lester, 'there will soon be another Beechcraft 18 joining you.'

Catesby could see that landlocked Laos was turning into a cauldron of opium-fuelled war. The global clash between capitalism and communism was on the backburner – at least for the time being.

The French captain belonged to an elite unit called the Groupement de Commandos Mixtes Aéroportés. He was the first member of the French military that Catesby had seen in Laos. The captain's job was organising a new unit of local partisans called Commando Nord Viet-Nam – and that, he said, was why he wanted to meet Junior. Catesby thought it odd that Junior, who was fluent in exotic languages few Westerners could get their tongues around, knew so little French. Catesby found himself having to act as translator.

'Our aim,' said the captain, 'is to recruit heavily from ethnic minority groups such as the Hmong, Khmu and the Nungs.'

'I could offer help with the hill tribesmen you mentioned, but not the Nung, who mostly speak a Chinese dialect that I'm not familiar with.'

Catesby could tell that Junior was not overly enthusiastic, but meetings were arranged between the French captain and Hmong leaders. In the end, thirty Hmong volunteered to join Commando Nord Viet-Nam and arrangements were made for them to travel north to the border town of Muong Khoua. The French captain asked Catesby to come with them. Déricourt agreed that it would be a good idea as it would be another week before they had enough opium for a return trip to Marseille – and Lester said it would be 'good to see what the Frenchies were getting up to'.

The captain was driving an American-made two-and-a-half-ton truck. The white US stars on the doors and bonnet had been painted over, but the underlying markings still shone through like pale ghosts. Lester called the two-and-half-tonner, a 'deuce and a half'. A dozen Hmong, the first draft of recruits, were riding in the open back.

'We have also been recruiting captured Viet Minh prisoners into a unit called the Black Tigers,' said the French officer. 'Viet Minh who change sides are very valuable soldiers because they know the tactics of the enemy – and they're useful for persuading their former comrades to desert and join us.' A frown crossed the Frenchman's face. 'But there are drawbacks. A few hardcore Viet Minh have infiltrated our units pretending to have changed sides. At first, they appear to be the bravest of our recruits – but, when least expected, their true allegiance makes itself known. Our best officer was murdered in his sleep by one of them. Roger is sorely missed. He gave his life for France two years after his brother was killed in action. They are a family of heroes.'

Catesby felt a pang of shame as he thought of his wife's two older brothers, both killed in the war. But at least that war had been worth fighting.

'The advantage of recruiting mountain tribesmen, such as the Hmong, is that they never betray you.' The captain gave a wan smile. 'Perhaps the Vietnamese have a more sophisticated culture.'

'Or perhaps they are more like us.'

The captain, thinking of his own country's collaborators, nodded in agreement.

Catesby was thinking of Déricourt.

'Things,' continued the French captain, 'have not been going well. The casualty figures still haven't been made public, but we suffered terrible losses in the fighting along Route Four.'

'How many?'

'Over five thousand troops, all French, were killed, wounded or captured. The enemy outnumbered us five to one and kept attacking. We have had to abandon Lang Son on the Chinese border and retreat to Haiphong. The Route Four defeat is, of course, one of the reasons that I am here.'

'So far, the only war I've seen in Laos is battles between drug smugglers.'

'I think that could soon change. By the way, we are not the only ones who are recruiting the Hmong. The communists are too – and have just named themselves the Pathet Lao, which translates as the Lao People's Revolutionary Army. Oddly enough, their leader, Prince

Souphanouvong, is a member of the Lao Royal Family and has a strong claim to the throne. Is that not droll?'

Catesby nodded.

'It would be as if one of your king's daughters became a member of the British Communist Party.'

'I think they prefer horses to Marxists.' For a second, Catesby had an image of two thoroughbreds, Dialectical Materialism and Laissez-Faire, galloping neck and neck towards the finishing line at Ascot.

The French officer gave Catesby a sideways look. 'You are in an interesting position. I believe that your young Lao friend Phoumi is well connected and could introduce you to Souphanouvong and other royals in Luang Prabang, a beautiful city where the Royal Palace is located.'

'It sounds like you want me to spy for you.'

The French captain laughed. 'And also for yourself or any others who may be interested in your observations.'

Catesby felt that his cover was completely blown.

The Hmong volunteers in the back of the truck had begun to sing in response to drumbeats and whistles.

'I know little of their language,' said the French captain, 'but it is a song of separation which they sing whenever they are taken away from their homes.'

The rhythm of the music and the swaying of the truck lulled Catesby into a gentle sleep.

The next day, after the Hmong had been delivered to a secret Commando Nord Viet-Nam training camp, the French captain gave Catesby a tour of the countryside around Muong Khoua.

'We are directly on the border,' he said. 'The town you can see in the valley is Dien Bien Phu. We are going to build a large outpost nearby which will accommodate ten thousand troops. It will be our impregnable anchor in the northwest of Vietnam. But my job at present is to establish a line of fortified outposts, here on the high ground, on the Lao side of the border. These outposts will be a string of isolated garrisons, manned mostly by mountain tribesmen such as the Hmong, which will delay a Viet Minh attack into Laos. The holding actions will buy us time to fortify major Laotian cities, such as Vientiane and Luang Prabang.'

'And what is your next fallback position?'

The Frenchman gave a grim smile. 'Algeria.'

As they walked back to the truck, Catesby asked a leading question: 'What do you think of the Americans?'

'We couldn't fight this war without their supplies and money. It's a question of French bodies and American dollars – but there are now American pilots supporting us too. They wear civilian clothes but fly supply missions under fire. There's a big US pilot, a huge man, that the Vietnamese call *Beaucoup Kilo*, but the other Americans call him Earthquake. He is very brave and will go anywhere.'

'What do you think of Lester and Junior?'

'They have their own agendas.' The French officer walked on – and then stopped. 'But as for Lester . . .' The Frenchman made a slashing sign across his throat.

Luang Prabang, Laos: June 1950

It was the first time in real life that Catesby had been in a royal palace, but as a teenager he had had a recurrent dream of, after a chance encounter, being invited back to Buckingham Palace for a night of fun – and then being chased out into the street by an elderly lady wielding a sword.

The Lao Royal Palace at Luang Prabang was not Catesby's dream come true – and his fluent French was more useful than 'proper' English. Compared to Buck House, it was a very modest affair. It was a single-storey whitewashed building that hadn't been completed until 1909. The best thing about the palace was its location. It was on a bank overlooking the Mekong River, which meant that visitors could be conveyed there by royal barge and immediately ascend the Italian marble steps to the entrance. The first thing that greeted you as you entered was a three-headed elephant sheltered by an ornate white parasol. It was the Lao Royal Family's equivalent of the Lion and the Unicorn. Without much ado, Catesby was led into the reception room where he met Prince Souphanouvong, who made no secret of being a friend of Ho Chi Minh and a supporter of the Viet Minh insurgency. 'We must,' he said, 'be independent of French rule even if it means dissolution of the monarchy.' The prince gave Catesby a close look. 'Would you not consider the dissolution of the British monarchy as a price worth paying for Britain's independence from America?' The prince raised his hand. 'I know what you are going to say, that Britain is not a colony of the USA in the same sense that Indochina is a colony of France.'

Catesby hadn't been going to say that at all but listened to what the prince had to say.

'Sadly, Britain is a puppet state of America. Washington forced your government to send British troops to fight in Korea – and the cost of that war means that your citizens will no longer be able to get free dentistry or spectacles on the National Health Service. You know that two cabinet ministers, Aneurin Bevan and Harold Wilson, resigned over that decision?'

Catesby nodded. He was deeply impressed by Souphanouvong's knowledge of British internal politics. He seemed more a university professor than a prince.

'But,' said Souphanouvong, 'I haven't asked you here to give a lecture on your country's subservience to America. I would like to ask a personal favour.'

Catesby maintained a blank face as he listened attentively. Personal favours were often more complicated than arranging assassinations, bribes in high places or exposing double agents.

'One of my nieces, a princess in her own right, is now under police protection in London.'

Pennies began to drop. 'I believe,' said Catesby, 'that I have met her.'

'She speaks fondly of you,' said the prince.

I doubt, thought Catesby, that she spoke of me at all – and, if she did, it wouldn't have been fondly. He remembered the princess looking at him as if he were something the cat had dragged in. But he decided to play along with the charade. 'Why are the police protecting her?'

'I confess to using the words "police protection" as a euphemism, but my niece has not been formally arrested. The Lao ambassador is quietly acting on her behalf, and it is a very complicated situation. The French, however, won't get involved because of my position as leader of the Pathet Lao.'

'I don't know how I can help. I no longer work for the British government.' Catesby smiled. 'My new boss is a drug smuggler operating under the cover of being a CIA officer – or maybe it's the other way around?'

'I am sure,' said the prince with a sly grin, 'that Monsieur Lester would not have taken you on if you were a person of no influence.'

'You still haven't told me what happened to your niece.'

'She was searched by a Customs officer at London Airport after a flight from Marseille and found to be in possession of a large amount of heroin – worth about one million US dollars.'

'Was the heroin intended for distribution in Britain?'

'No, that's why I quoted its value in US dollars. The princess was en route to Havana. She was intending to sail from Southampton when she had her unfortunate confrontation with British Customs. Nothing really to do with the British authorities at all.'

'Was Havana the ultimate destination for the heroin?'

'Of course not. The plan was to hand the drugs over to her American connections, who would pay her the agreed price before they smuggled the drugs to Miami. She had made the trip before.' The prince paused. 'What you must understand is that opium links together all the people of Laos: communist, capitalist; commoner, royals; Lao lowlanders, mountain tribesmen. It is our most valuable export.'

'Would it not have been easier for your niece to have simply sold opium to Lester?'

'I know that you work for Monsieur Lester – and probably owe him some loyalty – but he is a crook. Why are you laughing?'

'Please excuse my laughter,' stuttered Catesby. For a second he had been tempted to address the communist prince as 'your *altesse*'. 'But calling Lester Roach a mere crook is the most extreme understatement I have ever heard. He is the ultimate in evil: an utterly corrupt criminal who will do anything – including boiling babies in hot oil – for money.' Catesby smiled. 'But please don't tell him I said that.'

'I am glad that we agree on something.'

Catesby wondered if he had gone too far – but there was something about the palace and the prince that liberated him. He was among people who knew no fear but could still trade and bargain. The Lao Royal Family seemed to have divided up all the possible outcomes of the war between them. Souphanouvong was the Red Prince; another prince, Washington's favourite, was a strong supporter of America and the West – and a third prince supported a neutral non-aligned Laos.

'You asked why my niece does not sell opium to Monsieur Lester. The price he offers is an insult. He would offer her, a royal princess, the same rate that he pays starving peasants – and he does so as part of a plan. He wants to control all the drug smuggling out of Laos. I suspect that he planted an informer in London, which led to my niece being so thoroughly searched. His next step will be killing rival smugglers. But we are ready for that.' The prince smiled and drew a finger across his throat. The gesture was chillingly identical to that of the French commando captain.

Xieng Khouang Plateau, Laos: July 1950

It was the first time that Catesby had smoked opium. He didn't like smoking anything, but Lester nagged him into having a try. Catesby shrugged off his distaste and told himself that sampling the drug was part of his cover story. The actual opium pipe was a thing of beauty crafted from ivory and incised with floral motifs. The opium paste was prepared by a young Hmong woman and inserted through a small hole into a brass bowl on the end of the pipe, where it was gently burned into drug-laden smoke.

Lester pointed to a Chinese inscription on the side of the pipe. 'Junior says the characters stand for *zhenzhiyun*, which translates as "precious fungus cloud" – and the figures around it are the Eight Daoist Immortals. The boy knows his stuff.'

Catesby put his lips on the mouthpiece and breathed in the smoke, which tasted faintly of almonds. The opium made him soporific and very relaxed. He envisioned his family, his friends, the Director and Henry Bone dissolving into a pink haze. If you wanted to forget your worries, opium was a good way to go. The voices near him seemed disembodied and merged into atonal music. Catesby was soon asleep.

Parlez français, Schweinehunde! At first, Catesby thought the voice was part of an opium-induced dream, but then he noticed morning light creeping in through cracks in the Hmong mountain hut. The voice continued shouting in French, 'You're lucky this isn't Stalingrad or a prison – and now it's time to sing.' A chorus of voices began belting out a hymn that Catesby had heard before:

Tiens, voilà du boudin, voilà du boudin, voilà du boudin
Pour les Alsaciens, les Suisses et les Lorrains

Pour les Belges, y en a plus
Pour les Belges, y en a plus
Ce sont des tireurs au cul

Catesby didn't think it was fair that there wasn't any blood sausage left over for the Belgians – or that his maternal ancestors were malingerers who shot from their arses as they ran away.

When Catesby emerged out of the hut, part of him wondered if it wasn't an opium dream after all. The Foreign Legionnaires were all in battle dress. The only soldier not wearing camouflage and bearing a rifle was dressed in the ceremonial uniform of the Republican Guard, a slight compromise for a royalist – and carrying a sabre. It was Xavier-Honoré, and he was standing off to the side next to Lester and Déricourt. Catesby joined them.

'Good morning, Captain Dopium,' said Lester.

Catesby ignored the taunt and nodded towards the Legionnaires. 'It looks like reinforcements have arrived.'

'They're from the Second REP, a very elite parachute regiment,' said Déricourt.

'And except for the NCOs,' added Lester, 'they're all German – mostly ex-SS.'

Catesby had surmised as much from the shouts of the French sergeant.

'The Frenchies needed some persuading to lend us these troops and the Viscount de Saint-Breuil played an important role.'

Hearing his name mentioned, Xavier-Honoré raised his sword in salute.

'And,' continued Lester, 'we are in a difficult situation owing to clan rivalries among the Hmong – almost an entire clan has gone over to the Pathet Lao commies.'

'And now they're coming after us,' said Déricourt with a twisted smile.

Lester laughed. 'But don't think for a minute that these Pathet Lao Hmong are coming here to fight for communism; they're coming to fight for our opium – and we're going to take the battle to them.' Lester looked at the Viscount, who was wearing a plumed helmet and jackboots, and said, 'But you're not coming with us dressed like that.'

'I imagine,' said Xavier-Honoré sheathing his sword, 'that it would be unwise.'

There were two platoons of Legionnaires, about sixty men in all. The sergeant in charge seemed to rule by a combination of fear and sarcasm. He lined up his soldiers and told them that the coming battle was going to be sans Vaseline. Catesby wondered if the term for fierce combat also said something about life in a Legionnaire barracks.

As a point of pride, Catesby accepted an invitation to join the Legionnaires as they set off to attack a Pathet Lao encampment. He wanted to prove that the Belgian side of his family were not *des tireurs au cul*. The Legionnaires were certainly fit, because the first part of the operation involved climbing up a steep mountain ridge. Even though there weren't enough steel helmets to go around, Catesby still wouldn't have opted to wear one because of the extra weight in the tropical heat – but he quickly realised why the more savvy Legionnaires had grabbed them. The first rock, in fact, bounced off the helmet of the soldier in front of him. There was sporadic rifle fire and a few hand grenades mixed in with the rocks, but only one Legionnaire became a casualty. He had face and arm wounds from the shrapnel but laughed them off – *'Nicht so schlimm wie Stalingrad, besonders nachdem der Schnaps ausgegangen war.'* Predictably, the sergeant cried out, *'Parlez français, Schweinehund.'* The wounded German laughed and continued up the hill as one of his comrades called out, *'Sans Vaseline!'* There was a sprinkling of laughter. Part of Catesby was enjoying the sheer madness. The rocks continued to rain down and there was the sound of aircraft engines above. Catesby looked up – it was the Beechcraft 18. Déricourt was on station. There was no napalm this time, only the sound of small-arms fire from the plane punctuated by explosions. Déricourt's crew members were dropping hand grenades and Molotov cocktails on the ridge line. The rocks stopped falling and the Legionnaires moved on to the top – and Xavier-Honoré was among them. The Viscount had wisely donned battle dress, but was wearing his plumed helmet, now badly dented by a rock.

The sun was now low in the sky. Lester, who as always seemed to have appeared out of nowhere, came over to Catesby. 'Would you like a slug of bourbon?'

'I'd love one.'

Lester passed over his hipflask. 'Sorry, there aren't any ice cubes.'

Catesby took a sip. 'They didn't put up much of a fight.'

'There were only two or three of them and, as you can see, it's a very exposed position. Wait until tomorrow.'

Catesby handed back the hipflask.

'Meanwhile, get some food in you – and then some shuteye. We're bivouacking here tonight. See you later.'

Catesby spread out his sleeping bag. The sun was now fast dipping towards the horizon. He took out his 24-hour French army field ration pack. The contents were generous and contained three tins of meat as well as a half-litre of wine and a shot of brandy. There were also water purification tablets, but no water. A Legionnaire saw him staring at the tablets and bade him follow. He led the way past colleagues who were digging a toilet trench and down into a thickly wooded ravine where a stream oozed out of the earth. 'Are you an Englishman?' said the Legionnaire.

'Yes.'

'I owe you an apology.'

There was, thought Catesby, a long list.

'I was at Normandy, and I destroyed one of your tanks. A survivor leaped out of the tank, and he was on fire.'

Catesby thought of Strachan, his friend at Cambridge.

The German took Catesby's flask and filled it with water. They walked back to the encampment in silence.

It turned out to be a spooky restless night. Just as Catesby drifted off to sleep, he was woken by the loud thudding noise of drums coming from the jungle. There was also the sound of singing. A Legionnaire sergeant appeared out of the dark. 'They always sing that the night before an action.'

'Is it a battle song?'

'No. It's a funeral chant.'

They set off for the attack just before first light. The Legionnaires hacked their way down a thickly wooded slope. It was noisy and not at all surreptitious. After an hour they came to a well-used trail which no longer required the use of machetes. Catesby noticed that the Legionnaires took turns to lead the column. 'As you know,' said Lester, 'walking point is like playing Russian roulette. You always hope that your turn ends up on an empty chamber.'

'Are you going to take a turn?'

'Only if there's a lot of money on offer – and then I might. It's called risk-benefit analysis.'

'I ought to hire you as my financial adviser.'

'I don't think you could afford my fee.'

There were occasional pauses as Legionnaires headed off on either side of the trail to check the path ahead for ambushes. The thick undergrowth made it painfully slow work, holding up the progress of the column. Lester finally gave an order to stick to the trail and forge ahead.

'A bit reckless,' said Catesby.

'If we keep doing it by the book, we won't be there by Christmas.' Lester nodded at the Legionnaires. 'They're magnificent. They haven't any past or family or country. The Legion is their fatherland.'

'Lucky them.'

'Don't knock it.'

'I wasn't.'

Eventually there was the sound of aircraft engines overhead. Catesby guessed it was Déricourt. They must be getting close. A short time later a dog began to bark. A brown pye-dog with very long ears briefly appeared in the undergrowth.

'Kill the bastard!' shouted Lester.

A Legionnaire dived into the undergrowth wielding a machete, but the dog easily escaped.

'Was it a wild dog or a guard dog?' said Catesby.

Lester didn't answer and motioned for the column to move ahead. A moment later there was a loud explosion followed by silence. For a few seconds everyone stood stock still – and then there was the sound of someone moaning in pain at the head of the column. One of the French sergeants led the way forward, followed by Catesby and a medic. Just as they reached the casualties, firing broke out – and everyone hit the ground. The sergeant landed with a particularly loud thump as he had a bullet between his eyes. Catesby lay staring at the boots of the dead man. The image of Frances drifted into his mind. He saw himself sitting with his arm around her while the twins played on the sitting-room floor. He closed his eyes as the bullets whizzed and cracked overhead and thought, *Why the fuck am I so fucking stupid? How the fuck did I end up here?*

When he opened his eyes again, he saw the Legionnaires moving forward in crouching runs and firing from the hip – they were counterattacking. They liked it *sans Vaseline*. Catesby didn't want to be a Belgian *tireur au cul*, so he followed them, wielding the ancient World War One Lebel rifle that he had been issued. He hadn't gone far, however, when a Legionnaire raised his hand to signal a halt. Catesby looked forward and saw a landmine in the undergrowth. The Pathet Lao Hmong had covered their retreat by leaving mines and booby-trapped hand grenades in their wake. A young Hmong, who looked about fifteen, was lying dead with numerous bullet wounds near the landmine he hadn't had time to conceal.

The Legionnaires had formed a defensive perimeter, and the firing had stopped. A sergeant was standing over his dead comrade and saluting him. Another Legionnaire had found wires leading from the site of the explosion. He lifted them to show Catesby. 'A command-detonated mine placed at waist height,' he said. 'They wanted to blow off our balls.'

Catesby looked at the body of the Legionnaire who had been walking point. He must have ducked when he saw it because the blast had caught him full in the face. One eye was torn away and there were holes in his cheeks and forehead. The Legionnaire who had moaned in pain was no longer moaning. He had been hit in the balls and lower abdomen and was lying in a pool of his own blood. His breathing was marginal. The sergeant in charge looked at the Legionnaires nearest him. They nodded agreement. The sergeant took out his pistol and delivered the *coup de grâce*. One of the Legionnaires, who spoke German with a Bavarian accent, made the sign of the cross. Catesby followed his example. Once a Catholic.

While a group of Legionnaires began to dig graves, others were scouring the undergrowth around the site of the explosion and checking for mines and booby traps. 'It must be near here,' Lester said as he gave orders in his heavily accented French.

'What must be near here?' said Catesby.

'Their supply cache. That's why they ambushed us.'

Two Legionnaires gave triumphal shouts from the undergrowth.

'I think they've found it. Let's have a look.'

Catesby followed Lester through the brush, impressed by the American's complete disregard for any lurking mines and booby traps. It was soon apparent that greed fuelled his bravery. There was a scattering of weapons and explosives in the supply cache, but most of the booty was raw opium. Lester picked up a dark block of the drug and raised it to his lips. 'More precious than gold dust,' he said. 'And there must be over a ton of it.'

Xavier-Honoré had joined them. He was still wearing his ceremonial Republican Guard helmet but had stripped off the plumes and camouflaged it with mud and vegetation. Overhead, they heard the sound of aircraft engines. Catesby glanced up and saw the Beechcraft 18, which wriggled its wings and made a low pass to the west of their position.

'Shit,' said Lester, 'Déricourt's trying to warn us of a—' The shooting began before Lester had finished his sentence. 'The fuckers don't want us to have their opium.'

The Legionnaires had already formed a defensive perimeter. They were now receiving fire from machineguns as well as small arms. The fighting was more intense than during the earlier contact.

'I think they've had reinforcements,' said Lester.

As Catesby crawled forward to add to the defensive fire with his Lebel, he passed a Legionnaire dragging himself back through the undergrowth and making gurgling noises. He pointed to his mouth and then spat out a large quantity of blood. The soldier continued to crawl, and Catesby noticed a huge exit wound between the back of his jaw and his neck. It looked like the Legionnaire had opened his mouth to shout an order or a warning and a bullet had flown in and taken out a molar or two. The bleeding was bad. Catesby found a surgical dressing in a belt pouch and wound it tightly around the wounded man's head to staunch the flow. Meanwhile, Xavier-Honoré was singing the royalist version of 'La Marseillaise' at the top of his lungs:

> *Allons armée catholique*
> *Le jour de gloire est arrivé!*

Once again, Catesby wondered if he was in the midst of an opium-induced dream. The sense of unreality was enhanced by the thick white smoke of a grenade that Lester had popped. The deafening roar of aircraft engines flying overhead at a very low level nearly blotted out the sounds of battle. Déricourt was coming to the rescue.

The napalm was dropped so close that two Legionnaires were splattered with the burning gel, painfully but not fatally. Catesby wasn't burned, but he felt the intense heat on his face. For a few seconds it was difficult to breathe as the fireball sucked all the oxygen out of the air. The trees and undergrowth ahead of them were on fire. The Pathet Lao had been roasted. Their counterattack was over.

As the flames burned out, there was a debate over what to do next. Xavier-Honoré and the sergeant leading the Legionnaires wanted to pursue the retreating Pathet Lao survivors and finish them off, but Lester wanted to get the repossessed opium back to his base on the Xieng

Khouang Plateau. 'Let them go,' he said. 'We've taught them a lesson and they can spread the word.' Lester turned to Catesby and spoke in a low voice. 'And today's enemies can become tomorrow's friends.'

There certainly was a lot of opium to carry – and it took nearly all the unwounded Legionnaires to backpack it out. As there wasn't enough manpower to manage the weapons and explosives as well, Lester told the Legionnaires to booby trap them as best they could. 'Once you've got the drugs,' he said, 'you can buy all the guns you want – and the guys carrying them too.'

Laos and India: July 1950

The opium-laden trek back to Lester's plateau stronghold went without incident. The evening of their return was one of celebration. There was drink, dancing girls and opium, but Catesby restricted himself to drink. He was developing a fondness for *cher hue xue* wine. At the end of the evening Lester joined him, but he was still drinking the French beer.

'Get some good sleep,' said Lester. 'The plane's loaded and we're ready to roll at first light.' The American paused. 'You know what I'm really looking forward to?'

'Haven't a clue.'

'I can't wait to get back to civilisation so that I can have a relaxing shit on a nice clean toilet while reading a *Wall Street Journal* that isn't a month old. Pure bliss.'

At first, Catesby had found the toileting procedures a bit primitive, but finally he got used to it and could see the logic. The place where people relieved their bowels was next to a pile of well-rotted night soil. He was surprised to find how quickly human excrement ceased to be repugnant. After a month or two, you wouldn't mind grabbing a handful and spreading it around your roses. There was, of course, a splendid circular rhythm to what was happening. You ate the rice; then you excreted the rice that wasn't absorbed into your body; then the rice excrement was used to fertilise the paddies to grow more rice that you ate and excreted again to enrich the paddy fields. Catesby knew it would be impossible to introduce such a system at Stanhope Gardens, the backyard of the flat was too small and bricked over – and the neighbours wouldn't like it. But Frances's parents had a large place with a couple of acres of garden in the country near Dunwich. He would make enquiries.

'I bet you're looking forward to getting back to Limey-land even if you haven't got nice toilets.'

'King, family and pub. What more could you want?'

'But don't forget why I'm sending you there – and make sure she gets locked up for a very long time.'

'I'll do my best,' said Catesby as he swallowed another slug of Hmong wine. The heroin-smuggling Lao princess was his excuse for a trip to England. Her uncle, Prince Souphanouvong, had hired him to get her out of jail – and now Lester was sending him to London to make sure they threw the key away. That suited Catesby – he was happy to deceive both Souphanouvong and Lester into thinking that a word or two from him in the secret corridors of London could influence the police's decision. He didn't know what would become of Souphanouvong's neice, but his intuition told him that those who did wield secret power in Whitehall didn't like the idea of locking up a princess from a country at war.

'But who the fuck knows,' said Lester as he threw his empty beer bottle into the undergrowth, 'if you'll ever get to England – or we'll ever get to Marseille. There's a lot of shit brewing.' Lester's back looked bowed as he stomped off into the Asian night.

Catesby was enjoying his best night's sleep in some time. He was having a sex dream involving a passionate Frances. He was woken up by a hand on his thigh, but it wasn't his wife's. A spot of burning orange light punctuated the dark and there was a faint smell of burnt almonds. At first, Catesby wondered if Lester had sent a Hmong lady to give him pleasure – but the voice spoke native French. It was Déricourt, and his message was far from love. 'Things are reaching breaking point with Lester. You're going to have to make a choice – and I know that you will stick with me and Helen.'

Catesby thought it was cunning of Déricourt to bring Helen into the equation. He must have imagined Catesby was a knight in shining armour who would sign on to look after her.

'Another reason you should be on my side is that I'm a survivor and

Lester isn't. As you can see, he is out of his fucking mind. Sleep well.'
Déricourt got up and exited the hut.

Catesby reached for the Smith and Wesson .32 that he kept by his side in the dark watches of the night. Déricourt had given him the gun before their first flight. Was there a hidden message? Was the gun meant to take out Lester? Catesby smiled. It would be ungrateful to use it on Déricourt. He wished that London hadn't left so much to his own discretion. But the important message was, as always, no fingerprints.

Several dozen Hmong came to the airstrip to cheer them off with big smiles and colourful strips of fabric that they waved in the air. It was, however, a very bumpy take-off, and Déricourt didn't seem pleased with the way things were going. Catesby had questions for him but knew that he couldn't speak freely in front of Lester.

Two hours into the flight, Lester looked at Déricourt and said, 'Why do you always look so fucking miserable?'

'I'm not making enough money for the risks I'm taking.'

Catesby didn't know whether the remark was genuine or a red herring.

'I let you do some dealing on your own,' said Lester. 'Ain't that good enough for you?'

'We'll see.'

In order to avoid Indian radar Lester was already flying low when the red clay of the landing strip appeared. It wasn't far from their last refuelling stop on the way out, where they had been greeted by elephants and belly dancers. But this time there were neither – only an open-backed truck with a mounted machine gun that was firing at the plane. Déricourt banked away sharply with one wing tip nearly touching the trees. 'Putain, that was close!' Catesby didn't know whether the pilot was referring to the treetops or the bullets.

'What the fuck was that about?' shouted Lester. He turned to Catesby with anger in his eyes. 'I thought it was your job to be checking out safe refuelling places with Brit-loving natives.'

Catesby didn't answer. Selecting the refuelling stops had been a joint effort with Déricourt. Catesby suggested places where a helpful British consul or intelligence officer might be within shouting distance, but on this occasion Déricourt had overruled him.

Déricourt was now speaking English. 'Fuck, we're flying on empty. I'm going to have to put her down soon.'

'The land looks pretty rugged,' said Lester. There was a slight hint of fear in his voice.

'There's an Indian Air Force base we can just about manage.'

'I hope they don't come out shooting,' said Lester.

'I don't think gunfire will be our problem,' said Déricourt.

Something was churning in Catesby's mind, but he kept the thought to himself. Why had the blokes with the machine gun been so stupid? Why didn't they hide the gun under a canvas and pretend the truck was laden with aviation fuel? After the plane had landed, they could easily have shot the fuck out of it and killed everyone inside. He began to see what Déricourt was up to.

It was a small airbase. There were two jet fighters, a cargo plane and a pair of small single-engine aircraft that were probably used for observation. As soon as they landed, the plane was surrounded by armed guards in Indian Air Force uniforms.

A moment later an officer came striding up to the plane. He motioned to Déricourt to open the pilot's window and said, 'I want everyone out with their hands above their heads.' As soon as they had left the plane, the officer said, 'Sit down, but keep your hands up – and no talking among yourselves.'

As Catesby sat cross-legged on the sun-warmed tarmac, he felt what it must be like to be a prisoner of war. You did as you were told and kept your mind a blank. At least, that's what he would have done. He wasn't a hero.

An hour later a policeman arrived in a Humber Super Snipe. It was the same model of car that London cops tooled around in – but a bit too pricey for the Secret Intelligence Service. The policeman, bearded and wearing a red turban, told them all to stand up. As he read out the list of violations of which they were guilty, it was obvious that he was a person of the strictest integrity and devotion to duty. Déricourt's Beechcraft 18 was loaded with bags packed with American dollars and other currencies, but the turbaned policeman was clearly someone who would rather die than accept a bribe.

Turning to Catesby, Lester said, 'You handle this.'

'No talking,' said the policeman, 'unless you are spoken to. You will now hand over all your passports and identity documents.'

The request required a rummage back in the plane. As Catesby found his passport, he whispered to Lester, 'What's Chuck's Indian name and title?'

Lester took a card out of his wallet and passed it to Catesby.

'I saw that,' shouted the policeman. He reached forward and grabbed the card from Catesby's hand. The policeman frowned as he read the name and title.

'If you contact this—' began Catesby.

'No talking unless spoken to.' The policeman continued staring at the card. 'How do you know this person?'

'I was formerly a member of the British Secret Intelligence Service, a fact you can easily check – and I can assure you that what we are doing is in the interests of the Indian government.' Catesby didn't know how to pronounce Chuck's Indian name, so he tapped the card with his finger. 'I hope you will contact this person. It is not for me to give further details.'

The policeman was clearly very angry. He chewed his lower lip as he weighed up his options. He finally turned away without saying a further word and stomped off towards the Humber police car. He gave a curt instruction to the driver, and they drove off.

'Thanks for fucking nothing,' said Lester. He was now walking around the Beechcraft, kicking its tyres and shouting, 'Fuck, fuck, fuck.'

'What's gone wrong?' whispered Catesby to Déricourt.

The pilot didn't answer, but Catesby detected a slight smile of satisfaction on his face. After a few minutes, Déricourt said, 'I think we're going to be stuck here tonight.'

It was an uncomfortable evening, too hot to be in a sleeping bag, but Catesby used his as a thin mattress between himself and his portion of the aircraft's floor. A few 1.6 kilogram blocks of opium wrapped in a spare shirt served as a pillow.

Chuck arrived mid-morning, not in a government limo, but as a passenger in a single-engine Piper Cub. He was wearing a white suit, rather than Indian dress. He needed only the addition of a solar topee to make him look more like a member of the British Raj than a government official in post-independence India. He was greeted by the air base commander with whom he had a brief chat, then strode towards the Beechcraft with a confident smile. Chuck warmly greeted Catesby in a British accent, exchanged what seemed to be knowing glances with Déricourt, then began talking to Lester with an American accent. 'I don't normally drink alcohol, particularly at this time of day, but I would love another taste of that Tennessee bourbon that you once introduced me to.'

'I think I've got a bottle or two in my luggage.'

Catesby could see that the bourbon was an excuse for the two of them to have a private chat in the plane. 'Well done,' said Catesby, looking at Déricourt.

'What have I done well?' said the pilot.

'Never mind.'

The conversation between Lester and Chuck lasted twenty minutes. When Chuck emerged from the plane, he was carrying a leather case – and looking very pleased with himself. After another conversation with the base commander, Chuck got back in the Piper Cub, which quickly taxied for take-off. Meanwhile, Lester was still in the plane with his head between his knees mouthing a litany of fucks. He looked at Déricourt. 'That was fucking expensive. I don't want to do any more deals with that fucker.' He looked at Catesby. 'Your Indian friend is a duplicitous piece of shit.'

'I thought he was your friend. You introduced us.'

'Sure, whatever you say.'

Catesby could see that Lester's relationship with truth and facts was conditional. He also suspected that Chuck was more a product of Yale than India. It was still a new world to Catesby – an expanding universe of greed and power where verifiable facts and morals were disposable baggage.

There was engine noise and clanking outside the plane. An Indian Air Force bowser had pulled up alongside the Beechcraft and refuelling had commenced. They were soon topped up and cleared for take-off.

As they headed west towards the Persian Gulf and Iran, it was impossible not to notice a new coolness between Lester and Déricourt – but not one that had crossed the line into open hostility. Lester wasn't stupid. Catesby knew that Lester knew that he had been duped by Déricourt and that the pilot would be receiving a big backhander from Chuck. They flew on in silence, but Catesby didn't need to hear words to work out what was happening. Lester's face told the whole story – and Catesby already knew the sequels. Déricourt's sting didn't mean that Lester was going to part company with the pilot or have him killed. It was a finely balanced calculation, but Déricourt still had his uses. What happened next was positively eerie. The American suddenly turned around and looked at Catesby. 'He has more uses than you.' Catesby felt a chill run down his spine. Could Lester read his mind?

The rest of the journey to Marseille was relatively uneventful. There were no attacks by fighter planes, no gunfights, no arrests – and no mafia victims to be disposed of at sea. But the stock of opium decreased more than expected. The normal practice was to pay for refuelling and other services with either cash or drugs, but the Chuck–Déricourt sting had seriously depleted the plane's cash coffers and more payments than usual had to be made in opium. During one refuelling, when they were out of earshot of Déricourt, Lester confided, 'We need a lot more fucking opium. That's why I want to get more planes on this route – and with American pilots.' He looked at Catesby. 'Are you any good at science?'

'I know how to make explosives and detonators.'

'Well, maybe we can find you a job in one of my new labs. I want to produce Number Four Heroin, the purest shit on earth.' Lester laughed. 'But you've got to be careful, you need to use ether and hydrochloric acid for the final stage – and the ether gas is highly volatile. A chemist working in the first lab I set up got careless; the lab exploded and brought the house down on top of her. The Marseille mafia sent me a condolence card – and a note saying, "We hope we won't have to send you another of these cards".'

Catesby was about to say, *Sounds like a warning*, but decided to keep his mouth shut and let Lester dig his own grave.

'The mafia are wonderful guys, I love 'em, but they don't understand how a free market benefits everyone. If the Feds and the cops kept their noses out of it, Americans could consume two hundred tons of heroin a year. Are you good at math?'

Catesby nodded.

'It takes ten tons of opium to produce one ton of heroin. So how many tons of opium do we need to produce two hundred tons of heroin?'

'It sounds like two thousand tons.'

'Correct – and the maximum cargo payload of a Beechcraft 18 is one ton, so how many trips to move all that opium to Marseille?'

'Two thousand trips.'

Lester looked at the Beechcraft and shook his head. 'The maximum number of trips that baby can make is thirty or forty a year. We need a fleet of fifty planes and maybe ships too.'

Catesby looked at Lester's face glowing in the sun. He was a visionary. One could imagine his statue, gilt in gold, with outstretched hands on a candlelit plinth in the Holy Church of Greed.

'The total income from two hundred tons of Number Four Heroin could be one billion dollars a year – that's ten thousand times the salary of the US President, that's more than the total worth of Rockefeller. And it's not a one-off, it keeps rolling in year after year.'

Déricourt was walking back towards the plane. He had completed his own transactions.

London: July 1950

Catesby's trip to London was exactly the sort of spy-craft op he loved.
A jaunt undertaken under utterly false pretences to deceive the players
involved. The main purpose of the London op was to convince the Lao-
tians that Catesby was an influential figure who could determine the
fate of the Lao princess being detained for drug smuggling. In fact, the
British authorities had already decided what to do with the princess and
Catesby's arrival on the scene was just window dressing. Lester, who also
thought that Catesby was doing his bidding, wouldn't be happy with the
decision – but that was part of the game plan.

Catesby's first stop was the Lao embassy, which was located in a
modest terraced house north of Hyde Park. Despite the opium trade,
they didn't seem to have a lot of money to throw around on diplomatic
premises. Catesby had a long chat with the ambassador who, oddly
enough, had taken up fly fishing and was looking forward to a trip to
the River Tay with his Norwegian counterpart. The Lao ambassador was
busy researching which flies he should use on the Tay and asked Catesby
for advice. When they finally got around to talking about the princess,
Catesby lied that he would do everything possible to help – including
pulling strings at the Home Office, Scotland Yard and with his former
hush-hush colleagues at SIS – but couldn't promise a happy outcome. 'I
think,' said Catesby, 'the chances of her being released without charge
are nil – and even a light prison sentence is unlikely. The British government is doing everything possible to stamp out drug crime – and will try
to make an example of your princess.'

'I am very sad to hear that,' said the ambassador.

As Catesby got up to leave, the ambassador looked distraught – but,
as Catesby had a cover story to maintain, he couldn't impart that good

news was in the offing. 'Try not to worry, Your Excellency,' he said with a reassuring smile, 'I am sure you will hear something soon – and this time of year on the Tay, you might try a Sunray Shadow Riffle.'

'Thank you, I am most grateful.'

The next part of the act was visiting the Chief Constable, who had just heard that a decision to release the Lao princess had been made from on high. The policeman was furious. 'She should have been locked up for at least five years.'

'Secret matters of State,' Catesby said with an ironic smile.

'That's what the French police said when I visited Marseille – but this is even worse, it's a British decision.' The Chief Constable shook his head in seeming disbelief. 'I was there when they told her she would be free to go tomorrow. Was she bloody grateful? Fuck no, she wanted to clear off immediately.' The policeman shook his head again and laughed. 'What really got me going was what she said about the drugs? You wouldn't bleeding believe it.'

'What did she say?'

'It wasn't enough that we're letting her, a drug smuggler caught red-handed, go free. She wanted us to give the heroin back. She said it was her personal possession and we had no right to confiscate it.'

'Well, she is a royal.'

'For a second, I thought the Home Office toff managing things was going to give in – but he took one look at my face and knew it wasn't on.'

'Well done, let me buy you a drink.'

Going to the pub with the Chief Constable was another part of the charade. Catesby wanted as many people as possible to see him hobnobbing with people of influence to feed the rumour mills on the eve of the princess's release.

After the first pint, the Chief Constable leaned over and whispered, 'Come on, you can tell me. What's this all about then?'

'Sometimes you have to let a minnow go to catch a shark. Let's see what happens.'

The policeman winked and nodded. The conversation then shifted to the Chief Constable's own background. He was born and brought up in Hackney. His father had been killed the first day of the Somme and his widowed mother struggled to bring up her four children in 'respectable poverty'. 'If you want to cut crime,' said the policeman, 'make sure the poor have more money – and the rich less. Too much money makes geezers think they can get away with anything – and too little makes you desperate.'

The final part of the act was Catesby visiting the princess just before her release. He told her in no uncertain terms that he had secured her release as a favour to her uncle, Prince Souphanouvong. A Whitehall official was standing next to Catesby, nodding affirmation at his every word.

The princess was neither impressed nor grateful. 'I do not need help,' she said, 'from the leader of the Pathet Lao.'

Catesby already knew that shared ideology was not one of the things that bound the Lao Royal Family together.

'If you really wanted to help me, Monsieur Catesby,' said the princess, 'you would get the police to return the packages of drugs that they stole from me – or at least compensate me for their value. Their behaviour was totally unacceptable!'

Catesby's return to Stanhope Gardens wasn't as passionate as his previous visit. He was tired and stared into space with a half-empty glass of red wine in his hand.

'What's wrong?' said Frances.

'I feel filthy.'

'Let me run you a hot bath.'

'How do I wash my soul?'

The day before his return to Marseille, Catesby had a 'clandestine' meeting with Henry Bone on a bench in Green Park.

'Why do we meet here?' said Catesby. 'It's in the open and everyone can see us.'

'Because, if we met somewhere really secret it would look suspicious.'

'I must remember that when I'm back in Berlin.'

'You like Germany, don't you?'

'I like living among a people who have been defeated and humiliated – and have learned their lesson.'

'Do you feel a kinship?'

'No, I haven't learned my lesson.'

'There's still time. Why are you laughing?'

'Because I like your sense of humour.'

'Well, William, I think you will find my next joke utterly side-splitting. It's time for you to get on with the job. The situation is getting more and more out of hand. I don't like our being dependent on America any more than you do, but that relationship doesn't look like it's going to change in the near future. The best we can do is mitigate the type of America to which we find ourselves in hock. Why aren't you laughing?'

'I missed the funny bit.'

Henry Bone smiled. 'It was at the beginning, when I teased you about needing to get on with the job. And here's another. I've arranged a meeting for you with T-section at Aldermaston. They have been instructed to give you full and unrestricted assistance – which might include training as well as kitting you out with the latest weapons. Apparently, they are very keen on poisons and other biological agents. A thrust into the aorta with a Fairbairn–Sykes commando knife is so old hat.'

An image of Marie thrusting a knife into the young German Wehrmacht driver passed through Catesby's mind. 'He was,' she later said, 'such a pretty boy.'

'By the way,' said Bone, reaching into his pocket, 'someone sent you a present. It was addressed to SIS and said "Please forward". Of course, we had to open it and make sure it wouldn't explode.' Bone handed over a tiny jade elephant and a thank-you note from the Lao ambassador – and a postscript inviting him on a fly-fishing trip.

Marseille: July 1950

Lester had moved into a new property, a sprawling house which also overlooked the sea. He had sublet his luxury flat to Déricourt at nearly twice the rent he was paying. Lester's new home had a potager and well-manicured gardens as well as a tennis court. The house was shaded by trees. There were French doors opening from the sitting room onto a sweeping lawn that seemed held in suspension over the Mediterranean. As the sun set, Lester loved to stride through the French doors with a clinking glass of bourbon and walk across the lawn to the cliffs over-looking the sea. There were no neighbours or roads to get in his way. Lester may have been a king of the universe, but he knew there were troubles that needed sorting – and in a radical way. Kit Fournier, clad in a beige linen suit, was accompanying him on his early-evening prom-enade. 'What the fuck,' said Lester, 'did Catesby get up to in London? I sent him there to make sure Princess What's-her-Name spent a long time in a Limey home for naughty girls. And what happens? She walks free two days after he arrives.'

'Maybe,' said Fournier, 'he was overruled.'

'Bullshit! The Lao royals have turned him into an ass-kissing courtier.' Lester laughed. 'You always make excuses for Catesby because you're an East Coast preppy snob. You've been brought up as fawning admirers of the decadent going-down-the-drain British. They're finished, Kit, and the torch has been passed to us. Would you like another drink?'

'I'd love one.'

'Fuck, you're even beginning to sound like one of them.'

'It's because I'm from Maryland.'

As they began to walk back to the house, Lester glanced behind him and stopped.

'Is someone following us?'

'No, I want to watch the setting sun. This is the only place in Marseille where you can watch the sun set in the sea.' Lester stared hard at Fournier. 'You're surprised, aren't you? You think I don't have any sense of beauty. You ought to see my art collection.'

'Where do you keep it?'

'In a secret vault with a lot of other things.'

'Maybe someday,' said Fournier.

'If Catesby were a work of art, he would be an example of *trompe-l'œil*, an optical illusion that tricks the eye into thinking it's something else.'

Fournier refrained from telling Lester that he himself was an example of *trompe-l'œil*. Those who thought he was a brainless bully, which he certainly wasn't, often ended up dead.

'Catesby is a traitor,' said Lester. 'To use the company's current lingo, he needs "termination with extreme prejudice" – and you, Kit, might have to do the job.'

Fournier turned pale.

'We can put up with Déricourt a little longer. He pays the rent and still shifts planeloads of the shit.'

'But he also does jobs for other smugglers.'

'I'm glad you know that too – but how do you know it?'

'Phoumi ratted on him.'

'We need to watch Phoumi too. He's another double-dealing shit – that's why we need to bring more Americans into this game. I've already got three CAT pilots signed up.'

'"Any time, any cargo, anywhere"?'

'That's the one. We bought the airline from the Chinese Nationalists after they got beaten. In the near future, you'll see a lot more of Civil Air Transport in Laos. It's free market capitalism, we need to think big and get rid of the competition.'

Catesby hoped that the Marseille op was nearing its conclusion. He had savoured his forty-eight hours as a husband and stepdad and he wanted more. He was devastated when Frances told him that for a few days after one of his visits home the twins kept asking, 'Where's Will?' And then, after a week or so, they stopped. Life returned to normal.

His first stop in Marseille was a rendezvous with Vera Atkins in her hotel room. Her first words were, 'Are you going to kill him or should I?'

Catesby knew that she meant Déricourt. She had grown worryingly obsessive about taking him out.

'I have an army friend,' she said, 'who was trained as a sniper – and we've already reccied the best place to do it.'

Catesby didn't want to give the nod without knowing more. 'So where have you got in mind? I might have a look myself.'

'The American friend . . .'

'Lester Roach.'

'. . . has moved to a villa to the east of Marseille. It is a splendidly isolated property that backs on to a cliff overlooking the beach. There are several excellent sniper perches offering a quick getaway by sea.'

'So how is this going to help your friend pick off Déricourt?'

'The traitor often visits. They go for walks together. The problem is finding out when the visits are going to happen.'

'You need insider info.'

'Exactly – can you help me get it?'

'I'll see what I can do.' The words tasted sour in his mouth. Catesby didn't like lying to Vera. Marseille was his op, not hers.

The visit was more to recon the situation than to carry out a termination; but, when Catesby visited Lester at his palatial home overlooking the sea, he went tooled up with a 9mm Browning. He was greeted by a security guard, who looked and sounded like he came from the Middle East. The guard was carrying an American M3 submachine gun, better known as a 'Grease Gun'. It was issued at the end of the war as the US Army began to sweep through Germany. It was fondly referred to as the 'ultimate tool for cleaning up a room'. You fired from the hip and sprayed. If the guard showed any hostile intentions, Catesby would draw his Browning, fire first and then run like hell. Where? He didn't know. It was still a standoff when Lester arrived. He was unarmed, wearing a silk dressing gown and carrying a martini. His first words were, 'You fucked up in London. Did the princess give you something special?'

'The situation had moved beyond my control.'

'And you expect me to believe that shit?'

Catesby kept a stony face. 'I appreciate your situation and hope I still have services to offer.'

'Another trip to Laos wouldn't be a bad idea – but only if you manage to bring the Beechcraft back packed with raw opium. Too many girls at the labs are twiddling their thumbs.'

'I can manage that.' Catesby backed out of the door like a gunfighter as he said farewell. He knew that his next trip to Asia could be a final drink in the Last Chance Saloon.

As he walked down the track from Lester's palatial new home, he realised that taking out the American would be no easy matter. He was surrounded by tight security, and if Catesby knew Lester, they'd be making regular sweeps of the surrounding cliffs. Vera's plans for Déricourt seemed like so much wishful thinking.

Laos: August 1950

The flight from Marseille to Laos went smoothly except for a couple of clashes with Indian Air Force fighter planes. Catesby had the impression that the flyboys fancied themselves as fast bowlers trying to dismiss a cricket team who were unworthy of Indian airspace. Not all the gunfire unleashed seemed to be warning shots. As Déricourt put the Beechcraft into a steep descent for a refuelling stop, one of the pilots broke radio silence and spoke in a posh British accent: 'I'm sending my ayah to pick up your shit-stained underwear – and then you can fuck off. Cheerio, for now.'

Catesby wondered if the fact that Lester wasn't on board made things run more smoothly. It seemed that route helpers and officials on the ground knew that things were coming to a head and didn't want to delay the outcome. They were waved on with knowing smiles. Catesby felt he was racing towards a showdown. A long-distance Mexican standoff in which there would be only one survivor. The key to staying alive was keeping your nerve.

Déricourt's first job after they arrived on the Xieng Khouang Plateau was meeting Hmong tribal leaders. Some were suspicious that Lester wasn't there to take charge of things, but others seemed more than happy to deal with Déricourt directly. It soon became apparent that he was giving generous bribes to tribal leaders. In exchange, they wouldn't interfere as Déricourt doled out miserly amounts of Lao currency to Hmong peasants for their opium harvest – though slightly more than Lester had ever handed over. Everyone was happy. Déricourt's immediate aim wasn't cheap opium, but wrecking Lester's network and influence.

Two days after their arrival on the plateau, a messenger arrived inviting Catesby to the Royal Palace at Luang Prabang. Déricourt was more than pleased to wave Catesby off. 'Do your worst.'

*

Prince Souphanouvong welcomed Catesby into the reception room, where a table was set with an English tea service and cakes. 'I want you to feel at home,' said the prince, gesturing towards the table laid for tea. 'And to show my gratitude for your helping my niece.'

Catesby decided not to say anything about his niece's lack of gratitude.

'Now, Monsieur Catesby, is there anything that I can do to help you?'

Catesby had been expecting the return gesture and got out two items from the package of tricks that T-section at Aldermaston had given him.

Souphanouvong picked up the purple vial of poison gingerly. 'This, I assume, is to make sure that Our Mutual Friend is not only presumed dead, but actually dead.' The prince shifted to English. 'As Bella said, "Money, money, money, and what money can make of life".' Noting the blank look on Catesby's face, he added, 'As you know, Bella is a character in *Our Mutual Friend* by Charles Dickens. My reference to Monsieur Lester was a pun on the title.'

Catesby was embarrassed that Souphanouvong had read Dickens's novel and he hadn't. The reference to Bella was completely lost on him.

'The comparison with Monsieur Lester is, of course, not quite accurate.'

Catesby was still clueless.

The prince picked up a tiny silver tube from among the items that Catesby had laid out in front of him.

'That's a blowpipe,' said Catesby. 'It fires a tiny dart, so small it is almost invisible, which carries a lethal nerve agent.'

'How interesting. It is very similar to Russian devices.'

Catesby was concerned that the Sovs were showing – or even sharing – such top-secret devices with the leader of the Pathet Lao. It also confirmed his suspicion that much of the contents of T-section's assassination kit were copies of Soviet devices.

Catesby nodded at the poison. 'And he won't taste that in his bourbon.'

'I can't promise a result, but we will happily do what we can.' The prince paused and looked closely at Catesby. 'Our Mutual Friend has an unfortunate penchant for interfering in internal Laotian affairs. He has also launched terror attacks with burning fuel on our Pathet Lao freedom fighters. Sadly, a group of them has now deserted and been bribed to fight for Monsieur Lester as mercenaries.'

Catesby put the bone china cup of Earl Grey to his lips and washed down the last crumbs of a Fortnum & Mason tea cake. How such a quintessence of Englishness had ended up in Laos he wasn't going to query, but something far less quaint was emerging from the mist. He understood why Lester had told the Legionnaires not to finish off the fleeing Pathet Lao after they had been napalmed.

When Catesby returned to Xieng Khouang, he saw that big changes were taking place. The rough airstrip was being improved and lengthened. Tribesmen were pushing around handcarts of stones and heavy earth which were pounded into the runway and then smoothed over. Déricourt's Beechcraft 18 was parked in the corner of the airfield, being loaded with opium for its return flight to Marseille. There was another aircraft on the opposite side of what had been a dirt airstrip. It was considerably larger than the Beechcraft. Catesby recognised it as a Douglas C-47 Skytrain. He had made a practice parachute jump out of one as an SOE trainee. The planes had also been the main freight carrier during the Berlin airlift. The C-47 had Civil Air Transport painted on the fuselage – and someone in a cowboy hat was checking an engine. Meanwhile, a mule train was wending its way out of the mountain forest towards it. The cowboy hat crewman shouted, 'Hot damn, boys, they're here!' Two tall and languid men emerged from the plane wearing dark glasses and flying suits. Their voices were American. One said, 'About time too.'

Catesby watched as the muleteers unloaded crates from the heavily laden pack animals onto the plane. The Americans were shouting instructions that the tribesmen found incomprehensible, but the job was getting done. As soon as the mule train was unloaded, another appeared, and more cargo made its way onto the C-47.

Déricourt had joined Catesby and was also looking on. 'It looks,' said Catesby, 'like you might be losing your job. That baby must have twice the load capacity of your Beechcraft.'

'Actually, it carries four times the load and has twice the operational range.'

'Well, it looks like it's all over for you then. Has Lester given you formal notice?'

Déricourt smiled as the C-47, now fully loaded with four tons of raw opium, taxied for take-off. 'That plane – and any others that follow in its wake – will be Lester's death warrant.'

'Should I guess why? Or are you going to tell me?'

'I don't want you to get it wrong, because you will be playing a useful role.'

Catesby would rather have punched Déricourt in the face, but instead he put on a false smile and said, 'So what's happening?'

'Lester is cheating the mafia. The original deal was to thank the mob for their help in breaking the dock strikes by handing over forty per cent of the opium flown in from the Golden Triangle. It was a big cut, but they always take big cuts. The mafia have processing labs in Marseille, where they turn the shit into high-grade heroin – and Lester had set up his own, which was fine, as long as the mafia got their forty per cent.' Déricourt nodded at the C-47 Skytrain which was now airborne. 'But Lester is greedy, and he doesn't want to pay out. He has grand plans which involve setting up heroin factories in Turkey, Africa and Latin America. The C-47 can easily make the hop from Dakar to Brazil. Basically, Lester wants to push the mafia out of the global drug trade and be King of the World. And the mob aren't going to let him.'

Catesby knew what was coming next but decided to play dumb. 'Have you grassed him up to the mafia?'

'No, they wouldn't believe me. That's your job.'

The Beechcraft 18 still wasn't loaded the next morning. The opium was arriving in dribs and drabs, not delivered by mule train, but by Hmong peasants carrying their harvest on their backs or between two of them on poles. Catesby sensed something ominous in the air – and the drumming from the mountain forest did nothing to reassure him.

'You look worried,' said Déricourt.

'It must be something I ate.'

'What a pity, but if you get hungry again, I'll try to get you an invitation to the wedding feast.'

'What wedding?'

Déricourt smiled. 'Can't you hear the drumming? That's Hmong wedding music.'

'Who's getting married?'

'The groom is a friend of ours. The happy couple are going to turn up soon – if the Pathet Lao don't get here first.'

A few hours later, as the final consignments of opium were being stowed in every nook and cranny of the Beechcraft, a familiar figure accompanied by a woman emerged from the tree line. The Viscount Xavier-Honoré-Antoine de Saint-Breuil wasn't wearing his Republican Guard helmet – or any item of military uniform – but brightly coloured traditional Hmong clothing. The woman next to him, also dressed for a ceremony, was dripping cascades of jewels. They certainly weren't dressed for battle, but Xavier-Honoré was carrying a submachine gun and the woman a Mauser sniper rifle.

'May I,' said Xavier-Honoré, 'have the pleasure of introducing you to my bride, the Viscountess Xavier-Honoré-Antoine de Saint-Breuil?' His voice suggested that her Hmong name was a thing of the past.

Catesby gave a respectful bow; Déricourt remained upright. Meanwhile, a bearded figure in a black cassock was striding towards them. 'I would also like to introduce you to Father Louis Laneau, who united us in marriage. Father Louis is a Jesuit, who kindly made the trip from his parish in Vientiane to perform the ceremony.'

'There were,' said Father Louis, 'two ceremonies, which I always recommend: a traditional Lao wedding followed by a Catholic one. One must respect the local culture.'

There was the sound of small-arms fire in the distance, but no one seemed concerned.

'With a name like Catesby,' smiled the priest, 'you must be Catholic.'

'I admire your knowledge of British history.'

'I have always thought the Gunpowder Plot martyrs should be canonised and have petitioned the Vatican in that regard. Perhaps one day, I will celebrate Mass in the Church of Saint Guy Fawkes and Saint Robert Catesby.'

Catesby felt himself sinking into quicksand. 'I am not related to Robert Catesby. My family name is a coincidence.'

'But are you not a Catholic?'

'I was brought up as one but lost my faith just after puberty.' Catesby gave the priest a smug smile. 'I would describe myself as an atheist and a socialist.'

'Ah,' said the priest. 'That is far better than being a Protestant. The Reformation ushered in a work ethic culture inspired by greed.'

It was, thought Catesby, an odd conversation to be having next to a plane full of opium while bullets were beginning to whiz overhead.

Xavier-Honoré turned to Déricourt. 'I think, Henri, we had better get Father Louis aboard the plane. I have already set up a defensive perimeter, but the Pathet Lao are now attacking.'

Catesby could see a line of enemy Hmong readying themselves for battle in the tree line. You can't have a wedding without a firefight and some bloodshed. Catesby now knew that, as far as the Viscount was concerned, Déricourt wasn't at the airfield to fly out opium, but to give the priest a lift back to Vientiane. He also realised that the attack had been organised by Lester to take out Déricourt and himself.

'Let's get going,' said Déricourt as a bullet made a hole in the fuselage.

Catesby looked at Xavier-Honoré and his bride. They were both ducking and weaving towards the tree line. He settled himself in the co-pilot's seat as the priest crushed himself in with the opium. The plane was soon airborne and climbing rapidly. Catesby found a submachine gun at his feet. 'Can I take a few shots?'

'It's not worth the risk; I just want to get out of here.'

'I think we owe it to them.'

'Okay, but just one pass.'

As the plane banked, Catesby looked down. Xavier-Honoré was lying on his back and his bride, or widow, was leaning over him. She was tenderly holding his face between her hands.

Marseille: October 1950

Catesby was pleased with the scenario he envisioned. Lester was going to kill Déricourt – and it wouldn't be pretty – and then the mafia would kill Lester. Just step back and let the gangsters knock each other off – no fingerprints. But unfortunately, it didn't seem to be working out that way. He needed to play a more active role now that he'd returned from Laos.

The flight back to France had been uneventful – except for Déricourt shooting dead a fuel supplier who had demanded extra payment. His men were cowed and refuelled the plane without a murmur. A day later, Déricourt landed at the commercial airport in Marseille, where his Beechcraft 18 seemed a well-known visitor. It was a brief stop. Déricourt bid a terse farewell to Catesby and then took off again. Catesby hadn't a clue where Déricourt and the raw opium were headed. He wondered if the pilot was cheating both Lester and the mafia and setting up in business on his own.

Catesby checked into Madame Albertini's rundown hotel. It was where he had stayed when he first came to Marseille and, once again, he was the only guest.

'Is your book going well?' said Madame Albertini.

'How kind of you to ask. I've just returned from a trip to London, where I met my publisher – and she was very pleased with the progress. But I might still need some quiet time to reflect and revise.'

'I can certainly provide that, monsieur.'

Catesby knew that she, a gossip with mobster contacts, would be far from quiet – and that drumbeats announcing his arrival were already thumping along the Marseille jungle telegraph.

For the next three days Catesby kept his ear to the ground while pretending to write his book. He checked out every bistro and restaurant where Déricourt had ever hung out. He even bribed a corrupt cop or two to pass on any information or rumours about the pilot – but absolutely nothing. If Lester had taken out Déricourt, it had been a very quiet and unreported murder. The only inkling of info that Catesby picked up was from a waiter at the restaurant overlooking the fishing boats at the Vallon des Auffes. 'Monsieur Henri wants to know when the turbot are next in season. He and his American friend are frequent diners.' Déricourt was alive and hungry – and so was Lester. It was time to act.

Towards bedtime, Madame Albertini invited her lone guest to join her for a cognac and to ask how his writing was going. 'I need a break,' said Catesby. 'A long walk around the city.'

'There are so many inspiring things to see.'

'By the way,' said Catesby, 'the last time I stayed here you lent me a guide book to the cathedral.'

'Would you like to borrow it again?'

'Yes please, I'd like to have another look around.'

Madame Albertini padded off and returned a minute later with the thin black volume about the cathedral. She handed it to Catesby. 'It's best to visit after the morning services have finished.'

'Indeed. I think I'll go late tomorrow morning, just before twelve. Such fascinating architecture.'

As before, the Patek Philippe watch and the star-sapphire signet ring were better IDs than a diplomatic passport waved high at a Customs officer. As the mobster walked over to greet him, Catesby recognised him as the same person he had met before. Very sleek, perfectly suited and good-looking. If he hadn't opted for a career with the mafia, he could have made it as an actor or a model – or an expensive gigolo. 'Welcome back, monsieur. You seem to have developed a liking for the Basilica of Our Lady.'

'I was hoping that Our Lady might be able to give me a little help.'

'I hope, monsieur, that you are not making fun of our religion.'

'Apologies. I was brought up Catholic – and that wasn't a tactful way to put my request.'

The sleek man smiled and nodded towards a booth from which murmurs were coming. 'They are hearing confession. Would you like to make one now?'

'I think it would be better to do so after I've made my request.' Catesby smiled. 'Which I am sure might count as a mortal sin.'

'We all are sinners, monsieur.'

'I believe that Monsieur Lester is also a sinner.'

The mafia man remained silent.

'He's cheating you. Monsieur Lester is processing raw opium from the Golden Triangle at his own labs. Eventually, he wants to cut you out of the business completely.'

'Can you give me more details?'

Catesby did.

'We'll take it from here. *Capisce?*'

As the echoing steps of the mafia man faded away in the cathedral nave, Catesby looked at the confessional and whispered, 'Bless me, Father, for I have sinned.'

Marseille: October 1950

The head in the cooking pot didn't only ruin a marvellous bouillabaisse, it ruined Julot as well. Sure, he was a friend of the mob, but he'd had nothing to do with the killing or the decapitation. Nonetheless, in the weeks, the months, after the incident no one ever ordered his prize bouillabaisse again. The restaurant did end up having a certain ghoulish appeal, and people would pop in for a drink or two, but seldom ordered a meal. Eventually, Julot had to close his business. No one ever knew exactly what happened to him. There were rumours that he'd become a cook in a Trappist monastery – and may even have taken monkish vows himself. There was another rumour that he was running a bar in Tangiers. Catesby hoped it was the latter.

The evening itself, which had started off weirdly, gradually became surreal. The mafia had cleared the restaurant and Catesby found himself in the street, still holding a brimming glass of Ugni blanc. It was a wonderful wine, and he wasn't going to waste it – and he also needed a drink. Kit Fournier, who had vomited up his bouillabaisse after seeing the head in the soup, had been led out of the restaurant by Catesby and was still standing next to him.

'Are you all right?' said Catesby.

'I don't know.' Fournier wiped his mouth with a napkin. 'I need to contact Washington as soon as possible.'

A number of mobsters were shouting at bystanders to clear off. 'I think we should get away from here.'

'In fact,' said Fournier, 'I'd better get out of Marseille.' They started walking towards Le Vieux Port.

'Where are you staying?' asked Catesby, although he already knew.

'In Lester's mansion overlooking the sea. But I'm not sure I should go back there; it might not be safe.'

Catesby didn't comment.

'I don't know what's happening,' said Fournier.

'Did you know Lester had been recalled to the States?'

It was Fournier's turn to be silent, but he finally answered. 'Not permanently. He might have had to go back for consultations, but that was all.'

Catesby detected a false note in Fournier's voice but let him continue.

'Lester's travel plans are often a mystery – and for good reason.'

Catesby was still carrying the glass of wine and trying not to spill a drop. He stopped and had a swig. 'Excellent wine – even on a night like tonight.'

'I think I might get a train from Saint-Charles.'

Catesby could see that Fournier was running scared – and lying about Lester. They continued walking until they reached the harbour quay. Despite the late hour, an old man was fishing. Aware that Fournier was a fellow intelligence officer, Catesby said, 'You ought to use fishermen as watchers. They stay in the same place for hours and no one gets suspicious.'

'Shall we hire this one?' said Fournier with a grim smile.

Catesby finished his wine and then threw the glass out over the harbour, where it landed with a loud splash. The fisherman didn't bat an eyelid. 'Don't hire this one,' said Catesby. 'I think he's dead.'

'You think we're being followed.'

'Is that a statement or a question?'

'Both.'

'I don't know if we're being followed, but I do know I need a drink.' Catesby led the way to a small bar on the edge of Le Panier. It was a rundown place where workers and artists mingled. A woodcut print of Serge's hung behind the bar. It depicted a scene from the dock strikes. Catesby ordered a carafe of red wine. 'I hope you'll have some?'

Fournier nodded.

'When I drink spirits,' said Catesby, 'I end up getting in fights.'

'Like the one in the nightclub.'

'What do you know about it?'

'Not much. Lester said it was proof that you were a drunk and a degenerate and that not even the Russians would hire you. He said that dragging you out of the gutter would be an American thank-you for your war service.'

Catesby was pleased that the deception had worked – at least in the beginning.

Fournier looked around the bar. 'Is this dump one of your regular hangouts?'

'No, I come here because no one knows me. When people found out that I was working for Lester, my reputation was finished.'

'But of course, you weren't working for him. It was all a trick, a deception.'

'Shh,' said Catesby nodding towards the bar, 'I'm trying to hear what they're saying.'

'I find Marseille dialect difficult, but it sounds like they're talking about Julot's.'

'Indeed. News travels fast around here. They seem to think the mafia did it.'

Fournier took a gulp of wine – then stared hard at Catesby. 'But the mafia didn't kill Lester. You did.'

'No, you did. How did you know it was Lester's head?'

'I recognised his smile.' Fournier gave a sarcastic laugh. 'And don't bother lying – I know it was you. Are you going to kill me too?'

'No, you're not worth it.'

'Fuck you, Catesby.'

'It's a good thing I'm not drinking spirits.'

'You think you're a tough guy?'

'No, I think I'm a hungry guy. We didn't get much to eat before they threw us out. What about you?'

'I wouldn't mind a milkshake and some French fries.'

'I know just the place.'

They took a taxi to the bistro bar where Catesby had shared a drink with Helen, when she was still pretending to be the loyal wife of the British consul. It was an upmarket place and seemed to attract a lively evening crowd. Catesby could see why it appealed to Helen: swish and expensive, with a hint of the unconventional. Fournier seemed to like it too – and appeared relaxed for the first time that evening. A waiter passed them a menu – and immediately sashayed away as if he had far more important things to do.

'Anything,' said Fournier brushing the menu aside, 'except fish soup.'

'How about *confit de canard* with big side helpings of *frites*?'

'That sounds good.'

Catesby regarded the American. 'With a name like Fournier, your family must be French.'

'Maybe, a couple of centuries ago. I learned the language because my family are culture snobs and I majored in French literature.'

'And this evening is turning into *le théâtre de l'absurde.*'

Fournier raised his glass. 'To a fellow man of learning. And what could be more *ridicule* than eating salt-cured duck preserved in its own cooking fat an hour after seeing the head of a colleague elevated out of a pot of bouillabaisse – and sharing that duck with the person who killed him.'

'I didn't kill him.'

Fournier gave a deep sigh. Lester wasn't just the head in the soup, but the elephant in the room. And yet, the evening was to get even more absurd – and tragic too.

She arrived just after midnight and was in a terrible state: unkempt, drunk and barely able to string a coherent sentence together. The staff recognised her. At one point, before she'd left her husband, Helen had been a regular at the bistro bar. She always ordered a gin and Suze with a dash of Amaro and lightly flirted with staff of both sexes. It was a little escape from her marriage – and now she seemed to be escaping from something else. A waiter greeted her warmly, and seeing the state she was in, tried to lead her to a quiet corner where someone could look after her. But as soon as Helen saw Catesby and Fournier, she shook off the waiter and made a beeline for their table. She managed to knock over Catesby's glass of wine while Fournier rescued his and the bottle. The waiter quickly came to clear things up. As he did so, Catesby said, 'Can you call a taxi?'

Someone brought over a chair and managed to get Helen to sit down. She then leaned forward towards Catesby and Fournier and nearly knocked the table over. She spoke a lot of gibberish, but the only words that Catesby could make out were 'a threesome'. He knew it wasn't an invitation.

During the taxi ride back to the flat, the one that Déricourt was sub-letting from Lester, Helen vomited over Catesby's trousers – which were already soaked with red wine. Catesby apologised to the driver, who was more concerned about 'the lady being poorly' than about the state of his back seat. It was part of the trade, but Catesby gave him a handsome tip.

Between the two of them, they managed to get Helen up the stairs and into the flat – which was less of a mess than she was, but still a mess. For some reason the rug in the sitting room had been rolled up and shoved in a corner.

'How are you feeling, Helen?' said Catesby.

'Bed. I want to go to bed.'

'We'll give you a bit of a wash – and then tuck you in.' Her clothes were a mess. They undressed her and slid her into a bath. She seemed blissful as the soapy warm water covered her body. Catesby noticed that she had several bruises and a nasty bite mark on her inner thigh. 'She looks content, but we can't leave her in the tub, she might drown.'

'It's nice to find a killer with a caring side,' said Fournier.

'I want to stay here,' moaned Helen.

'No, we're going to put you in a nice warm bed,' said Catesby.

'With a teddy bear?'

'Maybe.' His mind jumped to the stuffed animal toys that Lester and his gang hollowed out and filled with smuggled heroin. Was she thinking of those teddies in her delirium?

They got her out of the bath and dried her off. Catesby noticed there were surgical scars above her pubis. He wanted to hold her and comfort her. He found a dressing gown made of thick cotton and wrapped her in it before they tucked her into bed. 'Just call if you need anything.' But she was already asleep.

Fournier took the spare bedroom, which was full of packing boxes. Catesby was about to bed down on a sofa near Helen's room when he noticed a splatter of damp stains at the base of the sofa. He touched them and sniffed his fingers. It wasn't wine, it was blood. He then partially unrolled the rug. Likewise, the stains weren't wine, but blood and what appeared to be fragments of flesh. He carefully rolled the rug back up. He had discovered a secret he wasn't going to share. As Catesby curled up on the sofa, he made sure that his 9mm automatic was within easy reach. Things were still at crunch point. The presence of the gun was a soothing reassurance – his own teddy bear – and he soon fell asleep.

The morning was deceptively calm, but there was still edginess in the air. Fournier had risen first and was making a racket in the kitchen. Helen was the second to emerge. As soon as he heard the bedroom door open, Catesby tried to conceal his weapon – but not soon enough. Helen looked surprisingly normal and healthy in her white dressing gown. 'Who are you afraid of?' she said, nodding at the automatic.

'I wanted to protect you,' he said with a feeble smile.

'Is that meant to be a joke?' There was no humour in her voice. She looked towards the kitchen. 'What's Kit up to?'

Catesby was surprised to hear her refer to Fournier by his first name. 'I think he's using his American ingenuity to brew up some coffee.'

'Then we should show our British good manners by drinking it.'

Catesby looked at Helen closely and whispered, 'You need to get rid of that carpet.'

She gave a weary nod. She didn't seem to mind that Catesby had uncovered her secret.

It was a breakfast as grim as it was polite. It was just warm enough to sit on the terrace overlooking the sea. Helen cradled her bowl of coffee and closed her eyes tightly. Ridges of pain seemed to radiate towards her temples. 'The first stage of the hangover is starting to kick in. It helps if I snort a bit of heroin. You can sniff the really pure stuff, but it looks like Henri packed away every ounce of powder when he cleared off.' She opened her eyes and looked at Fournier. 'That's why I was in such a state last night. Henri left me.' She sipped her coffee and tilted her head. 'So I had a few drinks and went out looking for him. I thought I would check out our usual haunts, but I was legless by the time I got to La Floriane. Thank you for bringing me back.'

'It was a pleasure,' said Catesby.

'Undressing me was a pleasure?'

'You had been sick, and we didn't want to put you to bed in soiled clothes.'

'I am sure you were a perfect gentleman.'

'We were both perfect gentlemen,' said Fournier.

The conversation had taken an awkward turn and Catesby intuited that Helen wanted them to leave.

Fournier looked at Catesby. 'This used to be Lester's apartment, but he found a better place and sublet it to Henri.' The American shifted his gaze to Helen. 'But you won't have to pay any more rent to Lester – he's dead.'

At first, Helen's face was totally expressionless. A few seconds later she smiled. 'Good. Lester was a total bastard. He deserved to die.'

'Then,' said Fournier, 'you have William Catesby to thank.'

Catesby and Helen exchanged glances.

Fournier continued, 'Your friend William went to the mafia and lied about Lester cheating and betraying them. I can't quote his lies verbatim, but I am sure that he concocted a convincing story. Unfortunately, Lester was an easy person to frame in the eyes of the mafia. He was engaged in a number of secret activities on behalf of the US government, which Catesby wove into a pattern of double-dealing against the mob. They are, of course, an organisation which deals quickly and harshly with anyone who crosses them. They wanted to make an example of poor Lester. A fake farewell dinner, with his severed head emerging from a steaming pot of bouillabaisse, was a clear warning to others.'

Helen turned to Catesby with an ironic smile. 'Thank you, William. That was a job well done.'

'The pair of you should be ashamed,' said Fournier. 'Lester was a great American, who – although he trod shadowy pathways – was making the world safe for democracy and freedom.'

Once again, Catesby noted something in Fournier's voice that didn't quite ring true. Was the American putting on an act and hamming up a script that he found a bit silly?

'I'm feeling tired,' said Helen with her head in her hands, 'and I'd like to spend some time alone.'

The two men got up to leave. Fournier reached the door first and didn't glance back, but Catesby turned to face Helen. She was now standing up and staring straight into his eyes. It was a look of understanding, complicity and, Catesby hoped, longing.

When the two men got to the street, Fournier turned to Catesby and said, 'Don't follow me.'

'I had no intention of following you – but where are you going?'

'I don't know but if I did, I would tell you a cunning lie and send you on a wild goose chase.'

'I wouldn't take the bait.'

'But I am sure,' said Fournier, 'that one day our paths will cross again.'

Catesby was tempted to quote the final line from *Casablanca*, but instead whistled a tune as he walked away. It was the tune that the band of the Royal Scots Dragoon Guards had played on the day he had been demobbed from the army, 'Time to Say Goodbye'.

London: November 1950

London didn't want to know. They didn't want to know a fucking thing, not the smallest detail. There wasn't even a top-secret file archived in a dusty vault under the 100-year rule. Catesby felt like the Ancient Mariner. He imagined himself years later, grey-bearded, clutching a half-empty bottle of cheap brandy and grabbing at wedding guests – or anyone else:

'There was a spy,' quoth he.

'Hold off! unhand me, grey-beard loon!'

It was, thought Catesby, probably the only way he would ever be able to tell the tale of what had happened in Marseille, Laos and the places between; of a CIA agent in the soup; of dockworkers being beaten and murdered; of war and corruption. But most of all, of a superpower out of control – and a foreign policy based on drugs and napalm. It was a tale that no one, certainly no one in power, wanted to hear or talk about.

Catesby's meeting with Henry Bone had set the tone. It took place the day after he returned from Marseille. 'Your report is in the burn bag,' said Bone. 'Please don't write another one.'

It was hardly a 'report'. Catesby had sent a brief encoded message of fifteen words informing Bone that Lester was dead. He had been planning to deliver a more detailed account when he got back to London.

'And,' said Bone, 'I don't want you to tell me what happened – even in hushed tones during a walk through Green Park. I do not wish to be burdened with such knowledge. What have you got to say?'

'Obviously nothing.'

'Good. You've got the point. Nothing ever happened. You were on temporary leave, went to France to write a book – and then packed it in.'

Bone smiled. 'Welcome back to Broadway Buildings. Your dry humour was much missed in the staff canteen.'

'And, Commander Bone, your dry irony was much missed during my time away.'

'Touché.'

Suffolk: December 2018

'Please stop looking so glum, Granddad, it's only football.'

'How did they manage to blow it?'

'They didn't lose. It was a draw – and we were lucky to hold on. Sheffield United had twice as much possession.'

'You're right,' said Catesby. 'It wasn't a peasants' revolution failing on the brink of victory. Only the Tractor Boys heading for relegation. Shall we get back to the memoir stuff?'

Leanna picked up her pad and flipped a few pages back. 'Last time we met, we were discussing the death of Lester Roach. You said you went to the mafia and grassed him up – but you didn't explain what happened after that.'

'Well, sadly, I can tell you now.'

'Why sadly and why now?'

'Because an old friend died last week – aged ninety-nine.'

'Why did their dying make a difference?'

'Because death is the great open sesame. The dead no longer have a right to secrets. Otherwise, historians would find a very bare cupboard. Surviving family can learn to cope.'

'History can be cruel.'

'And truth can take a long time to come out. The killing of Lester Roach was a difficult mystery to unravel because there were so many who wanted him dead: Henry Bone, SIS, the grown-ups in Washington; Teresa and Jack; the dockworkers of Marseille; the mafia, Henri Déricourt – and Serge, who wanted to turn his murder into a work of art. I didn't find out how Lester's head ended up in the soup until ten years ago.'

'You mean at Teresa's funeral?'

'Well spotted.'

'Granny joked you were rendezvousing with a secret agent.'

'And not entirely in jest. Are you ready to hear the story?'

'Do you want me to take notes or record?'

'Both.'

South of France: August 1985

It was a wonderful post-retirement holiday with Frances and the grand-children. Leanna was turning into a water sprite and had fallen in love with the river and its rapids. Catesby appointed himself Health and Safety Officer and jumped off all the rock ledges to check them out. On one occasion, Leanna shouted out: 'No, Granddad – that's dangerous!' He was pleased that he had made his point.

At the end of the first week, Catesby looked at Frances over the crois-sants. 'I hope you don't mind if I leave you with the children today, I want to go into Marseille to buy some presents.'

Frances gave him a searching look. 'What are you really up to, William?'

'I want to see an old acquaintance.'

'Serge?'

Catesby nodded.

'Henry Bone told you to leave it. So why won't you?'

'I was very fond of Serge.'

'And you also want to find out what happened.'

'Is that a crime?'

'Actually, the Security Service might think so. You were ordered to get off the case and shut up.'

Serge was now in his seventies – and not looking good. As Catesby entered the flat, he asked, 'How's Huong?'

'Not very well. She died thirteen years ago.'

Catesby wanted to drop through the floor. 'Forgive me for not knowing. I'm so sorry to hear that.'

'She didn't just die – she was killed.' Serge walked over to a bureau and took what looked like a military decoration out of a drawer. 'You helped convince Huong not to go to Vietnam in 1950, but she finally made the trip in 1967.' Serge handed over the medal. It was a twelve-pointed star in the middle of which were three women clutching rifles. 'It's the Quyet-Tam-Danh-Thang Giac My Xam-Luoc.' Serge smiled. 'It translates as the Defeat American Aggression Badge. It was awarded posthumously.' Serge gave a wry smile. 'Don't you think it should be upgraded to the Order of Ho Chi Minh?'

'She was a brave woman.'

'Too brave. She commanded an anti-aircraft unit defending Bach Mai Hospital. Huong was killed in Nixon's 1972 Christmas bombing of Hanoi – a petulant tantrum in a war America had already lost.'

Catesby could see that Serge's eyes were brimming with tears. 'Are you okay?'

'Huong would always come into the studio at the end of the working day with glasses, ice cubes and water. She never had more than one glass of pastis, as you know she wasn't a heavy drinker, but she wanted to show that she shared my life and tastes – if only in a small way.'

'Small gestures can have a big impact.'

'Ours wasn't a marriage between two people. It was a marriage between competing – but sometimes complementary – passions.' Serge picked up a bottle of cheap brandy and two glasses. 'Let's go into the studio.'

It was far more of a mess than Catesby remembered it. The floor was littered with tins of paint and brushes in bottles of white spirit. On the wall facing them were portraits of Huong's dead body.

'I wasn't there, but I know what bombs can do.'

Catesby found the paintings unsettling. They graphically showed the most intimate parts of Huong's body torn and dissected by bomb fragments. In the background were flames as American B-52 bombers crashed and burned.

Serge passed Catesby a drink. 'Why did it take you so long to visit?'

'It was a confusing time – and I didn't think I'd be welcome.'

'Tell the truth. You're here because you want to know what happened that day.'

Catesby gave an embarrassed nod.

'Well, I'm not going to tell you. I'm going to show you.' Serge set up an easel and disappeared into the chaos of the studio. There was the rattle of a padlock and the creak of a metal door being opened. Serge then re-emerged carrying a large canvas. 'Only two other people have seen this – and one of them is dead.'

Catesby wasn't shocked by the painting. But he would have been if he wasn't already acquainted with Serge's work. It was a vision of hell through the twisted lens of the Goya drawings Serge had been shown as a student – Catesby could only hope it was more a homage to the master than a true depiction of what had happened. Lester's face was twisted in agony. His amputated penis was being thrust down his throat at the same time as a plunger was shoved up his backside. And in the background shadows, the image of a man looking on with a demonic grin. Catesby was astonished to see that the face was his own.

Cimetière du Canet, Marseille: July 2008

It was a very French funeral. It reminded Catesby of President Mitterrand's; the mistress was there – and her presence was very welcome. Vivianne, in fact, had helped Jack nurse Teresa during the final two years of her life – and Teresa was now being buried next to her husband Marcel.

Cousin Jack had stayed on in France. He and Teresa had gone on to have one child of their own and three grandchildren. There were another two grandchildren from Teresa's marriage to Marcel, and two great-grandkids. All of which meant there was quite a family crowd at the graveside – and more than two hundred mourners spreading out beyond. There was a lot of singing: 'The Internationale', of course, and songs from the Spanish Civil War too. An elderly comrade of Teresa's from Spain raised his fist and shouted, '*No pasarán!*' The wake at the Labour Exchange beckoned.

As they filed away from the grave, Frances took Catesby's arm. 'Have you seen her?'

'Who?'

'Your acrobat girlfriend with the lovely legs?'

'Helen?'

'Oh, you haven't forgotten. She's looking this way. Why don't you go and say hello?'

'Will you come with me?'

'No, I don't chaperone the over-eighties.'

As Frances strode away, Catesby looked at the woman. It really was Helen – except that her hair was blacker than before, and her make-up was more thickly layered. She was staring at Catesby like a teacher waiting to give a reprimand. He walked over to her, and Helen spoke first. 'Why weren't you at Serge's funeral?'

'I didn't know he was dead until months after he had been buried.'

'Why didn't you keep in touch?'

'I didn't feel that he wanted me around, but I made occasional contact.' Catesby felt guilty that he had failed to answer Serge's last letter until it was too late. 'Are you coming to the wake? I'm sure we can wrestle up a gin and Suze.'

'No. I've got a car waiting.'

'Is it a Talbot-Lago Grand Sport?'

'No, Henri took that lovely car with him. I never saw him again after that awful afternoon. He got what he wanted and cleared off.'

'I heard he was killed in a plane crash in Laos in 1962.'

'You heard wrong. They never found his body or the drugs. But I hope he's dead by now.'

'You're looking well.'

Helen laughed. 'You want me to drink that gin and Suze standing on my head?'

'It would liven up the wake.'

'That's not why I'm here.'

'Why are you here?'

'I want to sew up the past.'

'And so do I.'

'I became close to Serge after Huong was killed. We both had loved her – and we briefly became lovers after her death. To get him in the mood, I used to wear Huong's dresses. But it never worked.'

Catesby suppressed a smile. It was an odd conversation to be having with a woman in her late eighties.

'When Serge was on his last legs, he named me as chief executor of his will.' Helen smiled. 'We celebrated with gin and Suze as he signed the document. After he died, there was some difficulty when a niece and nephew showed up out of the woodwork, but I saw them off and cleared the flat and studio on my own.' Helen paused. 'Serge told me he showed you the paintings.'

Catesby nodded.